"I shall also require compensation," Patrick told her.

Julianne looked up warily. "You want me to pay you to marry me?"

He closed the remaining three feet between them and then he was within striking distance. The scent of her damp hair rose up to greet him. "A kiss, to honor our bargain."

"We've had one," she countered. "Or have you forgotten?"

He pulled her to him. "I haven't forgotten." He half expected her to retreat, cry foul, retract the offer she'd thrown down. After all, these were nowhere near the same happy circumstances as their first kiss. This time, she believed him capable of murder.

His lips settled over hers in a kiss that offered no quarter and sought a raw truth. The taste of her was a flooding memory, sharp sweetness and languid heat. Christ, what man could forget such a thing? It carried a sting, this woman's kiss. Even with a plan and a stiff resolve, it was nigh on impossible to brace oneself for impact.

And that was when she pulled back, her hand a gentle reminder against his chest. "I trust this is adequate compensation until the vows are completed?" she said softly.

Patrick's palms fell away from the temptation of her night rail. She would be a willing participant in the marriage bed, that much was clear. No shrieking, no hysterics.

He lacked the audacity to think he deserved anything more.

By Jennifer McQuiston

MOONLIGHT ON MY MIND
SUMMER IS FOR LOVERS
WHAT HAPPENS IN SCOTLAND

Jennifer McQuiston

Moonlight on my Mind

AVON
An Imprint of HarperCollinsPublishers

This is a work of fiction. Names, characters, places, and incidents are products of the author's imagination or are used fictitiously and are not to be construed as real. Any resemblance to actual events, locales, organizations, or persons, living or dead, is entirely coincidental.

AVON BOOKS
An Imprint of HarperCollins*Publishers*
10 East 53rd Street
New York, New York 10022-5299

Copyright © 2014 by Jennifer McQuiston
ISBN 978-0-06-223134-5
www.avonromance.com

First Avon Books mass market printing: April 2014

Avon Trademark Reg. U.S. Pat. Off. and in Other Countries, Marca Registrada, Hecho en U.S.A.
HarperCollins® is a registered trademark of HarperCollins Publishers.

Printed in the U.S.A.

10 9 8 7 6 5 4 3 2 1

To my precious daughters, who remind me every day that life is not to be wasted, and who, though they may not yet be old enough to read my books, tell everyone they know to hurry up and read them so they can get another pony.

Acknowledgments

WHILE I MAKE no claims for legal accuracy in this book, I would be remiss in not acknowledging (and thanking) historical author Courtney Milan. Through a critique I was fortunate enough to win at a charity auction, Ms. Milan reviewed an early concept of this story and offered some excellent points that helped shape the final product. Many thanks to my husband, John, who reads far more books with suspense elements than I do and who brainstormed major plot points over bourbon cocktails one night. Thanks to my critique partners, Alyssa Alexander, Sally Kilpatrick, Romily Bernard, Tracy Brogan, and Kimberly Kincaid, who kept me focused and sane and, most of all, *moving* on this monster of a manuscript.

I am indebted to my fabulous editor, Tessa Woodward, who encouraged me to not lose sight of the romance and who graciously gave me the time I needed to rewrite major portions of the book, even though it meant she was reviewing pages on the eve of her wedding. As always, thanks to the fabulous team at Avon, especially Tom Egner and the Art Department, who created what I have to say is my favorite stepback art of the entire series . . . apparently, I am the kind of girl who would prefer a tryst in a moonlit folly instead of on a rocky beach or up against a wall. Who knew?

Moonlight on my Mind

Prologue

Yorkshire, England
November 1841

HE WASN'T IN the mood for a proper English miss . . . not that those words described the flame-haired hoyden lying in wait as Patrick Channing pushed his way into the foyer.

He almost cursed. *Out loud.*

Which was just another example that he lacked the capacity for social niceties this evening, no matter that his mother was in the midst of a crushing autumn house party.

It had been a hell of a day, starting with a lame horse that would probably have to be put down, and culminating with yet another argument with his brother over something so trivial as to now be forgotten. The woman in front of him wasn't the cause of his ill temper, but she was poised to be the salt in a wound that had long since started to fester.

She ought to be somewhere else. In the ballroom with

the other guests. Sipping champagne and dancing. That she was skulking about in the foyer suggested either a lack of common sense or an ulterior motive.

He was betting on a combination of the two.

As he shrugged out of his greatcoat, he tried to dampen the flare of irritation the girl inspired. She'd been under his feet all week. Her name was Jeannine Baxter. Or Josephine.

Something with a J.

No doubt she would expect him to recall it, and then use it with exacting precision.

"May I help you, Miss Baxter?" He supposed she was pretty enough to warrant a second look if he'd been in a receptive frame of mind. Pretty and petite, in a fresh-from-London sort of way. Green eyes framed by thick lashes. Impressive bosom, showcased by ivory lace.

But a second look would require effort, and he was quite tapped out for the evening.

"Never say you don't recall." The girl offered him a perfect pout and fingered the edges of her fan. It was mid-November and threatening to frost tonight. That she was holding an elaborately painted fan and shivering in a gown that looked to have been composed of dust motes was a perfect example of why he was not interested in continuing this conversation.

"Perhaps you could refresh my memory." He couldn't ignore her, no matter how insistent the urge. After all, he was speaking with the daughter of Viscount Avery, his father's good friend. He was not so ill-mannered or ill-tempered as to forget *that*.

The girl appeared unmoved by either his lack of memory or his curt tone. Her lips shifted to a practiced smile as she tapped her fan against his arm. "You promised me the evening's first dance, Mr. Channing."

Patrick knocked the mud off his boots as he tried to remember. Had he truly done something so ridiculous? He recalled a moment this morning when she had flirted with him over the breakfast buffet. Between the call of coddled eggs and the bleary hour, he had been vulnerable.

As if to confirm his idiocy, she canted her head toward the open door of the ballroom, from which leaked the opening strains of a waltz. "You've arrived just in time."

Surely she wasn't serious. God knew he wasn't dressed for dancing. There was dirt beneath his nails, for heaven's sake. He smelled of things best washed away, of horse and sweat and liniment. "I've just come from the stables and am likely to be poor company tonight. I imagine one of the other gentlemen might wish to claim this dance. My brother, perhaps."

Yes, that was a better idea all around. If his memory served, Miss Baxter had flirted with his brother, Eric, this morning too. He recalled now tamping down the sharp flare of jealousy, although not over the girl's interest in his brother, which was as predictable as the turn of a second hand on a watch. No, his discomfort had come from watching the attention Eric had commanded simply for being the *next* Earl of Haversham. It still chafed that his brother had returned home from London's gaming hells—with empty pockets, no less—to their father's proud smile, while Patrick floundered about the stables, looking for his place in life.

It had been almost six months since he'd returned from Italy. Four years of study at the veterinary college in Turin had prepared him for a profession, it seemed, but not for life as a second son. His father had tolerated his trip abroad, but Patrick had returned to England to discover his time away explained as "youthful wanderlust," never mind the fact he was almost thirty bleeding years old. He was relegated to his father's stables, and his new skills had been distilled down to a single gentlemanly allowance: improve the quality of horseflesh that resided there. No one knew of the nature of his studies, and worse, no one would be permitted to know.

Not that any of this concerned the girl standing in front of him. It was not her fault she personified everything his father and Society expected of him, and nothing of what he wanted for his future.

Miss Baxter pursed bow-shaped lips that threatened to lay waste to his imagination if he gave them half a chance. "I do not wish to dance with your brother at the moment, Mr. Channing. You've promised me this dance. And a gentleman does not renege on a promise."

"What makes you think," he asked, knowing that it was both an ill-considered question and something approximating the truth, "that I am a gentleman?"

Far from being offended, she threw back her head and laughed. "What makes you think," she said, her words an infectious slide of syllables and amusement, "that I wish to dance with one?"

Her words—and her laughter—caught his attention far more effectively than the tap of her fan had. He regarded her a long moment, his gaze coming to rest on cheeks that were pink with amusement or something more interesting.

Julianne. Her name came to him in an inspired flash. He'd expected a giggle out of her, though she was clearly out of the schoolroom. Perhaps a titter. Not that soul-inspiring laugh that seemed to build in her throat like a sweet, seductive mist. She was bold, this girl was. And propositioning *him*, not Eric.

Perhaps a third look was in order.

Knowing it was foolish but suddenly less inclined to care, Patrick allowed her to tug him toward the open French doors that led to the ballroom. He would probably track mud all over his mother's floor and sully the girl's gown with his ungloved hands, but apparently there was to be no help for it. He'd lost the heart for denial the moment she had laughed.

"One dance," he told her. "And then I am bound for bed."

JULIANNE PAUSED ON the threshold of the ballroom, scanning the crowd with a sense of anticipation. *Wait for the right moment*, she cautioned herself.

"I thought you wanted to dance?" Channing frowned.

Julianne ignored the irritation in her partner's voice. Men could be thick-witted in her experience, but with time and effort, most of them came around to dim understanding. "We must time our entrance for maximum effect."

"It's been a devil of a day, Miss Baxter. I do not have time for games."

She pursed her lips around a smile. What was life, after all, if not a delicious game? And Mr. Channing was her pawn, whether he consented to the indignity or not.

Most men—her father included—presumed the fairer sex incapable of competent battle strategy. For example, none would ever guess her maid had spent the entire morning lowering the bodice of tonight's gown, to stunning effect. The gentlemen at the house party had been distracted from their talk of hunting for a good ten minutes when she'd first come down to dinner. To Julianne's mind, those who underestimated the female mind deserved their fate.

Whether he approved or no, Mr. Channing was the only one here tonight who would serve the task at hand, no matter the stench of horse that clung to him like an aura. The first dance of the evening was far too valuable to waste on either of the other two gentlemen who had asked her to dance. Nephews of their host, Mr. Willoughby and Mr. Blythe had seemed affable enough young men, but the first dance of the evening called for a partner who would engender some competitive avarice in her true romantic target, and a politely pleasant cousin would do little to further her cause.

She squinted out at the dance floor, where a flash of color caught her eye. It was hard to make out details amid the blurry, swirling couples, but she thought she spied the green waistcoat worn by Mr. Channing's brother. Her stomach fluttered as she imagined his faraway gaze settling on them.

"There, you see? Not so long a wait." She placed her hand in Mr. Channing's. "And surely your bed can be put off five minutes or so."

"I am to lead a hunting party out at dawn. While it may seem merely a blink of time for you, Miss Baxter, I suspect five lost minutes will seem a regrettable length of time to me tomorrow."

Julianne prayed for patience as he began to steer her around the dance floor with smooth precision, suggesting that while he might look—and smell—as though he slept in those stables he had mentioned, he had at least taken a turn or two around the odd ballroom. "Surely thoughts of hunting can wait until morning," she chided, even as she craned her neck to catch that flash of green, taunting her across the dance floor.

"You are correct. My bed is the only thing I wish to think of at the moment."

His dry voice pulled her attention back to center. "Surely your bed is not the *only* thing you might think of when you finally make your room," she offered, letting a subtle but oft-practiced hint of suggestion leach into her words.

His attention jerked to her lips, as she had known it would.

Honestly, men could be so predictable.

But for heaven's sake . . . he acted as though it were an insult to grant her a few promised minutes. And was no one at this crowded house party able to have a conversation without bringing hunting into the mix? The sharp edge of fun had long since begun to wear off the week, given that most of the gentlemen were far more focused on firearms than flirtations. At dinner, one poor young man's eyes had practically rolled back in his head as he waxed poetic on the pleasures of stalking grouse. She expected such dullness in the gentlemen of her father's set. After all, what did aging peers attend house parties for but to point their rifles at things they didn't intend to eat?

But the younger men in attendance . . . they were proving a sore disappointment.

In fact, this very dance could be attributed to the boredom that had sunk its teeth into her almost from the start of the week. Her father had told her—quite sternly, in fact—that she was neither to pontificate on the importance of dancing over hunting, nor to foment small rebellions. Above all, she was not to publicly embarrass him.

Again.

Although really, the scandal sheets that had so enraged him this past Season had been rife with inaccuracies. It was quite an accomplishment, if you took the time to think about it. The obsession of London's gossip trade with her every smile meant she had arrived at the top of the social ladder, that she was a gem to be admired and—if need be—discussed over afternoon tea.

Her father, however, had not been impressed.

Well, neither was she impressed with her father's idea of fun. He had become far too circumspect since her mother's death nearly fifteen months ago, and she had hoped this house party would help shake him from his melancholy. But the reality of this holiday in the country was falling somewhat short of her expectations. If she was to keep a hold on her sanity, it was clear she needed more cerebral diversions than archery or picnics by the lake. And apparently, given the droning monotony of this house party, it was up to her to invent them.

That flash of a green waistcoat caught her eye again, circling her focus back around to the real purpose of this dance. "Tell me about your brother, Mr. Channing. Does he not require a good night's sleep as well?"

Her partner's brown eyes narrowed. "Are you always so forward, Miss Baxter?"

"Are *you* always so tired?" She arched a single brow, a move she had perfected in front of a mirror by the age of ten. When properly employed, it usually sent its recipients scuttling for the safety of other company, or, depending on the age and fortitude of the adversary in question, their mothers.

Mr. Channing did neither of those things.

"I can hold my own in most athletic endeavors." His lips held the promise of a wicked slant should they ever be fully unleashed, but he seemed to keep his expressions on a tight tether. "But I do find my aim improved by a solid night's sleep."

"I thought we were going to leave off with the discussion of rifles and the like."

"Whoever said I was speaking of rifles?"

Julianne knew a moment's gasping surprise. Was Mr. Channing *flirting* with her? He'd shown little propensity for banter this morning over breakfast, when his tongue had seemed as nondescript as his light brown hair. Only his height had been impressive. She'd been prepared for stilted dialogue and crushed toes in the name of advancing her cause. But this was proving more interesting than she had hoped. His words held a different essence than the topics offered by her usual dance partners. A drier wit, a sharper edge.

Perhaps not so dim after all.

Her eyes skirted the line of his jaw, and the hint of sandy-haired stubble that rested there. There were no easy smiles in sight. Then again, the easy smiles and clean-shaven faces of most gentlemen held ulterior motives.

She risked a glance at the couples spinning around them. Channing was nothing like the other men in attendance. The tedium of the house party sat like a threatened itch beneath her skin, and Channing's words rubbed her in just the right way. He had been up to more interesting things today than archery and a picnic by the lake, of that she had no doubt.

What could he show her, if she gave him half a chance?

Julianne looked up at him through half-lowered lashes. "I hope you plan to set your sights on something other than grouse in these athletic endeavors, or you'll be sure to earn a spot on the scandal sheets."

His lips twitched. Not a full smile, by any stretch, but still a notable easing of that tight control. "Have a care,

Miss Baxter. Or you might change your mind about the target in your sights, as well."

Julianne almost faltered her next step. Surely he couldn't suspect her motives tonight . . . he was a *man*. The gentlemen of the *ton* seemed largely oblivious to the workings of the female mind. But as she searched her memory she realized she had not seen him in London during either of her previous Seasons.

And he had warned her he wasn't a gentleman.

As the music began to build toward its conclusion, she sought a way to bring this conversation back around to its rightful direction. "During this evening's dinner where you failed to make an appearance, the other gentlemen professed their intent to join the hunt as well. *They* do not seem inclined to retire early. Your brother, for one, has placed his name on several young ladies' dance cards."

"But not yet yours, I'd wager. Isn't that why you are dancing with me, Miss Baxter?"

Julianne's feet almost tangled with her knees at Channing's dreadfully correct observation. She pressed her lips together, determined to avoid anything close to a confession, but he was apparently not through.

"There is no need to pretend otherwise. And truly, this is well played. There is no doubt his interest will be snared. Eric enjoys the chase. That you are dancing with me will be a temptation too great for him to ignore."

The music died out on a long, drawn-out C note, and Julianne stumbled to a stunned halt. Good heavens. She *had* plotted to dance with Channing to pique the interest of his older brother, whom she'd watched for the better part of the past Season. Any woman with an ounce of sense would set her sights on the heir to an

earldom, not the requisite but useless spare. But now—
to her horror—she realized those thoughts were turning
around to fall squarely on the surprise that was proving
to be Mr. Channing.

"Truly?" she asked, her heart thumping guiltily. She
stared at her partner, scarcely able to believe the man's
self-control. "You do not mind?"

He offered her his arm. "Not in the slightest."

A flare of irritation unfurled in her chest, even as she
permitted Channing to pull her toward the open doors
of the ballroom. Given that she was inarguably the pret-
tiest girl in the room, he really ought to be pleased she
had been willing to spend a few strategic minutes in his
arms. "Why ever not?" she demanded.

The muscles in his arm tightened beneath her fingers as they stepped into the cooler quiet of the hallway.
"Because I enjoy the occasional chase as well."

Julianne laughed. It was necessary to cover the shards
of uncertainty jumping beneath her skin. She was nervous. She was *never* nervous in such matters. But there
was no denying that this conversation was sending
thoughts of green waistcoats and other prey tumbling
to a far more distant place. Her father would not like
their disappearance from the ballroom, she knew, but
surely a moment or two alone with their host's son in
an open and accessible foyer could be no cause to sound
the alarm of impropriety yet.

"Are you chasing me, Mr. Channing?" She tossed a
quick look over her shoulder. "And more importantly, is
your brother watching you?" She could see little beyond
the smear of colorful gowns as the next set started. "I
can't see anything in this crush."

He leaned in close. *Too* close. She could smell the
earthy fragrance of horse and sweet hay on his clothing,

underlain by the sharper bite of something that smelled medicinal. His breath, where it tickled the edge of her ear, sent her stomach into a swirling state of confusion. "Eric is just there, near the edge of the line. Can you see? He's watching us now. Quite intently."

Julianne's skin thrummed with a curious anticipation. "Then why have we left the dance?" she whispered.

He stepped closer, until his trousers brushed her skirts and she could smell the heated linen of his shirt. "Because I imagine my brother's interest will be captured more fully now that he suspects I am going to kiss you."

Julianne's throat tightened around the thought. The relative indecency of the waltz fell away, forgotten in the face of this tempting new impropriety. She lifted her chin. "*Are* you going to kiss me, Mr. Channing?"

"Oh, of a certainty." He smiled down at her, and her knees locked up at the sight of his mouth, transformed from that stern slash of line into something shattering. His was not the sudden, sharp grin so preferred by the rakes of the *ton*. No, his lips stretched wide in a slow, seductive slide of promise, and it heated her from the inside out.

How had she not seen it? The man was far more attractive than she had first thought, with his lean lines and fathomless brown eyes. Why, if he took the time to bathe, he might even be handsome.

He moved closer still, and she felt the press of a welcome wall at her back. When had he maneuvered her into a corner? She blinked in delicious expectation. They were deeper in the foyer now, out of sight of his brother or any reasonable chaperone. Oh, he was far better at flirtation than she had first credited him.

And she was far more susceptible than she had first imagined.

Her gaze lodged on a smudge of dirt on Channing's right cheek. At least, she *hoped* it was dirt. After all, he did smell of horses. What was the matter with her, to be not only considering but welcoming the idea of such a thing, and from such a man? This would not do. He was neither strapping nor classically handsome. In truth, he was a little lean for her tastes. Worse, he was the second son.

An *unhygienic* second son.

And yet . . . as his lips lowered toward hers, she felt herself rising to meet him.

Because while the scandal sheets had certainly implied otherwise, she'd never kissed a gentleman in all her nineteen years. If she was going to be credited with having had the experience, she might as well see it done. So she tipped her head up and met him halfway, no matter the shocking impropriety of kissing an almost-stranger in an almost-public foyer, and no matter her original intention to merely use him to snare larger, more promising prey.

Not that she could recall such a thing now.

She could only press her lips against his and try to convince herself that Mr. Patrick Channing was not at all whom she wanted.

From the first touch of his lips, she felt as though the floor had been kicked out from under her. He might have dirt on his cheek, but he didn't taste like dirt. He tasted like sin, and it was a sin she wanted to lose herself in. He was a sharp surprise, wicked heat and barely restrained control, and his tongue teased the edges of her lips until she was gasping against his mouth. She might be inexperienced, but she was quite sure this was not the sort of kiss that should be shared between new acquaintances, or offered by a man seeking to declare his intentions to properly court a lady. This was an attack on her emotions, and it ripped the breath from her.

She made a small gasping sound that sounded painful to her own ears, and that was when he eased away, though his own chest rose and fell in a rhythm that matched her own. The fragility of their situation intruded back in, slow and unwelcome. The sounds of the music danced in her ears, and the laughter from the ballroom felt perforating in its nearness. She looked around, blinking, grateful to see they appeared to still be alone.

This had not been wise, in any sense of the word.

"Well." She swallowed, suddenly unsure of herself, and unable to keep a smile from claiming the lips he had so recently plundered. "I cannot decide if you are trying to help me or hurt your brother, Mr. Channing."

"Does it matter which?" The rumble of his voice worked her thoughts into a complicated knot, one she had no prayer of unraveling. "You'll have to try a bit harder, whichever of us you choose to pursue."

His words scraped against her already tender emotions. Did he think she walked around dispensing kisses like wishes? And worse, did he think the only reason she had kissed him had been to snare his brother? "I beg your pardon?"

"I am but a second son, and I doubt I can afford to do more than steal a kiss or two, however sweet your lips. And I suppose it would be ungentlemanly of me not to warn you. Eric has always preferred brunettes."

It was ungentlemanly of him not to have warned her of that before he took the liberty of a kiss, but Julianne discovered she could not bring herself to regret the oversight now, not with the taste of him still a melting surprise on her tongue. "I thought he preferred what *you* preferred," she countered tartly.

"I doubt it is the sort of thing he would call me out over, if that is part of your plan." Channing lifted a brow. "Now, if those curls were brown," he added, his eyes flashing with wicked warmth, "it might be another story."

She fought a moment's irritation. She'd just experienced her first glorious kiss in this man's arms, and now they were talking about her hair? It wasn't as if she didn't expect people to notice—after all, her vibrant tresses were either her loveliest feature or the bane of her existence, depending on her mood and the vagaries of fate. But to hear that his brother might dismiss her outright, merely on account of her hair, made her see . . . well, *red*.

"I'll wager I could change his mind," she retorted, though what she really wanted to do was change Mr. Channing's.

He studied her a moment, and his mouth returned to that straight line he'd worn at the start of their evening. "Well, it seems you may yet have a chance." He inclined his head toward the open door and stepped aside. "Congratulations, Miss Baxter. Your plan appears to have worked."

She turned in the direction he indicated. Her eyes found a green waistcoat, moving steadily toward them. "I . . ." She hesitated. "That is, I do not think—"

"My brother is officially intrigued, and I am off to bed. I've an appointment with dawn, and I'd hate to disappoint the grouse."

Julianne struggled to form anything close to a coherent thought in the face of his obvious dismissal. "Yes, I supposed they would be quite disappointed if you were not able to blow them to bits tomorrow."

The strain around his mouth eased, ever so slightly. Not quite a return to his earlier smile, but better than the frown, at any rate. He offered her a courteous nod, as if the entire length of his body had not just been pressed against her in so delicious and indecorous a fashion. "It has been a pleasure plotting with you, Miss Baxter."

Julianne brought a gloved hand to her still-swollen lips and stared after him as he strode away, leaving her open and vulnerable, standing in the foyer. Surely he didn't mean to turn her over to his brother, not when she was still reeling from the unexpected and unplanned heat of their encounter. For heaven's sake. She *liked* him.

What a terrible thing to discover about a man who was leaving.

"Miss Baxter?" The owner of that blasted green waistcoat settled in her line of vision, a charming, handsome, and now utterly unwanted heir. "I wonder if you might do me the honor of being my partner for the next dance?"

"Yes." Julianne sighed, risking one last wistful look toward the stairs. "I suppose I shall."

LATER, WHEN SHE looked back on that night and imagined what she might have done differently in her dealings with Mr. Channing, she would have immediately settled on the obvious: she should not have gone on to dance with his brother.

But hindsight often carries that blinding sort of clarity. If someone had told her then she would accuse Channing of murdering his brother on the morrow, she would have tapped her fan against his shoulder and laughed at such a jolly good joke. She had no way of knowing that the man who was now offering her his arm would lie dead before noon, or that her version of events—recounted through a shocked haze of tears—would expand so quickly to fill the void hewn by Mr. Channing's damning silence.

All she could think about was how attractive Mr. Channing looked, his thighs flexing with purpose beneath his riding breeches as he took the stairs two at a time.

And that perhaps there was more to hunt in Yorkshire than grouse.

Chapter 1

THOUGH IT WAS a thought she should have entertained far earlier, Julianne Baxter wondered if she ought to become a brunette before she sought out a man wanted for murder. A good instinct to have *before* she arrived in Scotland, but there was no helping it now.

It had been a hellish trip, first by train, then by four-horse coach with stops in Perth and Inverness. Now she was rattling into the little town of Moraig via a poorly sprung two-horse mail coach that was far better suited for hauling parcels than passengers. As the scenery outside her coach window shifted from pine forests to a smear of shop-lined streets, her mind twisted in this new—if belated—direction. Three long days spent sitting in trains and coaches, buttoned to the neck and hiding behind the brim of her bonnet, was enough to make even the kindest of souls cross. Julianne was admittedly not the kindest of souls.

Nor, regrettably, the cleanest.

The pretty green silk of her gown was now closer to a dull gray from the day's accumulated dirt, much of it from the interior of this squalid little coach. She yearned for a bath full of steaming water, and a feather bed on which to collapse in a well-earned stupor. But while Julianne was indeed bordering on a stupor from lack of proper sleep, she doubted a bath was something she would see this side of the next sunrise. She had things to accomplish in this nowhere Scottish town before her toes touched a bath or her head hit a pillow.

But at the moment, the thought of even five more seconds spent in the chokehold of her bonnet was too much.

Julianne eyed the coach's only other occupant, a portly man who had thankfully spent most of the eight-hour trip from Inverness sleeping. When he gave a re-assuring snore, she plucked at the ribbons holding her bonnet in place and pulled it from her head, intending to let her scalp breathe. She enjoyed two heavenly minutes of freedom before the man sitting across from her sput-tered awake.

He blinked a slow moment, his eyes settling on her hair with predictable tedium. And then he grinned, re-vealing teeth stained yellow by age and things best left unconsidered.

"Well, there's a pretty sight," he leered with a sleep-filled voice, filling the narrow space inside the coach with breath that suggested one or more of those teeth might be in need of professional care. "I dinna often see hair that bright, bonny color. I see you are traveling alone, lass. I'd be happy to show you around Moraig, personal-like."

Julianne withheld the curt reply hammering against

her lips. She was on a clandestine mission, after all, though she had little more than snatched bits of rumor to guide her. She was risking a great deal by coming here and following this lead without first contacting the authorities, but the shocking circumstances of the last week—from Lord Haversham's death and funeral to his family's desperate circumstances, the latter of which she feared could be laid firmly at her own feet—had forced her hand. Still, she did not relish the thought of discovery. No sense giving this stranger a voice by which to recognize her, on top of the copper-colored curls from which he seemed unable to detach his eyes.

When the passenger continued to ogle her, she determinedly settled the hated bit of straw and silk back on her head, this time leaving the ribbons untied. Deprived of his entertainment, the man finally looked away and turned his attention to a newspaper he pulled from a coat pocket. But the implications of his bald interest were not so easily defused. She hadn't given her hair much thought upon setting off on this journey, although, to be fair, she hadn't given any part of this journey a proper degree of forethought. Her father had ordered her home immediately after the earl's funeral, but instead of going on to London as she was meant to do, she'd dismissed her maid—a flighty girl on loan from Summersby's staff—and boarded the opposite train. And here she was. Alone and filthy, trying to avoid detection. She couldn't jolly well depend on a bonnet to keep her safe from recognition for the length of this trip.

But she didn't *have* to have red hair.

Indeed, for the purposes of this mission, it might be better if she didn't. That the man she sought—truly, the man half of England sought—was rumored to have disappeared into the farthest reaches of Scotland suggested he didn't want to be found. If he was warily watching over his shoulder, determined to avoid the gallows, the sight of her familiar red hair would give him a running head start toward escape.

Which meant her first stop in Moraig really ought to be a chemist's shop.

As the idea firmed up in her mind, Julianne cleared her throat. Her traveling companion looked up from his rumpled newspaper. "Excuse me," she said, remembering almost too late she was trying to avoid recognition. She readjusted her voice to a lower pitch and leaned in conspiratorially. "Perhaps I could use your help after all—"

A piercing blast from the outside horn cut her words short.

A sickening thud soon followed.

The coach lurched sideways, tilting Julianne along with it. Her head knocked against the latch to the door, making her teeth ache with the force of the blow. The vehicle hung in awkward indecision a long, slow moment, and then swung back to center before rolling several more feet to a stop. For a moment there was only the sound of her panicked breathing, but then a quick rap at the window sent both occupants jumping.

"Is anyone injured?" The voice of the coachman pushed through the thin glass.

"All is well." The portly gentleman settled his bulk more squarely on the seat and calmly folded his newspaper, as if this sort of thing happened all the time. "Struck another one, have we, Mr. Jeffers?"

Julianne rubbed her throbbing head, realizing with dismay that her untied bonnet was now lying in a heap on the filthy coach floor. Her eyes reached for it, but her fingers refused to follow. She could not imagine placing it back on her head. It bothered her to even set her boots upon those sticky floorboards.

The coachman opened the door and peered in, his eyes owlish in concern. "Are you injured, lass?"

Julianne's head ached liked the very devil and her stomach felt tossed by gale force winds, but she could feel no pain in her limbs suggesting an injury of grave magnitude. Still, she hesitated. The dust-covered coachman leaned farther in and his eyes lodged somewhere amid the strands of her hair, which, judging by the curls that swung wildly across her field of vision, had lost several hairpins in addition to the bonnet. Predictably, the driver's lips tipped up in empty fascination.

Suddenly, she was *not* all right. The strain of the three-day journey, her fear of being recognized, and the past few pulse-churning seconds coalesced into a spiraling panic.

No one knew where she was. If she had died here today, her head dashed against the Scottish dirt, her body crushed beneath the wheels of this fetid little coach, her father would have . . . well . . . her father would have *killed* her.

The contents of her stomach—a dubious shepherd's pie from the posting house in Ullapool—clawed for a foothold up her throat. She shoved past the driver, not even caring that she was abandoning all decorum along with her bonnet. She tumbled out into late afternoon sunshine, dodging the boxes that had come loose from the top of the coach. For a moment she swayed, breathing in the fresher air, willing her roiling stomach to settle. All around her, the town moved in an indistinct smear of browns and blues and greens, storefronts and awnings and people swirling in the maelstrom of the moment.

She almost missed it. In the end, it was the *lack* of movement that pulled her attention back for a second look. A small, still form lay in the street, perhaps thirty feet away. Behind her, strangers were already helping to heft the scattered boxes and trunks back onto the coach. She caught snatches of conversation on street corners, and the sound of clattering dishes and laughter trickling out of the open door of a nearby public house. No one seemed to care the afternoon coach had just mowed down one of their citizens, or that the body lay broken and unclaimed in the street.

The coachman picked that unfortunate moment to approach her. "I'll ask you to step back inside, lass. We're running late."

Julianne glared at the man. Surely he didn't expect her to just climb back on board, leaving the body in the street? "We have had an *accident*, sir."

The coachman nodded. "Aye. Happens all the time. Poor little thing darted right out under the wheels. Back in you go, now. The posting house is but a few blocks away."

Julianne took two deep breaths, praying for patience and calm—both of which she suspected would require divine intervention. "I am not getting back on that coach," she ground out, "until someone calls for help."

The driver lowered his voice to a more soothing tone, the sort she often heard used on frightened horses and recalcitrant toddlers. "'Tis a sad sight, I know, especially for a lady like yourself. But it's common enough 'round Moraig. Why don't you take yourself back inside the coach so you dinna see it? We'll only be a moment to get the last of these boxes back up."

Her thoughts flew around the driver's words. *It.* So uncaring as to not even assign the poor victim a gender.

This could not be happening. Good heavens . . . it was her coach. Her hurry. *Her fault.* Hadn't she asked the driver to cut short their time at the last posting house, going so far as to press a sovereign into the man's palm? She had come to Moraig find a murderer, not to turn into one herself. She gestured fiercely toward the form lying so still on the street. "A body's been struck down beneath your wheels," she hissed, "and you are worried only about the state of the *luggage*?"

The coachman paled. "I . . . I can't do anything for it myself, miss."

A new voice rubbed close to Julianne's ear. "Might as well take the coach on to the posting house, Mr. Jeffers. I know your pay is docked for every quarter hour's delay."

Julianne's hand flew up to stifle her gasp of surprise, and she whirled around so fast the earth quite tilted beneath her. She couldn't breathe, could only stare up, and then up some more. An awful sureness settled over her, a sense that someone, somewhere, was having a hearty laugh at her expense. In fact, they probably had a stitch in their side.

Because Julianne had found Patrick Channing—the accused killer she had traveled three days to find—within minutes, not hours. And it was a little too late to find a chemist's shop.

"Very good, sir." The coachman's voice echoed his relief to have the situation turned so squarely over to someone else. "I've a letter for you as well. Would you like to take it now?"

There was a beat of hesitation before Channing shook his head. "No, I'll retrieve it later. After I see to the dog."

Dog? The word bounced about in Julianne's skull for

three long seconds before settling into something coherent. She eyed the still form lying in the street again. The body was not human then. Embarrassment washed over her for such a mistake. Behind her she could hear the crack of the driver's reins and the creak of the wheels, but she scarcely registered the fact that her bonnet and bag were rolling away with the coach.

Instead, she suffered an almost painful awareness of the man towering over her.

He didn't much resemble the man she had once waltzed with at a Yorkshire house party. He looked common, she supposed. And thin. She could see the angular edge of his jaw, the wisp of stubble marring the surface of his gaunt cheeks. He was as tall as ever—some things, a body couldn't hide. But his coat hung loosely from his frame, and his sandy hair, once so neatly trimmed as to nearly be flush against his scalp, brushed the lower edge of his neck.

Did they lack barbers in Moraig?

Or was this part of his disguise, a diabolically clever way of hiding in plain sight?

Channing was studying her too, but the inspection felt clinical, imparting none of the wolfish appreciation offered by either her earlier traveling companion or the driver. And when he spoke, it was with a flat, disinterested baritone that made Julianne blink in surprise.

"Are you injured in some manner I cannot see beyond the state of your hair, miss?"

Julianne's hand flew to tuck an unruly curl behind one ear, as surprised by his lack of acknowledgment as the mention that her hair might be in need of intervention. "I . . . no . . . I mean, I struck my head. On the coach door."

He peered at her as if she was a specimen for dissection, rather than the woman who had once accused him of murder. "There is no visible blood. Your pupils are dilated, but no more so than might be expected after suffering a fright."

Julianne fought a building impatience. How could he be so . . . *impersonal*? Day or night, this man had occupied a central place in her thoughts for eleven long months. He had kissed her senseless and she'd never forgotten, though she'd spent the better part of the last year trying—and failing—to replicate the experience. She wanted to scream at him. Shake him to awareness. Make him look at her as more than just a patient.

Instead, she asked, "Do you not remember me at all?"

His eyes continued their impersonal march across her various and sundry parts before settling back on her face. "Of course," he said, his voice not changing inflection in the slightest. "You always did have a flair for a dramatic entrance, Miss Baxter."

Julianne's heart skidded sideways in her chest. However impassive the acknowledgment, he knew who she was. And yet, he hadn't bolted.

She wasn't quite sure what to make of it.

Without another word of explanation, Channing turned and made his way toward the injured animal. Julianne watched as he shrugged—quite *un*-diabolically—out of his coat, one blurry shoulder after the other. "He's unconscious but breathing," Channing called out. "But he's lost a good deal of blood. The leg will probably need to come off."

He returned to proper focus with a black and white animal wrapped in his coat and cradled in his arms. "I'll need to take him to my clinic and see what can be done in surgery. You might as well come along with me, Miss Baxter. That is, if you trust me."

It was the closest he had come to acknowledging the odd history that bound them together. "I . . ." She hesitated, feeling the stares of a few curious Moraig residents on her, even though she couldn't precisely see them. All she could see at this moment was this man towering over her, his arms full of beast and coat, a smear of blood wrapped around one wrist.

A memory snagged on the shards of her uncertainty, a groundswell of guilt and doubt that had begun at the funeral and chased her across all these miles. There had been blood on him the last time she had seen him too. A copious amount of it, vivid scarlet turned to rust. He had stood in his father's study as if hewn from granite, covered in his brother's blood. At the time, she had seen that blood and interpreted it as evidence of his guilt. But with eleven months of second-guessing behind her, she was no longer sure.

Now the old earl was dead, and the question of what came next was on everyone's lips.

She had entertained no plan beyond finding Patrick Channing and convincing him to return home. This journey had been naught but impulse from the moment she'd boarded the wrong train, still shattered by her first close-up look at Patrick's family since the infamous house party. Some of those in attendance had whispered the earl had died of a broken heart, and Julianne had shrunk against the bruised eyes and hollowed cheeks of Channing's mother and small sisters. It was clear they were devastated, and not only because of the Earl of Haversham's sudden death.

They needed Patrick, and they needed him whole.

And it was equally clear—as the inquest into the circumstances of his brother's death lumbered to life in the wake of his father's passing and the crowd's whispers turned to certain conviction—that she was the only one who knew where he was.

"Quickly, please, Miss Baxter. An animal's life may very well be at stake."

Julianne stared at his bloodied sleeve. The facts didn't match. *He* didn't match. That, more than anything else, cemented her decision, sane or not. "I will come with you."

She lifted her skirts, not even caring that she was probably exposing a good bit of ankle to the gawking townspeople. Perhaps, if she was lucky, that bit of stocking might distract them from the disaster of her hair, and discourage any speculation regarding why she was conversing—without a proper chaperone—with a man believed capable of murder.

"It's a half-mile walk." Channing's gaze roved downward and settled on the exposed heel of one of her boots. "Try not to twist something en route, Miss Baxter. Because I assure you, I'd rather carry the dog."

Chapter 2

JULIANNE. BLOODY. BAXTER.

She was here. In Moraig. About as far as a body could go in Britain and not plunge into the Atlantic. Which was really where he'd like to toss her, those tottering heels and fetching red curls be damned.

He still couldn't believe she was following him home. It was a foolish risk for a woman to take, particularly after the terrible crime she herself had accused him of. It was an even more foolish risk for him to invite her. But surely it was better than leaving the impetuous chit standing in the street. It would have taken all of thirty seconds for her to start poking about the afternoon crowd at the Blue Gander public house, asking questions, spilling secrets. No one in Moraig knew of the circumstances of his past, not even his best friends. Until he knew what his future might hold, he preferred to keep it that way.

Patrick knew there were those in England who still bayed like hounds on the trail of a fox, demanding his blood and justice. He assumed Miss Baxter was of the same mind as his detractors, especially given the nature of their last encounter. Several of his own relatives had called for an inquest into his brother's death, no matter his father's firm insistence it was naught but a terrible accident. The most recent correspondence he had received from his father had been a month or more ago, and unless today's letter carried some vital new information, it was not yet time for Patrick to return.

Miss Baxter's unexpected appearance, however, might just force his hand.

With the unconscious dog in his arms and those disturbing thoughts in his head, Patrick kicked open the door to his derelict house-turned-clinic. He hadn't needed to kick the door, of course. The latch didn't catch properly, just one of a hundred things that needed fixing about the tumbledown place where he laid his head and stitched up the odd farm animal. He could bump it open with his hip, and frequently did so when his arms were full. But the extreme physical reaction and the satisfying thud of his boot against the wood improved his black mood.

Better still, it made the woman trailing beside him jump like a bird flushed from the heather, and *that* made him glad, for no other reason than it gave him a brief upper hand in this situation bound for nowhere good.

As he stepped inside, a ball of yellow fur came hurtling down the steps and wrapped itself around Patrick's legs. Excited barking filled the air.

"Down, Gemmy." He skirted the exuberant and slightly off-balance antics of his pet, the very first animal he had treated upon arriving in Moraig. "Sit," he told the dog.

Gemmy stood.

His tail beat a furious rhythm in the air, and his pink tongue lolled happily. Miss Baxter removed her gloves, then crouched to rub the terrier's ears. "Who is this ill-behaved beast?"

"The mail coach's first victim," Patrick said dryly.

The dog's eyes all but closed on a satisfied groan as Miss Baxter's bare fingers worked some kind of female magic on him. Patrick stared in perplexed irritation. Gemmy had always struck him as a loyal dog, a *man's* dog. He liked to scratch himself exuberantly with his one remaining hind leg, and lick the area where his bollocks had been. He generally stayed on Patrick's heel unless there was a chicken or rabbit in close proximity.

But now this "man's" dog flung himself down worshipfully and presented the decidedly unmannish Miss Baxter with three limbs aloft and a belly to rub, which she proceeded to do with a familiarity that surprised him.

Though she bordered on slatternly this moment, with her hair falling down and her dress wrinkled beyond repair, Miss Baxter seemed a fussy sort of person, more concerned about the cut of her clothes and the curl of her hair than any reasonable person ought to be. To see her remove her gloves to pet not just a dog, but a three-legged mongrel, struck him as slightly absurd.

"How many mail coach victims have there been?" she asked, her voice tight.

"Four since the New Year. Mr. Jeffers is always running late, and the townspeople refuse to put their dogs on a lead. 'Tis bound to result in the odd collision."

"I see you make a hobby out of lopping off their limbs."

The reminder sent Patrick cursing under his breath. He had almost forgotten the bundle he carried, so disarming was the sight of Miss Baxter crouching in his dusty foyer. He strode down the narrow hallway that led to the kitchen. A plaintive bleating came from the part of the house that had once served as the front parlor, but though it was almost time for the orphaned lamb's bottle, he ignored it for the moment.

He settled the newest patient down on the kitchen table and carefully unwrapped his coat from the injured dog's body. Another jacket, ruined. This business was sending him to the poorhouse, sure enough.

Miss Baxter's heels clicked on the weathered floorboards behind him. "Do you live here all alone? Honestly, you are the son of an earl. You could afford a domestic servant or two."

Patrick didn't answer. No sense telling her he refused to accept a single sovereign from his father while he languished in this self-imposed exile. No doubt Miss Baxter had never turned down a farthing in her sweet, pampered life.

He forced his gaze to remain on the mess of the dog's leg instead of pulling to her. It was not an easy battle, because the sight of her was like a brightly colored lure, flashing end over end in turbulent water.

A lid clanged loudly somewhere behind him. "Do you even cook in here at all?" she mused. "These pans appear unused."

Irritation yanked at the edges of his temper. *By the devil*, would she not shut up?

"The kettle works." In fact, he kept it heated and at the ready, but his answer seemed to do little to deflect her prying. He swallowed his frustration over the feminine invasion and began a more thorough exam of his newest patient. The dog he had carried from Main Street was still unconscious, which concerned him. While there was no obvious damage he could see other than the mangled limb, the animal's sluggish return to wakefulness suggested it might have sustained an injury to its head in addition to its leg.

But its continued state of unconsciousness might also present an opportunity. If he moved quickly, he could take off the crushed leg without the animal waking. But quickly was a bit of a stretch, given his lack of an assistant.

He glanced dubiously at Miss Baxter, who had moved on to the side counter and was running a bare, elegant finger over his clean, washed tools. No, she would be no help. Quite the opposite. James MacKenzie, his friend and former roommate, had once helped Patrick with these more challenging procedures, but the man was probably sitting down to supper in his new house across town, wallowing in what appeared to be a healthy dose of marital bliss.

There was no one here but the infinitely nosey Miss Baxter.

"I thought you were taking the dog to surgery." She held up a long-handled implement with a vise clamp on the end. She raised it for a closer examination, squinting at it like a seventy-year-old woman who had lost her quizzing glass. She turned it left and then right, her lips pursed in study. "This is your kitchen," she continued. "Surely you don't see patients in *here*."

Patrick considered telling her he used the thing to castrate calves. Decided better of it.

After all, she might decide to use it on him.

Instead, he reached for the surgical instruments he kept in the nearby cupboard, right next to his meager tin of tea leaves and the shaker of salt. "One table's as good as another. I am not a particular man."

"Clearly." She laid the emasculator down on the far end of the table and came closer. Her eyes widened as she saw what was in his hand. "What is *that*?"

Patrick ignored her question, though that was not precisely the same thing as ignoring her. He hefted the bone saw—a monstrous, well-oiled thing with teeth the size of a man's fingernail—on the table, and enjoyed the quick blanching of Miss Baxter's already milky white skin as he placed it beside the unconscious dog.

For the first time since he laid eyes on her, he was tempted to smile. She believed him a killer, after all. He might even be—he wasn't completely sure of himself, or the tragic events that had destroyed his family and reshaped his future into a frail, furtive thing.

And that meant the next few minutes should prove entertaining, if nothing else.

SURELY HE WASN'T going to do it *here*, on the rough-hewn kitchen table where he took his meals. The very thought of it was enough to make bile sting the back of Julianne's throat. But as he fetched a needle and a length of thread and placed them alongside the torturous implement, it became obvious that he very much was.

"You might want to step away," he advised grimly, rolling up his shirtsleeves. "This next part's a bit tricky."

Julianne swallowed as he picked up the saw. She scrambled back, chased by the rasping sound of metal meeting flesh, only to have one heel twist out from under her on the uneven wooden planks of the farmhouse floor. She fell backward and lay a stunned moment on her back, listening to the heart-stuttering sounds of the saw at work and the fainter but no less insistent bleating of the lamb from somewhere in the depths of the house.

By the stars. It was a house of terrors.

The room spun around those two incongruous sounds.

As she tried to push herself to sitting, her bare hands made contact with a degree of grit and grime that made the floor of the coach seem pristine by comparison. She lifted one hand and peered at her palm in horror. It was dotted with bits of straw and sawdust and smeared with something that looked—and smelled—suspiciously like manure.

"Are you hurt?" Mr. Channing's voice reached down at her.

She breathed in through her nose as the saw scraped on. "No." Not physically, anyway. There was a bit of damage to her pride, she supposed. And her dress.

She supposed she ought to burn it now.

"Well, remove your boots. You're in a farmhouse, not a blasted ballroom. The floor's too treacherous for those ridiculous heels, and I can't be helping you up every time you pitch over."

Julianne rubbed her palm against the hopeless cause of her skirts, and then reached down to unbuckle her boots, all the while trying to seal her ears against the sounds of surgery from the table above. It occurred to her, as she worked the first boot off her foot, she was losing items of clothing with frightening rapidity around this man. She had no idea where her gloves had gotten off to, and her bonnet was still lolling about the floor of the coach. She smoothed a hand over her delicate silk stockings and contemplated removing them too. They had cost a week's pin money on Bond Street. Although, truly, the thought of placing those far-too-expensive stockings on the filthy floor seemed a small price to pay for the distraction from the grisly process above.

As she lined her boots up carefully on the least offensive patch of floor she could find, an inhuman moan pushed its way over the edge of the table. A muffled curse and clattering from the table above suggested that whatever else Patrick Channing was doing, he now had a new problem to contend with.

"Miss Baxter!" he barked, showing more passion in those two words than she had heard in an entire half hour's conversation. "I require your assistance. Quick as you can."

Julianne sprang up as if launched from a jack-in-the-box, pushed by the urgency in his voice. She flew across the floor—and truly, it *was* easier to move without the bother of those heels. And then she was standing beside him and trying very, very hard not to be sick at the sight spread out on the table like a Sunday dinner gone wrong.

The black and white dog lay prone on the table, its remaining limbs paddling slowly. Its mouth opened and closed in a grimace of pain, but it did not appear to be completely awake. There was blood everywhere—on the table, on the saw, on the man.

A thin sheen of perspiration dotted Patrick's forehead. "He's showing signs of returning to consciousness. I need you to hold his muzzle down on the table, in case he comes fully awake."

"Me?" she squeaked, sure he must be joking.

"Quickly, please. I don't have time to argue."

A high keening sound from the dog sent her scrambling forward, no matter her misgivings. She leaned over the table and wrapped her hands around the dog's yawning muzzle, the sight of its sharp teeth tightening the knot of terror in her stomach. "In this manner?"

He nodded, his hands pressed over the gaping wound along the animal's rear flank. "Aye," he said. "Hold steady."

The dog thrashed its head, and her fingers slipped dangerously close to its teeth. "I . . . I can't."

He lifted his eyes, and she felt his gaze like an iron brand. "You can, Miss Baxter. You must. Count to ten, if you need a distraction, but stop distracting *me*."

Julianne's hands shook against the animal's muzzle, but she renewed her grip. She began to count off the seconds in a firm, unwavering voice she barely recognized as her own. "One, two, three."

She could scarcely believe she was doing this.

"Four, five."

What if the dog bit her?

"Six, seven, eight."

What if the animal was mad, on top of being injured?

"Nine, ten."

What if . . .

It occurred to her the animal had stopped moving. Relief nudged the terror aside. She loosened her hold, but did not pull her hands away.

"Pinch the skin between his front toes, if you please."

Julianne looked up. Patrick was threading a needle now—when had she started to think of him as Patrick, instead of a more appropriate form of address? Probably somewhere around the time she had started to shed her clothing. "You want me to pinch him?" she asked, confused. "He's just gone off to sleep again!"

"It will test his reaction to pain, Miss Baxter. A good, sharp pinch. Use your nails. I want to be sure he's unconscious before I begin to suture the wound."

Though it went against her very nature to do something to purposefully hurt an animal, his voice brooked no argument, and Julianne reached a hand through the blood-matted fur and dug her nail into the skin between two of the dog's toes.

When the animal remained utterly still, Patrick murmured, "Good girl. Is he breathing?"

Julianne's knees trembled. There was no mistaking who the praise was directed toward, given that the dog was unmistakably male. She placed her palm against the animal's muzzle and felt its steady respirations. "Yes."

"I should be only a few minutes more. Hold steady, in case I need you to do it again."

As he began the process of applying the needle to the dog's skin, Julianne's emotions shifted from panicked compliance to unsteady wonder. He worked in silence, one sure pass of the needle after another. She had never seen a man do such a thing before, and the sight shocked her for its masculinity rather than its domesticity. With every push of the needle through the animal's skin, she could see the flex of muscle along the edge of his rolled-up sleeve. It was hard to believe she had once danced in those arms, flirtations and innuendo passing between them as they loped around the edge of a ballroom.

"I think we're in the clear now, barring internal injuries."

Julianne's gaze jerked up from the sight of his arms, her spine tingling with unwelcome awareness. The sight of Patrick Channing in shirtsleeves, covered in blood, stirred an unfortunate return to the same memory that had plagued her these past few months. His brother's death was a nightmare she was destined to relive, it seemed. The indisputable method of murder had been gunshot, fired from a distance. All were in agreement on this point. Any usual manner of killer would have slipped quietly away, his hands still clean. In point of fact, she was *quite* sure she had seen a man running away from—not toward—the scene of the crime.

But if Patrick had indeed shot his brother in a cold,

calculated fashion, why had he been covered in blood while standing there in his father's study?

Julianne forced herself to step away from the table and its bright, coppery smell of blood. She opened the stove's door and stirred the embers there, the need to be useful an unexpected pain. If only she hadn't said anything that fateful day . . .

She had come to Scotland determined to convince him to return to England and at least *attempt* to save his younger sisters, who—through no fault of their own— were facing utter ruin. And in doing so, she hoped to assuage in some small degree the guilt that still trailed her for her role in all of this. But the sight of all that blood rattled the bars of her memory, and the doubts that had chased her here firmed into something regrettably real.

Seeing Patrick Channing now, his hands laboring to save a dog whose worth was so little not even its owner had claimed it from the street, she could see he was a man who valued life.

And that meant she had made a grave, grave error.

Chapter 3

Patrick tied off the last knot in shadowed darkness, a testament to the day's steady march toward evening. As usual, he felt relieved. One never knew which direction surgery might go—not that the concern had ever kept him from trying.

He had every confidence the animal would live now, barring putrefaction of the wound. He should put some thought into locating the dog's owner and see if he could press him for a few shillings. Not that he regretted the extravagance of treating the dog, but money for supplies was a constant struggle. He considered whether he ought to ask Miss Baxter to pay for the materials he had just expended. After all, it was *her* coach that had caused the dog's injuries, and Patrick knew Mr. Jeffers, the coachman, struggled to put food on his own family's table. And for all the fact her shoes had gone missing and some of those red curls had abandoned their moorings, she radiated money the way his cookstove radiated heat.

But he abandoned that idea almost as quickly as it sprang free. He did not want to be beholden to this woman.

Patrick removed the glass globe from the lamp and

struck a match to light it before turning to face her. She was sitting on the floor, her feet tucked under her and Gemmy's head on her lap. Now that the immediate frenzy of surgery was past, he could turn his mind to what her presence here meant. Nothing good—that much was obvious.

Still, there was some relief in having the decision so firmly taken out of his hands. He was tired of skirting the demands of his moral compass. He missed his family, and the fresh, rolling hills of Yorkshire. The leaves had probably started to turn, and autumn had always been his favorite time of year to spend in the country. He missed his little sisters, Mary and Eleanor, and their bright, cheerful faces. Missed the stables where he had spent so much of his time.

Missed his brother, Eric, although there was no help for that.

Miss Baxter's discovery of his whereabouts was unfortunate, but it was not going to send the noose over his neck in the next five minutes. They had time enough for a conversation, before he decided what to do with her.

"How are you feeling?" he asked, breaking the long-fingered silence.

She drew an unsteady breath, and the motion drew his eye to the fine, high shape of her bosom. He was reminded, in that moment, of his former life, and his father's expectations for him. Miss Baxter's unwelcome appearance here did more than stir uncomfortable memories of dances and country house parties and the life he had once resented.

She reminded him of the brother he had lost, and the unfortunate argument that had preceded Eric's death.

"I am fine." Her eyes lifted to meet his. "Does the dog still live?"

"Aye." He moved on to light a tin lantern on the other side of the room, and then settled it on the edge of the nearby countertop. "I appreciate your assistance." And he did. She had surprised him today, with her help in surgery. She was not precisely the empty-headed flirt with a flair for drama and a penchant for mischief he had believed her to be.

No, today she had proven herself a levelheaded flirt. A more dangerous beast, entirely.

"I did too little to warrant any measure of thanks." Her words were deceiving, making her seem the complete opposite of the vivacious young woman who had stirred up brotherly jealousies at Summersby. She'd been trouble even before she'd kissed him in the foyer and then offered herself as the sole witness to his brother's murder. He ought to pull her to her feet and send her packing.

Instead, he slumped down on the floor beside her.

Gemmy squirmed a few inches toward him and nudged Patrick's hand with an insistent nose. He ruffled the dog's fur. After the stressful circumstances of the past hour, it was soothing to touch an animal whose life didn't literally rest in his hands.

"I had heard a rumor you were serving as Moraig's veterinarian." Her voice wavered. "But I wasn't sure I believed it. However did you learn to do all this?"

Patrick kept his gaze trained on his dog. No doubt she was as horrified by this aspect of his life as the other. Only *this* part of his life he had chosen. The other parts had been wrenched out of his control.

"What did you think I was up to these past few years, given my absence in Town? I was studying. In Italy."

Her pert nose wrinkled. "My father simply said you were traveling on the continent. Lazing away your days, spending money, if the rumors are to be believed."

Patrick rubbed the silken fur of Gemmy's ear, weighing the possible implications of confessing the details of his time in Italy to a woman incapable of a single guarded moment. His desire to confess *something* won out over his need for silence.

"I spent four years studying at the veterinary college in Turin. My father indulged my studies as a curiosity, but would not permit me to set up a practice. He considered it a hobby to pass the time, little more."

"So you are formally trained?"

"Yes." He shifted uneasily, surprised by the lack of censure in her voice. "Although it doesn't take much skill to amputate a leg. A bit of brute strength and a strong stomach are the only requisite traits. The town needed someone to doctor their animals, and I needed them."

"What did you need from Moraig?" Her voice softened to a whisper.

Patrick fanned his fingers over Gemmy's reassuring coat. It did not escape his notice that Miss Baxter's fingers swirled in similar circles mere inches from his own.

Damned lucky dog.

"Companionship." He shrugged. "I've friends from my days at Cambridge who live here, and they've been good enough to not ask questions. Moraig offered some degree of anonymity, I suppose, while my father works to deflect the questions. No one has thought to look for me here, and there is very little news that makes it here from London. It's a simple life. Adequate." He did not add that his life, though lonely, was something he no longer took for granted.

He exhaled forcibly. Might as well address the next question head-on, given that he needed to know whom to strangle. "How did you learn of my whereabouts, Miss Baxter?"

"I heard your name in passing when I was on holiday in Brighton this summer. Someone you know—Mr. Cameron?"

A curious mixture of relief and irritation settled in. Miss Baxter's discovery, then, could be laid at the feet of one of his best friends. He could not fault the man. Patrick had given David Cameron no cause—or request—for secrecy. "Cameron's one of those school chums from Cambridge. Serves as Moraig's magistrate at the present."

She inclined her head. "I must presume he is either a disreputable sort of magistrate, or else you have not told the good citizens of Moraig about your past circumstances." Her eyes glowed nickel-bright in the lamp's flicker. "I don't blame you for hiding here, Patrick. No one would."

He should have been too exhausted to respond to the low velvet scrawl of her voice. After all, this was Julianne Baxter. The girl flirted as easily as she breathed. But damned if she wasn't lowering her lashes in a manner that instantly inflamed his prurient interests, despite the grave nature of this discussion. "I'm not hiding, Miss Baxter. I've a life here, a purpose. I am not just playacting a role." He did not add that finding something useful to do with his hands had been the only thing that kept him sane following his brother's death.

"I can quite see that. What you did for that dog was nothing short of miraculous." Far from putting him at ease, the quick smile she offered stirred unfortunate memories. His understanding of this woman was shaped by history. She had once gifted him with such a smile, just after he had kissed her. And then she had turned around and tossed a similar smile in his brother's direction not two minutes later.

At the time, Eric had been the one ready to marry, and Julianne had been an eligible young woman looking to make an advantageous match. But *he* was the heir now, unless his father's efforts to dissuade his detractors failed. Her lashes were being lowered in *his* direction. And that meant Miss Baxter either had a tremendously fickle heart or a very mercenary spirit.

"I am sorry," she told him. "For all of it. Not that it helps you now."

Patrick's fingers tightened on Gemmy's fur, and his pulse bounded to hear her ill-timed words. The girl thought a simple apology, a mere "sorry," could fix what she had done? "You accused me of murder," he pointed out.

"I didn't accuse you, exactly. I merely related what I had seen." She hesitated. "I have thought about that day many times since, and I regret the pain I have caused your family. If I could do it again, I would choose not to speak against you."

The delicate tremor in her voice goaded him to belief. Perhaps the chit *was* sorry. She certainly sounded contrite. But "sorry" would not help either of them if she was called to provide testimony under oath.

"Do you think you would have a choice?" He dragged a hand through his hair, trying to reconcile her apparent naïveté with the sharp mind he knew to clack along behind those persuasive green eyes. "You could be compelled to testify, Miss Baxter. You'd have no choice in the matter at all if you were called as a witness. And all it will take would be one word from you to place a noose around my neck."

Even in the dim light, he could see the pallor that

descended over her. "I am not at all sure that is true. After all, the events of eleven months ago are somewhat in doubt—"

"Perhaps in *your* mind." He gave a short laugh that echoed like a gunshot over the room's exposed rafters and made him wince as the sound circled back 'round. He stared up at the ceiling. Aside from the danger she presented at the point of testimony, what did it matter if she thought he had murdered his brother? After all, he considered her a liar whose primary lot in life was to generate and propagate rumors.

Perhaps they were a good match.

He gained his feet, summoning Gemmy with a snap of his fingers. The terrier lurched to obey, but cast a longing look back at Miss Baxter. Patrick understood how the dog felt. But neither of them was going to spend any time in this woman's lap, no matter the temptation of her petite, silk-wrapped curves. The girl was like hives: popping up when least expected, impossible to shake off. Removing her from his house—and preferably from his life—was the first priority of business.

"We need to fetch your things from the posting station and get you to the Blue Gander where you can take a room. You cannot stay here tonight or tongues will wag. Moraig may be small and isolated, but rumors have a way of spreading here just as fast as they do in London."

"Oh. I suppose you are right." She shifted her feet from under her, and he had to force himself to avert his eyes from the shock of her pale ivory stockings. "I confess, I had not given any thought to where I might stay."

Patrick offered Miss Baxter his hand and pulled her to standing, determinedly ignoring how small and alive her palm felt against his own. He released her the moment she was steady. "It occurs to me that you scarcely give much thought to anything of importance before throwing yourself into the fray, Miss Baxter. But given that the hour grows late, and I still need to feed my bloody lamb, perhaps you ought to tell me why you are here."

JULIANNE GLANCED DOWN from the distraction of Patrick Channing's lamp-lit scowl.

Far from finding refuge in the moiré silk of her skirts, her gaze snagged on the grubby fabric. She felt like a different woman than when she had put this dress on this morning. Then, she had been thinking of nothing more than the pressing need to find this man and tell him the news he must hear. She'd hoped that in the process of finding him, she might find some measure of peace for her role in all of it.

Now, the dress that had borne those hopes was close to destroyed. The hem had ripped during her fall onto the kitchen floor, and a smear of blood stained the front of the bodice from where she had leaned in to wrap her hands around the dog's muzzle.

When she had boarded the train in Leeds, she had not considered how Patrick might *feel* about the news she carried, so desperate and important had her task seemed. But there was nothing to be done for it now. It would be far worse for all of their futures to withhold this information. She'd waited too long as it was. "I've come to find you because you need to go home, Patrick."

His jaw hardened. "Do not presume to tell me what I need to do, Miss Baxter. And do not call me Patrick. Our fathers might be good friends, but you are no friend of mine."

Julianne steeled her nerve against his scathing retort.

"Well then, you need to go home." She hesitated, this last bit of it painful for her to say, and likely devastating for him to hear. *"Lord Haversham."*

He took a sudden, whiplashed step back. She could almost see him wrestle his thoughts back to center. "What game do you play, Miss Baxter?"

"The earl . . ." She exhaled, and rubbed her sweating palms against her skirts, wishing the terrier's soft, reassuring fur was still within reach. "Your father died last week. I am so, so sorry."

He paled beneath the sandy fringe of his stubble, but appeared possessed by an almost supernatural calm. "I do not believe you."

She had expected his grief. Possibly his anger. But she hadn't expected doubt.

"I speak the truth," she told him, praying he believed her.

The calm with which he engaged this conversation began to show the faintest of cracks. "The *truth*." He stumbled over the word, as if it sliced his tongue to even utter the single syllable. "You, of all people, do not hold the truth in good stead. This is a ruse you have concocted to force my premature return, nothing more. Is there a reward out for my head, then?"

This time it was Julianne's turn to jerk backward as if struck. She felt ill, her stomach churning to hear the venom in his voice. Not that she didn't deserve some measure of it.

"Perhaps you seek the pleasure—the notoriety—of being the one to bring me in," he went on. "Or perhaps you have a moribund fascination to see the reduced circumstance of a man who might kill his own brother?"

Good heavens. Did he really believe she was capable of such a thing? "I'm here because I felt you deserved to know," she protested. "That you would *want* to know. There would be no reason for me to fabricate such a thing."

"What you fail to realize is that I am in regular correspondence with my father, and the letter the coachman mentioned is undoubtedly from him." He crossed his arms, though she could see his fists clench reflexively. "My father is the only person I trust, and I have no intention of returning until he sends word."

Julianne considered the possibilities, given her regrettable knowledge of the past week. "Are you sure the letter is from your father?"

"My father is the only person who knows where I am."

"Not the only person," she pointed out. "*I* learned where you were, after all. Perhaps someone else has sent you a letter. Your friend David Cameron. I believe he enjoyed an extended stay in Brighton after his recent marriage."

"Cameron and his new bride returned to Moraig a sennight ago."

"Well then, perhaps the mail was delayed en route to Moraig." She thought back to the solemn graveside service. It had been a beautiful ceremony, the leaves of the nearby trees just beginning to turn in color. But she had not spared much time admiring the beauty of a Yorkshire autumn. The countess's frozen vigil, and the tears of her two small girls, had held Julianne's attention far too well. "I saw him buried, Patrick. There can be no mistake."

He stared at her a long, fractious minute. "There can always be a mistake." His unspoken accusation hung in the air between them.

Julianne shook her head, anger beginning to simmer now at his refusal to entertain the truth. Her imaginings of this interaction—and she had entertained a few—had never gone like this. "You are the new Earl of Haversham, Patrick," she told him. "And because of that, you must return *now*."

His mouth opened. Closed. Opened again. "Do not call me that," he all but growled.

"Which? Patrick? Or Haversham?"

"Either."

"Then what should I call you? Channing no longer fits. You can deny it, you can hate me, but it will not make it any less true."

Somewhere in the house, the lamb found its voice again. He turned from her with a muffled curse and snatched a half-full bottle of milk from a nearby shelf.

"There's more," she offered to the hard slant of his shoulders.

He tied a slip of cloth over the bottle with a length of twine before turning back around to capture her in the steel band of his gaze. "You've told me my father is dead." His voice rang hoarse, a sure sign that the crack in his prickly, competent armor had widened to a chasm of canyonlike proportions. "How much more could there be?"

Julianne wished she had more than her voice to convince him, given that he seemed to distrust her so much. "An inquest has been called into Eric's death. I've been told I will be expected to testify."

His face betrayed no expression. "There has always been talk of an inquest, and nothing came of it. My father has assured me—"

"Your father cannot help you in this. Not anymore." Julianne drew a deep breath, praying the maddening man saw reason. "You *need* to return, Patrick, and fight these accusations through the proper channels. That is why I am here."

The little lamb called out again, fainter now, as if it had given up all hope of its dinner and was now considering crying itself to sleep. He snatched up the lantern and strode toward the door, his wide shoulders filling the frame. But something halted him, just on the threshold of the hallway. He turned his head over his shoulder, and she felt pinned like a scientific specimen by his gaze. "You told the authorities I murdered my brother. Were, in fact, the sole witness to the purported crime." His eyes burned like twin tapers in the lamplight. "It was an accident, Miss Baxter, as I have repeatedly attested. A terrible mistake, a shot gone wrong. Do you truly believe I am capable of such a thing?"

Julianne wrapped her head around the question. Discovered the ends of her thoughts would not meet flush at center. "You seemed . . . *uncertain* in your explanation to the magistrate. If your brother was shot by accident, why didn't you offer a stronger defense?"

"I was scarcely standing. For God's sake, my brother had just died in my arms. You'll forgive me if I wasn't thinking clearly."

Julianne stilled at his confirmation that he had been there when his brother had drawn his last breath. A scald of remorse washed over her, as hot as the water in the kettle upon the stove. Because if she believed him innocent—as she was increasingly prone to do—it meant she had done something so terrible as to be damned thrice over.

Not that his innocence mattered, in the total, awful scheme of things.

She raised her chin. "It scarcely matters what I believe. Because guilty or innocent, if you hang, your title reverts to the Crown. And that means your family loses everything."

Chapter 4

IF MISS BAXTER was to be believed—and he wasn't sure the girl's claims held more than a cursory brush with anything approximating truth—his father was dead. His sisters' futures were poised on the brink of ruin.

And Patrick was facing the fight of his life.

Another tentative bleat echoed down the hallway. His fingers fisted around the bottle. Bloody lamb. Bloody timing.

Bloody Julianne Baxter.

He stalked into the hallway and kicked the kitchen door shut on Miss Baxter's pinched face with an angry boot. Unlike the front door, this one stayed latched. He took an almost feral pleasure in leaving Julianne shut up in his darkening kitchen, with only the ghosts of her past wrongs and the recovering dog to torment her.

The little ewe lamb greeted the bottle with an enthusiasm that bordered on violence. Patrick leaned over the makeshift pen, still seething with resentment, and stared at the outline of the lamb's busy nose and tongue working hard against the fabric teat. His thoughts, usually so ordered, worked themselves into a similar frenzy.

Christ, but he didn't need this distraction. Until today, he had moved through the ordered nuances of his life in Moraig keeping the events of that day well buried. Now it seemed clear he had merely thrown a cursory bit of dirt over the details.

With Miss Baxter padding about his kitchen, it was far too easy to sink back into the past. His father had been the only one who believed him innocent in Eric's death, at least of the act of premeditated murder. The girl's statement to the magistrate, full of damning details that even *he* had trouble refuting, had much to do with the opinions that quickly turned against him.

Not that he blamed them. It had been his rifle, after all. His bullet that had struck his brother in the chest. His guilt to live with, even as his father had battled to save the remnants of what was now—but should never have been—his birthright.

"Hullo! Anyone home?" A baritone voice pushed at him from the parlor door.

Patrick looked up, startled from the torment of his memories. "In here." He chased the greeting with a foul, whispered curse. Covert expletives were necessary, given the man attached to the voice intruding on his thoughts. What in the name of all that was holy was the town vicar doing in his house?

Reverend Ramsey's girth offered a commanding presence from the pulpit, but squeezing through the narrow doorway, it made him resemble a turtle emerging from its shell. When he saw what occupied Patrick's hands, he pulled up short. The lamb chose that very moment to dispense of its last meal, wagging its tail vigorously as pellets of dung fell onto the parquet floor. The reverend snatched a kerchief from the depths of his black coat to cover his nose. "I say," he gasped. "If you'd come to church on a more regular basis, Mr. Channing, you'd know that cleanliness is next to godliness. 'Tis customary for a gentleman like yourself to keep beasts in a stable, is it not?"

Patrick eased back from where he leaned over the pen, disengaging the bottle from the lamb's mouth with a gentle twist. The lamb bleated its objection, but there was no helping it: the bottle had been sucked dry. He tossed the creature an armful of hay from the nearby sideboard as he considered his answer. No doubt the vicar and Miss Baxter would disagree, but he had always considered the warm, earthy smell of manure from a healthy animal one of the most natural things in the world. "It is also customary to knock first to announce one's presence," he finally said. "It seems we are both gentlemen who eschew convention."

Reverend Ramsey lowered his handkerchief in indignation. "The door was *open*, sir."

Patrick regarded his visitor steadily. They both knew the door wasn't open. It simply wasn't latched. "Can I help you, Reverend?"

"I heard from Stephens you might have my dog."

"Stephens? I don't recall the blacksmith being on the scene this afternoon."

"He said he heard it from the butcher, who had it straight from Mrs. Pue."

Patrick hesitated. Even after eleven months, the voracious machinations of Moraig's rumor mill remained somewhat of a mystery to him. "And Mrs. Pue is . . . ?"

"Mr. Jeffers's sister."

"Ah."

"He's a black and white collie. Spots on his nose. His name is Skip."

Patrick expelled a frustrated breath at the accurate

description. All hope of extracting some form of payment to cover the costs of the afternoon's surgery scattered like goose down on the wind. There was really no point in asking. The vicar was notoriously tightfisted with his own money, even as he expected the townsfolk to be generous with theirs. The knowledge that the hapless creature he had just snatched from death's jaws belonged to Ramsey was enough to make him want to take up bricklaying instead of vetting.

It was hard enough not to get attached to the beasts he helped. Turning them over to unworthy—and nonpaying—owners was harder still.

"Well, I've a black and white dog recovering in my kitchen. You'll have to take a look and see if he's yours. He's lost a leg and will need to be watched carefully for infection, but he's a good chance of pulling through." Patrick didn't add that there would be a good deal of fecal matter to deal with in the near future, at least until the animal was steady on its remaining three feet.

Sometimes the Lord worked in mysterious ways.

Ramsey's heavy shoes shuffled on the straw-strewn floor. "He's lost a leg, then? I'm not sure . . . that is, I don't think . . . He's a working dog, Mr. Channing. Perhaps it would be better to put him down."

Patrick's thoughts flew to Gemmy, and how the scruffy, damaged terrier twisted his heart up in knots. "So Skip's a working dog, eh? Gathers your flock and all?" He almost snorted. The vicar's idea of "work" was about as far from his own as the distance from Moraig to the moon.

And Reverend Ramsey's flock was more of the pious, human variety.

"Aye." The man lifted a finger to tug at his white

clerical collar. "And he's no good at all to me with only three legs. Perhaps it was God's will that he die."

Patrick unfurled his fingers, testing his patience. "He'll still make someone a fair companion. If not for you, perhaps someone else." He wiped his palms on his trousers, dislodging the worst of the filth and blood that had accumulated over the course of the evening before stooping to pick up his lantern. "And I'll not put him down after I went to the trouble of saving him. Besides, you haven't confirmed he's yours yet. Plenty of black and white dogs running loose in Moraig. Come on to the kitchen and take a look."

He strode down the hallway with Ramsey lumbering along behind him. He had no doubt the dog belonged to the vicar, but it would be interesting to see if the man tried to claim it was a stray. If he searched his memory, he could even remember seeing the animal now, lurking about the churchyard the few times he'd taken himself to Sunday service. The dog had been a bone-thin, furtive thing the last time he saw him, scarcely more than a puppy, but the confluence of spots around the dog's muzzle matched the ones in his memory.

He opened the kitchen door, girding himself for the difficult business of discharging the dog to a recalcitrant owner, but froze as a far different dilemma inserted itself front and center. Miss Baxter stood with her back to the door, leaning over the cookstove in a state that went somewhat beyond simple dishabille. She was still missing her shoes.

But now she was also missing her bodice.

No, not missing it, exactly. She was holding it. *In her hands*.

No matter the room's meager light, the sight of her blinding white chemise and beribboned corset felt like a stick in his eye. Even as he watched, she poured hot water from the kettle onto the bunched fabric and began to rub the two sides together. He was struck by the absurdity of her efforts. Any usual variety of fool knew pouring hot water on a bloodstain only made it set up faster.

Not that Miss Baxter appeared a usual variety of anything, standing in his kitchen in only her skirts and unutterables.

Too late, Patrick thought to warn her. "Julianne," he said curtly, only to wince as he realized her given name had escaped his lips instead of the far more appropriate formal address.

She whirled around, giving them a firsthand view of what under other circumstances could objectively be called a delightful, cotton-clad bosom. He risked a glance down at Ramsey's balding pate. The florid color staining the man's scalp told Patrick that no matter his own sparse attendance at church, the not-quite-naked Miss Baxter was the one now being judged here.

And despite the certain danger to her reputation, despite the fact he had cautioned her of just such a possibility, Patrick found himself enjoying the turnabout.

JULIANNE'S HEART FLUNG itself against the confines of her chest.

The same chest she was all but displaying like an exotic curiosity to the new Earl of Haversham and . . . *merciful heavens* . . .

Was that a vicar?

Her eyesight wasn't the best—not that she would admit that to a single, solitary soul—but she could still make out the dark coat and white collar that marked the new arrival as a man who relied on his Maker to decide his wardrobe instead of a valet. She had been very foolish to think she could quickly deal with the stain and be properly clothed again before anyone was the wiser. She had thought . . . well, she had thought a lamb might take a bit of time to go through a bottle. An hour at least. Apparently she didn't know the first thing about farm animals.

Or vicars, for that matter.

She had thought them kindly gentlemen, more interested in the state of one's soul than the size of one's breasts. Clearly she had been wrong, given the man's unswerving focus in that very area.

"We've a visitor." Patrick stepped closer, bringing his too-thin face into focus. He motioned about his chest in a parody of what she needed to do. "You might want to . . . er . . . cover yourself."

"I . . ." She stumbled over what to say. She had never stood in this state of undress in such close proximity to a man in her life. For her first experience to be undressed in the vicinity of *two* men took the scenario from damning to hysterical. "My dress is . . . that is, my bodice is—"

"Missing?" For the first time this entire dreadful day, a devilish gleam flashed in Patrick's usually stern eyes.

"Stained," she finished weakly. Her hand fluttered over the neckline of her chemise. Too late, she realized the motion merely drew the visitor's unwelcome attention more fiercely. If she hadn't felt like snarling an oath, she would have laughed. She had endured three London Seasons cringing over the attention her hair sometimes caused, when all along she had unknowingly possessed a more formidable distraction. "I've misplaced my bag with my clothing, and as we need to head straight to Summersby on the morning coach, I cannot afford to let the stain set up." She lowered her voice to a whisper. "I had thought you would be delayed a bit longer with the lamb and its bottle," she added crossly.

The vicar finally seemed to shake himself to lucidity, though his eyes did not leave her chest. "I confess, I had not pegged you for someone who would consort with a woman of questionable virtue, Mr. Channing."

Julianne's irritation shifted into peevish territory. Nothing untoward had happened here, and she refused to act as if it had. This gentleman might be a vicar, and she might be a girl who hid her poor eyesight from the world, but even she could see hypocrisy when it was dangled in front of her nose. She fitted a smile to her face, summoning her three years of experience dealing with London drawing rooms. "Why, how refreshing it is to hear a man stand in judgment of a woman. And how *original* of you, sir."

A wheezing sound gripped the vicar's throat, and his eyes bugged round in his skull. "Reverend Ramsey," Patrick said hurriedly, taking the man by the arm and steering him toward the sleeping dog. "I realize this seems a bit . . . *improper*. But Miss Baxter is an old family friend, the daughter of the Viscount Avery." He glanced over his shoulder, and motioned with his chin toward the fabric she clutched in her hands. "She is here only because she assisted with your dog's surgery today."

Julianne lifted a brow. That wasn't precisely true, and they both knew it. Then again, she supposed he'd scarcely burn in hell for the sin of lying to a vicar when he had other more impressive ones at the ready.

As the pair bent to inspect the black and white dog, Julianne turned back to the stove and wrung her lingering irritation out on the wet bodice. The bloodstain was still there. If anything, it was even more noticeable, now that the other layers of dirt had been loosened. With no other choice on the horizon, she slipped the damp fabric over her shoulders, though her skin practically screamed in objection. Only when she felt she could face them with some degree of respectability did she turn back around.

"It's not my dog," the vicar was saying. "Skip is . . . taller."

"The dog is lying down." Patrick's voice echoed with a dry wit she remembered from their oft-remembered waltz, so many months ago.

"Well, it looks nothing like Skip. You'd know that if you attended church more often."

"I attend as much as my conscience bids me." Patrick's voice remained flat, the picture of disinterest. "And for all that it was a puppy the last time I saw him, it strikes me that this animal is either your dog or its twin."

How does he do that? Julianne wondered. How could someone remain so steady in the face of such derision? Despite the underlying sarcasm evident in his choice of words, Patrick outwardly appeared no more ruffled than if he was flicking a fly off his evening meal. She wanted to rake her nails across the vicar's face, and she was only watching the interplay.

Julianne drifted closer, trying to unravel the odd pieces of the conversation. To cover the fact she was hovering, she picked up the bloodied saw that still sat upon the table, ran a dish towel over its length, and replaced it in the cupboard. A sudden silence sent her peeking over her shoulder. Patrick was staring at her, an unreadable expression on his face.

The good vicar, however, was glowering. "Miss

Baxter, wasn't it? You certainly seem at home here, for someone who is merely visiting a spell."

"Jul— that is, Miss Baxter is not staying," Patrick said quickly. "I had planned to deliver her to the Blue Gander so she can take a room for the night."

Ramsey smiled nastily. "It is clear she has assisted you with *something* here this afternoon, Mr. Channing, and I'll wager it's something more than surgery. Although I suppose the Gander is as good a place as any for a tryst. It's a veritable den of iniquity."

Julianne had heard enough. She slammed the cupboard door shut and conjured the frosty Society miss she kept bottled for special occasions. "There has been no seduction, Reverend, no matter your slavering imagination on the topic."

Patrick took a step toward her. "Miss Baxter—"

Julianne dismissed him with a sharp wave of her hand. "I shall forgive you for not knowing that this man is the new Earl of Haversham, given that the news has not yet reached Moraig. However, from this point on, you will address him as my lord, as is his due."

The vicar began to sputter.

"Julianne—" Patrick said, more sharply this time.

"And next time you choose to question *my* virtue, you might consider averting your eyes. I am sure the good Lord would not wish you to risk permanent damage to your vision."

The vicar's face turned a frightening shade of red she had only ever seen in overripe berries. He looked from Julianne, to Patrick, back to Julianne again. And then he stormed out of the kitchen, leaving the dog to its admittedly brighter fate.

Patrick exhaled loudly as the bang of the front door echoed faintly from the front of the house. His gaze settled awkwardly on her mouth, which had the unexpected—and unwelcome—effect of making her skin flush warm, no matter the travesty of her cold, wet bodice. "You've quite the tongue on you, Julianne."

She bit back a smile at his automatic use of her first name. "A consequence of my education at the hands of the *ton*, I'm afraid. That man is a bully."

He nodded slowly. "Aye. He is that. But I'm afraid Reverend Ramsey also holds the ear of every rumor-monger in town."

She tucked an errant curl behind one ear, wincing as she realized exactly how much of her hair was springing free. She probably *did* look as if she had just tumbled out of bed. Still, she doubted Reverend Ramsey held quite as much sway in the town as Patrick credited him. "Honestly, the man is a lecher. And if you've been able to hide in plain sight for eleven months, it suggests the information flow in Moraig is predominantly circular."

"Still, I suspect everyone here will know of this by morning."

Julianne smiled tightly. Even should the information leak forth, she could not imagine it reaching London. "How fortuitous, then, that we shall not be here come morning."

His lips tipped downward. "Oh?"

She nodded. "We'll be on the coach to Inverness, and then on to Summersby."

Patrick's eyes probed hers, suddenly cold for all their rich brown color. "I've agreed to nothing of the sort, and well you know it."

Julianne looked away first and smoothed an uncomfortable hand over the front of her ruined bodice. No, blast the man. He'd not agreed to it. Not yet.

And that had her very, very worried.

Chapter 5

PATRICK LEFT JULIANNE at the Blue Gander in the hands of the innkeeper whose eyes had brightened at the arrival of a moneyed guest from London, even one wearing a filthy, wet dress. Guilt trailed him for depositing her there, but he told himself he wasn't abandoning her. For Christ's sake, she'd traipsed across the entirety of Scotland without a chaperone. She could survive a bloody night on the Blue Gander's sheets.

At least here she'd find servants to order about. Indeed, as he headed for the posting house, the sound of her voice trailed him out the door, already demanding a hot bath and tray of food to be brought up to her room.

The quiet of the street should have felt like a balm to his soul after the last few hours in her stinging presence, but instead, the darkness sent his thoughts tumbling. He'd lost a brother in the last year, and Julianne's claim that he had now lost his father was still untenable.

It was easier to keep grief at bay when one considered whose lips had delivered the news. He reminded himself he'd seen this woman lie before: beautifully, flawlessly, with tears in her eyes and the perfect, thin waver to her voice. Then, she'd been describing how she had seen him point his hunting rifle at his brother and pull the trigger.

Annoyance coiled beneath his skin as he stepped into the posting house. He was willing to admit a role in his brother's death. Grief had not clouded his judgment in this regard—he blamed himself almost every day. The truth was there, and he was man enough to take responsibility for his actions. But not for the account she had provided to the world—and, more importantly, to the magistrate.

Mr. Jeffers had already gone home for the evening, but Julianne's bag and his own letter were produced by a dutiful clerk. Patrick returned to the Blue Gander with no clearer a plan than when he had left Julianne there, but he *did* take a childish pleasure in at least denying her the courtesy of dry clothing while he indulged in a much-needed drink. He carried her bag to a table at the farthest corner of the inn's public room, dropped his limbs into a chair, and ordered up a whisky he couldn't afford instead of the pint he ought to have.

He searched her bag first, though his actions gave him the merest moment's pause. His fingers tripped over filmy nightclothes and silk stockings and endless handfuls of neatly folded frocks that looked better suited for garden tea parties than a sojourn to northern Scotland in autumn. He took pleasure in shaking them apart, destroying the evidence of her care in packing.

Childish, perhaps, but one had so few chances to get the best of Miss Julianne Baxter.

When he had firmly established she carried neither a weapon nor a sensible cloak with her, his impatience and his conscience finally gained enough ground to move on. Pulling the letter from his coat pocket, he studied the address. By tacit agreement, his father's letters had been forwarded through a trusted third party to avoid detection by the authorities, though they had all been written—and addressed—in his father's hand. His stomach turned over as he admitted to himself this missive was already different. The other letters had been addressed in a tight, neat scrawl, his father's mark of efficiency.

This one held loops and flourishes. A feminine hand.

His mother's hand.

He broke the plain wax seal with his lungs sealed tight, then scanned the pages with an almost fatalistic sense of expectation. *Regret to inform* . . .

Dire circumstances . . .

Please come home.

He read the last line three different times, scarcely able to make sense of it. What, exactly, was he to come home to? His mother believed him guilty. Or at least she had, once upon a time. Worse than the puzzle of his mother's words was the irrefutable proof that Julianne appeared to be telling the truth, at least in the matter of his father's death.

He scrubbed a hand across his face, wondering how his mother had even known where he was. She *must* have, all these months when he'd thought she wanted nothing to do with him. And yet, she'd not set the authorities to his path, though she'd believed him well guilty that day he'd left. Too afraid to lose yet another son, even one such as he?

Or had forgiveness finally found its way into her heart?

The grief he had held at bay this full hour past surged upward like a welling tide. His family had always been close, and Eric's death had been hard on all of them. He could not imagine what his mother and sisters must be

going through in this moment, dealing with such an unexpected blow as his father's death alone. He swallowed
the anguish that lodged thick in the base of his throat.
By the devil . . . his father. Gone. The title in question.

The estate in the balance.

As if summoned by his inner turmoil, Patrick's
friends James MacKenzie and David Cameron strode
through the door, jostling and joking and sliding about.
They threw themselves into the chairs opposite him.

"Heard you carried off Reverend Ramsey's dog to
surgery this afternoon," MacKenzie said with cheerful
deviltry. He eyed Patrick's glass and signaled for the
serving girl to bring him one of the same. "I trust you
charged the bastard double if you are celebrating with
whisky."

Patrick schooled his features into what he hoped was
some measure of calm. He was usually the quieter one
of the group, the studious counterweight his friends
relied on to balance their more volatile natures. But in
the hours since Julianne Baxter had bounced into his
life, he'd been turned on end and inside out, and now
he felt close to exploding. "Why are you both here?" he
growled. "Did your wives toss your tiresome arses out
already?"

"They are both attending this evening's meeting
of the Ladies' Philanthropic Society." James grinned.
"Which leaves us free to have a wee drink."

David Cameron snorted. "*Wee* drink? I'd suggest
we start with a full bottle, and proceed posthaste from
there."

His words rang with the same brogue as James's,
marking them both as Moraig locals. Though he'd been
here eleven months, at times Patrick still felt like an outsider. He'd felt that way sometimes when they had all

attended Cambridge, the youngest of the group by three years. Although James and David had been at each other's throats for much of the past year, they appeared to have forged a happier peace in recent days. The sight of their new camaraderie would have warmed Patrick, if not for the grief that numbed his bones.

David held up a finger to the serving girl. The servant predictably inclined her head as if to say she'd be happy to serve up a bit more than the requested drink, but he did no more than return his attention to the table and grin at the two of them. Patrick raised a brow that his friend should so flawlessly pass such a blatant test. He would have once laid money David would have been the last man standing in their small circle of friends, happily whoring his way through life.

It was disconcerting for Patrick to realize he was now the odd man out.

The Gander was not yet busy, given the early hour for drinking, and his friends' whisky arrived before Patrick could make any real headway on his. David raised his glass and smiled across the table. "What shall we toast tonight, gentlemen? The future?"

James held up his own glass. "Aye, I think the future could use a toast. Mrs. MacKenzie has given me permission to share the news, at long last. Looks like I'll be a father, come February."

David clinked his glass against James's. "Oh, I say, that is brilliant news! Given the way Channing cocked up the job sewing you up a few months ago, he'll need those few months to practice for the wee one's delivery."

The smile fell away from James's face.

"Georgette will not need help of that sort," Patrick assured him, seeking to assuage the swift flare of panic in his friend's eyes. He had suspected this for some time, given Georgette's changing shape, but it was good to hear it from his friend's lips. "Georgette is young and healthy and I have the utmost faith in Moraig's midwife."

James nodded, but sipped his whisky a bit less exuberantly.

"And I regret to say I won't be here for the happy occasion." Patrick dislodged his friend's surprised looks with a grim smile. "I've received a bit of news today. I am to be charged with murder, it seems."

There was a moment of awkward silence. And then David laughed. "Is this about that business with McBride's horse again? Honestly, someone had to put a bullet in the animal's head. It had been down for a week. And how much whisky have you had? It's not like you to start without us."

"I am not jesting." Patrick stared moodily into his glass. He had carefully kept the details of his brother's death hidden from his friends, but things were already sliding to hell and gathering speed. They would hear about it soon enough, and he preferred to be the one to impart the information, rather than the gossip-prone beauty lounging in her upstairs bath.

"My brother died this past November." He raised the glass to his lips and took a hearty swallow. "We'd been hunting—arguing, actually—and a shot went astray."

"Eric is . . . *dead*?" At Patrick's nod, James exhaled slowly. "That's a bit of terrible news. You always spoke of him with such affection when we were at Cambridge. I remember being envious that you actually seemed to get on with your family."

David nodded his agreement. "Condolences seem a bit tardy, all things considered." His gaze turned sharp. "All this time, some eleven months, you've been walking around Moraig tending our cattle and sewing up our dogs, and you've been the heir to an earldom?"

Patrick answered with a curt nod, the all-too-natural question scraping at his conscience.

"Why didn't you tell us about your brother's death when you arrived?" David pressed. "We're friends, Channing. We would have helped."

"Because . . ." Patrick shook the cobwebs of regret and hesitation from his head. "It may have been an accident, but mine was the bullet that struck him."

There was a long silence as his friends wrapped their heads around his explanation. "Bugger that," David finally breathed, his knuckles white around the glass in his hand.

"There were questions, naturally. My father had somehow suppressed much of the talk, probably because of his influence and friendship with the local magistrate, but his recent death has loosened the control he'd kept over the process."

His two friends regarded him a long moment, then cast surreptitious glances at each other. David spoke first. "Your father has died too?"

"He died last week." Patrick gestured to the letter that still lay open on the table beside him. "I've had a letter from home. Now that my father is gone, an inquest has finally been called. I suspect it's a mere formality until I'm charged with murder."

James regarded Patrick a long, studious moment, appearing every inch the solicitor he was trained to be. "But if it was an accident, it seems more appropriate to classify it as manslaughter, not murder."

Patrick felt jerked back to the pain of that day. "A witness claimed she saw me aim for my brother. In the eyes of many, there was a logical motive. Eric was the heir. His death left me in line for succession." Indeed, it seemed few had refused to entertain the possibility of his complicity in a darker plot.

James drummed a stern finger on the scarred table. "Our first priority is to see you don't hang. We need to work toward reducing the charge to manslaughter instead of murder."

"Are you offering to assist in my defense?" Patrick asked his friend, surprised. MacKenzie was trained as a solicitor, not a barrister.

James waved a dismissive hand. "You've saved my own sorry arse on more than one occasion, and a solicitor's life in Moraig is so deadly dull as to justify killing someone, just to stir things up. You'll not deny me the chance, even if I'm relegated to the sidelines." His green eyes narrowed. "Is there only the one witness? Perhaps we can discredit her testimony."

"Aye. Just the one." Patrick took a cautious sip of his whisky, welcoming the noxious burn. "But Miss Baxter's word will be devilishly hard to dispute."

David's jaw tightened. "Miss Baxter? *Julianne* Baxter?"

"Aye." Patrick offered his friend a half-hearted scowl. "No thanks to you, she's shown up here in Moraig."

David returned a conciliatory grimace. "Ah hell, I am sorry about that. She was far too curious when your name came up in Brighton." He paused, and then lifted a brow. "Pretty bit of skirt, though, and you're still unattached. Perhaps you could seduce the truth out of her."

Patrick eased back, his muscles slowly uncoiling. "Well, that pretty bit of skirt is upstairs right now. She came to tell me the news of my father's death and the looming inquest. And I'd as soon strangle her as seduce her, thank you very much."

James's mouth turned down in his predictable solicitor's frown. "I am trying to understand Miss Baxter's motivation. Why would the witness whose statement could well send you to the gallows come to Moraig to find you?"

This was the part Patrick himself didn't understand. There was no reason for Julianne to be here, to have delivered this news. No possible logic could have propelled her to traipse across the country to confront a man she had accused of murder.

Then again, logic had never been Miss Baxter's style.

"She came to deliver an apology, of sorts, although I can't credit her with having much of a conscience. If she did, she wouldn't have lied in the first place." Patrick studied his glass. "She'll pay for it though. With her reputation, I'm afraid. Reverend Ramsey saw her at my house this evening in a state of . . . *undress*." He smiled tightly against the memory. "The man almost had an apoplectic fit."

David chuckled, a whisky-rich sound. "I thought you said you didn't want to seduce her."

"I didn't touch her." Patrick swirled the pale liquid around his glass a studious minute. Perhaps he *should* have touched her. He'd certainly enjoyed kissing her, once upon a time. He felt an acute discomfort in the thought of her near-certain downfall, though it was scarcely his fault she'd shed her bodice in his bloody kitchen. When word of this misadventure reached London, her reputation would be as close to destroyed as an unmarried woman's could be, lacking an actual babe in her arms.

"You mentioned Miss Baxter had come to apologize," James said slowly. "Could she have changed her mind about what she saw that day?"

Patrick considered their conversation on the kitchen floor. She'd not said anything about changing her mind, not even when he'd directly asked her if she believed him capable of murder. "No, I don't think so. It is more that she regrets seeing what all of this has done to my family. But there is no undoing it. She's been called as a witness for the inquest. I really don't see any way around it."

"A wife cannot be compelled to testify against her husband." James shrugged. "Privilege of marriage, and all that."

"Given that I don't have a wife, I fail to see—"

"Yet," James interrupted. "You don't have a wife *yet*." He leaned forward. "You claim she is sorry for her role in all of this. Did she provide a sworn statement after Eric's death?"

Patrick thought back to that terrible day. The local magistrate had been there—that much he recalled. But he could not remember her giving anything resembling a sworn statement. "No, I don't think so."

"If you can convince Miss Baxter to marry you, you'll have dispensed of the sole witness to the crime and neatly dealt with the problem of her damaged reputation."

The suggestion made Patrick feel as if *he* were the one who had been shot. "She accused me of murder, MacKenzie. I assure you, she won't have me."

"Don't dismiss the possibility outright," David cautioned. "If the girl came all the way to Moraig, it suggests she might feel something for you. Guilt, attraction—what does it matter, if it works in your favor?"

"I could never—"

James's hand slammed down on the table, cutting him off and rattling their glasses. "You need to stop thinking that way. You could *hang* for this, Patrick. This isn't a lark we are talking about. It's your goddamned life."

"You think I don't realize my neck is two steps shy of a noose?" Patrick retorted. "But to trick her into it . . ." He trailed off, abruptly stepping over that first, gentlemanly impulse that he would never do something so calculated, and then veering right to the spot where his friends were urging him. The thought of spending a lifetime saddled with the woman's sharp tongue and shallow thoughts might make the gallows seem an attractive option, but there was no denying his body approved of Julianne's ample physical charms.

His conscience aside, he *might* be able to do such a thing, might be able to justify such a terrible means to achieve a much-needed end. There was an odd symmetry to such justice, he had to admit. The unfairness of the situation did more than chafe—it rubbed great, gaping wounds in his soul. If things continued gathering speed along this treacherous path that stretched before him, his sisters and mother—who were undeniably the innocent victims in this drama—would be turned out of the house they had always known, near penniless. And there was that small, trifling matter that he would very likely be hanged for a crime he did not commit.

The repeated reminder of what he stood to lose—namely, his neck—made his pulse thump uncomfortably in his veins. Who was to say he couldn't marry a woman under such dire circumstances? *Particularly* the woman who had caused all of the trouble?

"I would be the worst sort of bounder," he said hesitantly.

"Better a bounder than a corpse," James argued.

Patrick tossed back the remnants of his whisky

before raising his eyes to meet his friend's intense gaze. "You are maddeningly persistent."

"A good trait to have in a solicitor."

"Well, in a friend, it is proving nettlesome. You don't know her like I do. I might prefer the noose." Although, as soon as the words tumbled from Patrick's mouth, an unbidden thought came to him, of Julianne, flushed and flirtatious, waltzing in his arms. Of the small sound she had made, there in her throat, as he'd deepened that ill-advised but unforgettable kiss.

He'd felt more than a marginal attraction to her then.

"Then you'll condemn her," James said quietly.

Patrick's gaze jerked up from the distraction of his empty glass. "How will *I* condemn *her*?" he demanded.

"Offering false testimony against a peer is a serious offense. Potentially a *hanging* offense." James chased his chilling words with a nonchalant shrug. "You claim she lied about the events of that day. Marrying the girl to prevent her testimony would protect her as well. If you don't, she'll be compelled to give a statement under oath. And I swear to you, I am going to do my damnedest to prove her claims false."

Patrick's thoughts cartwheeled against the threat James had flung out so mercilessly across the table. Until now, his neck was the only one he had considered at risk. "But I was not a peer when my brother died," he protested.

James raised his glass in a jest of a salute. "You are a peer *now*, in case you haven't sorted it out yet in that thick skull of yours. The charge is still pending, and there is no legal means to prevent your recognition as heir. You will be tried in the House of Lords."

Patrick slumped back against the hard back of his chair. He was a second son, had never expected to claim a place in the peerage. For so much of his life he'd kept his nose in his books, outside the rank and file. The thought of being shoved into their midst left him feeling numb.

But that was nothing compared to the thought of Julianne with a noose placed about her long, pretty neck.

"Being tried in the House of Lords is your best chance to survive this. It is devilishly hard to prosecute a peer who is guilty of murder, much less one whose crime is more correctly considered manslaughter. And with the new law removing the privilege of peerage, those who sit in the House will probably be more reluctant than ever to find others of their own class guilty." James hesitated. "But if she testifies against you, it won't go well for her there."

Cold fingers of worry squeezed Patrick's chest. "There's no time. She's underage, and if she's to have her way we're both off for Yorkshire on tomorrow's coach." And more to the point, Julianne was the toast of London and could have her pick of nearly anyone she wanted. Compelling a woman like that to marry a man she believed capable of murder would be about as easy as threading a rope through the eye of a needle.

"Hang that." David rolled his eyes. "You are in Scotland. The sodding truth is you can be married within the hour if you want to. Or have you forgotten the disgraceful circumstances of MacKenzie's marriage?"

Patrick somehow found a grim smile at that. No, he had not forgotten his friend's drunken night and hasty wedding, which had somehow—against all odds—turned into a marriage to envy. "I really wish you wouldn't use that word."

"Sodding?"

"Hang. I prefer to avoid the reminder, if you don't mind. And I cannot be married tonight if she refuses me. Which I assure you, she will if she believes I offer marriage for a devious purpose."

"Then delay the journey." James leaned forward, his hands splayed on the table. "Woo her. Convince her of your affection. Convince her of her ruin. But for God's sake, don't return to England without fixing this."

Chapter 6

WAS IT POSSIBLE to require a bath after a bath?

If one made a habit of traveling in mail coaches and rolling about on filthy floors, it seemed likely. Julianne's bathwater quickly turned a weak-tea shade of brown, and as faint-headed as she felt that so much dirt had been permitted to accumulate on *her*, the idea of soaking in such water was worse still.

But even dirty water was preferable to slipping back into her gown. It lay in a foul green heap, sullying the floorboards beneath. She climbed out of the cooling bath and eyed her only clothing with a dawning sense of horror. Sliding back between those sticky, bloodstained layers wasn't just a poor idea: it was close to a physical impossibility.

She wrapped herself in the threadbare excuse for a towel the maid had left and, lacking even a proper comb, tried to pull her fingers through her wet, tangled curls. All the while, she felt dragged under by the events and revelations of the day. She'd hoped, she supposed, she would have arrived in Moraig to find Patrick Channing as unlikable and unredeemable as the London gossips claimed him to be. Then it would have been easier to forgive herself for her role in all of this. Instead, she'd found a man who devoted his life to saving those whom fate had frowned upon. She'd ruined his life, and he'd gone on to make a new one. A *good* one.

She glanced down at her nails, the tips of which were ragged as a result of her ill-timed journey. Not for the first time, she cursed the impulsiveness that seemed to trail her despite her best intentions to keep it firmly harnessed.

And where on earth was her bag? She had expected it to be brought up a quarter hour ago, and had left explicit instructions regarding its prompt delivery.

Its absence sent her mind careening in a dangerous direction. Had it been stolen from the posting house? Its imagined loss was as much a cause for panic as the thought she might have to wear the green walking dress again.

A firm knock at the door granted a reprieve from her mounting panic. "Just a moment!" she called out, securing the towel in a hasty fist across her chest, her skin itching in anticipation of a clean night rail. "Come in."

But it was not the hotel maid who came into view as the door tipped open. Patrick stood on the threshold, his head skimming the top of the door frame. His brown-eyed gaze locked on her face, a fact that should have seemed comforting, given the other bits and parts of her that might have drawn his attention. But this was Patrick, and she was almost naked, and even that safest of visual exchanges jarred with the ferocity of a thunderclap.

Despite the chill in the air, heat licked along her limbs. Heavens, but standing in close proximity to this man did unexpected—and not entirely pleasant—things to her stomach. She filled her lungs with the necessary outrage. "I am not dressed, Patrick!" She wrestled the towel higher, praying she was not revealing worse in the process of ensuring her bosom was covered.

"Then you should not have invited me in."

Her gaze settled on the hard line of his jaw. On another man, the expression might have been easy to dismiss, but for Patrick, who wore his emotions on the inside, he might have well been shouting. Why did *he* look angry? She was the one standing with only a towel to protect her from total ruin. The man ought to avert his eyes, at the very least.

He held up her bag in this right hand. "I've brought your things from the posting house." His lips flattened into a straight-line frown. "The way you demanded."

Julianne's eye fell on her valise even as the distinctive scent of Scottish whisky—that vile drink that was becoming so fashionable among the *ton*—floated toward her on the air. Comprehension dawned. He'd been downstairs drinking, all this time. Probably holding her bag hostage to vex her.

Well, if he was going to play at being a slothful ladies' maid, she would treat him thusly.

Securing the fingers of one hand against her towel, she pointed to the floor with the other. "You may leave it."

His face remained impassive, but he placed her bag—a little too agreeably—on the floor.

She waved her hand airily behind her. "And you may take my supper tray as you go."

He eyed her a long, slow moment, seeming to come to some decision. He dutifully moved inside the room. But then he stopped. Closed the door.

Turned the key in the lock and held it up for inspection.

Julianne took a scrambling step backward. She

glanced around the room for evidence of what he meant to do behind a newly locked door, cataloging the various blurry pieces that might be his intended destination.

Bed. Hip bath. Bureau. Window.

Her eyes jerked back to the bed. Worse than what he meant to do, what did her treacherous heart want him to do?

His eyes were little more than brown shadows in the dimly lit room, but there was no mistaking the glint of the key in his hand. He examined it a moment, and then slipped it into his pocket. "You had the means to lock the door, and yet did not. Do you always abandon yourself to fate without thinking?"

She tilted her chin upward. "I do not believe in fate."

"No? You have a means of tempting it, Julianne. You left the door unlocked during your bath. That could have ended badly . . . not all gentlemen knock first."

"You, sir, are no gentleman."

He reached down and picked up her bag again. "I believe we established that during our first meeting." He took a step toward her, and Julianne's pulse leaped to life beneath her skin at his approach. Not because she was locked in a room with a man suspected of murder, but because she was locked in a room with *Patrick*, and her pulse had ideas of its own.

He tossed her bag on the bed. "Put something on. There are things we need to discuss."

"I cannot dress if you stay here," she protested. The screaming inappropriateness of this scenario made the earlier interaction with the vicar seem the very definition of propriety.

He made no move to extract the key from his pocket, but he did angle his body toward the wall, offering her his back. "I promise I won't look." His voice softened. "That is, unless you give me leave."

Julianne shivered against the onslaught of that deep, rumbly baritone that she suspected, if properly applied, could make women's clothes everywhere fall off their shoulders.

If they were wearing any, that was.

With that pointed reminder, she rummaged through the bag that seemed suspiciously more mussed than she remembered, and yanked out the first thing her fingers closed upon. "Why are you here, Haversham?"

"Please don't call me that."

She shook out her white night rail with a vicious snap of fabric. "Then what should I call you?"

"Patrick would be preferred, I suppose." He exhaled loudly. "I've just come from the public room," he offered to the wall. "Others . . . *know*."

Her fingers tightened over the thin fabric. "Others know what, exactly?"

"About us." His voice bounced off the faded wallpaper and gained momentum. "And the matter with the vicar."

She shook her head against his cautionary warning. "I am not worried about a few rumors from the vicar. The man commands a flock of Highlanders, for heaven's sake, not a London ballroom." Julianne cast a wary glance at Patrick's still-proffered back, then dropped the last shred of her dignity along with her towel and jerked the cotton night rail over her head. "Moraig is but a rustic slice of Scotland, Patrick. It will soon blow over."

"Moraig has wider circles than you might imagine. David Cameron already knows. It stands to reason his new wife does too. I believe you are acquainted with them both?"

Julianne found her comb in her bag and went to work on the damp tangles that were threatening to take permanent root in her scalp. "You may turn back around now," she told him, trying to reconcile the little town she had glimpsed this afternoon with any sort of gossip trade, much less one substantial enough to send out ripples to be felt in London. "And Cameron is of no consequence. His wife—while lovely—isn't even a proper lady."

Patrick turned to face her in a slow slide of a circle. "Perhaps he's of no consequence by London standards, but in Moraig he holds a position of respect. There is the Earl of Kilmartie, who lives nearby. His son, James MacKenzie, already knows of the matter."

She lowered the comb. "But a Scottish peerage is surely not as well respected—"

"MacKenzie's new wife is the former Viscountess Thorold," Patrick interrupted, tersely. "Mrs. MacKenzie knows many influential people in London."

Julianne struggled against a rising tightness in her chest. This was the Scottish Highlands, for heaven's sake, not London. It boggled the mind that Patrick could escape notice for almost a year in this town, but she couldn't hide for the space of a day. She had not thought . . .

Heavens. Like the key in the lock, she had simply not *thought*. She drew in a frustrated breath. "If I could just speak with her and explain—"

"Your reputation has been compromised. Speaking with her will not change that fact."

"And you think standing in my room while I dress will help matters?"

"There is also the matter of how we would travel together to Yorkshire—as you have so summarily insisted we must—without further damage to your character."

The comb fell from her hand and hit the wooden floorboards with a soft click. Well. There *was* that. She had to admit, she hadn't given any more thought to the constraints of traveling with Patrick to Yorkshire than she had to traveling here alone.

Decent, well-bred women did not travel with men who were not their husbands, much less with murder suspects. But despite her lack of forethought on the matter, the fact that Patrick was concerned about such a predicament was encouraging, to say the least. She had been prepared to cajole, bribe, or lie to get him on that coach come morning.

"Does this mean you have decided to accompany me back?" she asked cautiously.

He crossed his arms. "I will not do anything that further sullies your reputation."

She almost laughed. Had he no notion at all that she regularly flirted the edge of propriety, or that the London scandal sheets had chronicled her antics for the better part of two years? "It's my reputation, not yours, so if you would just—"

"I am afraid, as one of the parties engaged in the matter of your pending ruin, it is my responsibility to protect you. I cannot travel with you under the current circumstances. Only one solution would get me on that coach come morning, no matter how distasteful we might find it."

The implications of what he was saying sank through the cracks in her thinking. He was suggesting a fix that would both save her reputation *and* make her a countess, even though she'd all but destroyed his life. No wonder he had seemed angry upon entering the room.

Her thoughts spread around his words with an eagerness she wished she could control. This was a proposal—of sorts—from a man half of England suspected of killing his brother. But her flagging memory of the event had become distorted even before the surprise of the man she had discovered in Moraig. She could not believe he was guilty.

In fact, over the course of the last few hours, she had more than convinced herself he was not. His explanation of his brother's death being a terrible accident had the solid ring of truth to it, no matter that he had been unconvincing in his defense on the day it had mattered. The side of Patrick she had seen today—the veterinarian who wrapped his own jacket around the bloodied body of a dog, the protector who had defended her in the presence of the irate town vicar—was not the sort of man who could purposefully kill his own brother, not even in the most heated of moments.

She eyed him warily, trying to sort out his feelings on the matter. He couldn't mean it. Couldn't mean to toss away his future on her, the woman who had jeopardized his family's future simply because her mouth had run on several steps ahead of her brain that day. And he certainly didn't *look* like a man who was happily contemplating a vow to honor and cherish her.

If there had been only the matter of her reputation to consider, his scowl would have been enough to convince her that such a plan was foolhardy, at best. Truly, she cared less for her reputation than ought to be prudent—hadn't she come to Scotland without chaperone or permission, well knowing the risks she was taking? No, her reputation was not the reason she was actually considering marrying this man.

He was an earl, even if he refused to act the role. That would be a delicious enough incentive for most women. But Julianne could envision his future, and without someone to guide him on this path, he was bound for failure. Her chest squeezed tight at the thought. It was clear Patrick wasn't prepared for the title. He'd spent his entire life avoiding the social network of London. If she were his wife, she would be poised to help him.

But not even that measured empathy could fully explain her quickening pulse.

No, the problem with this proposal was how it made her feel. All during the long, weary trip to Scotland, she'd had but one goal: inform Patrick of his father's death and the inquest, and convince him to return to fight the charges. Her motivation had been born of the guilt festering inside her, and honed by new doubts. She'd realized, once she'd battled her way through self-absorption, that her role in this had not just affected him . . . her meddling had also orchestrated the ruin of at least three other innocent people.

But seeing him today had done more than convince her of how wrong she had been. It had also reminded her of how she had felt, hanging on the end of his kiss, the kiss she had tried—and failed—to forget. She'd abandoned her pursuit of Patrick's brother on account of that kiss, had risen before dawn just to catch a love-struck glimpse of a mere second son.

She'd at least attempted to carry on after that fateful day. During her latest London Season, she had pushed the boundaries of propriety, seeking to rediscover the quiver beneath her skin that Patrick had somehow conjured with little more than a slow, building smile. She'd tried on gentlemen like new shoes, only to discover that the wrong fit pinched. All through the lines of men who flirted and smiled and offered the occasional moonlit kiss, she had felt absolutely nothing. She couldn't claim the same bland effect in the presence of this man.

And the memory of that kiss they had shared—every bit as potent as any measure of guilt or doubt—now turned his proposal from something worth considering into something she was afraid she could not refuse.

She ran her tongue over her lips, trying to quell the way those thoughts made her skin flush warm. "You *must* accompany me on the morning coach, Patrick. Your future, and your family's future, depends upon it."

He did not move. Did not speak. Just regarded her in that familiar, stern way of his, his long face immobile.

She prayed her mouth continued to work well enough to finish this last bit, because she was quite sure she lacked the courage to repeat it. "So if that is the only course available to us, we need to marry. Tonight."

PATRICK STARED AT the woman who had just demanded they marry and wondered if he wasn't about to make the second biggest mistake of his life.

His cock, damnably independent organ that it was, disagreed with the question posed by his brain, and moreover demanded an equal stake in the debate. Because beyond all the myriad reasons both for and against this foolhardy path, he had neglected to consider a very greedy one.

Julianne was a beautiful woman.

Robbed of the distraction of the soiled green dress, the curve of her neck drew his eye. Beneath the scant layers of cotton, her bosom was indeed every bit as high and fine as he had imagined it would be. She was a painful sight. Patrick had kept to himself these past eleven months in Moraig, avoiding both the obvious interest of several lusty widows and the ready train of serving girls who plied their skills in the alley behind the Blue Gander. But as his body surged to life around the tempting image Julianne presented, he was reminded of a very basic fact: he was a man. And she was a woman who—despite the foolhardy nature of the emotion—piqued his masculine instincts.

There were worse reactions one could suffer from a wife.

His wife. He massaged that thought a moment. She'd fallen right into his thinking. Truth be told, he'd hoped she wouldn't. The Julianne he was coming to know didn't seem to care about her reputation nearly as much as this sudden acquiescence suggested. She was clearly an intelligent girl. She had demonstrated a sharp wit beneath that fashionable exterior on numerous occasions—most recently with poor Reverend Ramsey.

But on the other hand, she'd boarded a train lacking both chaperone and common sense . . . not exactly a point in her favor.

It wasn't gentlemanly of him to trick her into it, even if she deserved it. Hell, even if she *owed* it to him, for sending his life spiraling so far beyond his control. His conscience was intact enough—even after three rapid-fire whiskies—to admit some discomfort in using her in this manner, but he was hanged—quite literally—if he could think of another way to go about it. He had exaggerated the implications of their discovery together, although he hadn't precisely lied about the *potential* in James's wife's connections, or the dangers of traveling together lacking a wedding band.

But the image of Julianne in her nightclothes did not appeal to the gentlemanly side of his nature. She had made her own bed—messy though it might be—when she left behind her maid and boarded the train to Scotland.

And a very ungentlemanly part of him was looking forward to lying in it with her.

"If you are sure," he told her slowly.

"We need to do it quickly, if we are to make the morning coach." She turned away from him to rummage through her bag, and her night rail swung dangerously about her hips. "Is there someone who can do it at this late hour?"

"The blacksmith." Patrick swallowed. Thank God for Scotland and the irregular marriages made possible by the country's lax laws. "He officiates half the weddings here. No doubt he'll charge more to see us so late, but he'll appreciate the business." He took a step in her direction, probing the boundaries of her quick decision. No matter the practical advantages of what was being discussed here tonight, no matter the fact that by marrying her he might better protect her, he would not exchange those vows with a woman who was unwilling to accept him in her bed.

And unfortunately, there was precious little time to test the theory of her acquiescence.

"I shall offer him fair compensation," Julianne said, pulling out a frothy blue confection of a gown.

He took another step, determined to keep his eyes on her face instead of her hips. But that proved every bit as distracting as her scantily clad curves, because his thoughts landed on a niggling incongruity and refused to budge. There, across the bridge of her nose, he studied the source of his confusion. There weren't very many . . . a dozen at most.

But definitely—decidedly—freckles.

Her freshly-scrubbed face glowed a healthy pink, and carried far more interesting layers than he had seen before. He felt like a prospector who had unearthed a promising vein of gold but lacked all tools to extract it. He'd studied her enough to know that those freckles were not granted egress by day. She must cover them each morning, with rice powder or something of that ilk. There was something jarring about discovering such an intimacy, a secret he alone knew.

"I shall also require compensation," he told her.

She looked up warily and wrinkled that fascinating, freckled nose. "You want me to pay you to marry me?"

He closed the remaining three feet between them and then he was within striking distance. The scent of her damp hair and soap-kissed skin rose up to greet him. "A kiss, to honor our bargain."

She licked her lips, lips he had tasted, once upon a time. "We've had one," she countered, clasping the dress she still held in her hands like a shield between them. "Or have you forgotten?"

He reached out and plucked the blue dress from her fingers, tossing it onto the floor. Her mouth opened in protest, but he pulled her to him. "I haven't forgotten." The thin whisper of her night rail met his jacket, and then his fingers circled around to cup the delectable, cotton-covered curve of her arse. A gasp escaped her lips, but she didn't shrink from the contact.

A wicked surprise claimed his focus. He'd half expected her to retreat, cry foul, retract the offer she'd thrown down. After all, these were nowhere near the same happy circumstances as their first kiss. This time, she believed him capable of murder.

He gave his hands permission to roam northward, skirting the edges of night rail, belly, and breasts to finally settle on her face. He lowered his mouth, urged on by the encouraging beat of pleasure in his ears. His lips settled over hers in a kiss that offered no quarter and sought a raw truth. The taste of her was a flooding memory, sharp sweetness and languid heat. Christ, what man could forget such a thing? It carried a sting, this woman's kiss. Even with a plan and a stiff resolve, it was nigh on impossible to brace oneself for impact.

Her lips moved confidently under his, her breath mingling with his own, her unbound breasts a soft pillow against his chest. His body responded to eleven months of denial with predictable speed, and it rocked him to have such a physical confirmation of his need. She was warm and pliant, and his control was like a curtain being yanked from its moorings. He sought a more complete claim to her mouth, his tongue sweeping against hers.

And that was when she pulled back. Her hand was a gentle reminder against his chest, though the flush on her cheeks and her accelerated rate of breathing provided pleasurable testimony to her body's reaction. "I trust this is adequate compensation until the vows are completed?" she said softly.

The muted tenor of her voice was comical, really. She might as well have shouted.

She'd been inexperienced during their first kiss, though even untutored she'd been beautifully responsive. But that had been a restrained sort of kiss, an exploration of what she could learn to be. This was a fulfillment of the promise. Because the woman who had just wrestled control of the situation into her own small hands was not the same green girl she had been eleven months ago, experiencing her first kiss. Julianne knew the lay of the land now, and she was shouldering her way along a well-trodden path.

As his palms fell away from the temptation of her night rail, he tried not to think of how she knew this, or

from whom she had learned it. She was a coquette and a
flirt. It should not surprise him that she knew something
of matters between a man and a woman.

Had she kissed his brother this way, once upon a
time? Eric had certainly regarded the delectable Julianne Baxter in a proprietary fashion. They had even
argued over her in the minutes before the accident that
took Eric's life.

He shook his head clear of those damning thoughts.
Claiming now the woman his brother had wanted then
was just one more egregious sin to add to his mounting
tally of reasons to burn in hell. And no matter his dislike of the idea of her recent experience with kissing or
worse, the issue was moot, given the pressing need to
dismantle the danger she posed to his family and his
future. She would be a willing participant in the marriage bed, that much was clear. No shrieking, no hysterics.

He lacked the audacity to think he deserved anything
more.

"It will do for now." His voice, thankfully, retained
its faculties, even if his head felt pelted by lust and
doubt. He stepped back, breathing hard. She made him
feel unhinged, and *that* made him uneasy. The thought
of knocking her off her composed pedestal once they
finally tumbled into bed gave him a dark pleasure he
didn't care to examine overmuch.

"But make no mistake, I expect a complete marriage,
Julianne. If you marry me, you shall be mine, and no
one else's. I refuse to be a cuckold."

He could almost see the cogs turning in the depths of
those green eyes. There would be no outside lover. No
opportunity for a later annulment. He was reminding
her of who he was, and what he expected *they* would be.

Miraculously, she nodded by way of an answer.

"My father will not be happy we've done it in this manner." She inhaled deeply, flattening her palms against the front of the night rail he had just been contemplating removing. "But I suppose it is a match he will not be able to dispute. You possess a title, certainly. He was good friends with the late earl, and your father certainly believed in your innocence."

He searched her eyes for some kernel of truth. Her kiss had convinced him that a marriage would not be all jaw-gritting duty, but neither did it tell him what he needed to know. "And what of you, Julianne? What do *you* believe?"

She looked startled by the question. "I believe I shall enjoy being a countess."

Patrick held himself steady, but he could admit some disappointment in Julianne's ready evasion. So this was how it was to be. He was to marry a woman who believed him capable of murder. Of course, without that bit of it there would be no need to marry her at all, so why was he warring with his emotions on this matter? He would spend the rest of his life side-stepping the suspicion in his wife's eyes, and she would be granted a title and an estate as fair compensation. It wasn't as if either of them harbored hopes for something more.

"But given that the future is unclear," she added, stooping to snatch her blue dress from the floor where he had tossed it, "it would be best to organize a settlement that protects me in the event of an unfavorable outcome."

Unfavorable outcome. That was one pleasant euphemism for hanging, he supposed.

The lingering heat from their kiss cooled thoroughly with such talk. "Most of the estate is entailed, but I can ensure a respectable income, at the least. My friend James MacKenzie is a solicitor. We can have a settlement drawn up tonight, if that is your wish." If the worst happened, he would leave her financially protected. And if the best happened and by some miracle he was able to evade the noose . . . well, he would deal with the consequences of their union then.

"Might I have a moment to dress?" She held up her dress by way of answer. "I would prefer to meet the solicitor in something more substantial than my night clothes."

"Of course." He pulled the key out of his pocket and handed it to her. "I'll be waiting downstairs. But lock the door, if you please. The Blue Gander has a bit of a reputation for unruliness."

"Apparently, so do I." She smiled sweetly at him, and he was nearly struck dumb by the blinding simplicity of her unadorned night rail and those upturned lips.

He pulled the door shut in a muddled fog, trying to dissect why something as simple as a smile from his future bride should bother him so much. He landed on an answer just as his feet made contact with the top step and he *still* hadn't heard the key turn in the lock.

Her smile hadn't appeared friendly in the slightest. It was a deceptive strategy, a means of distracting her prey so she could bend the situation to her will. Good God, what a complicated woman. But simple or complicated, it no longer signified. The only thing that mattered was that she had agreed to marry him.

And then he could keep her from testifying against him.

Chapter 7

ᖴOR JULIANNE, THE ceremony was a blur.

A *laughable* blur, given that it was conducted over a still-smoking forge and presided over by a great, burly beast of a blacksmith who still had the remnants of his dinner clinging to his beard. For the first time in her life, Julianne was glad her mother was no longer alive to see what had become of her daughter.

Patrick's friend Mr. MacKenzie had come along with them. She had expected frowning disapproval, considering the scandalous circumstances of the event unfolding with such blinding speed. But the dark-haired solicitor was cordial to her, if not outright encouraging.

If the details of the ceremony were difficult to recall, the walk to Patrick's house from the blacksmith's shop was equally dim in her memory. No doubt it was cold. And dark. She allowed that there might have been stars. Heavens, there might have been wolves for all that she paid attention. But any physical perils to be encountered on the walk paled in comparison to the emotional dangers of the journey. Every step seemed fraught with the sort of tension that can only occur when one of the married parties was less than enthused by the prospect.

And it was clear that *she* was not the one with the most misgivings.

As Julianne stepped into Patrick's pitch-black foyer and breathed in the unpleasant things that waited in the darkness, all she could think was that he seemed angry. No matter the earth-shattering kiss he'd offered to seal this devil's bargain, he'd been closed off and silent from the moment the blacksmith had pronounced them husband and wife. Not that she blamed him. If their situation had been reversed, she might have liked to know the person she was marrying believed in her innocence.

Or, barring that, regretted his role in the suspicions others held.

But no matter her feelings, no matter her thoroughly hatched doubts, she wasn't sure what to say in this moment. *Something* had happened that November day, something terrible and unchangeable. Marrying Patrick carried a sizable risk, one she hesitated to examine overmuch. She faced far greater ruin if he was eventually convicted of murder than she would have by remaining a soiled spinster. But her shifting memories were leading her to a completely different conclusion regarding his guilt. Surely others would be able to see it as well.

And while Julianne could perhaps be faulted for often leaping into the fray without proper forethought, she knew this small truth: their wedding night was not the time to dredge up such painful memories.

The direction of her thoughts was disrupted by eager paws and an even more eager tongue.

"It looks like Gemmy is happy to see me again," she offered to the darkness.

She heard the unmistakable thud of her valise hitting the floor. A metal tin rattled, and then somewhere in the darkness a match flared. The meager bit of light settled around Patrick's shoulders as he set the flame to the wick of a lantern that hung on the wall. "Gemmy doesn't know you like I do."

She struggled to keep a rein on her own spark of temper. "You do not know me as well as you think."

That, finally, earned a backward glance in her direction. "I imagine I shall know you well enough by morning."

She swallowed hard. She could admit to herself that she was nervous about things to come, but to hear that *he* was thinking about it was disconcerting. "Perhaps you'll even discover something you like."

He chuckled. The heavy sound blanketed the narrow walls of the hallway with its sheer unexpectedness. "And perhaps the dog Skip has sprouted a new limb. I'll need a moment to check for this miracle." He held out the lantern to her. "Stay here, please. And then I'll escort you to bed."

Julianne took the proffered light and then her new husband disappeared around the corner. *Stay here. Lock the door.* He might chase the words with a "please," but it did not change the nature of the commands. He was already ordering her about like one of his canine patients. Clearly, he needed a lesson in the way things would go on between them.

She picked up her bag with her free hand, though the weight of it gave her pause. He had insisted on bringing it with them. Which meant he intended to spend their wedding night here, in a house better suited for a barn. The issue of cleanliness aside, the coming night sent her thoughts spinning on an uneven axis. She wanted to wrestle back the upper hand she had briefly enjoyed in that room above the Blue Gander. She wanted to strip away Patrick's hard façade and make him lose all coherent thought.

And, if she was honest, she wanted to give in to the wicked fever that threatened to consume her, as well.

At her feet, Gemmy whined and scratched at her skirts. "Does he order you about as well?" she murmured, lifting the bag higher and wondering if she possessed the strength to haul it up a flight of stairs. "I imagine you don't want to stay in this lonely hallway either."

She received a nudge from Gemmy's nose in return. She wondered how the scruffy animal would get along with her elegant little dog, Constance, who was probably missing her by now. But wondering would not provide the answer, and so she dragged the bag over to the stairwell. Gemmy scrambled along by her feet, his nails clicking on the floorboards.

"Does he sleep up here then, fellow?"

Gemmy squeezed past her, and then she was following the little dog up the stairs, hefting her bag up each mile-high step. At least *someone* knew where they were heading. She would have a look at the room where she would lay her head tonight. And her gruff new husband would learn she was not planning to be a biddable sort of wife.

HE ALREADY REGRETTED it.

Not the act of marrying the woman who had accused him of murder. No, that, in the end, had been surprisingly easy. But the subterfuge behind these vows didn't sit well. He was a man who had always prided himself on hard work and truth. None of those things had accompanied him into this marriage, and that guilt made him edgy. His instincts urged him to tell Julianne the truth, confess the reasoning behind this plan. Perhaps she'd even understand—the need to protect *her* neck was every bit as tied up in this drama as the need to guard his own.

But he needed to be careful. For all her antics, he'd also seen a side of Julianne today that suggested a sensitive heart beat beneath his new wife's very fashionable exterior. She had been kind to Gemmy, and quick to help an animal in need. She had admitted remorse over the trouble she had caused his family. Had traveled all the way to Scotland to find him on account of that guilt. It would not do to hurt her feelings, merely because of his own festering emotions.

And he needed his wife happy with him if MacKenzie's plan was going to work. Because not being compelled to testify against him was not the same thing as not being *willing* to. And he had a feeling that if scorned, Julianne would prove a formidable enemy, indeed.

He turned up the lamp he had left burning on the kitchen counter, to find the black and white dog awake. He crouched down, relieved to find the wound still closed and the sutures tight. The dog's tail thumped once, twice. A good sign, but not surprising. He had every confidence Skip would be up and walking come morning. He had long since ceased to be amazed by the power of animals to recover from wounds that would have felled the strongest of men. It was one of the reasons he had studied at the veterinary college in Turin instead of seeking out a medical program.

As a species, humans left much to be desired.

He set down a bowl of water, which the dog lapped gratefully. "It appears you'll recover." He rocked back on his heels, eyeing the dog objectively. He couldn't logically take an injured dog with him on the journey Julianne had planned for them. David Cameron owed him, particularly after the trouble the man had tossed

Patrick's way. He grinned, imagining his friend's reaction to a few new pets. "Tomorrow is a new day," he told the animal. "I've in mind a permanent new home for you, as far away from the vicarage as possible."

And given Cameron's long, sordid history with Reverend Ramsey, it seemed sure those two would not cross paths in this life or the next.

Skip blinked up at him. Patrick stifled the urge to continue the conversation, and instead settled for the requisite pat on the dog's head. He told himself he didn't care if Julianne overheard him, or whether she would think him deranged to hold a conversation with an animal. He often did such things—his profession had a way of turning the strangest of creatures into sounding boards.

But of course, he didn't want the *dog* to think he was touched in the head.

Patrick left his patient to its healing and stepped into the hallway, only to realize Julianne was nowhere to be seen. And she'd apparently taken Gemmy with her. It seemed the little dog would follow anyone with a gentle hand and a pretty smile.

As he headed up the stairs, anticipation and irritation warred with every footfall. He nudged the door of his bedroom open with his boot, his eyes confirming his suspicions. Julianne sat on his bed dressed in her night rail, the frothy blue gown she had worn to the blacksmith's folded meticulously beside her. Gemmy's head rested on his new mistress's lap, and the faithless terrier eyed Patrick warily, as if he knew his master's intentions to evict him.

He stared at her, his body already stirring to life. The marriage required consummation to be considered legal. MacKenzie had been most clear about that—something about Scots law, and that he should leave no cause for an outsider to question the validity of the union. He was still numbed by the whirlwind turn of events that now found him married to one of the most notorious gossips in London, but not so numb he couldn't admit a delicious anticipation for what came next.

Of course, he was angry that he *wanted* to bed her.

Hell, he was angry she made it so easy, negotiating the terms of a marriage settlement wearing only a filmy night rail. But it was an interest that would not be dissuaded, no matter his stern mental lectures on the topic.

The sodding truth was she made a beautifully tidy package there in the clutter of his room, buttoned up and prim amid the comfortable rumple of his bedclothes, as if she was waiting to be unwrapped. She had taken her hair down, and he had to swallow his surprise at the sight of it, half dried and curling against her shoulders. Her hair didn't fall in a neat, orderly pile. No, nothing about Julianne would be so predictable, or so obedient. Each copper-colored coil writhed with life in a separate but downward journey. He wanted to catch one in his hand, run his fingers over it before moving on to touch other interesting parts of her.

Instead, he set the lamp he had carried from the kitchen on the top of his bureau, then shrugged out of his coat. He tossed it over a chair littered with open books and periodicals, causing a small army of paper to slide onto the floor in an ungracious heap—not that a few more made much difference on his hazard-strewn floor. The brewing altercation made the blood in his veins contract. "I asked you to wait in the hallway for your safety, Julianne. The stairwell is in disrepair, and half the boards need to be replaced. I am amazed I didn't have to step over your broken neck to get here."

"You didn't *ask* me to wait." She smiled, and he was struck again by the sense that despite the graciousness of the gesture, she was merely baring her teeth. "You ordered me to."

A potent melding of exasperation and lust claimed Patrick's focus. Trying to force Julianne to do anything was a bit like playing at the hazard table: one never knew what was going to turn up on the dice. He was her husband, and just an hour ago, she'd promised the blacksmith she would obey him. But she was proving a handful to steer in a straight line, and that made him uneasy on the matter of convincing her to withhold her testimony.

Her gaze lowered to the terrier still lolling happily in her lap. "And I confess some surprise to hear you care about my safety," she continued, her lips more a hesitant quiver now, "given that you derided Gemmy for greeting me with any measure of affection."

Christ. Is *that* was this was about? There was no denying she was a bloody, beautiful mess when she was angry. Indeed, she appeared nigh on luminous in her nightclothes, her unbound curls twitching about her shoulders. But there was nothing of affection in his reaction to such a sight. Did she expect platitudes and whispers of love?

Because if she did, she had sorely overestimated his esteem.

"I like you well enough, Julianne," he replied, his voice a cautious drawl. And he did. Or rather, he liked her as a solution to his problem. He supposed he should soften his tone, but the woman brought something out in him. It seemed they were always sliding on the razor's edge of a row, her words as sharp and cutting as any knife.

But his cock did not seem to care. It had embraced its

own ideas from the moment he'd seen her sitting in the middle of his unmade bed.

"How does the patient fare?" Her words burrowed beneath his distraction, pulling him back to the intellectual dilemma she presented.

"Awake. Drinking. All good signs."

"What will you do with him in the morning? Surely you won't give him back to that odious vicar?"

Patrick shook his head. "No, David Cameron owes me a favor, after having such loose lips in Brighton." He smiled grimly. "Skip will be in good hands with him. I'll try to convince him to take the lamb too."

"And what will you do with Gemmy?"

At the sound of his name, Gemmy's tail thumped hopefully against the bed. Was she really so heartless to imagine he would leave his dog behind? "Gemmy will come with us," he said firmly. He would entertain no opinions to the contrary, no matter how dazzling her smile.

"I am relieved to hear that." She ran a hand over the dog's fur in a manner that made Patrick's stiffened spine relax a fraction of an inch. "I confess I've grown attached to him." Clearly returning the sentiment, the terrier rolled over and offered her his belly, wriggling in the sheets. She stared down, and her brow pinched in thought. "When was the last time your bed linens were changed?"

"Are you offering to wash them for me?" He began to work the buttons of his shirt. "Because you might want to wait until after we've soiled them properly."

Her eyes met his in an ominous flash of green heat. "I've seen stables with cleaner floors than yours. For heaven's sake, you're likely to give Gemmy fleas. You need a housekeeper."

"I've a wife." He shrugged out of his shirt and tossed it away, perversely enjoying the way her eyes widened to follow the article's deliberate, ceremonious path to the floor. "I've been told they are nearly one in the same."

At her strangled gasp, Gemmy hopped down from the bed and slunk for the shadows. *Smart dog.* Patrick took advantage of the newly vacated space on the bed and sat down to tug off his boots, hiding his grin behind clenched teeth. Then he eased back onto the mattress, holding fast at the invisible battle line that stretched between them.

He cast up a brief prayer she wouldn't clock him over the head with something for his insolence. Proximity was necessary for the coming business, and whether she realized it or not, he was working his way toward her, slowly but surely, the same way he would approach a skittish animal that required his ministrations.

He dwelled a moment on her scent. Even her fragrance was a poor match for him. She smelled clean, like soap and spice, heated to the point of combustion. He smelled of his daily activities: sheep, sweat, and probably something worse.

And yet . . . as always, there was this odd, nettling attraction he felt in her presence, a surprising flare of interest that defied a scientific explanation. His thoughts were usually more ordered than this. More focused. Certainly more logical. For some reason, being around Julianne made him less like himself.

Or was it that she made him feel more?

He paused over that a moment, there on the bed beside her. His life in Moraig was orderly. Predictable. Perhaps, to some, it might even be considered tedious. He preferred it that way. It suited his character, this steadiness of spirit. But if he was pressed to point to the most enjoyable parts of his life, he could not deny he found more inspiration in the rare, heart-pounding moments—such as the need to save an animal whose life was literally in his hands.

The thought of the coming skirmish with Julianne made him feel much the same way.

She had once informed him—quite suggestively— that he'd think about her when he finally made it to his bed. And he *had* thought of her that November night, alone in his room, the memory of her quick wit and tempting smile every bit as potent as the kiss he had so brashly claimed, there in the foyer. If he was being truthful, he'd thought of her more than was sensible, even after she'd accused him of murder. The chit had made damned sure she was not someone he would ever forget, no matter the havoc she had wrought in his life.

He concentrated on breathing a moment. Reminded himself she was the means to a necessary end, not a treat to be savored. She was neither a hopeful wish nor a regrettable memory. Tonight she was here. His for the taking.

And still in far too many clothes.

Chapter 8

"I<small>T OCCURS TO</small> me that I have seen you in far more a state of undress when we were veritable strangers, than I have now that you're my wife," he drawled, enjoying the way his words made her skin flush red.

"I am not sure undressing is a good idea, all things considered."

Patrick rolled onto one elbow, though he sensed his leisurely approach was piquing her temper. Why did he enjoy needling her so much? Because no matter the strange fever that gripped his tongue around her, his body certainly wanted to further their acquaintance. Even now, even as she bristled with anger and the air sparked dangerously between them, he was stirring with marked interest. "*Now* you want to retain your clothes? It seems you have been shedding them much of the night. Why, I've scarcely blinked tonight and not found you close to naked."

"All the more reason to keep my night rail on. I would hate to have you avoid blinking. I've heard it is a condition that can be quite painful."

He reached out a lazy hand and ran it over the folds of her gown, gathering the fabric in one hand until the pale curve of one leg beckoned. The condition she would cause him by remaining clothed threatened to be far worse. He traced his fingertips lightly over her calf, brushing in light circles. He could feel the emotion threading just below her skin's surface, her body's instinctive softening to his touch.

"There is no need to stage a seduction, Patrick. I understand what the night brings. Neither of us needs to enjoy it, as long as it is done." Her voice had taken on a lower, huskier tone that told him he was heading in the correct direction, even if her words contradicted her physical response. It was difficult to sort out whether this latest discussion was about maidenly nerves—which he doubted—or Julianne's unbending need to control her world and everything that came with it—which had more the ring of truth to it.

He raised his eyes to meet hers. "An odd reaction in a woman who kisses like a courtesan and eagerly took her vows. No one forced you to do this, Julianne. In fact, I seem to recall it being your idea." A pale cousin of the truth, perhaps. But she *had* voiced the idea out loud first.

Her lips firmed portentously. "It was the only way to ensure your return to Summersby."

"Surely you don't think this is only about Summersby." His fingers tightened over the temptation of one lovely knee. "Because if you do, I would suggest that you apply your imagination and consider that it could be more. If you are going to talk about Yorkshire, the coming business is going to be difficult." Even now, the thought of what awaited him on their return to his father's house was enough to provoke a state of paralysis.

Not the effect one desired when attempting to bed a new bride.

She worked her lower lip between her teeth in a manner that made his body jerk back to life within the confines of his smallclothes. Slowly—decisively—she eased back onto the mattress. "I'm sorry." She sighed, though she did not sound sorry in the least. "It has been a long day, and I confess my *imagination*, as you so eloquently put it, had foolishly anticipated something less tedious than the coach ride from Inverness."

Hell's bells. Nothing like having one's abilities compared to an eight-hour coach ride to deflate a man's enthusiasm. He leaned over her newly prone form, and closed the few inches that separated them with a deliberate angling of his body. But he stopped just short of kissing her. Because it would be a hard kiss. An *angry* kiss. A kiss that bespoke all the aggression he felt for her, and yet all the want she kindled in him.

Besides, despite her clear expertise on the subject, she looked none too interested in kissing him. Her eyes had fluttered shut—a promising sign—but her lips remained the farthest thing from pliant.

"Julianne," he told her, his lips mere inches from her disapproving mouth. "This business between us . . . it can go quickly, if you want."

Her body squirmed promisingly below his. "Have you not been listening to a word I said?"

Patrick knew his own enjoyment would be but seconds away if he just followed her instructions and hurried this along. But whether she understood it or not—and he was still unsure of the extent of her prior experience with kissing and the like—haste would not heighten whatever small bit of pleasure he could provide her this first time around. And given the less than honorable circumstances that forced them here, he was at *least* determined to offer her that.

He leaned down, tipping his forehead against hers, trying like holy hell to keep his instincts in check as the tempo of her breathing sped up in a favorable way. "But I would recommend another option. A *slower* experience."

Her eyes opened suspiciously. "I am not sure—"

He silenced her with a finger to her lips. The conversation she seemed interested in having wouldn't serve his purpose tonight. He should have felt too guilty to do this, to turn his mind to seduction as if theirs was a happy joining and a hopeful union. But he was discovering he was not above accepting this as his due, the consequences to his soul and their future be damned.

He wanted her. A simple enough emotion. That he could be angry with her before their coupling, and suspicious of her when it was over, was proving irrelevant.

And he had an entirely different idea in mind for that famously sharp tongue.

PATRICK TOSSED HER gown—the one Julianne had carefully folded to avoid wrinkles come morning—onto the floor with a callous flick of his wrist. She started to protest, but the blasted man curtailed her objection with a neat bit of trickery, stretching out beside her on the bed and pulling the coverlet up around their necks until she could scarcely breathe for want of space.

She struggled against an instinctive urge to both welcome and war with this man who would claim ownership of her body tonight. In retrospect, she should not have come above stairs alone. Not because he had told her to wait, but because the few minutes alone with her thoughts had given her far too much time to think about what was to come. She both wanted and resented his necessary attentions this evening, and could not wrap her head around what she *ought* to feel.

And yet . . . despite the duality of her emotions, she could not steer herself clear of a burgeoning curiosity in the process.

His lips met hers in a questing search, and she welcomed the press of his lips against hers. It wasn't enough, though. Her body felt awkward, a strummed instrument not fully tuned. She wanted *something*. And it irritated her to no end that she could not place her finger on the nature of that want.

She kissed him back, putting everything she knew into it. She'd learned how to kiss properly this summer, taking full advantage of Brighton's relaxed rules and fast set, away from the sharp eyes of her father and the perils of the London Season. But those had been muted forays into impropriety compared to the raw nature of this kiss.

It should have gone against her nature to kiss like this—openmouthed, tongues dancing—but it was also strangely exhilarating, like she was shedding her skin, stepping into another world. He smelled of sharply masculine things she could not identify. She could taste the whisky on him. It reminded her that he had tossed back several glasses with friends earlier this evening, while she had waited above stairs for her bag. At the memory, she took his lower lip between her teeth and nipped hard, intending to mete out punishment.

It had the opposite of her intended effect. A groan escaped his lips. His fingers tangled in her hair and she could feel them tremble against her scalp, a sign of his loosening control. She was grateful, now, for her daring this summer, those kisses she had accepted and experimented with. Because with the kiss she now employed with tactical skill against her new husband, she was wrestling the situation clean out of his hands.

Not that she was proving immune to the process.

Julianne's skin felt stretched across her frame, quivering in need of this man's touch. His tongue was both an invasion and a discovery, stroking her mouth, promising dark heat and wicked skill. In truth, her Brighton experience with kissing had been a pale, civilized facsimile of this. And in the shift of his thigh, the slide of his tongue, Julianne found her skill eclipsed and turned on end. Now she struggled to keep up, to avoid being swept away by the delicious pull of desire. *Good heavens* . . . no wonder women of good sense and breeding risked ruin.

To be kissed in this manner was to stand on the edge of a cliff wearing only paper wings and believe you could fly.

She only barely swallowed the small, gasping sounds trying to work their way out of her throat. He was already confident enough. She refused to give him the satisfaction of hearing how he sent her sanity spinning out of control.

His hand at her breast proved a lovely distraction through the cotton of her night rail, as did his busy mouth, which was now tracing a path of fire down the column of her neck. His tongue pressed against the hollow of her throat, warm and wet.

Julianne's expanding pleasure promptly stuttered to a halt.

Was he . . . *licking* her?

The realization burrowed deep beneath the very skin he laved. Her body shuddered as he continued his torturous, languid path, down one side of her cotton-clad breast, up the other, leaving a trail of cooler air in the wake of his attentions. Surely this wasn't a necessary part of it. The thought of being licked by another human should have sent her bolting for the washbasin.

But it seemed she lacked the capacity for protest. He turned her into someone unrecognizable, someone she wasn't sure she liked. Because she not only tolerated his tongue there against her skin, she wanted him to continue with a desperation that frightened her.

She opened her mouth, prepared to lodge a protest. But then his stern, sensual mouth closed over her nipple—still wrapped in its cotton prison—and she was lost to sentient thought. She sagged back against the mattress, the feel of his mouth on her breast sweeping her balance clean out of reach. She hadn't known . . . she hadn't *imagined*, that a man might do this to a woman. She had thought herself worldly, had counted kissing as a skill well learned. But now she realized she had experimented with the clumsiest of boys. Patrick's mouth—working some kind of black magic on her breast—told her just how little she knew.

The moans she had struggled to keep buried now pushed out from between her stunned lips and hung in the air between them. The sound pulled his attention regrettably away from her breast, and the loss of his warm mouth felt cruel, somehow.

He straightened over her, a looming scepter that surely spelled her doom. "You don't *sound* as though you think this is tedious."

His knowing gaze felt like a heavy blanket over her soul, and she wanted to thrash about and throw him off. She exhaled hotly, wanting his mouth to return to its torturous—if unhygienic—path along her breast. She refused to give voice to that wish. She wanted what came next, and she was honest enough to admit that she was not someone used to waiting. The man seemed to actually take *pleasure* in the torture.

Inspiration struck. "It is a cold night. I'd hate to risk

pneumonia because you meandered your way through this."

He frowned. "Meandered?"

"I understand what is expected, and would prefer to arrive there a little faster."

"Julianne, there is pleasure to be had if only you—"

"Now." She might be a wife, but she was also a woman who would be in control of her destiny. She straightened her shoulders, welcoming the scratch of the coarsely spun sheets against her neck. "If you please."

If she could credit him with any emotion, she might swear it was disappointment she saw in his eyes. But he fumbled beneath the covers to remove his smallclothes. Bent her legs and settled himself between them.

And then he seated himself inside her.

A sharp flash of pain erupted, pain she had been prepared for, and yet went so far beyond what she had expected. She gasped her surprise at the stabbing loss of pleasure.

Not that *he* seemed diverted from the path. He moved against her then, a rush of muscle, a slide of skin, and she was wrapped around him and praying for it to end. Miraculously, he obliged her, for once. She had no idea how long he labored, but it thankfully fell on the side of minutes rather than hours. And then he collapsed on top of her with a muffled groan. "I am sorry," he breathed against her neck, his words an exhausted echo of her own feelings on the matter. "If we had gone slower . . ."

A haze of tears—all the more embarrassing for how unexpected they were—stained her vision. It was clear he'd been planning to take a more leisurely approach. But then, true to form, she'd opened her mouth and ruined it, just jumped in without thinking and forced his hand.

As well as other pertinent parts of his anatomy.

A droplet of sweat trailed down his nose to land on her cheek. Distaste kicked whatever residual pleasure she had enjoyed from the kissing part of it completely out of reach. "It was my choice, Patrick," she told him, pushing her hand against his shoulder in an unmistakable demand. It was his rough, sweaty body causing her this pain, and now that he was through, she felt a desire to wrestle the situation back to heel. "You only did what I asked."

"Yes." He obligingly lifted his weight off her. "But I am beginning to realize you do not know your own mind." He detached himself from where they were still joined, and that proved an indignity all of its own. She fumbled for the coverlet, the sheet, anything to cover her from his postcoital scrutiny. The warmth she had felt earlier had been extinguished like a guttering candle, and there would be no rekindling of it tonight.

"Julianne . . ." The mattress shifted as he moved to sitting. She gave in to the urge to look at him, but regretted it almost instantly. His eyes probed her face, and her night rail felt transparent beneath his inspection. If he was looking to identify some hurt, he really ought to look a little lower.

Or a little deeper.

He smoothed a wisp of hair from her brow. "Next time will be better. I promise."

She accepted his touch, though it carried none of the flash of fire from his earlier caress. "I believe you," she told him, putting on her false smile, the one she had practiced in front of the mirror for hours, the one that told the world she was just fine, thank you very much, and required neither sympathy nor assistance.

Only she *didn't* believe him. If they restricted themselves to the kissing, or even—heaven help her—the licking, she might be inclined to trust his words. But the breaching was not something she could ever see herself ever growing accustomed to.

"Wait here," he told her, which almost pulled a hysterical laugh from her, because really, where would she go? She was in *Scotland*, for heaven's sake. In Patrick's bed.

And he was legally entitled to keep her there.

He brought a washcloth from the nearby basin, and with deft hands washed the stickiness from her thighs. The thought struck her as slightly absurd, such tender ministrations in the wake of such a mindless, messy business. But she tolerated it, much as she had tolerated the coupling.

And then he stretched back out beside her, pulling the coverlet high over her shoulders. Gemmy jumped up to wriggle his way between them, clearly used to sharing this space with his master. Julianne suppressed a shudder at the thought of fleas from the little dog, unsure what morning would bring but certain of this:

She was going to be sore on the morrow.

And while her new husband might have gotten the kissing right, *this* part of marriage was proving a disappointment, at best.

Chapter 9

Patrick's luck held out the first two nights of the journey to Yorkshire . . . not that luck was something perched on his shoulder of late.

He used the weight of his new title to justify separate rooms at the posting houses where they stopped each night. James, who was traveling with them as far as Leeds, had greeted the fact of those separate rooms with a raised brow, but wisely held his counsel on the matter of Patrick's sleeping arrangements with his new wife. Separate rooms were expensive, but Patrick reminded himself that he was no longer a mere country veterinarian.

And surely it was a justifiable expense. His own conflicted thoughts aside, there was a slight stiffness to Julianne's gait that made him feel like a bounder. He had wondered if she would come to their wedding bed an innocent, but then had treated her as if she was not. He'd hurt her, though it was her own insistence it be done that way.

He'd give her some time to heal before he mauled her again.

But luck and good fortune were not the same thing.

Three days of sitting next to Julianne in cramped coaches and railway cars had left Patrick's emotions in a frustrated snarl. There was no biologically plausible reason for the near-constant state of adolescent arousal he felt around her. No scientific explanation could explain the fact that no matter how far they traveled, no matter the press of sweating passengers on all sides or the smell of coal smoke from the steam engine, the damned woman smelled like a cake. The omnipresent scent of cinnamon seemed to hover beneath her skin.

What was the matter with him? He'd *had* her, for devil's sake, even if he'd quite cocked it up. He was not a man prone to obsessive vices. One taste of a dessert usually left him satisfied. He had presumed that bedding Julianne would be little different. He would indulge in the novelty of her, and then cease to want her.

He had been stupidly, staggeringly wrong.

As they watched James's train depart for London in a belching cloud of black smoke and screaming iron, Patrick heaved a sigh of relief. The plan was holding so far. James MacKenzie would begin the process of lodging the petition for Patrick to be recognized as the new earl. Patrick and Julianne would finish the trip to Summersby. Tonight offered one last chance for sleep and reflection before the challenge of facing his family tomorrow.

But as fate would have it, sleep and reflection were not foremost in his mind.

It occurred to him, as MacKenzie's train rumbled out of the station, that he was finally, for the first time in this journey, alone with his wife—a woman he was legally permitted to strip naked and worship at his leisure, though his conscience bid him to keep his hands and other interested parts to himself. Of course, "alone" was a figurative consideration, at best. The yard at the local inn was elbow-to-elbow with men making boastful wagers on the outcome of the annual horse race in nearby Wetherby. The smell of spilled ale and sweating bodies hung thick in the air. Apparently unwilling to wait for their sport, two men had stripped off their shirts in a corner of the yard and were exchanging punches in front of the jeering crowd.

He promptly abandoned his initial hope of procuring two rooms and instead insisted on one. Because there was no way he was leaving Julianne alone in her room tonight, given the way his temper flared against the ungentlemanly whistles that followed her into the inn.

His gesture seemed a little less gallant, however, when he saw the room they were given. Patrick tossed Julianne's bag onto the narrow mattress and eyed it with a groan. His hope for two beds had come to naught, it seemed. Gemmy faced a more peaceful night than he did, already curled up in a pile of straw in the stables at the direction of the innkeeper. He ought to join the terrier there. But one look at Julianne, and he knew he wouldn't. He'd not missed the speculative looks cast her way by the men downstairs, nor appreciated the stab of jealousy such attention spiked in his blood. The lace shawl draped over her shoulders provided some cover, but it could hide neither the low cut to her bodice, nor the fact that hers was an impressive bosom, by anyone's estimation.

"Were you going to prepare for bed?" he asked, already unbuttoning his own shirt. The noise of the crowd could still be heard below stairs, but the solace of the room promised some respite from the muffled roar of inebriated patrons.

She averted her gaze to the hopeful white curtains

that hung on the room's windows. "Perhaps you could go down and instruct them to send someone up to help me undress."

Patrick shrugged out of his shirt and unbuttoned his trousers, even though his fingers itched to be offered access to a different set of buttons.

Namely the ones on his wife's bodice.

"Given the crowd we left below, I doubt they can spare someone tonight," he told her. "I can help you with your gown."

Two bright spots of color stained her cheeks, whether as a consequence of his emerging state of undress, or his offer to facilitate a similar state for her, he couldn't discern. "You are an *earl*, Patrick. 'Tis unseemly to be engaged in such menial tasks. And if you explain your position, they'll likely do anything you ask of them."

Her presumption that undressing a lady was something a man considered menial was something he itched to correct in action, if not words. "My title is uncertain until I petition the Crown and present evidence of my claim," he pointed out. "And while they might leap to do my bidding below stairs, you saw the crowd they are facing. I would not ask it of them tonight, not when they are so busy."

"Your claim is presumed when the line of succession is direct. I daresay a petition isn't even needed, unless you plan to take your father's seat in the House of Lords. And if you had been a little more forceful below stairs, it seems assured we would be enjoying the pleasure of two rooms tonight instead of arguing here in one."

Patrick kicked off his boots, then stepped out of his trousers. She couldn't know it, but petitioning to take his father's seat was not just important—it was an outright necessity, according to MacKenzie. And just as concerning, Julianne's obvious worry over the single room told him that she was as hesitant to repeat their wedding night as he was. Of course, his hesitancy was because he didn't want to hurt her.

Hers was because he already had.

Tomorrow would see them delivered to Summersby, where they would face the disaster of her father's outrage and his own uncertain reunion with his mother and sisters. He would be distracted at best, arrested at worst. If he was to convince Julianne that their marriage bed was more than a duty, this room and this night might be the only opportunity he would see for weeks. A selfish part of him wanted to prove he was a better man than the fumbling idiot who had hurt her on their wedding night.

Patrick stepped toward her, and was relieved when she did not shrink from his approach, although those flags of color on her cheeks expanded to suffuse her entire face. He leaned in, sliding past the temptation of her flushed skin to find her ear.

"What bothers you more, Julianne? That your husband doesn't act like an earl?" He took her earlobe between his teeth and laved it gently, enjoying the gasp of surprise the simple motion wrenched from her lips. He released his prize to whisper, "Or that you might discover the sharing of one room is far more pleasurable than two?"

"Most definitely the former," she said, but her words ended on a breathy undertone.

He leaned back to a safer vantage point and studied her, from the flush expanding southward down her neck to the curve of the ear he had just held between his teeth. She was a mind-numbing set of contradictions, a living puzzle he was not sure he could ever sort out. She housed an armada of inappropriate frocks in her bag, any one of which might have been worth more than his entire year's salary as a veterinarian in Moraig. And yet he'd also seen her give an entire guinea to a ragged child begging at the entrance of the Glasgow train station. She claimed she was uninterested in the sort of pleasure he was offering, but the cues of her body were telling him otherwise. These details had begun to define her as someone different from whom had he expected when he had taken those damnable vows.

But they did not yet provide a clear picture of who she was.

"If you would simply trust me, and turn yourself over to what I have in mind, you might find you actually enjoy it," he told her.

For a moment, her mouth opened in surprise. But then her chin thrust out and she offered him an indelicate sniff. "Well, whatever else you have in mind, I pray it involves your bath."

A raucous cry of victory went up in the yard, just outside their window. Someone had won a round, apparently. It was clear Julianne thought she had won too. He smothered his own answering grin as he turned toward the washstand.

His wife would soon learn that winning a round was not the same as winning the fight. The state of his hygiene was something he could fix.

And given that this room was roughly the size of a pauper's cell, she was just going to have to bloody well watch.

JULIANNE STRUGGLED TO remind herself that this was her *husband* pouring water from the pitcher into the washbasin not two feet way. She'd spent a frustrated few days, wishing for even a single moment of privacy in which she might apologize and beg his forgiveness.

But always, always, there was an audience. A public room meal, taken elbow-to-elbow with veritable strangers, or else Mr. MacKenzie's constant, grating shadow, interrupting what she needed to say. And at night, when she ought to have been sleeping in her husband's arms, there had been solid walls and turned keys, ensuring her confession must hold for another day.

Now they were finally alone, but Julianne was hard-pressed to find the presence of mind to form a complete sentence, much less a carefully constructed apology. In this tiny room, Patrick's every movement was delivered in perfect, torturous focus. And while she couldn't decide if she recommended the experience, she lacked the good sense to avert her eyes.

He dragged the cloth over his chest, and her eyes wanted to linger over the way his muscles bunched and knotted across his back. The other men who had paid her court these past three Seasons—well-groomed men, appropriately pale, the silver buttons on their waistcoats already straining against the soft middle that would eventually claim them—had never made her body tighten in such delicious anticipation.

She was acutely aware of the rattle of the window-panes in response to the crowd below, but that was nothing in comparison to the scrape of her pulse. Her senses were heightened to the point of pain. Even the usual press of her clothes felt heated and unnatural.

He completed the cursory swipe over his shoulders and neck, small rivulets of water running down his back and disappearing into the waistband of his smallclothes. And then—unbelievably—he wrung out the washcloth and turned around to face her.

"You cannot be through," she protested.

A slow grin claimed his mouth, and he held out the washcloth. "If you have something different in mind, by all means feel free to provide a demonstration."

Julianne's stomach churned, though it was an agreeable sort of distress. "That isn't the role of a wife." Although truly, she had no idea whether it was or not. She had no maternal figure to ask, and this was *not* the sort of thing one asked a father.

"You would relegate the business to a servant then? Perhaps the maid you asked for earlier?"

He was teasing her, of course. She was beginning to sort out the nuances of his tone, the stern disapproval from the humor that ran below his stony surface. Somehow, the thought of Patrick disrobing in front of a servant made her feel oddly ill. She swung her legs off the bed and stalked toward him, aching with a strange, sullen need to show him—in no uncertain terms—she would not be compared to a maid.

Or, at the very least, she would not be compared to one and found lacking.

She snatched the cloth from his outstretched hand and plunged it into the washbasin. With hard, jerky moves, she began to scrub him down. He stood stock-still for her, letting her do her worst. She focused on his back a good minute, reasoning that if he couldn't reach it properly, she would. She refused to let her hand—or her imagination—wander too far afield. It seemed safer, somehow, to stick to the obvious parts.

But as she moved around to his chest and its scattering of light brown hair, she began to forget the indignity of the task she had been assigned. Her hand slid over the architecture of his torso, traced the masculine contours of muscle and bone, and she felt a complementary tightening in her core, a feminine spooling of want that left her mouth dry and her fingers shaking.

"Ah . . . you might . . . that is, I think my chest is now quite clean." He lifted a hand and motioned in a southerly direction. "Were there other parts you felt needed washing?"

His voice pulled her determined focus from his chest and aimed it toward the more perilous parts of his person. He was practically daring her to touch him.

The feel of his heart thudded below where her fingers clasped the washcloth. The promising start to their wedding night had been eclipsed by messiness and pain by the end, but tonight she felt tossed back to those beginning strains of desire. The rhythm of his heart beneath her palm, the in-and-out cadence of his lungs, these things had hold of her now. And so despite the fact she had no idea what to expect, or what to do with what she might find, down his abdomen she went, the cloth tripping over ridged planes of muscles that brought to mind a washboard.

Not that she knew what to do with one of those either.

Her free hand dipped scandalously under the drawstring of his smallclothes and, after a moment's hesitation when she warred with her instinctive aversion to all things . . . well . . . *messy*, her fingers closed over his heated, hard length. It surprised her, this first touch of this most private part of him. She'd paid it scarcely any mind that first night. It was smoother than she had imagined, and far more potent in its capacity to disarm her.

She tightened her fingers, almost experimentally, and caught his indrawn hiss of breath that suggested her touch had surprised him too. He wanted her. This was no nagging suspicion, no beautiful doubt. She held the evidence firmly in her hand.

"What do you want, Julianne?" His voice was a question, and yet it was a demand.

What *did* she want?

More. The word whispered in her ear.

She wanted this marriage to be more than a solution to save her from ruin, more than a means of forcing Patrick's return home. She wanted his forgiveness, and yes, his admiration. Since leaving Moraig, she'd been plagued by the unsettling certainty that her reputation had not, in fact, been in imminent danger. All during three long days of travel, she'd sat in the coach beside him and wondered what he was thinking behind his serious mask.

And all through two lonely nights, she'd slept in a bed without him and wondered what he was thinking behind his private walls.

Why had he married her, if not to preserve her reputation? Could he have wanted to?

Could he have wanted *her*?

The clinical scent of the soap provided by the posting house breached the space between them, and she felt nicked by the sharp, unfamiliar edges of the fragrance. She slowly withdrew her hand, afraid to continue touching him in this way without voicing these thoughts. She could grasp what should come next. Marital relations were part and parcel of being a wife, perhaps the only part of the position she truly understood. She had viewed the loss of her virginity on their wedding night as something wholly necessary. Her innocence had been dispensed with in proper British fashion: quickly, the completion of a contract, an apology issued thereafter.

But the way her heart was flinging itself against her ribs felt nothing like a contract. And now that she hoped his emotions ran deeper, the idea of repeating that intimacy felt wrong without some explanation of her feelings, some acknowledgment of what she had done.

She dared to meet his eyes.

It was like being pulled from a dark hole and flung into full-on daylight. Whatever composure usually defined this man had been stripped clean away. This was not the man the rest of the world saw. In this moment, he appeared neither the complicated, serious veterinarian nor the scowling, resentful second son. This was the man she knew existed beneath that clinical exterior, the man who had flirted with her on a dance floor and who had shown her hints of passion on their wedding night.

And then he was crushing her up against his very bare, very clean chest, proving beyond a shadow of a doubt that her imagination was a pale shade of truth compared to the actual man.

Chapter 10

As seemed to be the rule where this woman was concerned, Julianne's kiss was a welcome madness. Then again, whatever madness she was inflicting upon him seemed to have possessed her in some small measure as well.

Patrick encountered a good deal of frustrating fabric in his quest to pull her closer still, but the layers and flounces were secondary distractions to the heat of her mouth. The din outside their door receded into nothingness, muffled by the blood rushing through his veins.

A distant part of his mind regretted not taking the time to unwrap her properly, but the control required to reach for the buttons that marched down the back of her bodice refused to be found. She had driven him to this state of derangement merely by her ministrations with the washcloth, and the heat and taste of her mouth now sent him pitching straight over the edge.

He backed her against the wall, their lips separating for the merest fraction of an inch to refill starving lungs. And then they were back to that frenzied rush of a kiss that sucked all the air from the room and all the logic from his brain.

He lifted her against him, pulling her legs around his waist and pressing her back against the wall. His hands found purchase in the folds of her gown and shoved the layers up rudely. The thought of the lush, soft curves waiting just behind the infinite expanse of silk threatened to unhinge what minimal hold he retained on his sanity. The feel of her body became a jeering taunt, and he broke briefly away to explore the boundaries of her neckline with his mouth. As if agreeing with his frustration, her hands twisted in his hair—whether to find an anchor, or to punish him for waiting too long, he could not be sure.

"Patrick." The single, gasped word seemed to drop from a height of some ten thousand feet, bouncing off his lust-hardened thoughts. As inconceivable as he might have once found it, he liked the sound of his name on his wife's lips.

He abandoned the fragrant temptation of her neck, the sweet curve of her jaw, to submerge once more in the pleasure of her mouth. "What do you want from me, Julianne?" He spoke the words flush against her lips, and he felt her tremble in response.

"I want you to listen a moment."

He stilled. "Now?" he asked stupidly. In the name of all that was holy . . . he had her pinned against the wall. If not for the indignity of so many skirts, he would already be inside her.

"Yes. I need to say this now, before we do *this*. Again." It was a whispered hitch of a word, one she seemed to reach for.

He smoothed his way up her body with hands that ought to have no right to touch her, lingered over the generous swell of breast that waited above her corset. He could think of a dozen things more important to do at the moment than talk, and all of them involved removing her clothing. "Are you quite sure this conversation cannot be delayed an hour?"

Her face bloomed up at him, her skin a beautiful, flushed rose. "Regrettably, yes."

Comprehension dawned, nudging its way between them. With it came the return of their surroundings. The shaking floor, from whatever revelry had commenced below stairs. The distant shouts and whistles from the yard outside.

His stiff, frozen wife, who only moments before had been molten in his arms.

She was not jesting. Julianne wanted to have a conversation before he tupped her against the wall. At least she claimed to regret the decision.

He lowered her legs to the ground, though his body almost groaned in protest. Her heels made audible contact with the floorboards. With that sound came the merest sliver of shame—he hadn't even given her time to remove her shoes. And yet, he couldn't quite find the decency to regret the mindless, rutting beast she turned him into.

His gaze lingered over her rising chest, her flushed skin. He could see the pulse point on the curve of her neck, the unspoken evidence that the blood rushed in her veins. Not that such evidence of her arousal mattered . . . she was likely still healing from his rough handling on their wedding night, and the experience they'd been grappling toward tonight was anything but gentle. So instead of kissing her again, he waited.

Something about the wrinkle between her brows, the way her lips pursed in thought, unsettled him. He hoped she wasn't going to do something awkward, like confess some girlish notion of feelings. He smoothed a strand of hair from her eyes, tucked it behind one ear. Reminded himself that keeping her happy was not only his role as her husband, it was necessary for this plan to work.

"Tell me," he told her. "Whatever has you tied up, I will listen." And the sooner she purged whatever was bothering her, the faster he could divest her of her clothes.

Her chin lifted. "I do not believe you murdered your brother."

Patrick exhaled slowly. Not a confession of love, then. He felt strangely deflated. Or perhaps not so strangely. She wanted to discuss their past, not their future. Not precisely a conversation conducive to bedding one's wife. He supposed he really ought to put his trousers back on if this was where they were heading tonight.

"Given that I did not, in fact, murder my brother, that seems a solid conclusion to reach." He didn't like revisiting this memory, even in private, but going there with Julianne seemed a sharper kind of pain. His gaze pulled to the dark crescent smudges below her eyes that suggested recent sleepless nights. "You've spent the past three days bending my ear about the opera, the scandal sheets, the latest fashions from Paris as we rattled our way from Moraig to Leeds. Not once did you bring up the events of Eric's death. Which begs the question . . . why are we having this conversation now?"

She owl-blinked up at him. "We've not had a private moment before now. I did not want you to think I would do . . . *this* . . . with someone I believed capable of murder." She sagged back against the wall, her hands pressed behind her. "We've been pretending this piece of it doesn't matter, when it feels as though it taints everything we touch. How can you kiss me in this way, when by rights you ought to hate me for what I have done to your family?"

His mind wanted to wrap around her words like a greedy vine. Once, he would have given up his soul to hear her say such a thing—preferably in front of a magistrate. But given her timing, the confession seemed more of an irritation than a balm. She was such a contradiction in his head that it hurt to sort out which pieces he liked and which he didn't.

He certainly liked the taste of her. The feel of her in his arms. He even liked their banter, the wickedly cunning heat of her words.

Their history he could do without.

But that history wasn't something either of them could escape, particularly not if she was going to dredge it up now.

He took a step away from her, the most sensible thing he'd done yet tonight. He dragged two hands through his hair. The gesture did little to ease the ache she caused inside him, but he doubted running his hands through *her* hair was going to serve, not when she was searching his eyes, waiting for an answer he did not know how to give.

"I do not hate you, Julianne." He realized with a small start of surprise it was the truth. "I'll allow I ought to. But you have a habit of working your way into one's head."

Three days of traveling beside her had shifted his perceptions. If this was a journey to hell, hell was a far different place than he had once imagined. He'd just endured three days of torture, constantly confronted with her scent, her laughter, the curve of her lips. His head was slowly becoming desensitized to the shock of her, even as his body sharpened around the promise of having her again. He could not escape her.

And he was discovering—much to his annoyance— that somewhere along the way he had ceased wanting to.

She drew a ragged breath. "Why did you marry me, Patrick?"

An easy enough question to answer. A harder question to answer truthfully.

"I married you to save your reputation," he told her, sticking to the original plan.

"I've been thinking about this for three days, and I cannot make sense of it. I cannot believe my reputation was so endangered. Nothing happened, after all. We had options other than marriage that might have ensured some respectability. Mr. MacKenzie's wife could have come with us to Summersby, for example."

"She is expecting, Julianne. I would not have asked such travel of her."

"Oh." She flushed violently. "I had thought . . ." Her voice went hushed, a trickle of a whisper he had to strain to hear above the background noise of the inn. "I had thought that meant you must have *wanted* to marry me."

Comprehension was a cold bed partner in this train of logic. What was she after here? Hers were not the words of the infamous London beauty who conjured gossip simply to suit her moods, or kissed one gentleman just to spark jealousy in another. He well knew Julianne was a woman prone to theatrics—didn't she time every bloody entrance for maximum effect? Apparently, she was prone to fanciful thinking too.

Because she had imagined his insistence on marrying her meant he felt something for her, something more potent than lack of hate.

Good sense told him to simply reassure her, whisper something appropriately sentimental. Shout, if necessary, to be heard above the din of noise still wafting up from the crowd downstairs. There was a plan to follow, laid out by James MacKenzie across the Blue Gander's table, fueled by whisky and good intentions.

No, he didn't hate this woman.

But that leap in logic was not the same as admitting he *cared* for her.

"Why does it matter?" he asked, willing himself to see the situation through her eyes. "No matter the reasons why, it is done. I married you in spite of our history. Isn't that enough?"

She shook her head, fiercely enough to dislodge several loosely pinned curls. "I married you *because* of our history, and there are parts of it you do not know." She exhaled, a long, shuddering breath that turned him cold, for all he knew there was heat in her lips. "I was not entirely truthful to the authorities, Patrick. I did not see you kill your brother. I didn't see much of *anything* that happened that day."

Chapter 11

BARELY A FLICKER of emotion crossed his face.

Actually, that was not true. Julianne imagined she saw a reversal of emotion, the shuttering of eyes she now knew could display a remarkable amount of feeling. In an instant, he was wearing that same blank expression he had displayed in his father's study.

The woman she had been even a week ago would not have cared. She'd viewed the world through her own distorted lens, flitting between petty intrigues with all the consistency of a hummingbird. Even her flight to Scotland had been a self-absorbed impulse, a desire to right the wrongs her impetuousness had caused his devastated family. But the experience of traveling to Scotland, and discovering a man of honor instead of a murderer, had quite clipped her wings.

"You told the magistrate you saw me aim my rifle at my brother." His voice felt like a blow, delivered as it was in such a precise, low-pitched tone.

"I saw something." She spread her hands helplessly. "*Someone.* I just . . . the truth is . . ." Her voice sank into a whisper. "I don't see well."

He took a decided step away from her. "Your eyes appear to function well enough when you need them to."

"I don't see well at a distance," she clarified. "Things become blurred and indistinct."

"Do you wear spectacles then?" His face was still hard, expressionless. But the clip of his words revealed an angry rhythm.

She shook her head quickly. "No." *Never that.* She well knew what became of women who wore spectacles. Three London Seasons were good for something beyond husband-hunting.

His eyes narrowed. "So you lied about what you saw that day?"

"I did not divulge the entire truth, but I did not precisely lie. It all became hopelessly twisted when the magistrate interviewed me." She shrank against the awful memory. "I was initially questioned about why I was out walking at dawn. And I suppose, in my haste to explain away those pointed questions, I led them away from me."

He muttered a foul oath, something she didn't even understand, and reached for his trousers on the floor. "Why *were* you out that morning?"

His question had remarkable aim, and she felt far too clumsy to dodge it. "I was following you. I thought at that hour I might find a chance to speak with you. Privately."

His face hardened. "Of all the stupid—there was a hunting party out in the fog that morning! You could have been killed."

Of course she realized that now. But that morning, she had been too focused on finding him and telling him to take any notice of the danger. "I hid in the folly when I heard you arguing with your brother." She remembered crouching on her knees, her ears trained on the escalating voices.

He yanked on his trousers. "Which folly?"

"The Grecian folly, on the east lawn near the edge of the lake." She sighed in exasperation. "You've already heard all of this, Patrick. I explained all of this to the magistrate, that day in the study."

"And yet, you've just admitted your statement was less than accurate. You'll forgive me if I seek a recounting of events." He buttoned the fall of this trousers with an almost feral intensity. "How far can you see clearly?"

"Twenty feet. Possibly less." Shame plucked at her. She had never confessed this to anyone, not even her father. "I've never measured," she admitted, "but most things become smears of color and movement around that distance."

"When you stood before the magistrate in my father's study, you described how you watched me point my hunting rifle at my brother's heart. How you saw me aim, re-sight, then pull the trigger. It would have been— what, a distance of at least *a hundred bloody yards*?"

"I saw movement," she countered. "Someone running away, through the smoke from the rifle. And do not forget, I heard both the argument and two shots, in close succession. It was not as much of a stretch as you might imagine."

"I assure you, my imagination is stretched to the limit, and still I cannot envision what possessed you to claim you had seen such a thing."

A perverse part of her welcomed this man's shift toward righteous anger—anything was better than the frozen silence he'd displayed that day in the study. "Prudence filled in the missing pieces. Your height, the color of your coat. She said she would lose her chance at a permanent position if she was forced to testify, and it was my fault she was out there—"

"Julianne." His slow, dangerous drawl startled her as much as the question in his voice. "Who, exactly, is Prudence?"

She would have taken a step backward, had the wall of the posting house room not already been pressing against her back. She tried to remember through the fog of confusion, the doubts that had begun to choke her understanding of the events of that day, almost as soon as she'd recounted them to the magistrate. "My usual ladies' maid is a poor traveler, and my father consented to let me use one of the maids provided by Summersby. Prudence was the maid who had been assigned to me for the week," Julianne remembered. "She wasn't a regular servant at Summersby, though she had hopes of being brought on permanently. I believe she had been hired to help with the house party, out of Leeds."

"There's another witness?" Patrick's words seemed edged with flint, sparking dangerously.

The thought occurred to her—belatedly, perhaps—that if he'd thought to ask even a fraction of these same questions that day in his father's study, they would not be in this position now. "Yes." She sighed, knowing those sparks were about to come closer to the tinder of the truth. "But Prudence believes you are guilty."

"GODDAMN IT!" PATRICK'S hand slammed hard against the wall next to his wife's head, startling even himself.

Blood pounded in his ears, his head, his fists. This could not be happening. He'd laid a plan, followed it through. But MacKenzie's well-intentioned orders were unraveling like a poorly woven rug, and the pieces were coiling about his feet, thick and ropy and ready to trip him with one misstep. "You led everyone in that room to believe you were the only witness!"

"No one asked if there was someone else," she exclaimed, lifting her chin. "The poor girl was terrified. I had the privilege of my father's position to guard me. I thought I was doing her a kindness, and she seemed so sure of what she had seen."

Patrick's fingers twitched in want of something to strangle. "Tell me the truth about what happened that day. Not the truth you imagined, but the truth your maid recounted to you." Given that this maid, this *witness*, might hold either the key to his hanging or his freedom, he wanted to be clear on every inglorious detail.

"She described . . ." Julianne hesitated, seeming to struggle with the distant memory. Not that he felt sorry for her. The least she could do was apply a little exertion to remembering the bloody truth. "She saw a man wearing a coat of the same color as yours, aiming his rifle at Eric."

"A brown tweed hunting jacket?"

At her nod, he gave in to the snarl that had been simmering in his throat. "For God's sake, that describes half the men out on the estate that morning. The maid did not even identify me by name?"

"She was so new she did not know the family well enough to understand who she saw. But I *heard* you, just before the shot. Arguing with your brother, your voices raised in anger."

Patrick's thoughts bounced off his skull for a frustrated, frenetic moment. He remembered that argument all too vividly, and hoped to God she hadn't heard all of it. It had been the most heated argument he'd ever had with his brother, and they'd come nearly to blows with loaded rifles in their hands.

And it had been about goddamned *her*.

"I'll allow I was arguing with my brother. I'll even allow I was angry. But it was an accident, Julianne. Your maid mistook what she saw. I did not purposefully aim my rifle at my brother!"

"I believe you, Patrick. Truly, I do not think you are capable of such a thing, not now that I know you. But Prudence seemed so sure of what she had seen . . . and with her description, and the pieces of it I saw and heard myself, I felt I had the right of it." She swallowed. "When I finally saw you up close, you were standing in your father's study covered in blood. You *looked* like a killer."

"At twenty feet, perhaps," he told her coldly. "But I assure you, the picture would have been much different at three hundred!"

She spread her hands in a silent plea, the same hands that been fisted in his hair a few short minutes ago. It occurred to him that the possibility of returning to that place was impossible now. That, finally, sent him looking for his shirt.

"I am so, so sorry," he heard her whisper. "I will correct this when we return to Summersby. I will tell the truth during the inquest—"

He jerked up, alarm spreading like a flame through spilled whisky. The thought of Julianne relating these details during the inquest would be a disaster. "And point them straight to the second witness, who could very well tighten the noose about my neck? My God, Julianne. I know you are impetuous, but surely you can see the only way to help me is to stay silent now."

"But . . . how can I remain silent about this?" She

threw up her hands. "If I don't tell them the truth, you could be found guilty of murder. Because of *me*."

The moment slowed down in his mind to a pulsing heartbeat of truth. "Your statement from that day is not admissible because it wasn't provided under oath. I cannot be convicted on that, not without further testimony." He paused, searching her eyes even as he hardened his heart. "I came to your aid in Scotland, Julianne, and married you to protect your reputation. Now I need your help. There is another way to make amends, if you really want to undo the damage you have caused."

Her eyes shone bright with unshed tears. "I'll do anything," she told him, her voice close to breaking.

He stepped toward her. This, finally, was why he had married her, wasn't it? "Perhaps the circumstances of our improper marriage might be good for something beyond protecting your reputation." He lifted his hand to touch her cheek. "You cannot be compelled to testify against me if you choose not to, Julianne. They cannot force it of a wife."

He did not add it was an expectation he had carried from the start.

For a moment he thought she was going to fit all the pieces of this damnable puzzle together and see him for the bounder he was. But her face remained a canvas of self-loathing, and he knew a moment's relief in her perpetual self-absorption. She was too focused on her own sins to consider his. "But . . . if I stay silent," she said, the faintest quaver to her voice, "no matter the outcome, there will always be those who believe you are guilty."

Patrick's hand fell away. Time to press this home, while the blade of surprise was still sharp. "Better the judgment of fools than a guaranteed trip to the gallows.

I am not asking you to lie. Far from it. Without your testimony, they have no evidence. If you recuse yourself from testimony, I will owe you my life."

She sagged against the wall, the wall he had almost taken her against not ten minutes before. He could see she was considering it. Applying that bright, whirring mind to the work of the moment. He felt guilty applying this degree of coercion. But was there any other way? She'd proven herself immune to orders. There was nothing left to do but beg.

And so he waited.

Waited to hear the words from her lips, and which direction his future would go.

"Of course." Her words were a whisper, and then she was straightening her shoulders and nodding. "*Of course*. Anything. I would save you in any way I could."

He felt a slamming relief to hear her words, and a disbelief it could be so simple to gain her acquiescence. He breathed in deeply, and the air was laced with her omnipresent scent. It called to him, tempting him to stay and bury this argument with a mindless tup. She was feeling guilty right now. Vulnerable. He could see it in her pinched features, and in the tears she held back. If he chose to resume their interrupted kiss and toss up her skirts, he had no doubt she would let him. But in the end, he knew that would make them both feel worse, not better.

So instead of kissing her, he shrugged into his shirt. Her pale silence pulled at his conscience as he dressed, but he resisted the urge to take her in his arms. Her determination to help him might be welcome, but her timing was to rot. Mother of God, he had *married* her, and it could not be undone now. He'd made bloody well sure of it, hadn't he?

The door beckoned escape, and he was not in the mood to second-guess the instinct. He'd hold sentry in the hallway if he had to, protecting her from those inebriated men who might be bold enough to wander upstairs, but protecting himself from the temptation of her touch. "Lock the door behind me." He pulled the key from his pocket and tossed it onto the bed. "The men downstairs would not overlook an unlocked door with a prize like you behind it."

Her voice reached for him, just as he stretched his hand toward the door. "Patrick, wait."

He knew it was a mistake, but he looked back. Her hair tumbled about her shoulders, mussed and wildly arousing. It occurred to him that he had done that to her, even as she had done this to him. What a confusing mess this marriage was.

"How will you let yourself in without a key?"

"There is no need to wait up. I'll not be returning before dawn." He hesitated, though he wanted to kick himself for the weakness. "You asked earlier why I married you, but I would ask the same of you now, Julianne. Why did you marry me?"

She swiped, almost angrily, at one cheek. "I came to Scotland already doubting your guilt, but knowing that I was guilty too." Her face turned red and splotchy, and it made his feet itch against the floorboards. He had two young sisters, one of them was always on the verge of a good cry. He knew the signs, and he wanted none of it.

"But when I arrived, I could see you could never have done it. Not purposefully. I thought I could make things right again. The whispers in London, the endless gossip . . ." She sighed, and then her chin thrust out. "You can't imagine what you are facing on your return. I thought, if I were your wife, I could help you."

"You married me because you wanted to help me?" Patrick's mouth suddenly felt dry. He couldn't fathom it. This was Julianne Baxter, for God's sake. Sharp-tongued gossip, self-absorbed beauty. He would have liked to imagine she'd married him because her reputation had crashed on the shoals of Reverend Ramsey's eager eyes, and that he'd been the only piece of flotsam within arm's reach she could find to keep afloat.

But the sort of motivation she had just divulged required a good dose of empathy to go along with her infinite supply of recklessness.

She shook her head, setting errant curls in motion and a trail of tears spilling down one cheek. "You are a decent man, Patrick. A good man. *That* is why I married you. Not because of my reputation, or even because of our past. I married you because I wanted to. And I do not regret doing it."

Patrick preferred to imagine those tears weren't real, that she could produce them at will, like her myriad, shifting smiles, but her sorrow-clogged voice sounded far too authentic for comfort. He could see her reaching blindly for a truth that didn't exist.

This, finally, chased him into the hallway and yanked shut the door. He slumped down onto a floor that smelled of mildew and urine and held his breath until the sound of the key finally, hesitantly, reached his ears. She had chosen to listen to him in this, it seemed. To protect herself from the men downstairs?

Or to protect her heart from the man who arguably had worse intentions?

Because he was not decent or good. Not even passably so.

His earlier anger drained away, leaving only a hollowed out space in his heart. Inevitably, guilt flowed in to take its own rightful place. Julianne's conscience might now be clean, but his was miles from absolution. Because no matter how contrite she seemed over her role in the events of eleven months ago, it was still *his* finger on the trigger, *his* bullet in Eric's heart. Decent men did not argue with their brothers just moments before killing them. Decent men did not hide like cowards in faraway towns while their families mourned.

And decent men did not marry a woman—even a woman as beautiful and maddening as Julianne—to remove her as a potential witness.

Chapter 12

THE LAST LEG of their journey wound through the market village of Shippington, then took them through five miles of rutted roads flanked by newly fallow fields. The monotony of the late afternoon sunshine was broken up by the occasional dark forest where the oak trees met overhead in a yellow riot. In another few weeks, Patrick knew, the spindled limbs would lose their leaves to frost, but for now they kept a firm grip on their dying charges.

Though he'd made the trip in reverse scarcely eleven months prior, he no longer felt as though he remembered the way. Perhaps it was because he was arriving in a coach pulled by a team two breaths shy of the knacker, rather than his father's well-sprung coach and matched set of bays. Or, perhaps it was because he was arriving with Julianne, the very woman whose accusations had chased him away nearly a year ago, and whose tearful confession had driven him into the stairwell last night. She'd been withdrawn most of the morning, keeping even her false smiles tightly cloistered. It seemed a night of sleeping alone did not sit well with his wife.

A night of sleeping in the inn's rank stairwell had

not improved his view either. He'd overcome the initial surge of anger she'd conjured with far less difficulty than he would have imagined, dousing its spread with a healthy dose of introspection. It was impossible, if one applied logic, to blame Julianne for his current circumstances. Her attempt to protect a vulnerable servant might even border on admirable in the eyes of some. She'd believed the truth of her words at the time, even if her decision to protect her maid from scrutiny was ill-considered. And truly, she seemed to *want* to do the right thing now, to the point of being willing to admit her mistake in a very public way.

But he could not let her confess the truth at the inquest. If she did, she might reveal that there was another potential witness lurking somewhere in Yorkshire, one who apparently *did* think he had murdered his brother. Better to keep the original plan intact, and prevent Julianne's testimony from coming to light.

And for the near future, better to focus on dealing with the inevitable wrath of her father, even as he steeled himself to deal with the staggering loss of his own.

The coach disgorged them onto Summersby's manicured lawn, the same lawn where he had played as a child and grazed his horse as a rebellious young man, much to the consternation of the head gardener. The springy earth beneath Patrick's soles felt foreign after eleven months gone. When he had returned from his studies in Italy, excited about his future and convinced he could persuade his father to loan him the money to open a veterinary practice, he'd scarcely paid the lawn any attention. But now that he was returning to set his feet upon soil that belonged to him, he felt as though he were sinking.

The driver clattered off with a quick slap of reins,

and a glance toward the bank of east-facing windows confirmed the source of the driver's haste. The manor stretched high above the hopeful swath of green lawn, reaching three slate-tipped stories into the sky. Never the most hospitable of visages, Summersby Manor's front windows were draped in black today, yawning black holes sequestered behind glass.

A mourning wreath hung on the door, a macabre sort of welcome, and the hair along his arms pricked to attention at a burrowing memory, one of his last moments at Summersby. A pair of red-eyed maids had been covering the windows with black crepe as he'd left. Grief had not been reserved for the immediate family. The entire staff had loved Eric, even with his reputation as a bit of a rogue. He'd flirted with the maids and played dice with the footmen, no doubt fleecing them with the skills learned from his time in London's gaming hells. His death—so sudden and unnecessary—had been devastating to them all.

And Patrick was the man who had destroyed it all with a single, careless mistake.

He had no idea what to expect inside, except this: his mothers and sisters needed him. But needing him and welcoming him were not the same thing. His father's letters these past few months had touched on his mother's ebbing grief, but he wasn't sure how much his father had been hiding from him. Certainly, his father had never mentioned his own declining health, or that his mother had known where he was hiding.

Patrick gained the front steps with Julianne's bag in his hand, but as his hand reached for the door, her fingers grazed his arm.

"Wait," she said. "You should knock and have us announced."

He gritted his teeth around the absurdity of the request. "Such formality is not needed, I assure you."

She tilted her face upward, the brim of her bonnet shading her eyes to obsidian. "Nonetheless, I'd appreciate the opportunity to be presented. I was not exactly welcome here during your father's funeral. When I left this house a week ago, your mother still viewed me as the girl who'd orchestrated your downfall. She needs to see we are returning of an accord."

"This is hardly the time or place to plan a grand entrance, Julianne."

"It establishes our circumstances without fumbling over explanations." She paused a brief second before adding in a softer tone, "And it shows your mother she must accept me as your choice."

It occurred to him—belatedly, perhaps—that his new wife didn't just *look* like a countess. She thought like one. She was the person more experienced with social customs, more adept at the execution of manners that would need to come with this new life he did not want, but could not avoid if he was to ensure a decent future for his mothers and sisters. He'd always presumed such things would be Eric's domain. His refusal to take an interest in the estate, in politics, in manners, was part of the friction that had so frequently existed with his father.

That he was arriving with Julianne on his arm was the height of irony. If nothing else good came of this marriage, he had at least gained the sort of wife of whom his father—though apparently not his mother—would have approved.

He moved his hand from the door handle to the knocker. The sound seemed final, hammering at his ears. Gemmy sniffed his way up to the door and added his own demand, scratching against the wood and whining anxiously.

The door swung open to reveal Mr. Peters, Summersby's butler, dressed in solemn black. The elderly man's eyes widened in recognition. Patrick had known Peters his entire life, and yet had no idea how to present himself at the moment. As the prodigal son, returned home to disrupt the tranquillity of the grand manor?

Or as the new earl, come to take his far-from-rightful place?

Gemmy showed no hesitation on the matter. The terrier darted between the butler's legs.

"Oh no!" Julianne moaned. She elbowed them all aside as a ferocious explosion of snarls and growls rose up from the foyer.

"I thought you wanted to be announced," Patrick called out in confusion, as frozen by the tempting flash of ankle his reckless wife was displaying as by her lack of manners.

"Gemmy has already done it for us." Her panicked voice reached Patrick in a rushed blur of vowels and consonants. "And I would hate for my dog to kill yours."

CONSTANCE AND GEMMY were locked in a fierce battle for supremacy as Julianne skidded to a stop in the middle of the foyer. The two dogs tumbled across the black and white marble tile in a ball of flying fur and clicking teeth. She became aware of an undulating smear of black at the edge of her vision, evidence of a gathering crowd dressed in the somber hues of mourning.

And yet, no one stepped forward to offer assistance.

Perhaps they felt that a canine palaver of this magnitude would soon be over. To an uninformed bystander, bets would have probably been laid in Gemmy's favor, even given the dog's missing limb. He outweighed Constance by at least twenty pounds, and carried the ancestry of ferocious ratters in his blood. Those bystanders, however, would have been wrong.

Constance might be a fluffy white dog that fit in her mistress's arms, but Julianne had seen her pet chase down a mastiff in Hyde Park and come out victorious.

Poor Gemmy didn't stand a chance.

Julianne reached for the scruff of both dogs' necks, trying in vain to pull them apart. A high-pitched yelp—was it from Constance or Gemmy?—sent her panic soaring, but she couldn't see her way to a good handhold on the twisting animals. "I need help!" she called out.

Patrick materialized by her side, a large vase of flowers in his hand. She glared at him, her hands full of writhing dogs. He'd spent the entire day ignoring her, and last night had left her emotions so tattered she'd spent a night tossing in disturbed dreams. *Now* he was standing before her with flowers? But then he tossed the flowers aside and a spray of shockingly cold water from inside the vase rained down on all of them.

It occurred to her—in a sputtering fit of pique—that her husband was quite capable of using water for things other than washing when the situation called for it.

Gemmy scrambled away to cower between Patrick's legs, his tail pinned contritely against his body. Constance blinked up through her water-clogged lashes, holding out a pathetic, wet paw. Julianne's heart did that odd flopping thing it always did when Constance looked up at her that way.

"Oh, you poor, poor thing," she moaned, dropping to her knees and scooping the damp, furry bundle into her arms. She buried her nose in the Constance's thick coat, breathing in the familiar, musky smell. She'd not wanted to leave her pet when she'd been sent back to London after the funeral, but her father had insisted that Constance would have been too much for her to manage on the train alone. Little did he realize what she'd managed to accomplish anyway.

"What in God's name is going on here?" Her father's voice pulled Julianne's gaze up from her undistinguished position on the floor. Now it was her stomach's turn to do its own flopping thing that always accompanied her father's disapproval. Eyes of nearly the same piercing green as her own glared down at her, framed in white-bearded formality.

And, as per usual where she was concerned, her father's mouth was turned down in a distinct frown.

"Father." She rose on guilty legs, and her fingers curled into the comfort of Constance's fur. "I . . . that is, we . . . came as soon we could."

"How quickly you've come seems irrelevant, if you consider the fact you're supposed to be in London."

Julianne shifted Constance to her other arm as the dog's wet fur began to seep through her bodice. "If you would but listen for a moment, I am trying to explain—" Her voice tapered off as the countess, Patrick's mother, stepped out of the blurry sea of faces.

No, that wasn't quite right. *Dowager* countess.

Because Julianne was the countess now, even if no one yet realized it.

Lady Haversham stared up at Patrick, her hand lifting to cover the surprised oval of her mouth. Julianne had not realized it during the funeral, but now that mother and son were standing together, she could see the similarities between them were startling. They possessed the same thin, angular face, the same far-too-serious brown eyes. The woman's hair was threaded with gray, but it showed evidence of having once matched Patrick's own light brown color.

Much as Julianne had once mistaken Patrick's lack of expression as evidence of his guilt, she was at first tempted to interpret Lady Haversham's stony features as evidence of the woman's disapproval. But if she had learned anything from the past few days, it was that such quick impressions could be wrong.

"Mother." A subtle vibration could be heard in Patrick's voice. "I received your letter. I was so very sorry to learn of Father's passing."

The dowager countess's hands clenched in her black skirts, and her mask slipped, ever so slightly, to reveal the anguish beneath. "Thank you for coming home. You are welcome here."

"That remains to be seen." Julianne's father took a menacing step toward Patrick. "Please explain why you have arrived with my daughter without a single chaperone between you. I may have been your father's good friend, but by God, if you have compromised my daughter's reputation in any way, I will demand satisfaction."

Patrick stiffened, and Julianne laid a gentle hand on her husband's arm. Her father was not to blame, for any of this. And if Patrick endangered either himself or her father in something so foolish as a duel she would never, ever forgive either of them.

Patrick cleared his throat. "I suppose it depends on how you would define compromise, sir. If you are thinking of calling me out, you might want to consult Julianne first. I doubt she'll appreciate being made a widow."

Chapter 13

GASPS RANG OUT on four sides, but Patrick's attention was focused solely on his mother. He regretted delivering the news in so ignominious a fashion, but really, was there a better way?

She looked as though she'd been through hell. The dark circles beneath her eyes, the new prominence to her cheekbones—these things he had already noted. It was easier to focus on the clinical signs of mourning instead of the hurt surprise that flashed in her eyes at his announcement. But that did not mean he didn't notice.

"It cannot be true," she told him, her voice a hurt scratch against his conscience. "She was just here for your father's funeral, and said nothing at all of this."

Patrick nodded grimly. "We were married in Scotland four days ago."

"I do not understand." His mother's voice, usually so calm, seemed as gnarled as her hands, knotting and unknotting in her crepe skirts. "How could you marry the woman who . . ." She swallowed, and her voice dropped to a whisper. "Who accused you of killing Eric?"

The understandable question reached through his ribs, searching for an answer that would not be a lie.

Patrick hesitated. The black-frocked crowd in the foyer showed no signs of dwindling, but it was far too late for regrets.

Or, it seemed, properly constructed explanations.

"She no longer believes that, Mother."

His mother stared at him a long, telling second before glancing toward Julianne. Her lips formed a thin façade of a greeting. "Then it seems I must offer my congratulations. The new Lady Haversham is, of course, welcome here at Summersby as well."

"Has everyone here lost their hold on their sanity?" Jonathon Blythe, Patrick's cousin, shouldered his way out of the crowd.

It was not all that surprising that Blythe was apparently still here a good week after the funeral, publicly mourning the death of the man whose favor he had always sought in life. From Patrick's earliest recollection, Blythe had always been underfoot, descending on Summersby for entire months at a time. But it annoyed Patrick that the younger man should now stand in what was arguably *his* foyer and toss out such accusations.

And Blythe's gaze seemed far from familial at the moment.

"He's murdered his brother, for God's sake," the younger man snarled.

Patrick struggled to contain his temper. Blythe might be the first to speak it out loud, but he would not be the last, or perhaps not even the loudest. Now would begin the parade of angry relatives. He'd expected it, of course. His father's letters had hinted at the residual animosity, and Blythe's loud objections had been chief among them.

"Someone should fetch the magistrate," a disembodied voice echoed in agreement.

"He belongs in gaol." This from Aunt Margaret, his father's sister and Blythe's mother.

Other voices rose in agreement. It was like being thrust into the November house party again, only this time the arrows were being aimed at him instead of the targets set up on the front lawn.

"Is this any way to treat the new earl?" A single, contrary voice rang out. "He's not yet been charged."

Silence fell, and the crowd twisted around. Patrick shifted with them, searching out the source of such dissidence. The relative who had uttered those words stepped forward, and Patrick recognized George Willoughby. Another cousin.

And apparently his only supporter.

Most of those in today's crowd had been at the November house party, eager to enjoy the comforts of Summersby at someone else's expense. He'd considered Willoughby chief among those interlopers at the time. He felt guilty for such quick judgment now.

Here was a man who *ought* to hate him as much as Jonathon Blythe. On the simplest level, both Blythe and Willoughby had likely lost some social standing after the events of eleven months ago—not that either had ever held much. After all, one did not boast a murder suspect in the family without suffering some from the association. Things became more complicated if one considered that both men were considered equal contenders for succession after Patrick. Neither would be looking forward to the prospect of having the title stripped from the family's reach and returned to the Crown.

Patrick extended a cautious hand. "Willoughby."

His cousin hesitated, but then clasped Patrick's. "Haversham."

A collective easing of tension rippled out through the

crowd at George Willoughby's very public acknowledgment. The butler finally collected his wits and closed the front door, nodding toward Patrick as he bustled past. "Welcome home, my lord."

Patrick had heard Mr. Peters utter those same words a thousand times, always to his father. To hear them directed toward himself sounded horribly wrong, and for a moment he wondered if he wasn't making a tremendous mistake. He didn't know how to be earl.

He didn't *want* to know how to be earl.

He wanted only to free himself from the pending murder charge and ensure his family didn't wind up destitute. But to do that, he needed to accept this mantle that, like it or not, had been lowered onto his shoulders like a heavy yoke.

Mr. Peters began to herd the servants back to their posts, instructing one wide-eyed maid to clean up the water that still lay upon the floor. The guests began to drift away too, though judging by the disapproving looks a few tossed behind them, Patrick was still front and center in their thoughts. With any luck, the morrow would see most of them returned to London.

Then again, family had a way of staying longer than they ought.

As the guests left the foyer, Patrick felt as though he was finally able to breathe again. Only his mother, Julianne, and Lord Avery remained. His mother was watching him with a sheen of moisture in her eyes, but those tears were far removed from the ones that had fallen the day of Eric's death. He felt like a bounder to have caused them. "You should not have had to deal with Father's death alone," he told her gently.

"I had your letters to comfort me. But I am so, so glad you are home."

Patrick blinked. "My . . . *letters*?" He had not written his mother, thinking the contact would be unwelcome.

"Your father read me each of your letters. I have them, in safekeeping." Her smile turned brittle. "In case we need to use them in your defense, proof of where you have been these past months."

Patrick blinked. "You knew Father corresponded with me?"

"I understood it was necessary to be so careful, until the facts were sorted out. I felt better knowing you were safe, instead of sitting in a prison somewhere stricken with gaol fever." She reached out a hand and squeezed his arm. "Mary and Eleanor will be so pleased to see your safe return. Your sisters cried for weeks after you left."

The thought of his ten-year-old twin sisters mourning his disappearance stung. Patrick had imagined his family still blamed him for Eric's death, that his absence was necessary for their healing. He'd envisioned a family torn, his culpability in his brother's death dividing their loyalties and pitting husband against wife. But apparently, his disappearance had been nearly as hard on them as Eric's death.

Lord Avery swept an angry hand toward the hallway. "The study would be a better place to continue this conversation, Haversham." He stopped Julianne's forward motion with a firm hand. "I wish to speak with him alone. You will go upstairs and see yourself settled."

Julianne flushed. "But—"

"*Now*, Julianne." Her father's tone brooked no argument.

Patrick well knew the tight smile that swept over his wife's face, and it did not bode well for an easy acquiescence. Not that he didn't see the reasoning behind

Avery's demand. A man liked a smaller audience when his liver was about to be delivered in pieces, roasted on a platter.

"Perhaps it would be best," Patrick agreed. "It will be an unpleasant sort of conversation, I'm afraid. I would spare you the indignity."

"But I *wish* to be present," she said, her voice rising in both pitch and volume.

The urge to resort to Avery's methods and order Julianne above stairs gnawed at him. He was her husband, a man she had sworn to obey, even if he suspected those vows had emerged from her lips as more sentimental drivel than actual fact. But while his new wife might still be a bit of a mystery to him, he had at least discovered this about her: no one made Julianne do anything she did not wish to do.

She shifted the dog in her arms. "I am every bit as culpable here, and—"

"Are you aware your dog is injured?" Patrick interrupted as he spied a red smear on her otherwise pristine lavender bodice. He searched for the source of blood, and spied a small wound on the dog's right shoulder. *Well done, Gemmy.* An uncharitable thought, perhaps, but given the hold Julianne's dog had taken on Gemmy's throat, Patrick couldn't help but be glad his dog hadn't completely disgraced himself.

"Constance?" Julianne glanced down and her face turned as white as the dog's fur. "Oh my word," she gasped. "She is bleeding!"

Patrick examined the wound more closely as the little dog bared its teeth at him. Constance appeared to be the by-blow of something disreputable, at best, and judging by the little dog's temperament, a sewer rat likely figured somewhere in its ancestry. The wound was reassuringly shallow, but it was enough to foment an idea. "It does not appear overly deep. Still, unwashed wounds have a tendency to fester. It should be cleaned straight away."

Julianne lowered her cheek to her pet's head. "Is it so very serious as that? Perhaps we could have one of the servants do it."

"I'd hate to risk lethal injury to the staff," he said tellingly.

Her eyes narrowed on him. "Constance *can* be a terror at times."

"A fact I am sure Gemmy can now respect. In this case, I think only someone who knows her well should attempt to see to her injury."

Her smile faltered, which Patrick took as a good sign. She had clearly sorted through his scheme, and was weighing her options. But finally, she nodded. "Of course, you are right." She leaned in close and her voice lowered to a whisper. "I might as well practice my nursing skills, as I suspect you may need them when my father is through with you."

"I can escort you above stairs to Patrick's room," his mother offered. "'Tis the same as he left it, medical supplies and bandages scattered about. I am sure you can find whatever you need there."

"Thank you, I would appreciate that." Julianne's eyes pulled to her father. "But . . . please be kind to Patrick, Father. He has had a difficult few days."

Avery bristled. "Then one more difficult hour shouldn't make much of a difference."

Chapter 14

THE EVENING SUN was fading as Patrick faced Lord Avery over his father's desk. It had been difficult enough to stand here eleven months ago, facing his father's grief. Standing like a delinquent schoolboy in front of Julianne's father, about to confess to some sugarplum version of his sins, came close to the same misery.

"Damn you, Haversham!" Avery pounded on the desk, nearly setting the inkwell over. "I think I deserved the courtesy of at least being asked for my daughter's hand."

The familiar scents of cigar and brandy and leather-bound books nudged at Patrick's senses. They were things he had always associated with his father, and for a moment he was jerked back to a dark, foreboding place.

Christ above, would he never be given an opportunity to properly mourn?

But Julianne's father was waiting for an answer, and so Patrick forced himself to focus on the white-haired man who had been his father's closest friend. Avery appeared in something less than a benevolent frame of mind, sitting in Patrick's father's chair. Not that he blamed the man. Despoiling a man's only daughter was a wrongdoing on par with murder.

And in this sin, at least, Patrick was all too guilty.

"Why was she even in Scotland, for God's sake?" Avery raged. "And why did my staff in London not send word she'd gone missing?"

For all his blustering, anyone could see Lord Avery was a father who loved his daughter, and he deserved an explanation that provided hope for his daughter's future. Still, Patrick could not see the sense in adding nonsensical exultations of love to the mess of this marriage. Given the circumstances, he doubted Avery would believe them, anyway.

"Were they expecting her?" Patrick asked. "She told me she came straight from the funeral."

That set Avery's white brows at attention. "She never made it to London?"

"By the timing of things, I would wager not."

"I sent her to London a week ago, with a borrowed ladies' maid. Her presence here was proving distressful to your mother and sisters, particularly after all she had done." Avery's fist thumped on the desk. "But *why*, damn it? Why would she do such a dangerous, foolhardy thing? And why would you bloody make it worse by marrying her? She's underage, for God's sake!"

"I believe she felt guilty, sir, and sought to rectify her role in things by coming to Scotland to find me. And no matter how she was sent, she arrived lacking a maid or proper escort. Preserving her reputation through marriage seemed the least troublesome solution."

Avery leaned back, his knuckles turning white against the edge of the desk. "That is little enough cause for such a hasty decision. You're suspected of *murder*, Haversham."

"Julianne understands the seriousness of the situation." Patrick willed himself to keep a tight rein on the temper that wanted to take the bit in its teeth. Lord Avery was more than Julianne's father, he was a strong potential ally in the House of Lords, and Patrick suspected he was going to need one. "She has expressed some reservations about what she recalls from that day, reservations that have convinced her of my innocence, thank God. She did not marry me believing me a murderer, if that is your worry."

Avery rose, and the air seemed to bend around his anger. "Hang it all, Haversham, why did she marry you at all?"

Patrick recoiled against the muttered oath that so literally reminded him of all that was at stake. Did gentlemen usually toss the word about so liberally? Or was it only that his neck was increasingly feeling the sting of the threat? "Her lack of chaperone caught the notice of the town rector." So had her lack of clothing, but perhaps the point was well enough made without revealing that piece to her father.

Avery stalked around the side of the desk, but his ire seemed to be deflating with every step. He tugged at his cravat with a frustrated finger. "She's an impetuous chit, but that doesn't excuse your behavior in encouraging it."

"I claim full responsibility. You should not blame her for the outcome." Patrick paused, then added a gentle half truth that would ease Avery's mind, even as it pricked his own conscience. "Not that it was anything close to a hardship to offer your daughter my protection, sir. Anyone would be proud to take Julianne as a wife."

The older man's eyes softened, ever so slightly. "You will learn," he said, his voice thickening at the center, "that managing Julianne does not mean it is necessary to indulge her. My daughter is—" He seemed to reach for the right word.

"Headstrong?" Patrick supplied.

"Determined. As determined as her mother was. Keeping her out of the scandal sheets was nigh on impossible." He eyed Patrick with something close to a grimace. "She'll be a difficult wife, I'll wager. Perhaps I should thank you, in the end. God knows I've had my doubts as to whether there was a man out there who could both meet her expectations and be willing to take her on."

"She certainly pursues her own mind," Patrick agreed, realizing that in this, at least, he spoke a large measure of truth.

"Goaded you into it, did she?" Avery's hand plucked at his beard and he studied Patrick a disconcerting moment. "It is admirable of you to take the blame, of course, but you forget I know my daughter better than anyone." He paused. "You've married her without my permission, and she's a month shy of her majority. You realize you'll not see a penny of her dowry. I am not obligated to provide it, given the circumstances."

Patrick clenched his jaw against the thought of accepting payment for deceiving Julianne into this marriage. "I do not seek it." He settled a hand on his father's desk, and his finger trailed over the papers and correspondence that littered the top, correspondence it was now his godforsaken duty to manage. "I have planned a respectable settlement for her, should the worst happen. But it will not come to that. She will have the protection of my name, I swear it."

"Protection?" Avery's voice cupped around the word in disbelief. "How do you propose to protect her if you are turned over to the gallows? You will drag my daughter to hell with you."

Patrick stepped around the edge of the desk and lowered himself into his father's chair. "I'll not be found guilty, Lord Avery."

"The devil take you, Haversham." Julianne's father stared down at him with eyes of chipped ice. "You will need more than bravado to convince the assizes, son."

Patrick looked up at Avery with a calm assurance he did not yet quite feel, his new position both telling and terrifying. "I'll not be tried in the assize courts."

Avery's eyes glittered across the space of the desk. "It's to be the House of Lords, then?" At Patrick's nod, those eyes narrowed. "A startling change in fortune—some might even call it *good* fortune. Your father's suspicious death, and a chance to be tried as a peer?"

Avery's words made cold fingers of worry shiver up Patrick's back. "Was my father's death suspicious? Julianne did not mention such a thing."

"There are some who believe so. By all accounts, the earl was in perfect health, even days before his collapse. Damned convenient thing, you showing up now to take up the title."

Patrick's lungs funneled shut. The insinuation was vile, as horrifying and unimaginable as the crime he had been accused of committing against Eric. "Are you suggesting I had a hand in my father's death?"

Avery stroked his beard with a deliberate thumb. "There will always be those eager to question the neat sequence of events that have landed you in your father's chair." His jaw softened. "Not that I believe it myself, Haversham. I never believed you capable of purposeful violence. But I want you to be prepared. A trial in the House of Lords is based more on appearances than evidence, son. 'Tis a long road you face to freedom."

The older man's words echoed the guidance Mac-

Kenzie had provided, and in this, at least, Patrick felt prepared. "I am grateful for your advice, Lord Avery." He hesitated. "And, if I may dare hope, your support."

The older man reached for a tray on the desk, and poured a generous glass of the old earl's best Scottish whisky. He handed it over to Patrick. "Of course you have my support. I never believed it of you, no matter my daughter's claims to the contrary. The stubborn chit's never been able to see ten feet in front of her." He shook his head, and a half-smile flitted about his face. "But you need to be prepared to fight for your birthright, son, as well as the truth. Because if you don't, I imagine they might try to pin your father's death on you too."

Chapter 15

NIGHT HAD FALLEN by the time Patrick finally made his way out of the study. Something Avery had said still bothered him, a piece of the puzzle that refused to fit. His father had been close to sixty. It was not a surprise that a man of that age might experience a decline in health, but Avery was right: his father's precipitous death was sure to attract notice.

Worse than the thought of what his father's death meant for him was the very fact of the loss. It hurt to think of the ignorance he had shown to his father in those months before Eric's death. He would gladly give up his own life if it meant he could have Eric and his father restored to the family, but after the uncomfortable conversation with Lord Avery, he was worried he might be required to give it up regardless.

The glass of whisky he had tossed back with Lord Avery at the end had restored him to good graces with Julianne's father, but it had done little to ease his mind. And unfortunately, it had near shredded his wits. He wanted nothing more than to stumble his way to his bed and a good night's sleep. But as his mother was waiting for him just outside the door to the study, his wits would need to be reassembled, and his bed would have to wait.

"Am I to presume your discussion with Lord Avery has thwarted the possibility of a duel?" she asked.

Patrick fought a smile, the one his mother had always been able to wrench from him, even when he was in the blackest of moods. "I believe Lord Avery understands things better now. And I would not have permitted him to call me out. I think you've been through enough this past year without losing another son, don't you think?"

"Indeed." She studied him a moment. "Thank you for coming home, Patrick. Heaven knows this past week has been difficult enough, losing your father, penning that awful letter. Such necessary subterfuge." Her calm façade slipped, just enough to reveal the devastation beneath. "I just . . . I hope you will be careful. I will not be happy if I have called you home to lose you to the gallows."

Patrick inclined his head, his throat swelling around the question he needed to ask. "Do you believe me guilty then, Mother?"

She shook her head without hesitation, and it brought a lump to Patrick's throat to see it. "No, dear. Never. You are so much like me . . ." She lifted a hand to his face, a face Patrick knew was in need of a razor and three weeks of solid meals to be restored to the son she remembered. Her hand felt cool against his skin, and he wanted to lean into his mother's strength. "You keep your emotions too well contained. But I knew. A mother always knows. You were as devastated by Eric's death as any of us. You were in shock, and those who would be suspicious misinterpreted it as an expression of guilt."

Much as he had interpreted his mother's frozen silence as a belief in his guilt, it seemed. "Thank you," he told her, his heart coming to rest on its side.

His mother's hand fell away. "But the new Lady Haversham's explanation didn't help matters that day, did it? I confess I am surprised by your choice for a wife."

Patrick clenched his fists, feeling oddly protective. "She is more than she seems."

"Well, you are a man grown, capable of making your own decisions. The earl now. I only hope she proves worthy of your trust." Her serious brown eyes met his, the same as those he saw in a mirror when he took the time to look. "Your father always thought she would be a good choice for Eric, but I had my doubts. She seems quite . . . *fashionable*."

Patrick hesitated, resenting the slice of jealousy his mother's innocent words conjured. Julianne was admittedly not the sort of woman he would have once imagined marrying, and he could well believe she would come as a surprise to his mother, even without the history of her accusations against him. And yes, she cut quite a sharp figure, one he had watched more closely than he would like to admit these past few days.

But she was also loyal and brave and altogether maddening. All told, "fashionable" was somewhat low on the list.

"I was just heading up to see her."

"Don't you think you have at least one more interview to complete tonight before returning to your wife?" His mother's words were gentle but firm. "Mary and Eleanor are waiting. I told them of your return."

Patrick nodded his agreement, even as he wondered if his sisters' reception would really be as welcoming as his mother imagined. "You are right, of course."

Even if he dreaded the accusation he feared in his sisters' eyes, there was little he could do now except apologize to the earnest hearts who had probably been the most damaged by Eric's untimely death and his sudden departure.

Gemmy was lying on the stairwell's first landing as Patrick made his way up, the dog's nose poking between the banister slats. "Poised for a quick retreat, no matter which direction she comes from, eh?" Gemmy's tail thumped on the smooth wood of the landing. "You don't look half as contrite as you ought. Perhaps if you didn't go barging in, hackles raised, Constance might have greeted you in a more civil fashion."

Gemmy's ears drooped. Patrick understood how he felt. It was the same way he'd felt after mucking things up with Julianne in their wedding bed. So far he'd failed to banish that dishonorable memory, and given the way this night was going, he doubted he'd find a way to erase it from either of their minds any time soon.

"Come on, then." He snapped his fingers and headed up the remainder of the stairs. "Perhaps things will go better for me at this next stop with you in tow."

With Gemmy on his heels, Patrick found the door he sought and knocked in an unmistakable pattern. Two slow knocks, followed by three sharper raps in quick succession.

"Who is it?" The voice that reached him through the door was achingly familiar, and rightfully suspicious.

"Bonny Prince Charlie," he quipped, lapsing into the familiar game they used to play.

The door opened to reveal a face heartbreakingly older than the last time he had seen it. Mary was already dressed for bed, her hair in plaits and a white cap covering her light brown hair. Despite his worry, Patrick felt a smile steal across his face at the sight of her. "Miss me, sprite?"

Recognition widened Mary's brown eyes, and she launched herself at him with a small, soft cry. Eleanor hit him next, a second kick of surprise. Patrick swooped them up, one in each arm, so full of family he couldn't draw a breath. And then he was setting them down and they were pulling him inside, almost hopping with excitement.

"Mama told us you had returned," Mary exclaimed. "But then you didn't come."

"This funny little dog came by to visit us though," Eleanor added. "He only had three legs, and I thought, oh, Patrick would like this dog."

"And then I said what if it *was* your dog—" Mary interjected.

"And then we both prayed it was your dog—"

"Quite hard, actually. Elle gave herself a headache."

Patrick bounced between his sisters' erratic thoughts, his interpretation skills a few months rusty. He smiled as Eleanor threw her arms around the little yellow terrier, who had wormed his way between them and was wiggling almost as much as the little girl.

"So Gemmy found you first, did he?" Patrick chuckled at the mention of his dog's wanderlust. He could well imagine the dog had spent much of the last hour prowling the house, urinating in corners, looking for places to hide from Constance.

"So he *is* your dog?" Eleanor smiled up.

"Of course. Who else do you know who would have a three-legged dog?"

Mary smiled. "And his name is Gemmy? I think it's a lovely name."

"That's because you like gems," Eleanor pointed

out. "I prefer horses. You should change his name to Trotter."

Mary gasped. "I like horses too, Elle, and you well know it."

"Although I suppose you can't name a three-legged dog Trotter," Eleanor tumbled on, "because the poor dear thing would limp, and it would hurt his feelings to have to live up to such expectations." She paused for a breath, then regarded Patrick with a somber expression—far too serious for plaited hair, at any rate. "Why did you come back? Was it because Papa has died?"

Patrick tugged at a brown braid, setting Eleanor's nightcap askew in his attempt to make her smile. "No, sprite. I've come because of *you*. I am so sorry you had to manage all of this without me. Father would be proud to see how well you've taken care of Mother."

"I am *so* glad you have come to see us tonight," Mary said, leaning against him as if she were afraid he might suddenly disappear again.

Eleanor nodded. "Yes, it would have been ever so cruel if you'd made us wait for breakfast." Her face scrunched up. "We'd have had to sit in our chairs and look at you, but ne'er say a word."

"I'm glad I've come too." And he was. How could he have forgotten what it felt like to be silenced by the chatter of a sister, or hugged by small arms? "I wanted to be the first to tell you both. I've brought home a wife. You'll meet her at breakfast."

"A wife?" Both girls stared at him, their mouths wide enough to catch dust, had the maids at Summersby been permitted to let any settle. "But . . . *why*?"

Patrick hesitated. "She's going to help me fight the suspicions regarding my role in Eric's death." He wondered if he ought to say more, but decided it was as much explanation as was needed. Simple, perhaps, but true. He could see his sisters' heads trying to wrap around the notion, and it occurred to him that—unlike real life—they no doubt considered marriage something magical, a fairy tale of princes and true love. Julianne herself must have once been such a mysterious creature. And just like that, he was reminded again of his duplicity.

Christ, but he was a cad.

He'd raged at her last night, when she'd been brave enough to face such a difficult confession. He'd ignored his new wife much of today, when she probably would have appreciated a smile to help pave the way into Summersby. He'd spoken the truth to his sisters. Julianne *was* helping him fight these charges, helping him stay with his family. No matter how angry he had been with her last night, no matter how frustrated he sometimes felt toward her, Julianne was the reason he had come back to Summersby.

And he had treated her poorly, all things considered.

"Who is she?" Mary asked, her voice curious. "Is she pretty?"

"Very pretty. You probably know her as Miss Baxter. She attended mother's house party last year."

Eleanor cocked her head, her freckled nose wrinkling. "The lady who said you killed Eric?"

Patrick shifted uncomfortably. When he had departed so hastily eleven months ago, chased by his grief and those who would have his head, he hadn't considered what his sisters might know, or what they understood. "She made a mistake, Elle. And she is very, very sorry."

Mary smiled up at him. When he'd left, her front teeth had just been coming in, but they'd emerged in full and now appeared too large for her face. Like those teeth,

Patrick could see a new startling maturity in her eyes. "As long as she loves you like we do, we shall like her."

"But she won't make you leave again, will she?" Eleanor asked suspiciously.

Patrick truly had no idea what the morning might bring, but he was loath to admit that to his wide-eyed sisters. And the mention of love from his sister's innocent lips made him squirm uncomfortably. No, Julianne didn't love him. He'd be lucky if she came to tolerate him. "She brought me home to you," he said evasively. "So I rather doubt she wants me to leave."

Mary's brown eyes seemed to swim in her face. "Have you been to see Eric's gravesite?" she asked.

Patrick found himself at a loss for words over the question. "No, sprite. I've just arrived, after all."

"You should go. He is buried by the lake, where you always went fishing. Papa said he should be in the family plot in Shippington, but Mama insisted on the lake. She said he would be happier there, and we could visit with him whenever we wanted."

Patrick had presumed his brother would have been buried in the family crypt at Shippington's cemetery, where generations of Havershams lay in some semblance of rest. He'd left too quickly, knowing he would be unwelcome at the funeral, chased by the suspicions others held of him. The crypt was a cold, foreboding place.

The lake, however, was not.

Mary smiled. "I planted flowers there this spring."

"And I tried to catch a fish," Eleanor broke in. "But I couldn't figure out how to tie the lure the way you showed me."

"I'll go there tonight," he promised. He might be weary, but this was not something to be put off. No matter his explanations to his sister, no matter his plans for Julianne, he had no idea what tomorrow would bring.

And he owed his brother this much, at least.

A SCRATCHING AT the door jolted Julianne awake, and for a moment, the strangeness of her surroundings, pressed in on her. But then Constance yawned in her lap, and Julianne's eyes adjusted to the almost violent light surrounding her, and she remembered where she was.

Summersby. Patrick's room.

She'd fallen asleep in a sturdy reading chair, unwilling to disturb the bedclothes before he returned, anxious for some news of how the interview had gone with her father. As the room had fallen dark, she'd lit every lamp she could find. After the care she had seen him exercise in minimizing waste on oil and tallow, the extravagance would probably make Patrick frown. But she'd needed light to clean Constance's shoulder, which had thankfully turned out to be little more than a scratch. And it wouldn't hurt to show Patrick that he no longer had to pinch pennies, that there was no shame in being the new Earl of Haversham . . . and indeed, that he had as much right and strength of character to occupy the position as anyone else.

When she cracked the door, Gemmy nosed his way in, whining anxiously. She cast a quick look down the dark corridor, but could not see Patrick anywhere.

"He's abandoned us both, hmmm?"

Gemmy cocked his head, but she shook a finger at him in warning. "If you come in, you'll need to behave yourself. No attacking Constance again, or I won't be held responsible for what she might do to you."

Thankfully, Gemmy showed no signs of wanting to further his acquaintance with Constance. The scruffy terrier hugged tight against Julianne's skirts as he walked into the room, refusing to make eye contact with the other dog.

"Sit," Julianne ordered. For once, Gemmy appeared to be in a mood to obey.

Constance approached with a quivering nose. Poor Gemmy met the smaller dog's interest with as much dignity as a terrified, three-legged dog could muster. There was much sniffing. A comical baring of teeth. And then Constance backed away, apparently satisfied the interloper posed no threat to either her person or her mistress's affections. She leaped up onto the bed. Gemmy claimed the chair Julianne had just been sleeping in and turned in three awkward circles before flinging himself down with a soft *whuff*.

Julianne exhaled the tight breath she had been holding. This, at least, was laudable progress. Her husband's absence—for the second night in a row—was not.

Where on earth was Patrick? Was he sleeping in another room? She knew he'd spent last night in the posting house stairwell because she had unlocked the door and peeked out just before dawn. She found him there, a sleeping sentry guarding her against whatever evil had threatened to come up the stairs. But he wasn't outside her door tonight, and the house had taken on the still silence reached only when its guests claimed their beds.

If he was in the house, wouldn't Gemmy have stayed with him?

She made her way to the window and stared out onto the shadowed vista of Summersby's front lawn. The moon was bright overhead, splashing its way across the blurry landscape. She recalled from last November that the ground sloped so gently by the lake as to be suitable for croquet, and that the breeze off the water was apt to catch arrows and sling them off target.

At least, that was what she had told everyone. At the time, she hadn't wanted to admit she couldn't *see* the target.

A thin sweep of light caught her eye, heading east. She almost missed it in the reflection off the window glass, and so she blew out all the lamps in the room and returned to the window, trying to see more clearly. There was a full moon tonight, enough to cast shadows across the lawn, but even had it been daylight she knew she could not have made out the person below her window. But the juxtaposition of light against darkness was a far easier thing for her flawed eyes to see. Logic told her she could still be mistaken. Her eyesight had a way of playing tricks on her, of convincing her she could see things that did not exist. She thought she'd seen movement that day in November too, heading away from the scene of the crime.

And yet clearly she had been wrong. Patrick had been covered in Eric's blood that day. He had run *toward* his brother, not away from the scene of a crime. The enormity of what she had presumed, and what she had done, felt like a lead weight sewn into the hem of her skirts, waiting for her to find enough water to drown.

The light bobbed steadily, cutting a sure path to the east. It could be anyone. One of the other guests, heading outside to smoke a cheroot, perhaps. Someone who couldn't sleep. But she knew it was Patrick. Knew it in her heart, that fickle organ that wanted to lean out the window and shout for his attention. He would be hurting after such a long interview with her father and after the dubious homecoming he had received.

And so instead of leaning out the window, or curling her weary muscles into bed, she sent her feet to the door.

Chapter 16

ʜᴇ ᴋɴᴇᴡ sʜᴇ had followed him, even before he saw her.

Knew it by the way the air changed around him, and the way his muscles tensed in preparation for whatever fight she'd brought with her. He's seen the lights go out in his room as he'd stared up from the lawn, had hoped it had meant she'd grown tired of waiting and taken herself to bed. Instead, she'd followed him to the one place at Summersby where he'd hoped his guilt would flow out instead of in, but where instead he'd found a scraping, slapping emptiness that refused to be filled. There was no peace to be found at Eric's grave. And even had there been, her appearance here was bound to shatter it.

He rose up, the feel of the cold marble headstone still on his hand, his shoulders already bracing for the impact of whatever ill-hatched need had brought her out this time of night. The light from his lantern fell squarely across her face, and he almost doused it as a means of self-preservation. Her cheeks were pink with cold and exertion, and those dark red curls were flying loose about her head. His exhaustion was no match for the pull of attraction the sight of her always incited, but it at least provided him the excuse to resist succumbing to the temptation.

"What are you doing out here in the dark, Julianne?" She'd not even brought a light with her to trek across Summersby's darkened paths. Then again, was he really surprised? This was Julianne, after all. Planning and forethought were sorely lacking in his wife's arsenal of life skills.

"I came to find you." Her voice cut through the night like the sweetest of blades.

He studied her, trying to sort out what she wanted with him, with the world. He was glad to see she had at least donned a shawl, and that for once she'd shown enough sense to gauge the weather before tumbling into trouble. He'd left the warmth of the manor in his shirt-sleeves, and the cold now came close to tearing holes in his lungs.

He waited for the conversation to turn around to her true purpose. He expected her to rail at him for leaving her alone in her room. Demand to know what matter of discourse he'd had with her father. Instead she took up his hand, a shock of warmth and comfort he hadn't known he needed. She drew him away from his dark vigil and toward the specter of the Grecian folly, waiting nearby like a stone sentry in the moonlight. She pulled him up beneath its high, arched ceiling, sat him down on a bench with her small, vital hands.

And then she blew out the lantern he carried, plunging them into darkness.

"Julianne—" he started, but fell silent as she sat down too. She lifted the shawl from her shoulders and placed it around them both. Her head tilted over onto his shoulder and her hand crept up to twine tightly with his. And there she waited, like water at rest in a glass.

Four days of marriage and a dozen vivid arguments had not made him anything close to an expert in the dilemma of this person who was his wife. But this newest layer was difficult to decipher. This was Julianne, toast of the *ton*, darling of drama. How could she sit here so quietly, offering such comfort, waiting to share this grief? No one deserved that sort of burden.

"Tell me what happened that day," she whispered.

He exhaled, and she was so close he could feel how his breath ruffled her curls. The moonlight spilled through the open sides of the folly, casting fantastical shadows across them, and he imagined they grew teeth in that moment. He did not wish to speak of this. An accident, he'd told her. Surely that was enough for her to know.

And yet, he found himself speaking. "We were hunting."

She exhaled delicately, as if she had been holding her breath. "Grouse, if I recall."

"Yes, well, the grouse were not cooperating." He hesitated, unsure of his own words. She felt essential there, where her hand lay joined with his. During the brief length of their marriage, he had lifted her into coaches, his hands spanning her narrow, corseted waist. He'd helped her down from the smoke-obscured steps of the train, steadying her against the soot-slick surface. But he couldn't remember just *sitting* with her, her body quiet against his, her hand clasped firmly in his own. It was an unbearable intimacy.

"You already know I had been arguing with my brother. I was in a most disagreeable frame of mind in those months after I returned from Italy. I was angry with him, and with my life, and I said something to Eric I regret to this day."

"He accused you of wanting something that by rights belonged to him." She lifted her head and offered him a tremulous smile, as if they were both pretending this had a neat, happy ending when they already knew how it turned out. "And you told him to go to the devil and take his future countess with him. I heard that much when I was hiding here, in this very spot. He was talking about me, wasn't he?"

Julianne's interruption—and her accuracy—rattled him. Yesterday's confession that she hadn't truly seen what had happened had led him to hope that she hadn't understood anything that had happened that day. Clearly, she knew more than she ought.

He nodded. "He was jealous."

She sighed, and then readjusted the shawl around both their shoulders. "I have always regretted that dance."

He could well imagine she did. "Then you should not have asked me."

Her head popped up, and he could feel her gaze probing through shadows. "I did not regret dancing with *you*, Patrick. I regretted dancing with Eric. I did not want to be the source of such discord between brothers. I probably should have accepted your cousins' offers to dance, instead of pursuing you that night."

A spear of envy found its mark. "My cousins asked you to dance?"

"Yes." She sighed, and he felt the motion echo through him, where her body pressed up against his. "But I didn't want to dance with Mr. Blythe or Mr. Willoughby. I didn't think they would catch your brother's attention in quite the same way that a dance with you would. I was so, so naïve."

Patrick's thoughts proved too raw to form anything

coherent of her confession. "It was but the latest in a long series of arguments between my brother and myself, Julianne. Truly, you were not to blame." And she wasn't. Patrick was sure, even without her flirtation as a ready excuse, he would have found *something* to argue over with Eric that morning.

He tried to focus on what he had been feeling that day, more than what he had been doing. "I remember stalking away from our quarrel, seething with resentment. And then a stag stepped out of the brush, not even twenty feet away. I pulled the hammer back and sighted on the animal's heart."

She squeezed his hand, her fingers curling over his, waiting for him to go on as if she trusted him to tell the whole of it.

And yet, this part he couldn't rightfully explain.

He hadn't been thinking clearly, his finger hovering over the trigger in anger. He'd thrown his shot wide at the last moment—*too* wide—shaken by how close he'd come to killing something with his anger toward Eric so flush in his thoughts. The second shot had reached his ears a scant second later, coming from somewhere behind him.

"We both took the shot," he finally told her. "I aimed away from the buck at the last moment. Our rifle blasts were close together in time, but I could hear them both. My first reaction was disbelief. Eric had taken his shot, despite his position behind me, and despite the very real possibility of hitting me in the process."

Some parts of his memory were blurred, as cloudy as the black smoke that had filled the air after he had sacrificed his shot. But the next part of it remained all too clear. He remembered turning in a circle, searching for his brother through the thick of the smoke, the tirade already filling his lungs. He had found Eric on the forest floor, the blood spilling from his brother's body. In the end, four years of training in Italy had come to naught. He hadn't been able to do a damned thing to stop the hemorrhaging the one time it had truly mattered.

Not that he hadn't tried. Eric's blood had stained his hands that day, all too literally.

"When I realized he'd been hit, I ran to him and tried to help, but there was little to be done." He remembered the calls of the other men, crashing through the underbrush. He recalled his attempts to stanch the flow of blood from his brother's chest, the sensation of being dragged forcibly from his brother's body.

"Patrick." Julianne's voice dug into his self-flagellating thoughts. "I believe I saw someone running from the scene."

He shook his head in weary denial. "You've admitted you don't see well. You must have seen the stag bounding away."

"The motion of a man and a deer are quite different," she said doubtfully.

"Then perhaps you saw one of the members of the hunting party running for help," he sighed. "Dr. Merial was summoned, if you recall."

Not that the doctor had been able to revive Eric either.

He extracted his hand from hers. "I hate reliving this. I know the facts are rather damning. I cannot see how you believe me, all things told. You must know I would gladly trade my life for my brother's."

Her palm crept up to press against his chest, and he was quite sure she could feel the rude thump of his heart. Her voice floated toward his ear. "You were in shock, that day in the study. You felt guilty. I suppose, all things considered, it is not surprising you would have acted guilty. But that does not mean you deserve to be charged with murder, Patrick. I believe you when you say it was an accident."

He leaned back into the bench, welcoming the chill seeping through the layers of wool and cotton, even as he welcomed her trust. They floated a quiet minute. Or perhaps it was ten minutes. He lost track of time, focused only her gentle breaths, in and out, and her quiet, unexpected strength. But soon enough, she was moving, and this, finally, was the Julianne he knew, the woman who could not be still. She lifted his hand to her chest and held it there, her heartbeat a dim flutter beneath his palm.

And then she lowered it to her breast.

His world all but shuddered to a stop. He'd just confessed the most terrible piece of his life. He was still racked with emotion, sliced open. He hadn't expected this when she'd followed him here tonight. Hadn't asked for it.

She was offering it anyway.

Her eyes met his, unwavering in the moonlight. She wanted this, and that was a revelation. Always, always he had initiated the contact with Julianne. Always he'd had to convince her of the path, with seduction both his tool and his destination.

But tonight, he was helpless to deny her.

He raised his hand and cupped her cheek, trailing a gentle finger down one side of her jaw, but refusing to grant his fingers access to the buttons they longed for. It was late October, and cold for that. They were out of doors, in a folly designed for beauty over function, open to the night air and the elements.

Anyone might see them.

Seemingly unbound by the same caution, she leaned in to kiss him, and *oh God*, the taste of her seemed to have sharpened into something lethal during the last few days of frustrated celibacy. She was cinnamon and heat, exotic yet familiar, the very definition of something so decadent he should not have it more than once. But he could tell his future with this woman was not going to be simple.

And once was not going to be enough.

"Patrick," she breathed, her breath sweet and warm against his lips. "I do not want you to regret marrying me."

He *didn't* regret marrying her. Particularly not in this moment, not with the surprise of her on his tongue and the feel of his own need snaking to life inside him. The denial rose to his lips, but it was swallowed by her deepening kiss. He wanted to bury himself inside her, lose his mind in the tangle of her lips. But the night was too cold, his senses too dulled, his grief too sharp to fully take advantage of what she was offering, no matter the jarring interest of his body.

And yet . . . the thought of leaving her unfulfilled again tore at him.

He broke off their kiss, resenting already the intrusion of cold night air where her lips had just warmed him. He gently pushed her back until she was reclining against the seat of the stone bench, then searched his way through maddening layers of cotton and silk to find her body already slick, the most beautiful of welcomes.

Patrick hovered there, his palm pressed against her heat, waiting to see what she would do. She arched upward into his touch. But clumsy fingers were neither what he wanted nor what she needed. And so without asking permission, he set his mouth against her instead, seeking the edge of her soul she had denied him the first time they had done this.

He ignored her cry of surprise, refused to be thwarted from this path. He followed her mute, thrashing protest with a knowing tongue, unwilling to let her accept a lesser fate. He sought to teach her what her body needed, to make her understand there was as much pleasure to be had in the climb as she would soon find in the fall. Strove to make her understand that by skirting her own pleasure during lovemaking, she lessened his own.

He felt it the moment she gave in. Her body, always so restless, always so *reckless*, stilled. And then she was moving again, this time finally straining toward where he would lead her. When she let go, Patrick did not draw back. He settled instead for the feel of her, bucking and pulsing against his tongue, embraced the pull of her hands clutching at his hair, and reveled in the bittersweet acceptance of his own denied pleasure as she fell back down to earth. He remained there a long moment, loath to release her completely from this spell. No matter the burden of holding himself back, he was tempted to toss her back up into oblivion once more.

He would have her remember this—remember *him*— if it all went to hell on the morrow.

THE COLD TRIED to creep in, insolent and unwelcome. Julianne drifted away from it, determined to float forever on this haze of desire. She understood, with the clarity that so often comes with a new discovery, what Patrick had meant on their wedding night.

Why he had *meandered* the first time.

She hadn't trusted him enough. She had been reaching for something unknown, thinking he was holding it out of her reach on purpose, not understanding that the journey was what would carry her there. He had not found his own release just now, but he had given her quite a lesson in how to find hers. His fingers stayed pressed against her where his mouth had just wrought such delicious havoc, and she arched up toward him, wanting more. He seemed in no hurry, though she was all but inviting him in. His deft touch trailed the tender flesh at the juncture of her thighs, teasing and testing, promising and denying. She sensed he held himself back, but she knew he *needed* such emotion tonight.

It was her role to give it to him, after all, as his wife.

But even as the thought occurred to her, she recognized it for the falsehood it was. This need, this want, was nothing close to a role. The feeling clutching at her now was no demure wifely chore, no sense of reluctant duty. This was something that left her inverted, gasping on the inside, vulnerable parts exposed.

She lifted her body up from the bench. It was far too cold to undress, and she felt too frantic to take the time. Her fingers reached for the buttons of his trousers, and then he was springing free into her hand, clearly wanting.

She stared down at his body in the moonlight, remembering how he had reacted to merely the touch of her hand at the inn. Time seemed to slow down to a crawl. The night sounds roared in her ears, muffling the pounding of her own heart. Slowly, daringly, she lowered her mouth over him, seeking to give him the same sort of pleasure she had just endured, rejoicing in his resulting groan of frustration.

This time, *she* meandered. Ran her tongue along his length. The masculine scent and taste of him stirred her body to rising passion again. He proved a remarkable study in patience, letting her do her worst, but in the end, it wasn't enough for either of them.

Too soon—or too late, it was hard to know which—he clasped her head in both hands and drew her up to meet his lips in a searing blaze of a kiss. She felt out of her skin, another woman entirely, to be kissed in the breaking shards of moonlight by a man whose mouth had just done such deliciously wicked things to other parts of her body.

"I do not regret marrying you, Julianne."

Her heart jerked painfully toward the sound of her name on his lips. The promise in his words felt every bit as heady as the promise in his kiss. It was not a declaration of love. But for now, for *her*, it was enough.

He pulled back and searched her eyes, and she was drawn into the rawness of his scrutiny. She wanted him to stay this way forever, unshaven, disheveled, his eyes sparking with lust and something more promising. It felt as though something was shifting between them, something portentous and clarifying and too sweet to refuse.

"Show me," she whispered, willing to beg if necessary. "Love me tonight."

This time, he obliged her desperate plea. There was no pain, no hesitation on either of their parts. She gasped out loud, welcoming him inside her, welcoming even the feel of the cool stone bench against her back as his weight pressed down on top of her.

He moved slowly at first, but when she raked her nails across his back in encouragement, he began to move more purposefully, until she was driven toward that bright, dancing spark once more. It became a want beneath her skin, now that she knew what this feeling was about, and it unfurled within her like a cresting wave. Julianne cried out from the sheer surprise of it crashing over her, sure that she would break in two before she ever grew tired of this man's touch.

And only then, when she caught her breath and offered him a brilliant smile that she hoped bespoke everything he had done to her heart, did he finally turn himself over to his own oblivion.

Chapter 17

PATRICK AWAKENED TO an unexpected trinity of sunlight, servants, and Julianne.

The beam of sunlight poking its way through the bedroom curtains was more a curiosity than a puzzle. He knew the sun came up. It bloody well did every morning. It was more that it usually came up *after* he began his day. Likewise, he could hear two servants scratching about somewhere in the room, stirring the fire, pouring water, speaking in hushed tones. It had been almost a year since anyone had done those things for him, and he resented both the presumption and the intrusion.

Unlike the servants and the sunlight—which were jarring but understandable—waking in a bed with Julianne was a conundrum he could not wrap a coherent thought around. He lay still a long moment and stared at this puzzle who was his wife, unwilling to blink lest he shatter the moment into too many pieces to reassemble.

She lay on her stomach, her face to one side and her arms pushed up under the pillow. It had been late by the time they had returned last night, but he was surprised by how soundly she still slept. Her hair glowed like polished copper in the light of dawn, and a dappled skein of sunlight fell across her nose, illuminating the scattering of freckles there.

He was reminded of the moment he had discovered those freckles, at the Blue Gander. Then, he'd seen only the evidence of her vanity. Now he held a deeper appreciation for her myriad, maddening layers. He'd made a study of her in coaches and rail cars these past few days, and understood that while she ruthlessly denied those flaws egress by day, they were apt to slip out in private moments. She might have a well-earned reputation for giving people the cut across a crowded ballroom, but it was likely because she couldn't actually *see* them. She was flighty and steadfast, cold and passionate.

Predictable in her unpredictability.

He wrapped a long red curl around one finger, lingering over the pleasure of it against his skin. Her deep, steady breaths lulled him right up to the abyss of hope. Last night had been a revelation, but had it changed things between them? He wanted a future with this woman, beyond the lies and the conundrum of a likely murder charge. He wanted her in his bed every night. And, if he was honest with himself, he wanted to visit that folly again, but this time with an armful of blankets.

As the sound of the servants' exit reached his ears, he leaned in to press a kiss to Julianne's nose, tracing the path of those freckles with his mouth. The warmth of her body beneath his lips told him this was no lovely, transient dream, and the soft, satisfied sound she made further told him she might be amenable to more.

She stirred. Opened her eyes. Smiled.

"Good morning," he told her, his heart stretched taut by those upcurved lips. And it *was* a good morning. The press of grief he felt over the loss of his brother and father had not been completely assuaged. He suspected it would be months, if not years, before he felt whole again. But last night's moon-soaked coupling had dissolved the last five days of frustration. It had been something he had not planned, and an understanding he had not dared hope for. She had given him a staggering gift, far more poignant than the mere offering of her body. She had given him hope for the future, and that was something he had not had in eleven hard months.

As he stared down at her, Julianne lifted a hesitant hand to her nose. Her smile faltered, ever so slightly. "You are staring."

"You are beautiful."

"Then you are deranged," she scoffed, a husky sound that sent his body stirring. She sat up and her hands lifted to comb through her hair, but taming those wild tresses was a hopeless cause, and they both knew it. "I must look a fright."

Patrick nodded solemnly. "Better to lie back down and let me muss it up some more."

"Both dogs probably need to be turned out. I'd prefer not to contend with a puddle on the floor." She lifted a brow, and certain parts of his body lifted right along with it. "We haven't missed breakfast, have we?"

"I think it is likely we will be late." And yet, he lingered, his mind refusing to focus on words like "puddles" or "breakfast." He was far too interested in the bunched neckline of her night rail. The freckles on her nose had unearthed an unholy curiosity in what other breathtaking discoveries she kept hidden. When they'd returned to their room last night, they'd undressed in darkness, forced by the cold night air and utter exhaustion. Sleep had demanded a place of priority. But now it occurred to him he'd never properly seen Julianne's body.

That was a damned tragedy for a married man to claim.

Gemmy chose that inopportune moment to jump up on the mattress. "Gemmy, no," he commanded, remembering her earlier concerns about fleas and such.

But Julianne only laughed and patted the mattress. "Let him come, Patrick. The poor dog had a devil of an arrival yesterday."

Gemmy crawled toward her, his tail a pitiful thump against the bedclothes. Julianne bent a kiss to the terrier's nose, which caused Constance to stalk up from the foot of the bed and nose in between them with stiff-legged suspicion. "Behave," Julianne warned her pet, and miraculously, Constance lay down with a soft huff.

He took a moment to inspect the shoulder Gemmy had laid open on the little dog. "You did an excellent job cleaning her wound," he observed.

"Being obsessive over cleanliness has its advantages." Julianne cupped both dog's muzzles in her palms and murmured nonsense to each one in turn, and Patrick's chest tightened against the irony of his fastidious wife offering these admittedly smelly beasts good morning kisses. He felt a bit like the dogs, desperate for a kind word, a touch.

A kiss.

Patrick pointed to the floor. "Down," he commanded. "It is my turn."

The dogs' tails beat a muffled rhythm against the blankets.

"Down," he tried again, but the dogs did no more than grin happily up at him.

"Get down," Julianne's voice rang out. That, finally, sent both dogs jumping to the floor.

Patrick glared down at them. *Impertinent beasts.*

"Gemmy listens far better to you than he does to me," he groused.

"That is because you are not animated enough with your delivery."

He inched closer to her. "I was not aware dogs preferred nuanced orders."

"Dogs require a master with some enthusiasm. You tend to hide yours."

He reached out a hand, grasping the edge of the ribbon that beckoned at her neckline. "I have plenty of enthusiasm, Julianne. And I would show you a taste of it this morning."

"How enthusiastic, precisely?" Her words teased his ears, and made his fingers itch to touch more than just the ribbon on her night rail.

"Enthusiastic enough to think we should ring for a tray to be sent up," he murmured, unwilling to relinquish the prize of Julianne in his arms for anything as trite as mere sustenance. He found himself wanting to make each second he had with her stretch into ten.

She gasped as he nipped at her newly exposed neckline with his teeth. "But . . . everyone will be waiting for us. They will imagine we are . . . well, that we are . . . too busy for breakfast."

He could feel her teetering on the edge of acquiescence, and her indecision merely fueled his desire. "I would *like* to be too busy for breakfast," he whispered against her skin, wondering if he ought to silence her objections the proper way: with a long, heated kiss. "And what better way to convince the cynics downstairs that this is a love match?"

She stiffened, and he felt the motion all through his body, a harbinger of looming disappointment. He drew back, searching her eyes for the source of her sudden shift in mood, unsure of exactly what he had said to break the spell of the moment.

"Julianne—" he started, but she halted his protest by pulling her night rail closed and retying the ribbon firmly.

"I would like to avoid speculation among the guests and staff on our first day here," she said, her earlier interest deflating before his eyes. "And have you forgotten the dogs need to be let out? Constance will happily relieve herself on your shoes if she happens upon them on the floor, which seems a certainty given your slovenly habits."

He tried once more. Lifted a finger to her chin and raised it up. Her eyes met his, a beautiful sun-splashed green. "Are you so sure you won't regret the loss of the morning?"

"Your family and guests will surely be waiting for our appearance." She pulled gently from his touch. "You are the earl now, with responsibilities waiting for you. And I have not yet met your sisters. Your mother said I would have a chance at breakfast."

Patrick's hand dropped to his side. She was right. Mary and Eleanor would be unleashed from the nursery this morning to show off their blossoming manners to their new sister-in-law. And his mother would expect them, if for no reason other than protocol. In the end, it was his sense of familial duty, rather than the thought of Constance piddling in his shoes, that had him pulling back the sheets. He dressed quickly, and the dogs responded with a clatter of nails, vying for a position of supremacy to be the first one out. "I'll only be a moment," he told her as he reached for the door. "Shall I meet you downstairs for breakfast?"

Her lips curved higher, and he was struck by their

wistful arch. "That sounds lovely. And perhaps, because you have conceded me this, I can promise you tomorrow's breakfast as forfeit."

Her words chased him from the room with a smile on his own face, but he was also left with a sense of loss. *She* might comfort herself with the thought that tomorrow would bring another breakfast, another kiss.

But Patrick was reluctant to take a single second of their time for granted.

A WHITE-CAPPED MAID arrived before Julianne could even locate the bellpull and began bustling about the room, opening curtains and such. Julianne lifted a hand and blinked against the sun, scarcely able to believe that not only was she *up* at the yawning mouth of dawn, she was about to be dressed and ready for battle.

Though by London standards it was several hours too early, Julianne indulged in her usual morning ritual, making up the bed with sharp, efficient movements. Such a thing might be less than befitting a countess, but she didn't trust anyone else to do it according to her specifications. Shrugging off the maid's wide-eyed protests, she moved on to pick Patrick's discarded clothing up off the floor. Only then, when she could look around the room without her chest going tight, did she turn herself over to the business of washing.

Patrick's earlier words stayed snarled in her thoughts as she padded on bare feet to the washbasin. She retained a delicious soreness in places that made her breath catch, but it was not a painful sort of feeling. Indeed, it had hurt far more to hear him encourage the façade of a love match—as if the real possibility of it was so foreign an idea.

Last night's lovemaking had been a revelation for

her, a splintering of her preconceived notions of marriage and intimacy. She'd awakened to the pleasure of a husband's touch, and she wanted his love in truth. But while he certainly seemed willing to tumble her, the degree of his regard remained uncertain. She was not too proud to admit to herself that she was well and truly smitten. But she was far too proud to be willing to risk it alone.

"Shall I lay out your gray silk?" The maid held up a dreadfully dull frock, pulled from the depths of Julianne's bag. "It seems to be most suitable for mourning."

Julianne sighed at the reminder. She didn't want to spend her first six months of marriage clad in somber tones, no matter that propriety called for that very thing. She'd packed her gray silk two weeks ago in London with no thought other than what a fashionable young woman might wear to an earl's funeral, but at the time, she'd not anticipated coming back to Summersby as Patrick's wife. "I suppose it will have to do," she was forced to agree. "Perhaps you could hang up the rest of my gowns while I am at breakfast? They are becoming terribly wrinkled."

"Of course, miss."

Julianne gave herself over to the servant's ministrations, knowing this single dress would not serve until her things could be fetched from London. A solution came without warning, and the inquiry was out of her mouth before she could even consider what she was asking. "There was a maid who served me during the November house party who was handy with a needle. Her name was Prudence Smith. Is she perchance still employed at Summersby? I would talk to her about possibly making over some of my gowns into something more appropriate for the family's state of mourning."

The maid shook her head. "The name is not familiar to me, Lady Haversham."

Though Julianne knew she should not, she itched to ask more. *Surely* it was important to establish whether Prudence was lurking somewhere on the estate, waiting to pop out from a corner like a veritable bogeyman. But she was quite sure Patrick wouldn't see it the same way, and so she reluctantly tucked the instinct to ask more questions away for a later time.

He was waiting for her in the foyer. His hair was mussed and he'd needed to shave days ago, but her stomach skittered with heat as his eyes met hers and held. "Are you *sure* you would not wish to return to our room?" His voice was a delicious rumble over the distant clink of cutlery and the low laughter that echoed down the hallway. When he reached for her hand, the brush of his fingers against her wrist made the fine hairs on her arms stand at attention.

"I . . . that is . . ." she stammered, trying to remember why they were not already dashing up the stairs.

"From the sounds of things, they are already seated, and will presume we are abed anyway," he coaxed.

She shivered against the feelings he seemed able to pull from her skin with a mere touch. "We must face them." Missing breakfast, she knew, would be a tactical misstep. She gently tugged her hand away. "There will be time enough for that later, Patrick. I refused to provide the guests with anything more to speculate about." Including what wicked things might have kept her abed with the new Earl of Haversham—even if a part of her wanted nothing more than to return to bed and speculate on those things herself.

Patrick offered her his arm, and together they stepped into the dining room. Julianne normally enjoyed a well-timed entrance, but the rush of eyes felt like a scald of heated water, and her smile faltered. Conversations fell apart and chairs everywhere scraped as the men gained their feet.

Greetings were murmured, introductions hastily made. She spied her father as she made her way to her seat. She caught the ghost of his frown, and mentally sorted through the long list of his likely disapprovals, starting with her inappropriate wardrobe and ending with the fact she had married a man who most of those in attendance suspected of murder.

As she sat down, two young girls watched with openly curious faces. They showed promise of maturing into future beauties, but for now they were still coltish and unrefined. These must be Patrick's sisters, Julianne realized, trying to refrain from squinting in their direction. They'd run rampant during last year's house party, but they had grown in the eleven months since she had last seen them, and were sitting perfectly still, hands folded neatly in their laps. She found herself surprised by their maturity. Then again, much else had changed. It should not surprise her that two little girls might change too.

As the gentlemen sat down, Julianne put on her paste smile, the one she adopted when dancing with gentlemen whose hands seemed to sweat through their gloves. She turned herself over to the ghastly business of trying to enjoy herself.

Or at least, *appearing* to enjoy herself.

Apparently, the guests' lingering grief was to be fed on coddled eggs and pastries, because the table almost groaned under the weight of the food. As she fumbled her way through a plate of a smoked herring, Mr. Blythe, Patrick's cousin, leaned closer to address her directly.

"Lady Haversham, I find myself curious about the circumstances of your arrival. Has the magistrate been informed?" His voice brimmed with faint hostility. "Given that you've been summoned to provide a statement at the inquest, I feel sure he will want to know you have returned."

Julianne examined her plate as she considered how to respond. She remembered meeting Mr. Blythe during the November house party, and had presumed him a rather uninspiring young man. Her impression had not improved with time. "By all means, you should feel free to share the news with the magistrate," she finally offered, addressing him with the full force of her disapproval. "Although you should also tell him I will not be providing the statement he seeks. A wife cannot be compelled to testify against her husband." She could hear the hushed whispers, flowing up and down the table in response to her announcement.

Mr. Blythe, however, appeared to have no use for whispers. "What vile subversion of justice is this?" he demanded. "You were happy enough to accuse the man of murder eleven months ago." His venomous gaze darted to Patrick. "Has he forced you to it, then?"

"No one has been forced into anything," Julianne retorted. "But if my decision makes you uncomfortable, you are welcome to leave."

Next to Mr. Blythe, a heavyset woman in a black turban set down her fork. She addressed Patrick in a familiar manner, her mouth fixed into a straight line. "My brother always welcomed us at Summersby. Are you implying that will now change, Haversham?"

Patrick's expression remained difficult to read. "Nothing has changed in that regard, Aunt Margaret. You and Jonathon are of course welcome to stay here, as you always have been. My wife, I am sure, speaks only of wanting our guests to be comfortable."

"I am glad to hear that," Aunt Margaret said stiffly. "I'd hate to think you'd abandoned your family on account of your wife's ill manners."

Julianne gripped her fork, scarcely able to believe that not only had Patrick just openly contradicted her, but that Mr. Blythe's mother, of all people, had accused *her* of being ill-mannered. And that was when Julianne realized that this was one of those times her mouth was going to quite run ahead of her good sense.

She offered her new aunt a tight smile, three Seasons' worth of experience coalescing into the oft-practiced gesture. "Perhaps, if my manners are so *ill*, Aunt Margaret, you might feel more comfortable eating elsewhere. Your own dining room in London, perhaps?"

Patrick's sisters—who, despite their tender age, were clearly scholars of sarcasm—dissolved into giggles. Aunt Margaret's mouth opened wide enough to catch a three-tined fork. As it were, Julianne felt as though she were being quite magnanimous to hurl only a well-timed insult instead of the cutlery.

The older woman abruptly stood up. Chairs scraped as gentlemen up and down the long table were forced to once again abandon their plates. "I find I've quite lost my appetite," Aunt Margaret said archly.

"Oh dear," Julianne said with feigned politeness. She, of all people, could recognize a theatrical bid for attention when she saw it. And judging by Aunt Margaret's girth, she doubted the woman would stay afflicted for long. "I hope you are not taking ill. Why, *that* might force a premature leave-taking, and I can assure you we would all be quite devastated for the loss of your company."

The woman's face turned as red as the jam waiting to be spread on the toast. And then she swept from the room, and Mr. Blythe was throwing down his napkin and stalking out after her. Julianne heaved a relieved sigh. "Now then. I imagine our digestion will now be much improved. But if anyone else finds their appetites similarly upset, you are welcome to leave as well."

"Although," Patrick countered, his eyes flashing a cautionary warning, "we of course welcome those guests who have come to honor my father, and encourage them to stay as long as they wish."

Julianne battled a flare of anger, though she also knew she had perhaps plunged too far afield of good manners with the last of it. After all, while the table had not been precisely welcoming, no one else beyond Mr. Blythe and his mother had bordered on rude. She dotted her mouth with her napkin, hovering on the bitter cusp on an apology when George Willoughby spoke up to save her.

"As the new mistress of Summersby, your wife is well within her rights to ask us to leave, cousin."

Julianne experienced again that sense of relief she had known when Mr. Willoughby had so publicly come to their aid yesterday. And again, she felt that odd sense of regret that she had misjudged the young man once upon a time, refusing even to dance with him as she stalked the larger, more promising prey at that November house party. She smiled at him, and this time it was her *real* smile, the one that she could not control in the slightest.

"It is none of your concern, Willoughby." Patrick's stern voice nudged in, poking holes in her victory.

Julianne's smile faltered. "He is only trying to help, Patrick—"

"I do not require my cousin's assistance," came her husband's surprisingly cool reply.

Willoughby's gaze swept the crowd before finally—almost apologetically—coming back to rest on her. "Someone needs to speak out on your behalf, Haversham. The title has passed to you, and you have not yet been formally charged with any crime. Your wife should know there are those here who do not wish her ill." His voice rose, this time addressing the table. "Haversham deserves our respect, as does his new wife. And if there are those among you who would disagree, I suggest you follow the way of Aunt Margaret."

Chapter 18

"JULIANNE, WAIT."

But she was off immediately after breakfast, storming up the stairs at a pace that left no doubt at all to her mood. Patrick followed her. Bloody impertinent girl, making him feel as though he had done something wrong, when *she* was the one who had practically ordered his entire extended family to leave. His father had just been buried, for Christ's sake. Tossing out family who practically lived at Summersby was unthinkable.

The devil take it, she was like an unschooled horse, intent on having her own way, trying to throw him at the slightest provocation. Well, she would soon learn he was an excellent rider.

He caught up with her in the upstairs corridor, just outside their room. He grasped her elbow, but she promptly used it to deliver a swift jab to his ribs.

"What in the devil is wrong with you?" he hissed, rubbing his side and casting a furtive glance down the hallway. A maid exiting one of the rooms several doors down ducked her head in embarrassment and hurried off with her ash bucket. Bloody hell, they were causing a spectacle for the servants. It would be just his luck to have Willoughby or Blythe come across them in such a way, brawling like a fisherman and his wife. "Why are you angry with *me*? I'll wager it ought to be the other way around, after your performance at breakfast."

"To which performance do you refer?" Julianne offered him an overly sweet smile that made his teeth ache more than his ribs. "My attempt to defend you against those family members who would spread vicious rumors? Or perhaps my struggle to sit quietly while my husband permitted those same people to speak so disparagingly about me?"

Patrick wasn't fooled in the least. While she could certainly *be* sweet, when the stars aligned and her world tilted right, the smile stretched tightly across her lips did not begin to plumb the depths of feeling that ran beneath his wife's skin. She was a consummate actress—this, at least, he was learning. She could control the curve of her lips and the tilt of her brows like a master puppeteer. But her eyes gave her away. At the moment, they were flashing at him like a smuggler's beacon.

Infinitely more interesting than sweet.

"You do realize I can discern your smiles?" He tried to glower, though he suspected he wasn't half as good at pretending as she was. "The ones that are genuine versus the ones you use merely to get your way?"

Her brow arched. "Then I encourage you to pay close attention to which I am employing right now."

He couldn't help it. His lips twitched, ignoring the signals his brain was sending. Damn it, he couldn't keep hold of his annoyance with her. She was a woman defined by fierce loyalties, willing to defend to her last breath those whom she cared for. It was difficult not to admire her, or respect her intentions. But the reality of being married to a woman like Julianne was like being tied to a summer storm: unpredictable, at best.

Liable to kill you if you didn't approach it with caution.

"I apologize if my words hurt you," he told her. "I know you meant well. But my father prided himself on being generous to friends and relatives. Summersby has always been open to anyone who wished to stay here, for as long as they wish. Aunt Margaret and Jonathon spend every summer here, and George Willoughby has been known to sleep in a guest room for a good six months of the year. Permitting them to stay is an important part of honoring my father's memory, at least for the near future."

A puff of air escaped her lips. "Oh," was all she said. As if it had never occurred to her he might have a good reason to permit his hanging-on relatives to stay as long as they wished. And then she turned the door handle and plunged into their room with nary another word.

Patrick stalked after her, annoyance winning out over bemusement in his choice of emotional responses. Apparently to Julianne's mind, apologizing to him—when he had just done the unthinkable and apologized first—approached an act of treason.

He kicked the door shut behind him. The hinges squeaked in protest, and he frowned at the distraction. In Moraig, he wouldn't have given creaking hinges a moment's thought. Hell, he wouldn't have blinked if the bloody door had toppled off its frame. But this gave him an uncomfortable pause. Because it was his door. *His* problem. Probably Summersby had people on staff for this sort of thing, but it bothered him that he didn't know. All during breakfast, when he hadn't been contradicting his wife's sharp tongue, he'd been confronted by the realization that everything at Summersby—from the silver cutlery, to the staff removing their dishes—was now his responsibility. The enormity of the task before him made him twitch.

As did his beautiful, infuriating wife.

He pulled up, unsure of what, exactly, he should say next to her. What few choice words he might have managed became even more muddled as he considered whether he was even in the correct room. It was neat as a pin, for one thing. His clothing had been picked up from the floor and folded neatly on his reading chair. The bed where he had awakened this morning was now made up with military precision. The squared edges of the coverlet sneered at him, proclaiming that any further mischief on its pristine surface would be ruthlessly denied. The various medical supplies that usually stood atop his bureau had been removed, and now small crystal bottles and ivory-inlaid brushes and an entire army of hairpins lay scattered across the top.

"Did you do something to my room?" he asked tersely.

"*Our* room, I should think. I straightened a few things. And I may have asked the maid to unpack my bag."

An awful suspicion took root.

Patrick strode over to his wardrobe, the one that held his jackets and riding boots and such, things he had left behind when he had departed for Scotland, and threw open the doors. A cloud of sachet-scented air puffed out at him, generated, no doubt, by the sea of gowns that now hung there, glittering like jewels in what heretofore had been an incontrovertibly masculine domain. There had to be at least a half dozen or more, in varied rainbow hues, with lace and ribbons sprouting like weeds from every crevice.

"What have you done with my clothes?" he demanded.

"I am sure the maid folded them away in one of the drawers. I shouldn't think it would matter. It is not as though you ever hang anything up."

Damn it to hell and back. She had invaded his thoughts and his life, like a miasma on the wind, and now she had taken over his bloody room. He turned from the travesty of his repurposed wardrobe, prepared to argue for a return of his space and his things, only to discover that his wife was now working to reach the buttons on the back of her dress.

Well. She'd certainly become more . . . *comfortable* around him. Perhaps there were some benefits to the intrusion he had not considered. And the prolific nature of her clothing and the loss of his personal space aside, he couldn't deny she looked so bright and tempting and unexpectedly *right* undressing in his room, his bones hurt at the sight of her.

"Can you help me with the buttons?" she asked, seemingly oblivious to the torment she was causing with merely the suggestion that her dress might soon be removed. "I need to change my gown."

He stalked toward her, irritated with himself for not being more irritated, and regretting the realization she wasn't expressly undressing for him. He frowned at the gown she intended to shed. "Why, when you have just put it on before breakfast?"

"A countess cannot wear the same gown for afternoon that she wears in the morning."

"What would you propose to wear instead?" he asked, genuinely confused. Did women really *do* that? Take off one perfectly clean, perfectly functional gown, just to put on another, based on the turn of the hour hand? He'd never stopped to consider it before.

He didn't want to consider it now.

"I was considering wearing the blue silk, the one with the lace redingote. I know it is ill-suited for mourning, but as the gown I wore to breakfast is the only one I have that might be considered suitable for bereavement, I need to have a care with it." She turned away from him, offering her back and the buttons waiting there. "Clearly, I need to have more gowns made."

Patrick knew, in that moment as he began to unbutton her, two distinct things. One: He did not want to know what in the bloody hell a redingote was. And two: His wife needed a caning more than she needed a new wardrobe. The number of gowns she had pulled from her bag in the space of the few days he had known her made him feel vaguely ill.

"If I might beg the question," he said, trying to circle this conversation back around to something sane, "you knew you were coming to a house in mourning. Did you not give any thought to the matter of what to wear when you arrived?"

"I packed a gown appropriate for attending a funeral." Her eyes flashed a green warning over her shoulder. "But I certainly didn't expect to arrive as mistress of Summersby. Convention calls for six months of mourning." She stepped out of the gown and laid it carefully across the bed, leaving her clad only in her crinolines and corset. "Perhaps we could take a trip into Leeds tomorrow to find a seamstress. I would like to invite a few close neighbors over for dinner at the end of the month, but I would need something appropriate to wear."

His response was instinctive, rather than well-considered. "Have you forgotten my father just died? A dinner party seems a poor idea just now."

Julianne moved toward the wardrobe. "I disagree,"

she argued. "You've been tried and convicted in the eyes of your own relatives, and that does not bode well for your eventual defense. This morning's breakfast has shown me we need to plan an offensive strike, to turn public opinion. Surely you will need character witnesses to stand up for you if you are charged."

"And you think a dinner will change their minds?"

She paused, her fingers running over the blinding array of gowns before finally settling on one. "A small dinner that includes neighbors and acquaintances from town will help us sort out who among your family's friends might be relied upon for support. But I certainly agree we need to tread carefully and respectfully. That is why I'll need just the right gown for it."

That reference to "us" and "we" again. By the devil, but his new wife was a meddler. "Are you claiming the right gown does not exist among the hundred or so you have stuffed into my wardrobe?" he asked dryly.

"*Our* wardrobe." She turned and smiled far too sweetly, a swath of blue silk clutched in her hands. "And no matter how many gowns I may own, none are appropriate. I need mourning gowns, not ball gowns." Her smile softened into something warmer, and marginally more real. "It is the way it is done, Patrick. It will be expected of your wife."

He stared at her a moment, struck again by that earlier sense of not knowing the way of things in the world into which he had been tossed. He knew almost nothing of social matters, having spent his life mostly in the company of books and animals. This was, admittedly, Julianne's area of expertise. But did they have to have this conversation while she was standing in her corset and stockings? Because it was damnably hard to think when his brain was being denied its fair share of blood.

He forced his fingers to unclench. Perhaps a dinner party wouldn't hurt. Indeed, there were elements to Julianne's arguments that made perfect—if reluctant—sense. "Aunt Margaret will probably have an apoplectic fit when she hears you are planning to honor her brother's memory with a dinner party," he warned. "She is a martinet about such things."

Julianne smiled, and this time it was her real smile, the one that made him feel as though the sun were breaking over the horizon. "I don't give a fig for what Aunt Margaret might think, or her detestable son. With any luck, they have already departed." She stepped into the new dress she had chosen, some complicated thing that he could now see came in several pieces. "Do you think George Willoughby will stay, though? I hope I did not imply that I wished *him* to leave."

Patrick sighed as his wife's bare skin disappeared into yet another gown. "Yes, well, while you certainly put some effort behind it, I don't think you can count on anyone leaving, at least not as far as my aunt and cousins are concerned. They spend practically half the year here, and autumn is a favored season in Yorkshire." And given Willoughby's mooning looks toward Julianne during the latter half of breakfast, Patrick half suspected she had unwittingly ensured the young man's stay had just been extended until Christmas.

"Aunt Margaret usually stays through the start of snow, if memory serves. She is not such a bad sort," he added. "You might try being a bit more understanding of her."

An unladylike snort escaped Julianne's lips, one he was quite sure her swains in London had never been permitted to hear. "The way she has tried to understand *your* position? She has been quite quick in her judgment. And her son clearly hates you."

He hesitated, wondering how to explain the odd mix of family politics that always swam just below the surface at Summersby. There was jealousy at the heart of it, to be sure. Perhaps a vein of cruelty. But his trouble with Blythe was more complicated than that.

"I do not believe he hates me. Or if he does, he likely believes he has good reason. Blythe has always been . . . difficult."

Julianne raised a brow, clearly waiting for more. Patrick sorted through which pieces to share. Amid the usual family squabbles, one, in particular, teetered at the top of the list. He'd always considered his earliest memory of arguing with Jonathon Blythe to be trite. Almost silly. But when he trotted it out for a new inspection, it still made his fingers curl in objection.

"When I was nine years old, I loosened one of my father's courser bitches in with the foxhounds because I was curious what sort of puppies would result. I confided what I had done to both of my cousins. Willoughby kept silent, but Blythe told his mother, who in turn told my father. But when my father showed no inclination to punish me for the deed, Jonathon set about ensuring I suffered what he felt was a fitting punishment for dishonoring my father."

Julianne's eyes narrowed. "What did he do?"

Patrick hesitated. "He drowned the puppies in the lake, just days after they were born. He felt it was justified. After all, their birth—and therefore their deaths—had occurred solely on account of my own mischief." Patrick recalled how he had discovered the water-soaked flour sack filled with sodden, still bodies, there on his bed. How guilty he had felt, and how he'd been convinced of his personal culpability in the outcome.

Julianne gasped in horror. "And you call that merely being *difficult*?"

"He thought he was righting a wrong, I suppose. He is not necessarily a bad person, but he approaches zeal-otry in his quest for justice." Patrick shrugged off the flare of misgiving that thinking of his cousin always wrought. "His dislike of me is simple to explain, really. He thinks I have done wrong, and he's determined to see me punished for it."

She pursed her lips, though she remained a trifle pale. "It is a shame that Mr. Willoughby is the only one of your close relatives who believes you are innocent, but thank goodness someone does."

Willoughby, again. The name alone made Patrick want to gouge his eyes out. Or, better yet, gouge out Willoughby's.

"Willoughby has not said he believes I am innocent, Julianne. He merely encouraged everyone to wait for the results of the inquest." And given the choice be-tween which of his two cousins he liked least, he'd be hard-pressed to place one over the other.

The damnable thing was that while history had given him a sense of Jonathon Blythe's character, he was not precisely sure what to make of George Willoughby's. Because while Willoughby hadn't drowned any pup-pies, he'd certainly lurked in the shadows and watched events unfold, then demanded recompense for his silence. So while Patrick was grateful for the younger man's seeming acceptance now, he could not help but feel some hesitation over his cousin's motives.

"I would like to pen the dinner party invitations this afternoon," Julianne said, working her fingers over a row of front-facing buttons that—regrettably—needed no help at all from the male quarter. "With your approval, of course," she added as a murmured afterthought.

Truly, did it even matter whether he offered his approval or not? He could not envision a world in which Julianne would fall into line like a typical English wife. Hell, he wouldn't be surprised to find she'd already put pen to paper. "I agree that perhaps you need a new gown or two for this party. There is a seamstress in Shippington, if memory serves. My mother or the housekeeper should be able to point you toward her."

Her fingers paused over the buttons, and Patrick congratulated himself on his deft handling of the situation. This was where she was supposed to thank him. Instead, she pursed her lips. "I would prefer to find a seamstress in Leeds."

"Shippington is closer. Leeds would require an overnight trip, and my presence is needed here." His eyes lingered over his wife's face, noting the faint flush of . . . *something* there. What was she up to? And why this mulish insistence on Leeds?

He could see it then, in the tilt of her chin, and the pull of those expressive brows.

Trouble.

"Prudence mentioned she had once worked for a seamstress in Leeds before coming to Summersby, and the girl was brilliant with a needle. I am rather particular about such things," she added, as if that was all the explanation needed.

Patrick's jacket suddenly felt three sizes too small. While she seemed to have a point to make here, he was quite sure it had little to do with either a needle or a new dress. He met his wife's innocent-eyed gaze with a darker one of his own, even as his fingers returned to what was fast becoming a perpetual clenched state. "What is this really about?"

JULIANNE STRUGGLED TO think of a rational argument that might nudge this conversation in the direction she needed it to go. Rational arguments were not often her forte. Still, while she knew she could be impulsive at times, there was nothing rash about this latest idea.

Why, she'd thought about it for at *least* a good hour or so.

"Knowing the location of one's enemy is the key to a strategic defense," she said determinedly as she slipped the lace redingote over her shoulders. "I learned that lesson on the battlefields of London's drawing rooms."

"This isn't a bloody musicale, Julianne. You are talking about tracking down a woman whose testimony could hang me."

"I don't think we should find her for the purposes of having her testify," she qualified. "But we should know where she is."

His eyes flashed an ominous warning. "It is too dangerous."

"I would argue that *not* finding her is too dangerous. Surely it makes more sense to determine if she is lurking about, waiting to point her finger at you. I've ascertained she isn't at Summersby, at least. I think we ought to look for her in Leeds."

She held her breath. Patrick had handled her request for a dinner party surprisingly well. Indeed, he had handled the entirety of the morning—from the slights she had lobbed at his family across the breakfast table, to the suggestion of a new wardrobe—far more agreeably than she would have predicted. Perhaps she was overthinking it, and her new husband was actually a malleable spouse who would let her carry on however she pleased.

And perhaps kittens might sprout wings and fly.

"No." He issued the single word as though it were a verdict, instead of something they might discuss reasonably.

"Why won't you even consider the idea?" she protested.

"Because there is no guarantee that finding her will go the way you think."

"I would not say anything to endanger your defense—"

"My worry, Julianne, is that you often say and do things without thinking. Finding Prudence could well seal my fate." He hesitated. "Or is that your intention?"

She sucked in a startled breath. *"No!"* How could he even think such a thing? She was determined to save him. Hadn't she promised him she wouldn't testify? But the dark question in his eyes was punishing. If she meddled, he believed she would tighten the noose around his neck.

"I am trying to help, Patrick." She cringed to hear her voice ring with the faintest edge of desperation. "I've just discovered you. It might be selfish of me, but I am loath to sacrifice you to things we might control."

"There is nothing for *you* to do. MacKenzie will come to Yorkshire as soon as he is finished with my legal affairs in London. We let Prudence stay hidden, wherever she is." His eyes softened a small degree. "And if I am arrested ahead of MacKenzie's arrival, you must wait here at Summersby, and try to stay out of trouble."

Julianne choked back a cry of surprise. *Arrested.* The very word sounded like the vilest of curses, slipping darkly in her ear. "Could that happen? I thought you would be safe from such an outcome, given that I am no longer going to provide a statement."

He waited a fraction of a second too long to answer. "I do not think you should worry overmuch. If your testimony is removed, it stands to reason they will lack evidence to recommend me to trial. MacKenzie's efforts in London are purely cautionary. He wants to be prepared, just in case."

Julianne felt a faint stirring of unease. Why had MacKenzie presumed his legal machinations in London were cautionary? When he'd boarded the train to London, they'd not yet even discussed the removal of her testimony. But her thoughts were too unformed to resist the distraction of her husband, who was taking a determined step toward her. Her world narrowed down to nothing beyond the warmth in his eyes.

"Julianne." His voice dropped to that low, delicious rumble, the one that made pleasure swim drunkenly in her chest. "I am glad to hear you do not wish to lose me."

"Don't do that," she warned. "You are trying to distract me."

"The way you distracted me last night?" His mouth spread in a languid smile, the one that made her stomach stamp its feet and turn in confused circles. "You have proven yourself quite adept at distractions. Surely you can see that turnabout is fair play."

"There is nothing fair about the way I feel about you," she bit out. But her petulant words only made that smile stretch higher. Infuriating man. Almost as though he was *enjoying* her upset over the thought of his possible arrest.

When he at last spoke, it was with measured care. "I

know you wish to correct past wrongs. Your desire to make things right is an admirable sentiment. But if you care for me at all, surely you can see this way is better."

That made her blink. "I do care for you," she told him, the words too hoarse, and too quick, to be anything but honest. "Last night was . . ." Her voice trailed off, trembling on its downward trajectory, until she found the right sentiment. "Far too short."

"And cold," he pointed out, stepping even closer. "For example, it was too cold to take the time to undress. We could rectify that now. In fact, I've a mind to undo those buttons you just worked so hard over, and to muss up that beautifully made bed."

She slid precariously on the thought. How easy it would be to close her mind to the more sinister possibility of their future, and just enjoy the moment. How much kinder it would be to surrender to his ideas for how they ought to spend the day. She felt as if there was a string between them, and he was slowly, expertly pulling it taut.

But that string could choke her, so easily. He'd not even been home a day, and he was already calmly discussing his looming arrest. But he was here with her now, and in the end her thoughts and objections were too easily shoved deep.

Patrick's hands lifted to her face, and his fingers were nearly a searing pleasure against her skin. She closed her eyes and leaned into his hand. She couldn't help it. When he touched her like this, it was though he was setting a torch to her reservations.

Not that she'd ever had any around him.

"I suppose I could make the bed up again," she breathed, and was rewarded by the touch of his lips on hers. The kiss chased the unpleasant conversation to quieter corners of her mind. There was only this moment, and her husband, working some sort of black magic on her emotions. She tried to remember what they were arguing about, truly she did. It was important, she sensed. But she was loath to jerk her thoughts away from the lush distraction he was posing.

And as he took what she offered and deepened the kiss, she forgot how to breathe, much less how to speak.

Chapter 19

JULIANNE GRASPED THE coachman's hand and stepped down onto Shippington's dusty streets, wondering if her husband yet realized where she had gone.

She hadn't set out to deceive him, exactly. But when she'd spied Patrick with his head bent over a mountain of paperwork in his father's study, agitated and cross and cursing under his breath, she'd realized that asking him to accompany her to town today would serve no good purpose. He had been thoroughly distracted by estate matters, and seemed none too happy about it.

Well, *she* was thoroughly distracted by her dwindling wardrobe. All week she'd struggled with the decision of which dress to wear, settling for which was the least objectionable, rather than which was most suitable. She'd worn her gray silk nearly every day, a nod toward propriety over cleanliness that had her cringing each time the maid buttoned her up the back. She had not been exaggerating when she'd said she needed new clothing. While Patrick had not disapproved her insistence on having some new gowns made, neither had he called up the coach and taken her into town.

Still, they'd only been married for two weeks. He'd learn the way of it, soon enough.

And she could forgive his obtuseness for the simple fact that despite her dwindling wardrobe choices, her new role as Patrick's wife was proving far more pleasurable than she'd imagined, especially after their inauspicious start. The past week had been filled with small, joyous discoveries. Such as the fact that his feet were ticklish. Or that he awakened in a state of readiness each morning that ensured they were nearly always late to breakfast.

But while he had been unfailingly attentive, seeing to her every pleasure, he remained maddeningly silent on the matter of their marriage of convenience. Which, to Julianne's mind, really wasn't proving very convenient at all, at least in matters relating to her heart. When she'd agreed to marry him, she'd thought—naïvely, perhaps—that feeling such strong attraction toward the man who would be her husband could only be a harbinger of their future happiness. She'd believed that she could convince him of her regard, and earn his in return.

But two weeks of marriage had shown her that happiness was not a simple thing one plucked from a vine. It was sharp-edged and shifting and had layers she had not anticipated. Despite the pleasure to be found in their bed, Julianne was beginning to wonder if such sensual attraction was enough. She wanted more than his passionate kisses and his willing hands on her body. She wanted him to open his heart. And while he had been unfailingly generous in other things, he kept that piece of himself under lock and key.

But such thoughts had no place in her day's mission. So she shook off her worries and set off at a brisk walk, searching for the seamstress's shop Patrick's mother had recommended. She pasted a sunny mask on her face as she stepped into the shop, and reminded herself that with this first proper foray into town, she must strive to neither call undue attention to herself, nor offend the natives.

The little bell on the inside of the door tinkled merrily as she pushed inside, but its hopeful sound could not improve the circumstances of its sorry existence. The seamstress's shop was exactly what Julianne had feared finding in Shippington. At most, there were a dozen or so bolts of fabric lining the shelves on the wall, only one of which—a coarse black cotton that seemed more of the sort to grace one's settee than one's shoulder— might be considered to emulate a status of mourning. The walls of the shop were decorated with nothing so much as the occasional knothole, and there wasn't a piece of furniture in the place.

Not exactly an establishment that invited lingering, or leisurely consideration of a new wardrobe. In fact, the only thing that came close to capturing her interest was the shopgirl, who was pinning a half-finished piece on a mannequin near the front window and refusing to look in Julianne's direction.

"Excuse me." The woman's dark hair and hunched shoulders knocked against the walls of Julianne's memory. The girl looked an awful lot like the missing maid she was not supposed to be thinking about. Then again, her thoughts had been a tangled web this past week. It should not surprise her she was imagining the girl everywhere she looked.

Instead of turning around and offering a greeting, as good manners and probably her position demanded, the girl ducked her head and stepped behind the curtain that separated the shop's showroom from its workspace.

Her curiosity now thoroughly piqued, Julianne started to follow, but just as her hand reached out to brush the dark velvet fabric, a woman roughly the size of a draft horse stepped out, muttering below her breath.

She stopped short when she saw Julianne. "Oh! My apologies, miss. My girl told me there was a customer out front, but she neglected to tell me you were a lady." The shopkeeper's hands fluttered over her apron, smoothing and worrying and finally untying it and shoving it beneath a shelf. "How might I help you?"

Julianne smiled, though this was a distraction she was no longer sure she wanted. "I am in need of a new gown, and I'm afraid my timeline can only be described as desperate. I am to host a dinner party at the end of the week, and I need a gown suitable to reflect the family's state of bereavement. I am willing to pay for a rushed order, of course."

"Then you are the new Lady Haversham, I presume?" At Julianne's cautious nod, the shopkeeper's already ruddy cheeks pinked up. "Mr. Blythe mentioned the events at Summersby to my husband, over a pint at the King's Widge. My congratulations on your recent marriage."

Julianne's own mouth firmed in response. Honestly. Had Shippington really named its public house after the king's . . . well . . . *widge*? And was Blythe staying there, regaling the locals with sordid tales of the new earl? He'd left Summersby nearly a week ago, though his mother was still very much underfoot, and over the course of the last week she'd given little thought to where the man had gone other than being glad for his absence. Her stomach tightened in irritation to realize he remained so close to Summersby.

"Let me hazard a guess," she told the shopkeeper.

"Has Mr. Blythe been spreading tales about town? Perhaps suggested Lord Haversham might sport scales and breathe fire?"

The shopkeeper's eyes widened. "I . . . er . . . that is . . . he did not . . ."

"He means to discredit my husband. I should have a care how much stock I put in his words, if I were you." She straightened her shoulders. "Now then. With respect to the gown . . . I was thinking of a similar style to the one I am wearing, but perhaps in black instead of this horrid gray. I need it completed by Friday morning and delivered straightaway to Summersby. I also wish to place an order for five additional day dresses—all black silk, but in varied styles, of course—to be finished by the second week in November." She smiled meaningfully, certain her business was not only welcome, it was direly needed. Why, the poor woman couldn't even afford enough fabric to fill her shelves.

The shopkeeper shook her head, worry lines radiating from her eyes. "I don't think I can help you, Lady Haversham."

Julianne waited for an additional explanation, but none appeared forthcoming. Honestly, no wonder the town floated in a backwater sort of nonexistence. What kind of self-respecting seamstress turned down an offer of work? Why, in London she would have already been seated on a plush settee, a cup of tea in one hand, the latest plates from Paris spread out before her and a veritable army of staff bringing bolt after bolt of fabrics for her to see and touch.

Here, they'd been haggling for what seemed an eternity, and her hand was still noticeably empty.

"In London, my modiste has always been able to accommodate my requests," Julianne said slowly, trying to make sense of this new, nonsensical world. For the first time it occurred to Julianne that perhaps the world she had married into—namely the alien territory of Yorkshire—was a different beast than London.

The shopkeeper shrugged apologetically. "Unless you'd planned to settle for broadcloth, we'd have to order the materials out of Leeds, and if you'll forgive me saying, you don't seem the broadcloth sort. If the fabric is delivered promptly, we could possibly have the first gown finished by Saturday next, and the rest by the end of November, but even that will be a rushed order, I am afraid. I've only the one girl to help me. While Miss Smith is fast of hand, we've other customers to serve as well."

Julianne's thoughts promptly abandoned her request for a new dress—which was clearly a lost cause—and shifted to the latter part of the woman's explanation. "Miss *Prudence* Smith?" she asked, daring a glance toward the curtain where the shopgirl had so recently disappeared.

"Aye." The shopkeeper clucked in annoyance. "Not the most dependable of creatures, but devilishly clever with a needle, which is why I've kept her." Behind Julianne, the door's bell rang out, and the shopkeeper's eyes pulled away. "Oh, good afternoon, Mrs. Duffies. We've finished those new drapes you ordered. I'll be with you in just a moment." The woman turned back to Julianne. "Shall I order the crepe from Leeds, Lady Haversham?"

Julianne's feet itched, but she forced herself to wait. "Oh, I think I'll just have a look at the broadcloth and think about what you have advised." She waved a nonchalant hand. "Please, I do not want to keep you from other customers with my indecision."

She pretended to study the meager selection of fabrics, waiting until the shopkeeper's attention was fully absorbed with the new arrival. Then she pulled back the velvet curtain and stepped behind it, letting it fall with a muffled rush.

In the rear of the shop, the atmosphere was markedly different. Fabric was offensively strewn about, with little rhyme or reason, and chaos was the order of the day. The air hung thick with the scent of silk and wool and lamp oil, and Julianne wrinkled her nose against the unpleasant scents. The girl with dark hair was bent over a pile of piecework in one corner, and Julianne's chest felt hollow as she spied her.

"Prudence," she whispered.

The former maid leaped to her feet, and the fabric in her lap slipped to the floor. "Oh!" Her hand fluttered about her chest. "You . . . you startled me." She sounded close to breathless. "You . . . that is, *customers* aren't allowed back here."

"Which is why you retreated behind the curtain, isn't it, Prudence? You should remember from last November, I am not so easily dissuaded."

"Please, Miss Baxter." The girl was trembling visibly now. "I . . . I can't risk getting sacked. Not from this job too."

Julianne knew the vivid flush of triumph. She'd not broken her promise to Patrick, and yet she'd stumbled across the maid anyway. "It is no longer Miss Baxter. I am Lady Haversham now. And what do you mean, sacked? The whole point of my speaking on your behalf in November was to make sure you weren't blamed."

"It is not so simple, miss. A house in mourning doesn't have house parties," Prudence choked out. "Or hire new maids. I've been out of work since November last. My mum is sick, and the doctor is expensive. I had to come from Leeds to take this job, even though I *knew* it was a poor idea to come back to Shippington."

"That may explain why you are working here, but why are you afraid to speak with me?" Julianne demanded. The former servant's cowardice had gotten them in this muddle, and a bit of explanation was the very least she was owed. "Perhaps you would prefer I fetch the magistrate so you may explain it to him?"

That, finally, brought a flush to the girl's pale cheeks. Her gaze darted toward a bolted door at the rear of the room, but Julianne stepped to the left, effectively blocking the girl's escape. By God, she would be caught in last year's fashions before she let the chit fly out the back door now.

Prudence wrapped her arms around herself, her chest heaving in protest. "Please," she moaned. "I can't speak with you about this."

Julianne slipped closer to the frightened girl and tried on a more soothing tone, the sort she typically reserved for first-year debutantes who had ripped the hems of their ball gowns or spilled punch down the front of their bodices. "Nothing is going to happen to you, Prudence. I just want to talk to you about what happened last November."

"Oh . . ." the girl moaned, tears spilling down her cheeks. "I *knew* this job was trouble."

Julianne only narrowly resisted the temptation to shake the former maid's thoughts back to center. "Focus, if you please, on the matter of what has you so upset to see me. And why do you so object to Shippington? It's just a *town*."

"Being so close to Summersby brings back terrible memories of that day," Prudence cried softly. "I told myself it would be all right, that you had gone back to London. But then I . . . I saw you. Walking in the procession for Lord Haversham's funeral. And that was when I knew I had made a dreadful mistake."

Julianne fought back an impatient huff. "What has seeing me at the funeral to do with any of this?"

Prudence swiped a hand across her eyes. "I didn't only see you. I also saw . . ." Her voice fell to a tear-soaked whisper. "I saw the man who held the rifle that day."

Julianne's heart began to thump in her chest. Surely she'd misheard the girl. Surely it couldn't be so simple. Patrick had not been at the funeral. "Are you sure?" she pressed, her mind racing with swift surety toward a new conclusion, one she'd never considered in all these long months.

"I'm quite sure I shall never forget that face," Prudence choked out. "I see him in my nightmares."

By the stars. It was unconscionable.

And yet . . . now that she considered it, Prudence's explanation made so much more sense than the one they had all presumed to be true. Julianne had seen someone running away from the scene. Prudence had been adamant she'd seen a man aim and pull the trigger. That she could have overlooked such an obvious fit to the events of that morning made her lungs feel heavy now with regret. "Do you know who the man is?" Julianne demanded.

"No." The girl shook her head, swallowing a hiccup. "I was so surprised, I just dashed into the nearest shop and waited for the funeral procession to pass on by." She swallowed, and accepted the kerchief Julianne handed her to wipe her eyes. "I was not of a mind to march right up and ask his name, mind you."

Excitement coursed through Julianne's limbs. As chilling as the idea was that someone might have purposefully murdered Eric, this, finally, was the proof Patrick needed to convince everyone of his innocence. She needed to tell him.

She needed *Prudence* to tell him.

Surely he couldn't be angry with her. She hadn't purposefully tracked the girl to ground. And Prudence *had* just named someone else as the killer.

Well, not named exactly, but still . . .

Julianne swallowed the lump of excitement swelling in her throat. "Where was this man standing when you saw him?" she pressed. Perhaps it didn't matter that Prudence did not know the man's name. Julianne had attended the funeral, after all. Perhaps she could name the killer herself, although she was loath to go down this particular, twisted path again.

Prudence shuddered. "He was standing near the family."

"Was he tall or short? Portly or fit?"

"I . . . I don't know. He was taller than you, I think."

Julianne recalled with frustration how she'd needed to similarly extract the description of the killer in November. That had turned out poorly, but this time, she was determined not to leap to an incorrect conclusion. "What color was his hair?"

"I couldn't tell. He was wearing a tall black hat. And . . . and a black coat."

Julianne struggled against a building impatience as she realized they were speaking of a man of unknown name and hair color, who would have the audacity to wear black to a funeral, and who was possibly—but not decidedly—taller than her. "If you cannot recall any of this, how can you be sure he was the man who pulled the trigger?" she asked in irritation.

" 'Twas his eyes." Prudence exhaled, shuddering with the effort. "I'll never forget them. So cold. Like he could see through me. He looked up toward the folly when the smoke cleared, and it felt like the hand of death was settling over me." The girl's voice rasped low. "He did the same thing during the funeral. Looked right at me."

Good heavens. Julianne supposed that explained Prudence's hysterics last November well enough, as well as her white-faced terror now. "Was he a guest at Summersby?" she pressed. "Or perhaps a servant?"

"He did not eat with the servants during the November house party. And . . . he wasn't dressed like a servant. His clothes were finer than that."

A terrible thought occurred to Julianne, like a gust of wind that scraped skeleton branches against windows in the dead of winter. Many of the guests who had attended the funeral were still in residence, a perpetual plague of Patrick's family and friends who would not leave.

Whoever this was, he could still be at Summersby.

She grasped the girl's arm. "Prudence, you must come with me. You must *tell* someone."

"Oh no, miss," Prudence protested through a fresh wave of tears. "I couldn't. I've told you all I know." She tugged against Julianne's ruthless grip. "I . . . I would like to go now."

"Go where? You've the shop to mind, or you'll lose your position. And you've said you need the money." An idea took root. "Let me help you. You said you wished you had not come to Shippington. I could help you get back to Leeds, if you will but assist me with this small matter. How much to pay your mum's doctor, and make sure you have enough to set by?"

Prudence stilled. "Oh . . . would you, miss? Perhaps

a few quid? If you'll grant me this, I promise, I shall disappear and you'll never see me again."

Julianne released her hold on the girl's arm to dig through her reticule. "I shall give you four—no, *five* gold sovereigns, but you must come back to Summersby with me and help identify the man who killed Lord Haversham's son."

"But . . . the killer could be there. What if he saw me that day? What if he tries to kill *me*?"

Her fearful tone ruffled Julianne's sympathy, but not her resolve. "Don't you see?" Julianne stretched out her palm, hoping the fistful of coins she had retrieved from her purse would be enough temptation for Prudence to stay. "The man, whoever he is, is most certainly dangerous. If you stay silent, someone else could be hurt by him."

Prudence reached out her hand and cupped the coins. She seemed to weigh them a moment, closing her eyes against whatever internal struggle claimed her. When her lids next opened, her face crumpled with new tears. "I . . . I am sorry, miss. I wish I could help you, truly. Please, have a care for yourself. I'd hate to see you hurt." And then she lunged to the door, threw the bolt, and fell out into a spear of sunlight.

"Wait!" Julianne cried, scrambling to give chase. She tossed herself after the terrified girl, her heart pounding a terrified hole in her chest. She had just found the woman who held the key to Patrick's acquittal.

She could *not* lose her now.

Desperation surged through her as she stumbled into a back alley. In her vastly inappropriate heels, the walls of the nearby buildings proved too narrow to do little more than lurch unsteadily a few steps at a time. A horrible smell wafted on the air, along with a swarm of

black flies. She could see the hem of Prudence's skirt
disappearing some hundred feet or so up ahead. Were
there five doors leading off into the flanking buildings?
Or were there six?

She aimed in the general direction where she imagined Prudence had gone, only to trip over a refuse barrel
from a butcher shop.

She tumbled to the ground, and blackness crept in on
the periphery of her vision as she tried desperately to
shake the bits of offal from her hands. Her body insisted
she scream, but she shoved the instinctive urge away.
Because being tangled in a barrel of intestines was not
the worst possible thing that had happened to her today.
Patrick's brother had very likely been murdered in cold
blood, and the deed had been pinned on Patrick. Prudence was gone, the five sovereigns with her.

And Julianne had no idea who the killer might be.

PATRICK KNEW SHE was looking for him, even before
he saw her.

His awareness of her was often subtle, a shift in the
atmosphere of the house. Julianne was a force unto herself, and it should not surprise him that the air would
bend to her will. But the rumpus down the hallway was
no bending of air. It sounded as though a herd of cattle
had been admitted to the front foyer.

She was probably feeling neglected and stomping
about to demand her fair share of attention. God knew
he'd rather put his hours to better use enjoying his wife
than sorting through Summersby's accounts, but if he
was to take over the estate and leave it well prepared in
the event things took a regrettable turn, this afternoon's
focus had been necessary.

He kneaded the knot that had taken hold in the back

of his neck as the sound of her heels clipped down the corridor. Perhaps an hour's diversion and then a return to the books would not be remiss. He glanced out the window and was shocked to see evening shadows stretching across the lawn. No longer afternoon, then.

Perhaps she had a reason to be angry.

He pushed back from his father's desk and the task that had occupied his attention for the entirety of his afternoon. He'd resisted sitting down to it at first. He'd presumed, as he had all these years, that the work of managing the estate was tedium personified. And indeed, he'd spent the first hour staring at the notes scribbled by his father's steward and gnashing his teeth. But as he'd slowly begun to apply a more clinical eye, he had been surprised to discover there was a pattern to the work, a need to sort out problems and apply an appropriate intervention. Not that different from the practice of veterinary medicine, really.

He'd spent the latter part of the afternoon working out solutions and feeling somewhat more optimistic about filling his father's shoes.

A knock came, firm and quick and so very *Julianne* that it sent a smile blooming on his face. He took a step toward the door, already contemplating how he might reap the benefits of his wife, spitting mad and looking for his undivided attention. By the devil, she had proven a surprise this week. He'd thought he was marrying her as the means to an end, only to discover that the means was the most pleasurable part of it.

He opened the door and his smile fell away, chased by the sight of her. She didn't look angry. She looked awful. In fact, she looked so awful his eyes simply didn't know where to land.

Her hair was coming down from its pins, and her

skirts were smeared with blood—clearly not her own, given the remaining bits of gore clinging to the fabric. Had she taken a spill off her horse and injured them both? Tried her hand in the kitchen, as both scullery maid and cook? Butchered a bloody cow?

"What has happened?" he demanded.

She closed the door and leaned back against it. "Would you happen to have some brandy?"

The scratch of her voice only plucked more violently at his misgivings. "What has happened that I should need a drink to hear your confession?" he asked slowly.

"It is for me, Patrick. Not you." She drew a haggard breath. "I've ordered a bath, but I wanted to speak with you before I went up."

He sniffed. Not even a *fresh* cow. She smelled worse than she looked, if such a thing were possible. And this was Julianne. If she felt this conversation was more important than bathing, something was dreadfully wrong indeed.

He poured her a glass of brandy. She drained it, sputtering only a second before holding it out for more. He added another finger and then waited for her to explain herself.

Her fingers curved around the delicate crystal glass. "I've been to town."

"I had not realized you'd gone out." Indeed, he'd been preoccupied with books the entirety of the day, and he'd neither seen nor heard her until now, with the sun almost gone from the sky. There was plenty to get a body into trouble in Shippington. Particularly if that body—delectable though it might be—belonged to his wife.

A pulse of worry rounded through him. God's teeth, what had she done, that she was tossing back brandy as though it was water? Something had happened on her trip into town, and he'd wager it wasn't anything as innocuous as meeting the vicar in her shift.

"I've seen Prudence."

A tensile silence descended over them. He could almost swear he could hear the irregular beating of her heart. Or perhaps it was his own, bounding in denial.

The afternoon's success in his father's chair fell away. It scarcely mattered whether he felt more competent now to assume the responsibility of the title if the gallows loomed once again on the horizon. But worse was the shattering sense of betrayal that snaked through him. Over the course of the past week, he'd begun to hope—and believe—in a future. With *her*.

He'd placed his life in her hands, despite better sense, despite even the tutelage of history to guide him. He ought to have known better.

"For the love of *God*, Julianne, you promised me not even a week ago you would not," he snarled, knowing he sounded like a wounded animal, and feeling little better.

"Please don't shout at me, Patrick. I've had a devil of a day." The finger she pressed to her forehead left an offensive smear on one temple. "I did not go to town intending to find Prudence. I only went to visit the seamstress, as we discussed. It is not my fault she had taken a position there. And *you* are the one who insisted I go to Shippington instead of Leeds, horrifying experience though it was. I had planned to ask you to come with me, but you seemed in no mood for coercion when I checked in on you this morning."

He uncoiled his muscles, but only just. The blood still pounded in his ears. He had indeed insisted Julianne utilize the services of Shippington's seamstress. But he had been speaking of a hypothetical use, trying to mitigate the potential damage of a trip into Leeds. And that was before she'd staggered into the study covered in offal and demanding brandy to assuage her guilt.

He forced his fingers to unclench. "Just tell me, Julianne. What about this meeting with Miss Smith has you so upset you would forgo a bath for it? And why are you covered in the worst parts of a cow?"

"She spoke to me about the murder."

His stomach tightened in denial, even as his thoughts clawed toward survival. Because that was the next step, wasn't it? The bloody maid still thought he had murdered his brother.

"Has she spoken with the magistrate then?" His mind began to toss over the chances of escaping this alive. He didn't like the odds.

"I don't think she's spoken with him, no. She's powerfully afraid to speak to anyone. She bolted when I encouraged her to come to Summersby and talk to you. I lost her somewhere between the alley and the butcher shop." She swept a reluctant hand down her dress. "This happened when I gave chase."

A harsh laugh escaped him like a cannon blast. Not that the thought of Julianne sprinting to catch the woman who would hang him was anything close to amusing. It was done, even if it hadn't been done purposefully. The second witness had emerged and now his chances to escape a conviction were shattered. The devil take all, it was his worst nightmare.

Because the woman he'd married in order to silence her testimony had––innocently or not––gone and found someone else to do the job.

Rage boiled through him, hot and in need of an outlet. "Why is *she* afraid, when it's my neck on the line?"

Julianne hesitated. "She feels very sure Eric was murdered. That his death was not an accident."

"Of course she does," he snarled. "She told you as much eleven months ago."

"She never named you in November. She only described what she had seen, and I filled in the pieces with my understanding of events. But today she told me she saw the man who killed Eric. *Recently*." She swallowed. "At your father's funeral."

Disbelief had a way of unmanning a man, making him impotent. Rendering him mute. Patrick struggled through that now, knowing he needed to speak clearly this time. "I did not attend my father's funeral," he somehow managed to get out.

"I know, Patrick." Her affirmation fell softly. "I was there." Her lips formed an apologetic frown. "But she is quite sure of what she saw that day, even if she is not precisely sure *whom* she saw. Which begs the question: who wanted your brother dead?"

Patrick suffered through the question, so painfully constructed it seemed impossible to contemplate. He'd spent the months since his brother's death in purgatory, almost paralyzed from the guilt. Such a burden was not easily lifted, not even for such a sinister possibility as acknowledging that Eric may have been murdered. "She seemed sure?" he asked hoarsely.

"Prudence did not know the man's name. And bitterly few details to describe him. But yes, she is utterly convinced she saw the killer at your father's funeral. Think on it. It makes sense. You claim you swung your rifle away from your target at the last minute, but how far would you have had to swing the barrel for that bullet to strike your brother, who was standing behind you? And do not forget I was there that morning. I saw *someone* running from the scene, and Prudence was quite insistent, even from the start, that she saw a man aim a rifle directly at Eric."

Patrick's mind raced back to that day. He was tired of reliving it, and yet he could never forget. He could still smell the ever present decay of dead leaf litter stirred up by his feet, the pungent smoke from his fired rifle. He'd imagined that day was the dawning of his own personal hell. But now, for the first time since this nightmare began, he turned himself over to a different thought.

A black but welcome rage rolled over him as he contemplated this new facet to his brother's death, his anger pointed at a nameless, faceless enemy. Was this the answer to his dilemma? Or, was he fooling himself, reaching for the explanation he wanted, instead of the one that made sense? What proof did he really have of his own innocence, beyond Julianne's white-faced insistence the maid had seen someone else?

And how could they convince someone to believe them? He wasn't sure *he* believed it. He'd heard two rifle retorts that day, and he'd always presumed one of them had been Eric's. The thought that there could have been a third party made his chest tighten in anger and hope.

"Surely we have enough to go to the magistrate now and stop this senseless inquest," Julianne pressed.

Patrick wanted to believe it. Oh, God, he wanted to think he hadn't killed his brother. But the sinister possibility that Eric had been murdered was simply too fantastical to accept without further proof. He reluctantly shook his head. "We've a phantom witness that you failed to identify eleven months ago, and who has now disappeared. If we raise the suspicion of murder, who is to say the deed won't be pinned on me? Continuing to claim that Eric was killed by an accidental gunshot, at least, provides an opportunity to argue a charge of manslaughter, instead of murder." He hesitated, sorting through options, discarding some, reconsidering others. "I think we need to wait and consult with MacKenzie when he returns."

"Someone killed your brother, Patrick. The killer was here, at Summersby, during the November house party, and he was here during your father's funeral as well. He could kill again." Her voice choked on the shimmer of a sob. "He could kill *you*."

"If someone killed Eric, that does not mean they would come after me. Eric had any number of friends in London. It stands to reason he might have acquired some enemies there too, particularly in his last months. He'd run up quite some debt, and had come home to ask Father for more funds. Perhaps someone got tired of waiting."

"That is *one* possible explanation." She shook her head. "But it is not the only one."

Patrick hesitated. He didn't just want to trust Julianne. He *needed* to, with an intensity that almost frightened him. "You are really worried about me?" he asked, more gently now.

"How could I not worry? Even if I sometimes want to kick you for your idiocy, I do not want to see anything happen to you."

He folded his arms around her, the sorry state of her person be damned. "Other than a bruised shin, that is?"

She breathed heavily against his shirt, and he could feel the warmth of her breath through the thin cotton. "I would aim my boot a little higher," she said, her voice muffled.

"I do not recall that a kick to the cods was part of

the vows you took," he said over her head, even as his thoughts struggled to coalesce into a plan of action. The key, he knew, was speaking with Miss Smith, wherever she was. He struggled—and failed—to bring the maid's face to mind, knowing he must have seen her at some point during the November house party.

Or perhaps not. After all, he'd spent most of his time sulking in the stables that week.

"Don't make light of this, Patrick." She sniffed against his chest. "How can you hold me like this? I . . . I smell."

"Aye. That you do."

She stiffened in his arms. The feel of her helped calm the vicious pattern of his pulse, though the smell of her was indeed ripe enough to turn his stomach. But he had come home nearly as filthy on any number of days when he had served as Moraig's veterinarian, and he tightened his arms around her. "Didn't you know?" he added. "The blacksmith made me promise to honor you, no matter the stench."

"He did no such thing," she protested, her voice muffled.

"You are fortunate I am not a squeamish sort." Now that the first fear of betrayal had settled, he was a little in awe of what she had gotten herself into, all on his account. He would not be surprised if the day's disgrace had caused permanent damage to his fastidious wife's psyche. That she had come to speak with him first, shrugging off the need for an immediate bath, told him her state of mind far more eloquently than any strategized confession.

He thought better of the instinct to place a kiss to the top of her hair, which was in want of some good lye soap. Instead, he whispered into her ear. "I am sure you never thought to hear these words from my mouth, but you desperately need a bath."

She shook, as if fighting off a laugh, then pulled back. Her red-rimmed eyes met his. "I think it is foolhardy to wait for Mr. MacKenzie's return before speaking with the magistrate. Such a man has the power to help us. It's his job to sort out these facts, after all."

For a moment, Patrick considered it. Could he trust her to remain steadfast in an interview with Mr. Farmington, Shippington's longtime magistrate?

And moreover, could he forgive her if she did not?

He knew her body now, and how it fit in his palms. Knew her sharp mind and her sharper tongue, and the way she said things that made his blood run too hot for comfort. But her words were every bit as ill-tamed as her hair. He had no way to predict what she might say if given an audience with the magistrate. MacKenzie had been quite clear in explaining this part of it: a wife could not be *compelled* to testify against her husband. But Julianne taking the matter into her own hands— even accidentally—was a different dilemma entirely.

He shook his head. "It is too early, Julianne. But do not mistake my desire to wait for any sort of apathy. We've at least two things to keep us occupied while we await MacKenzie's counsel."

"*We* have?" she asked carefully.

He nodded slowly. As if he could keep her tethered.

Hadn't she just proven herself incapable of leaving well enough alone? The idea that she might yet prove his downfall would not quite leave him, and that, quite ironically, made him feel like a bounder all over again. He had treated her poorly to have judged her so quickly when she had first staggered into the study and announced she had seen Prudence. Keeping her close, and

knowing what she was thinking and doing, would perhaps grant him a small—if unpredictable—measure of
control. And he owed her this, even if his instincts told
him to bundle her up and lock her in their room for her
own safety.

"First, we need to try to find Prudence, sort out what
she truly knows, and convince *her* to go to the magistrate. He will not be swayed by anything but the maid's
own free testimony."

Julianne nodded her approval with the plan he laid
out. "And the other?"

"We need to discover who might have wanted to kill
my brother."

Chapter 20

JULIANNE LOOKED OUT over the crowd and wondered which of Summersby's dinner guests might be a murderer.

It was a muted gathering, as befitted the family's circumstances, but that did not mean it was a drab affair. The drawing room was filled to the brim with family and friends, milling about, offering their condolences as they waited to be called into dinner. Despite the preponderance of black clothing—except, unfortunately, on her—there was a hum of anticipation in the room, and overhead, the beeswax candles burned brightly, adding light and warmth to what could have been a dark mood.

She wished Patrick was here with her, but he'd come in straight from the barn. She'd taken one look at him sent him back above stairs, declaring him in desperate need of a valet and a haircut. Now, as she waited for him to return in which she hoped was a more presentable state, she circulated among the guests, smiling here, listening there.

Mr. Farmington, the gray-haired magistrate who had questioned her so unerringly in the hours following Eric's murder, stood sentry next to her father. Aunt Margaret stood beside them, nodding agreeably at something the magistrate was saying. The woman was still clinging to Summersby with the persistence of a barnacle, but at least her perpetually sour expression had softened tonight with the arrival of her son among the guests.

Farmington's eyes shrewdly followed Julianne's progress through the crowd. He'd struck her as a fair man in November, offering his handkerchief when her tears had flowed during that first regrettable interview, but he seemed harder tonight. More the magistrate, less the sympathetic ear. She kept her distance, moving on after a few mild words of welcome.

Patrick had decided to trust her. To *include* her, confiding in her and discussing a plan of attack, as if her ideas had merit. It was a heady feeling, and it sent a bright bulb of happiness blooming in her chest. She would not squander that trust now by lingering overlong with the one man in the room who would certainly have more questions for her than answers.

Two dozen guests fanned out around her, and she considered each one's potential. She dismissed a group of people clustered around the dowager countess in one corner of the room. They appeared to be local gentry, and while she remembered their faces from the earl's funeral, she did not recall seeing those extraneous souls last November at the house party.

Instead, she focused on the gentlemen she remembered attending both the house party and the funeral. One of the men who fit the bill was the darkly handsome Dr. Merial, who was standing near the windows and listening politely to something George Willoughby was saying. She supposed she needed to keep Willoughby on her list of potential suspects too, but he appeared so young and earnest tonight, she felt an instinctive twitch of remorse at her duplicity.

In contrast, she didn't know much about Dr. Merial. She was inclined to dismiss Shippington's doctor as a suspect, even though he'd attended both events. It was not only because he was quite young to hold such an important position, or because he had the sort of face that made women stop and stare in stupefied wonder. It was because the doctor had purportedly attended the earl in his final hours, and labored mightily to save his life. She'd heard of his heroics from her maid, who had ended the story on a dreamy sigh. Not that Julianne blamed the girl. Once upon a time, she might have sighed a little herself.

Mr. Blythe, who had also attended both events, was standing by himself near the mantel, watching the crowd in much the same manner Julianne was. That held her attention a long moment. Was he a guest who felt only barely welcomed?

Or a killer searching for a new target?

The covert inquiries she had pressed around the room so far had come largely to naught, and only the hot-blooded Blythe seemed capable of something more nefarious than ill-spirited gossip. She moved toward him, her mind sifting through the possibilities

Blythe inclined his head at her approach. "Ah, the indomitable Lady Haversham has come down from her new pedestal. I understand I have you to thank for my belated invitation. I admit I was surprised to receive it."

Somehow, Julianne found a smile. Blythe's vocal efforts to discredit Patrick in Shippington had ensured—to her own mind, at least—that he was now a prime suspect, and she'd known of no better way to ascertain Mr. Blythe's potential involvement than seeing him interact with the family. "Consider it an olive branch," she told him. "Patrick feels it is important to respect his father's memory by honoring those guests he always welcomed in life. No matter our inauspicious start, you are always welcome here at Summersby, Mr. Blythe."

His face darkened, but before he could respond a murmur went up among the guests. Julianne turned away from his glower, seeking the source of so much distraction. Her gaze swept the swirl of indistinct faces, and she leaned in, depending on her ears to sort out what had stirred the crowd from its otherwise polite stupor. A shiver traversed her spine as she caught the low baritone of Patrick's voice, perfectly tuned to tug a reaction from her body.

And then her husband stepped into focus, and she had to look twice.

Gone was the scruffy veterinarian, with a face in need of shaving and hands in need of washing. He was clad in a splendid black evening jacket—a bit loose in the chest now, thanks to his leaner existence in Moraig, but the very sort of jacket he *should* have been wearing during that memorable dance so many months ago, and which she had begun to doubt he owned. His hair had not been trimmed, as she had ordered, but it *was* combed into respectability. Her fingers itched to touch the rakishly long edges, there over his ears, and a selfish part of her soul was glad to see it had not been shorn after all.

His eyes met hers, warm and frankly appreciative. While manners demanded he ought to stop and greet the guests who were parting before him, he headed toward her with singular purpose. The murmured voices hushed, and she knew everyone in the room was watching his progress with wide eyes and busy minds. But she could not bring herself to care. The moment slowed, pulsing with some elemental rush of emotion that—despite three Seasons of searching—she had only ever experienced with Patrick.

Attraction. Desire. *Want.*

Would it always be like this, her feet pointing themselves toward him, divining her way as if she had been fashioned to some degree for this man, and this moment? She felt spun back in time, to this same house and this same man, asking for a waltz and ending with a kiss. She knew there was a proper plan to follow, a need to smile politely and take his arm as they moved into the game of stealth that awaited them tonight. But that plan withered beneath an overwhelming urge to go up to their room and see where this look—this *feeling*—might lead.

He stopped in front of her. "Do I pass muster now?"

Her eyes cataloged the changes a half hour had wrought. Now that he was closer, she could see there was a small nick on the left side of his lower jaw. Infuriating man, shaving himself. She might have known he'd refuse her order to use a valet, much as he'd refused to cut his hair. Despite the obvious risk to life and limb, her eyes approved of this new version of her husband. Even her nose approved, the scent of him familiar but laced with the new fragrance of soap.

But most compelling of all, under the new layer of polish, he was still *Patrick.* Handsome. Deliciously disreputable, as if any moment he could toss off the yoke of convention and snub the entire room in favor of saving an animal's life.

"You'll do," she told him, then added, "You've always done."

His smile was slow in dawning, almost sheepish. "Why, Lady Haversham. Are you telling me you like the unkempt version of your husband?"

"I like both versions of my husband." She laughed. Although truly, there were more than two versions. She might like the man he presented to the world, but she treasured the man he became behind their bedroom door. Her cheeks warmed even now as she considered what he might yet do tonight, when their guests had gone home and they fell into bed.

And then Mr. Blythe cleared his throat.

Patrick's eyes lifted from her face. A sudden frown claimed the smile that had just stretched across his face.

"I was beginning to wonder if you'd deign to notice your guests, Haversham," Blythe drawled.

Patrick nodded curtly. "My apologies, Blythe. You are of course correct. I must offer my greetings to the crowd." He offered Julianne a thin smile. "I shall return to escort you in to dinner."

Julianne stared after her retreating husband. Her heart tugged to follow him, but pride kept her slippers sewn firmly to the floor. She turned back to the man who so paled in comparison to her husband's magnetic pull. She supposed she ought to speak more with the loathsome Mr. Blythe. After all, it was the express purpose of inviting him here.

"Your husband seems anxious to be away," Blythe observed.

Julianne was not the least bit embarassed to have been caught ogling her husband, but unfortunately, Patrick appeared to harbor some misgivings. "He has a responsibility to his guests," she replied coolly.

Blythe's suspicious gaze swept the length of her skirts before coming back to probe her face. "Perhaps he disapproves of your refusal to mourn the earl's death properly?"

A rush of heat claimed Julianne's cheeks. After the destruction of her gray silk in her argument with the butcher's barrel, she'd faced a near impossible task of selecting a gown for tonight's dinner from her remaining wardrobe. The gown she wore had a modest neckline, at least, but it far more befitted a London ballroom than a quiet family dinner. "I have not yet had time to acquire a wardrobe appropriate for bereavement, Mr. Blythe," she replied stiffly.

"A natural consequence of such an . . . *unexpected* marriage, I would think."

Julianne's brow shot up. "Do you have a point you wish to make?" she asked. "Because, truly, I cannot see how my marriage is any sort of concern for you."

"And yet, I admit to being concerned. Truly, in the matter of your decision to marry my cousin, I cannot decide if you are an idiot or an actress, Lady Haversham."

After a moment of cold appraisal, she decided to indulge him. After all, the entire purpose of this dinner was to acquire information, and at the moment she held his undivided attention. "I promise you, I am neither." She angled her body closer, daring him to continue down this ill-advised path. "But feel free to enlighten me, Mr. Blythe. Why might I be an idiot, when I've merely married the man my conscience bade me?"

"Your conscience?" His gaze dropped suggestively lower. "Or your circumstances? You see, I know my cousin well. A consequence of so much time spent here at Summersby, I suppose. He is a man who has always weighed his options carefully before acting, sometimes to the point of paralysis. It would take a powerful motivation to convince a man like that to marry in such haste." Blythe leaned in, until he was so close she could see the uneven slant of his front teeth. "It is entertaining to watch, as marriages of convenience so frequently are. But is it even Haversham's?"

Julianne had expected it, of course. There could be little other interpretation, and Mr. Blythe was proving himself a rather gauche communicator. Still, it made her gasp to hear him say it out loud. "Is *what* Haversham's?" she clipped out.

"Come now," he chided, shaking his head. "The scandal sheets have painted quite the picture of you these past few years. You are, of course, widely praised for your beauty and wit, but not widely known for your propriety."

The audacity of the man near left her breathless. "I assure you, Mr. Blythe, that the only thing you ought to be worrying about in that regard is that it is *none of your business.*"

"Perhaps I have spoken out of turn." His eyes remained narrowed. "But I do have *some* vested interest in ensuring a direct bloodline to the title. I have a great deal of respect for this family, and I would not like to think an injustice was being perpetrated on them."

Julianne struggled to keep a rein on her temper, though his thinking was logical, if a bit boorish. "Patrick is part of the family you claim to love," she reminded him. "Why do you hate him so much?"

"I do not hate him." Blythe's eyes flickered in hesitation. "But I admit a certain . . . distrust, if you will. He always looked down his nose at those of us who spent time actually preparing for the possibility of inheriting the title."

"Far less a possibility for you than him, I should think," Julianne pointed out, against better sense.

"All the more reason he should have taken that duty seriously. His father, certainly, tried to groom him in that regard. But Patrick always refused to pay court. When he tucked himself off for four years on the continent, it came close to breaking his father's heart. If my mother looked on me with even half the pride the old earl showered on his sons, I assure you, I would not ever take it for granted. But your husband has proven himself unworthy at the end, as he was always bound to do."

"Your argument lacks logic." Julianne knew she shouldn't vigorously engage a man as potentially dangerous as Blythe, but her ire was too high to leave off. "If my husband was so reluctant to prepare himself for the possibility of the title, wouldn't that suggest he had no desire to be earl? And therefore had no reason to kill his brother?"

Blythe's dark brows pulled down. He stared at her a long, searching moment, and while his eyes stayed wide open, she could have sworn he was blinking on the inside. Finally, he gathered himself. "Perhaps he changed his mind."

"Perhaps you should change *yours*, Mr. Blythe. It is clear you have leaped to judgment based on old grudges, rather than any clear examination of the facts."

She gathered her skirts in one hand, preparing to turn away, but found herself hanging on the second half of the man's original, impudent question. "At the risk of very much *proving* myself an idiot, why, if I might dare to ask, did you suggest earlier I was an actress?"

He looked down at her, and she could see a disarming resemblance to Patrick in the line of his jaw and the slope of his nose. "You are putting on a good show, I'll give you that. Some of the guests are even making wagers on the outcome, though the discussion trends toward *when* the blessed event will occur, rather than *if* it will. But if we're not bound to be toasting your good fortune in an indecently short amount of time, it seems clear you and my cousin have orchestrated this sham of a marriage simply to prevent your testimony."

Julianne reared back, her composure dangerously close to shattered. "No." However she'd expected this conversation to go, this went very far afield. Blythe was wrong. Patrick had never demanded her silence, though she'd been all too happy to offer it. *"No,"* she repeated again, her voice firmer now.

"Have you asked him?" came the man's well-oiled reply.

"I don't have to ask him, Mr. Blythe." Her knees felt close to buckling. "You are tilting at windmills. My marriage is a happy one."

Now the man's smile turned positively feral, and it made the fine hairs on her arms prick to attention. "Then perhaps that makes you an idiot after all, Lady Haversham."

PATRICK HATED EVENTS like this. Stilted, polite conversation. Food he knew had been prepared to perfection, but which might as well have been made from sawdust for all that he was enjoying it. Julianne was seated next to him throughout the interminable course of the meal, a tempting distraction to the forced pleasantries. But her nearness and falsely bright smile could not remove the fact that the eyes of every soul at the table were focused squarely on him.

At least with Blythe and Willoughby, a man knew where he stood. But Mr. Farmington was holding his cards quite close to his chest tonight. Although he had been a good friend of Patrick's father and had sat down for a dozen meals at this very table, the expression on the magistrate's face was indecipherable.

It went little better after dinner, when the ladies had left for the drawing room and the men were poured a glass of port. Through the open door, he could hear the appealing pitch of Julianne's laughter down the hallway. Patrick wanted to be there with her, the expectations of Society be damned. But this bit of masculine banality was expected by the guests, and he was forced by his new position to play host to the lot of them.

Willoughby, damn his imprudent tongue, tumbled into dangerous territory after only a half a glass of port. "How goes the inquest, Mr. Farmington?"

The room stilled, and all eyes turned toward the magistrate, who looked discomfited by the attention. "The coroner's report will be returned, soon enough," came the man's uneasy answer.

"I am sure we can all speculate how it's going, now that the only witness has cried off." Blythe lifted his glass to his lips and swallowed before adding, "Awfully convenient, that. A rather brilliant means to get away with murder."

Patrick's fingers tightened around the cool edge of his crystal. "I did not murder my brother, Blythe."

"You'll forgive me if I retain some doubt. Everyone knows you hated your brother. You argued with him all the time."

Patrick's pulse jumped angrily beneath his skin. It seemed Blythe was looking for a confession tonight, but he would not find one here. "I did not hate Eric," Patrick growled, though he could not deny their relationship had been tumultuous those last months. "Certainly not more than I hate *you*, and yet you are still standing before us."

"Perhaps you ran out of bullets," Blythe sneered. "Or perhaps you ran out of nerve."

"Gentlemen, *enough*." Farmington placed his own nearly full glass down on the table. "It is pointless to speculate, and ridiculous to argue. The only thing that matters in this moment is whether the coroner will determine there is enough evidence to commend Haversham to trial, and that is quite out of our hands now. We should speak of other things."

Patrick seethed with anger. It was a bloody nightmare that would not end, and the port was loosening whatever bit of judiciousness he'd once possessed. "I did not kill my brother. But *someone* did. And you should be trying to find him, Farmington, instead of chasing me."

A moment of awkward silence descended over the room. "You are changing your story now?" Farmington's gray eyes flickered warily.

A steady hand settled on his shoulder. "You've already admitted the shot was yours, Haversham," Lord Avery said quietly. "Have a care where you are going with this, son."

Patrick could hear the echoing undercurrent of dissension spreading throughout the room. The urge to mention the second witness sat like a barbed hook on his tongue, but he was not so naïve—or inebriated—to think that would go well in this crowd, especially without the witness in hand. Damn his questionable judgment. He'd spoken out of turn, without consulting MacKenzie first. Had he just irrevocably altered his defense? Or planted a seed of truth that would encourage Mr. Farmington to look farther afield for his brother's murderer?

"You provided a statement that your brother had also taken a shot that day," Farmington pointed out.

Patrick gritted his teeth. "Aye. I remember."

"The subsequent investigation showed your brother's gun was never fired." Farmington shook his head. "You can be sure the coroner's report has already focused on those irregularities in your statement. I would discourage you from adding more. Such inconsistencies in your story will not help your cause, Haversham."

While the aftermath of his brother's shooting was a clipped series of images, hazy and panicked, those moments before his death remained as clear as glass in Patrick's mind. "But . . . there *was* a second gunshot." His voice felt charred, but his memory swam drunkenly. "Did you not think to question anyone else about what they may have heard?"

"Are you telling the magistrate how to do his job, Haversham?" Blythe snarled. "Christ, you are an arrogant sod. Always thinking you are smarter than the rest of us. I was there, if you remember. And I only heard one shot."

"You were on the west bank of the lake that day, not the east, where Eric and I were hunting." Patrick ignored his cousin, focusing instead on the magistrate's reddening face. "I heard two shots, close in time but distinct. Julianne heard two shots as well," he urged. "Ask her, Farmington. She will tell you."

The lines of tension about Farmington's eyes reminded Patrick that the events of eleven months ago had affected him too. He'd seemed as stunned as anyone over Eric's death, but in the aftermath, he'd had the unenviable job of methodically sorting through the additional evidence.

Evidence that Patrick had not heretofore considered.

"Ah, but your new wife has recused herself from all involvement in this nasty business of testifying, hasn't she?" Farmington shook his head sadly. "She cannot have it both ways, Haversham. And neither can you."

Chapter 21

THE WEATHER IN Yorkshire could be uncertain in October, but as if mocking Julianne's own darkening mood, morning brought clear skies and an unseasonably mild temperature that invited a family excursion down to the lake.

Julianne sat on a blanket, her feet tucked up under her and the remnants of a picnic luncheon scattered about. A slight wind had picked up from the west, and it rattled the dying leaves in overhead branches and knocked against the worry brewing inside her. Patrick was bent over Eleanor's head, patiently working his fingers over some knot in his sister's fishing line, even as he explained the mechanics of tossing out a proper cast to Mary.

A muffled curse came from her right, and she turned her head to see George Willoughby tugging his line from an overhead branch. He smiled ruefully in her direction as he lowered his arms. "Never was one for fishing. Perhaps I should join you and stop mauling the poor trees?"

Julianne smiled and patted the blanket. "Come and sit then, Mr. Willoughby. Leave the fishing to the experts.

Perhaps we can both learn something from watching Patrick and Eleanor."

Willoughby settled beside her, stretching out his long, trouser-clad legs. "Surely by this point there is no need for such formality. I think given names are a must, now that you know how terrible I am at fishing."

She could see nothing immediately improper in the suggestion. He was family, after all. "Not so bad as that, George."

"I am a terrible marksman as well. They only invite me along with a goal of improving my aim. But all told, I believe any man would prefer the pleasure of your company to the hunt." He shifted closer. "I think today I will count myself fortunate to be such a poor sportsman."

"Er . . . thank you." Once upon a time, this was precisely the sort of attention Julianne would have wanted, a gentleman focused on *her* instead of the usual country pursuits. But today, it felt wrong. He was so close she could smell his hair pomade, some sickening scent of cloves. For a moment she considered lengthening the inches that separated them into ten.

But then Patrick glanced over his shoulder, disapproval clear in the slant of his brow. Julianne dug her fingers into the blanket, meeting her husband's gaze with the challenge in her own. Making Patrick jealous served no one's best interests, least of all Willoughby's. But George was harmless, and Patrick's bristling animosity was the closest she'd come to attention from her husband since their encounter at dinner last evening.

"You seem unusually quiet today." George leaned back on one elbow. "I remember following you about last November, listening to your banter. It was wicked good fun. Never knew what you might say."

Julianne frowned, a bit nonplussed by the man's admission. "I am just . . . preoccupied, I suppose. Mr. Blythe was bothersome last night." Indeed, she could not stop thinking of their conversation, though it was foolhardy to give the man any credence. "I had hoped this outing to the lake would take my mind from it," she admitted, "but instead I find myself with too much time for reflection."

Willoughby clucked sympathetically. "I would have spared you if I had known. Did my cousin discuss his theories on Haversham's guilt to you, as well? He was most vocal about it after dinner."

Julianne sighed. George Willoughby was not the man she should be discussing this with, and she already regretted traipsing down this path with him. But the facts contributing to her poor mood lay like a black pool of oil on the surface of the day, and they wanted expunging. "No. He questioned the reasons behind my marriage."

Willoughby's hand came up to pat her own. "You should pay my cousin no heed," he advised. "He has never been one to properly guard his words."

"I am less concerned about what Mr. Blythe is saying than others. He implied there was talk among the guests." She swallowed, knowing that if nothing else, George Willoughby was someone who would at least speak truthfully of these matters. "Wagers, as to my . . . *condition*. Are others truly saying such things?"

He hesitated a fraction too long. "Some are. I have defended you against such vile talk, of course, and encouraged those who might repeat it to leave." He glanced toward Patrick and his expression darkened. "And regardless, they should not blame *you* for any of it, Julianne."

She tugged her fingers out of the young man's grasp. "I did not *have* to marry my husband, George. I am enormously fond of him. That is all that should be said about any of it." And it was true, however hollow the sentiment sounded. Somewhere along the way, affection had indeed found her. Bound her tight. But now it was shaking her with great, bared teeth as it laughed at her predicament.

Willoughby tugged at his waistcoat, which had ridden up to reveal the beginnings of what Julianne had not previously realized was a middle that would soon lean toward a decided paunch. He flashed her a hopeful smile. "Still, if there is any truth to it, I hope you would tell me. I believe those wagers must be laid before the end of the month."

For the first time in all of her twenty years, Julianne found herself utterly without words. Good heavens. He not only believed the rumors, he wanted to *profit* from them?

An awkward silence descended, punctuated only by the rustle of leaves and the smooth encouragement Patrick was offering his sisters. Willoughby closed his eyes and soon began to snore, thank goodness. But though the sun was warm on her face, Julianne found herself too keyed up to do anything so restful. Another time, another day, she might have enjoyed the experience of watching Patrick with his sisters, the sunlight glinting off the sandy slope of his hair. But it hurt, watching Patrick engage in such a personal, tactile interaction with people he loved. Because she couldn't help but think that perhaps she didn't receive such public attentions because she didn't merit them. Not that he was a man inclined to public tomfoolery, but once upon a time, he had kissed her, nearly in public, there in Summersby's foyer.

Why the change, now that he was legally entitled to do so?

All morning—and arguably, since dinner last night—he'd been aloof, as though that moment when her world had ground to a stop and he had stood before her in the drawing room, spit-polished and shining like a new penny, had never happened.

She cataloged the myriad touches she had accumulated over the course of two and a half weeks of marriage. More than she could count on her fingers. Nary a one where anyone but she could see. Was it any wonder Mr. Blythe and George Willoughby were questioning the purpose behind their marriage? To the world, theirs must seem a cold sort of showing.

Julianne fought her mind's insistence on drifting back to the conversation with Blythe. She watched Patrick toss the delicate silk thread out onto the water and pull it back in cunning, short strokes, and could not shake the sharp new thought that perhaps her husband had done nearly the same thing to her. Because if Mr. Blythe had been right about the matter of the guests' speculation, what else might he have had correct?

Had Patrick really married her to ensure her silence?

It was a stinging idea, but it was persistent. She had refused to believe Mr. Blythe's vile claims last night, and she didn't want to believe them now. But had she reacted so strongly to Blythe's taunts out of loyalty to her husband, or cowardice? She'd always prided herself on being able to read people, to understand their motives. She'd never truly believed Patrick's explanation for marrying her was to save her reputation.

But she'd thought she understood his reasons for marrying her. She had presumed that, like her, Patrick felt this same driving, needy force that seemed to consume her every time she saw him. Every time he kissed her. She'd been pushed—almost blindly—by an emotion she could now see came grievously close to love. She felt blind still, groping her way through a darkness she'd not seen coming.

Stupid, stupid, stupid.

Her stomach jumped in time with the smooth, unerring flick of Patrick's wrist, spooling into a tangle of confusion. She might arguably be called a fool, but she had never before considered herself a coward. But she was beginning to wonder if true cowardice was refusing to see what was looming before her. She was rather afraid she did not want to dissect Jonathon Blythe's accusations or George Willoughby's explanations because of what she might find.

It took forever for the girls to admit they were not going to catch a fish that afternoon. Longer still to gather up the blanket and their picnic remains and set back toward the manor. As they began the long trek home, Eleanor and Mary chattered on like small sparrows, pulling George Willoughby by the hand as they skipped ahead on the path.

Only when the trio had disappeared around a bend up ahead did she feel Patrick's hand reach out and brush her own. When he pulled her down a side path, she didn't resist, not even when briars pulled at her skirts and her shoes became hopelessly smudged with mud. Just a few hours ago, she would have welcomed the opportunity for a stolen kiss. Heavens, just a few hours ago, she might have suggested the excursion herself.

But now, his quest for privacy niggled at her, like a key in the wrong lock.

He pulled her behind the trunk of a large oak tree and brought his lips down to hers. She sorted through the taste of her husband as he kissed her, sunshine and laughter and the turnovers they had eaten during the picnic, tart and sweet and faintly spiced. She wanted him to kiss her forever. But forever was a tricky beast, when there were questions burning her tongue as fiercely as his kiss.

He seemed to sense her hesitation and pulled back. "Is something amiss, wife?"

Julianne looked away, down the path they had just come down. She could hear the concern in his voice, sounding every bit as real as the faint shouts of the girls. It should have warmed her heart to hear such regard in Patrick's voice, and his ready use of the word "wife." But she, of all people, knew that concern could be conjured, words chosen with care to bend someone to your will.

"Why did you marry me?" she asked. It felt as though her soul was being split open to ask it, but she resolutely pushed her shoulders back. "Was it only to ensure my silence?"

His lips tipped downward. "Did George Willoughby tell you that, when he sidled up to you on the blanket?"

Oh, for heaven's sake. "This isn't about your cousin, Patrick. Why did you marry me?" she repeated. Louder now. A question and a demand.

But his eyes were unreadable, his jaw set to stone. "Why are you asking me this now, Julianne, instead of then, when it mattered?"

"I assure you, it matters now." Her chest felt muffled, as though her heart was wrapped in wet wool. "Was our marriage nothing more than a ruse to prevent me from testifying against you?" She waited. For an answer, for a reaction. Perhaps, if he didn't—couldn't—say those words, there was hope yet for them, a glimmer of something salvageable from what was fast becoming the wreck of her heart. But instead of handing her the answer she wanted—the answer she still foolishly believed and prayed he might give—he gave her the answer she feared.

"Aye," he ground out.

That single word cut with the surety of a saber. For a moment, she only blinked, sure she had misheard him. But one did not mistake an admission like that.

Blythe was right. It was a refrain chanting in her ears, deafening in its simplicity. And she realized she should have guessed it, from the start. After all, one did not marry someone he scarcely knew unless he had a very, very good reason for it.

"So it is true," she gasped, stepping away from the man she had married for no other reason than foolish, girlish fancy. She had once considered Patrick little more than a pawn in her grand game, though that sentiment had ended nearly as soon as it had started. It was disconcerting to realize she was now the one so used. She wrapped her arms around herself, her mind too numb to sort through all the implications of his admission.

Was the day warm, after all? She felt so cold.

"In my defense," he said slowly, his expression still too blank for comfort, "I have regretted the lie, nearly every day since."

In his defense. She wanted to cover her ears with her hands, block out the sound of those words. What did that mean, exactly? She only heard that he regretted it. He regretted *her*. And she felt cleaved in two by her naïveté.

"Why?" she whispered. "Why did you not simply tell me, from the start?"

He exhaled loudly, and one hand came up to scrape

against his already unruly hair. "I should have. I should have been more honest. But at the time, my choice seemed . . . fair."

Understanding nudged aside her mind's quest for denial. *Oh God.* He had married her for what, exactly? Expediency? Convenience?

Revenge?

And he'd done it brilliantly too. He'd never once insisted she withhold her testimony. But he'd certainly asked it of her, hadn't he? Gauging the perfect moment of weakness, no less, that night in Leeds when she'd been knotted with tears and desperate to make things right between them. And ever since, he'd implied she held the noose in her hands, reminding her—with subtle, frequent encouragement—of the vital need for silence.

She took another step back, wondering how far she would have to run to reclaim her pride. A mile? A thousand miles?

She waited for him to go on. To further explain his decision, to apologize. The sounds of the day intruded into the aborted conversation. Leaves rustled. The distant sound of girlish laughter hovered, somewhere up the path. But louder than all of it was the pressing clamor of Patrick's silence. She, of all people, knew what that hard quiet meant. He was guilty.

Or at least, he believed himself to be.

Her throat closed over the silence. And then she was stumbling away, choking back her tears, scrambling to follow the blurry path back to the manor.

"Julianne!" Patrick called out from somewhere behind her. "Wait!"

But there was no waiting for this. The memory of that first fumbling night came flooding back. And that glorious night in the folly, and every night since . . . she'd tossed herself on him, like an East End doxy. But worst of all was the haunting realization that she deserved this. All of it—the humiliation, the pain. Perhaps she even deserved worse.

Because hadn't she told the first lie?

Roots and limbs reached out to hinder her blind charge, but she plowed on, desperate to put as much distance between her and Patrick as possible. She had spent three years avoiding the sort of emotionless match that most in the *ton* accepted as their due, determined to find someone who would appreciate her for who she was, rather than who she pretended to be. She had thought . . . well, she had thought wrong.

She was in love with the blasted man. Helplessly, hopelessly in love with him. And he had sold his soul for her silence.

Chapter 22

PATRICK AWAKENED TO a dawn and a marriage bed much colder than he'd expected.

It took him a slow, blinking moment to sort out the difference. Instead of his wife being tangled in his arms, as she had been these few days past, Julianne was hugging the far side of the mattress, curled up tight, a wall of muslin and pale skin that told him her state of mind in no uncertain terms.

Damn it to hell and back. Yesterday had not gone well.

He had told her the truth, a decision that turned out to be far more difficult to manage than his usual inconvenient silence. He regretted not having told her the truth from the first, but he could not regret the decision to marry her. She was the single bright spot out of the entire unholy mess of his life. But how else could he have responded to her trembled accusation? He could no longer remember the reasons he married her, much less justify them.

He had flung himself into this marriage knowing his motivations were wrong, only to discover the sweetest of promises in her kiss. He'd latched on to the hope she would find their union pleasing enough to not question the reasons behind their marriage. And the rub of it was that regardless of why he married her, the reason to *stay* married had nothing to do with her testimony, and everything to do with how she made him feel.

He lay there a moment, adjusting to wakefulness, wanting to gather her in his arms and tell her. To prove that the reason why he had married her no longer mattered. But the sound of oncoming hooves snatched his attention, rattling the windowpanes like distant thunder.

He eased out of bed and pulled the curtains aside. Through the morning mist, he could see three horses— only two with riders—cresting the last swell of Summersby's long drive. He recognized the magistrate's familiar, lean frame, sitting tall in the saddle, and beside him, the stockier frame of someone who looked very much like his cousin, Jonathon Blythe. He could think of no explanation for the fact that the men were riding toward Summersby as if the very hounds of hell were nipping at their heels, except one.

Julianne approached the window, her arms wrapped stiffly around her. "Is it the magistrate?"

"Yes," he admitted, already turning to grab a pair of trousers from his bureau, where Julianne kept them neatly—maddeningly—folded. He might be unable to avoid the coming confrontation, but he had the right to greet the men who would arrest him clad in something other than his unutterables. "Blythe accompanies him. I imagine this means the inquest has returned a charge of murder."

Julianne's night rail billowed around her legs as she stepped up to the window and squinted out into the morning. She stood a long moment, though he knew she could likely make little sense of the view. "Why would Mr. Blythe come to arrest you?"

"Perhaps Farmington felt I might not go willingly." Shippington was a small town. So small, in fact, it had never needed to hire a constable. But a citizen who wished to press charges was legally entitled to make an arrest. "Blythe likely offered his assistance."

"Your cousin hates you enough to not only see you hang, but escort you to the gallows?"

Patrick hesitated. He didn't want to answer these questions, but the fact she was speaking to him—even of such difficult things—was a stark improvement over how they had ended things yesterday. "He has always been determined to best me."

And if not best him, destroy him.

He did not trust Blythe to leave Julianne out of whatever this was that simmered between them, and that sent his feet turning for the door. "Stay here," he told her, worry for Julianne's safety easily outweighing the desire to gather her in his arms and explain away the hurt that had lingered in her eyes since yesterday.

The approaching pair had a riderless horse in tow, for God's sake.

Whatever business brought them here, they did not plan to leave alone.

Patrick strode down the stairwell, two steps at a time. His boots echoed against the mostly silent house. It was early enough the lingering guests were all still abed, though he could hear the voices of some of the early servants, kindling the fire in the parlor. They looked up as he passed, but did not question his direction, and he supposed the dogs dancing attendance at his heels lent his mission some legitimacy.

Mr. Peters was not so easily fooled, however. The aging butler met Patrick at the door in his nightcap, his eyes drawn with worry. "Riders approach, my lord. Should I summon a few sturdy footmen?"

Patrick shook his head. Farmington was widely known as a fair and peaceful magistrate, but Blythe's arrival lent a decidedly different flavor to the morning. He did not trust this to go smoothly, and for better or worse, Patrick was responsible for everything and everyone at Summersby, from the broad-shouldered footmen down to the lowest scullery maid.

He would not see any of them placed in danger now.

"No footmen," he said firmly. "I would be grateful if you would personally summon Lord Avery and ask him to see that Julianne stays in her room." Patrick had a feeling he was going to need an ally in the older man this morning, even if from a distance.

And at the very least, he was going to need someone to hold Julianne back.

The butler nodded his acquiescence. "Very good, my lord. But please . . . have a care. We've just gotten you returned home safely. We would not have you removed from us so soon."

Patrick opened the door, calming himself with a deep draught of morning air. The men were sawing their mounts to a stop, their horses blowing hard. The pair must have departed Shippington when it was still dark, and judging by the froth flying from their mounts, they must have galloped much of the way. Gemmy and Constance nosed their way through the open door and bounded out to greet the dismounting newcomers, barking and jumping up on the men with grass-slick paws. In the uncertain light of dawn, he glimpsed the glint off Blythe's revolver as he raised the butt of it threateningly. Anger suffused through Patrick.

Only cowards—or idiots—threatened dogs with guns.

Patrick whistled sharply, calling the dogs back. Gemmy bounded back toward him, but Constance returned more slowly, her hackles on full display. *Damned ill-behaved dog.*

But not as difficult as her mistress, who even now was emerging in the open doorway beside him. She had thrown on a dress of bright, marigold yellow—living proof she could move quickly when she wanted to—but she'd missed a handful of buttons across the front, and her hair flamed defiantly around her face.

"Julianne, go back to the room," he growled. The looming danger required his full attention, and Julianne's distracting presence had a way of sending his wits to ground. Exasperation crowded into the keen edge of his worry as, far from obeying, she bent down and scooped Constance up in her arms.

"You cannot prevent me from being here, Patrick." She glared up at him over Constance's fur, her determined green eyes a distraction he did not need.

"Damn it, this isn't a social call." Indeed, that was now clear. Jonathon Blythe's pistol was now out on full, pointed display, and Patrick felt perforated by fear. Not fear over what might happen to him. No, the fear of losing his wife to a misfired bullet was by far the more terrifying possibility of the morning.

Julianne ignored his protests and pasted on what he could now recognize as her practiced smile, the one she trotted out for enemies and idiots. "Gentlemen," she called out from the top step. "Lovely morning for a visit."

The magistrate's eyes darted uncertainly between them. "We've . . . er . . . we've not come for a visit, Lady Haversham."

"Oh?" She continued to smile—far too sweetly. "Perhaps you've come for breakfast, then?"

Farmington tipped up the brim of his hat and wiped the sweat away from his brow with the back of an uneasy hand. "We have come to bring you in, Haversham."

"The jury returned a decision on the inquest late yesterday evening," Blythe's self-satisfied voice chimed in. "We've a warrant for your arrest."

Patrick's chest hollowed out beneath the weight of his cousin's words. It was done. The whispered threat that had chased him for eleven months was now officially a murder charge. He scarcely knew whether to laugh or curse at the obvious progress that had been made.

Behind him, muffled shouts rang out. Lord Avery all but tumbled from the house, Mr. Peters on his heels and panting hard. The viscount's hair was sticking out at odd angles, and he was heaving, as if he had jogged the entirety of the way from his room. Yet his eyes were still capable of flashing an aristocratic warning.

"What is this about, Farmington?" he demanded. "Haversham is a peer."

"He's a peer who's been charged with murder," Blythe replied hotly.

"This is an outrage," Avery blustered. "He should be permitted to remain here, at Summersby, or returned to London to await trial. You cannot throw him in gaol like a common criminal."

Blythe demonstrated his apparent disagreement with Lord Avery's opinion by pulling down on the hammer of his pistol. It seated with an audible click. "I assure you, we can."

Patrick cursed low under his breath. Worry for Julianne and all the people he counted among his responsibilities sent him stepping quickly in front of the imminent danger of that cocked pistol. He'd lost his brother to a bullet, for God's sake. He, of all people, knew the mistakes that could be made with a loaded firearm.

"Have a care," Patrick cautioned, holding out his hands in a move he hoped would pacify his hot-blooded cousin. "I'll not resist."

He tried to shut out the sight of Julianne's white face as the irons were placed over his wrists. He was boosted onto the back of the third horse, any chance at a proper good-bye or murmured reassurance yanked rudely from his grasp. Not that she would have likely permitted him such an indulgence, given the way things were being left between them.

As his captors mounted, he sought her attention, if only for the scant seconds he had left. "Wait here for MacKenzie to arrive, as we discussed, Julianne."

She met his request with a mulish silence that made his lungs contract far more efficiently than any thought of what awaited him in gaol. Gemmy whined anxiously and circled his horse's feet. The mare danced in agitation, and Lord Avery put a firm hand on the dog's collar and dragged the terrier back toward the house. Patrick hoped the man intended to show the same degree of sense when it came to his daughter, because there was no way in hell Patrick was going to permit Julianne to visit him in a louse-infested gaol cell, especially not with Jonathon Blythe and his too-easily-cocked pistol standing guard.

"Do not let her come to see me," he warned his father-in-law as his captors pulled his horse roughly into line behind them. "I do not want her involved."

Lord Avery's distant snort followed him down the drive. "You know as well as I that no one can bloody well force her to do anything, Haversham. You've made her a goddamned countess. There'll be no stopping her now."

Chapter 23

JULIANNE FELT HELPLESS as she strode back into Summersby's grand foyer.

The gleaming marble tile and bright, hothouse flowers sitting on the center table seemed madly inappropriate for the turn the morning had taken. Had she once imagined herself here, a grand countess amid such beauty and wealth? The reality—and the responsibility—of it was something far more terrifying.

The desire to strike something, do something, *fix* something proved a roaring counterpoint to her initial blind frustration. He thought she hated him. She'd *made* him think she hated him, when the truth of her emotion was far less black and white. She'd been impetuous and rigid in her attack yesterday, stalking away like a child, believing he deserved a dose of his own poison. But now he was gone and she might never see him again.

A crowd of gawking guests had gathered in the foyer, their hair still mussed from sleep. "Is it true?" one gasped.

"'Tis utterly scandalous."

Aunt Margaret stood at the foot of the stairs, her ridiculous turban left off for once to reveal a head full of gray hair. "I hear they suspect him of the earl's murder too."

That piece of it nearly made Julianne's pulse stutter to a stop. *By the stars.* Could someone really believe that of him? Patrick had been in Scotland these past eleven months, nowhere close to Yorkshire. He *couldn't* have killed his father.

But that did not mean others did not believe it, or that the motives people wished to pin on him were not shaped by a terrible logic.

"I ask that you all return to your rooms," she said drawing her fury up tight. "Mr. Peters, I would like breakfast to be moved to eleven this morning. Given the unsettling events of the morning, I think a light repast will be more than sufficient."

Peters inclined his head. "Of course, my lady. It shall be done."

Her gaze moved next to Patrick's mother. Julianne could not immediately tell if the woman's white face was due to worry over Patrick, or fury over the way Julianne had just assumed control over the household. "You do not look well," she said, reaching a hand out to squeeze Lady Haversham's hand. The older woman's skin was cool, clammy to the touch. In contrast, Julianne felt as though there was a fire kindling beneath her skin. "Is there something I can do for you?"

She half expected Patrick's mother to scream that she had done enough. After all, this was all her fault, in so many ways. But instead, her mother-in-law's brown eyes, so much like Patrick's, rose to meet hers. "No. You have it all in hand, as should be. I know you care for my son, and he cares for you as well. I am grateful to you, for more than you can know. Just help us, please. Help *him*."

Julianne felt humbled—and shocked—by Lady Haversham's trust. Clearly, Patrick had not explained his motives in marrying her to his family, any more than he'd explained them to her. It was obvious he loved his family. Their safety and happiness was the most important thing to him. Indeed, he'd married her to save them. No matter how she felt about him, or how he felt about her, she would not rest until she saw the door slammed shut on this tragedy she had kicked open.

"I will," she promised her mother-in-law. "I swear to you."

One more face came into focus as Patrick's mother made her way unsteadily up the stairs. Her father was standing near the front door, and for the first time Julianne realized he had been standing back, watching her bark orders. She flushed, imagining he must be about to chastise her in some way. Instead, he said, "What is your plan, Julianne?"

"My plan?" she echoed.

"I presume you and Patrick spoke of what might be needed in the event of his arrest?"

She hesitated, surprised her father had not inserted his usual authoritative opinion into this mix. She knew how to plan, even if doing so was not always her first inclination. She might have impulsively gone to Scotland to find Patrick on little more than a whim, but she'd also plotted for days how to procure that first initial waltz with him. She had an impulsive nature—a fact she refused to apologize for—but when her attentions and her inclinations were properly harnessed, she'd proven herself well.

She needed some of that same nerve at the moment.

"Aunt Margaret said Patrick was suspected in the earl's recent death. Is it true?"

At her father's nod, she swallowed the fear that wanted to sink its claws into her. "He couldn't have done it, Father. Patrick has been in Scotland these past eleven months. He's witnesses there who can prove it."

"He'll need them, I'm afraid."

Julianne's thoughts raced in time with her pulse. "James MacKenzie traveled on to London to take care of legal matters for Patrick. He will have need of his friend's counsel, and MacKenzie can also serve as a witness. Now that Patrick has been arrested, there is no time to lose."

"I suppose you think I should go to London to fetch him?" At Julianne's nod, her father stroked his beard, thinking. "Haversham is important enough to you that you would send me away at a time like this?"

The memory of yesterday's argument hung like a full moon in her mind. But even with all that had passed between them, the answer that came to her lips was still instantaneous, still sure. "He is."

Her father nodded. "Then of course, I'll go immediately." He smiled grimly as he turned toward the stairs. "I confess, you seem well capable of managing affairs here without me."

The praise slipped past her as her father left, a welcome surprise. She turned toward the study, determined to pen a letter for her father to carry to London in his quest to find James MacKenzie, only to pull up short when she realized she still had an audience of sorts.

George Willoughby leaned casually against the wall of the nearby hallway, looking as though he'd just been pulled from bed. She raised a startled hand to her chest. "Oh! Mr. Willoughby." At his raised brow, she corrected herself. "That is, *George*. You startled me."

He pushed off the wall with a lazy shoulder. "How

are you managing, Julianne? I regret Haversham has put us all through this. And did I hear correctly that your father is leaving too? You've been abandoned, left here all alone."

Julianne blinked. "I'm hardly alone. I've Mr. Peters and the dowager countess and family to think of, certainly." She lifted a finger to one temple, wondering if she could rub him out of her way. "Truly, I am fine, George."

His eyes swept her person, to the floor and back up, as if he did not believe her claim. "We've at least three hours until breakfast. I would spend them comforting you."

Julianne raised a brow. "*Comforting* me?"

He shrugged. "Offering my assistance. You must know I would do anything for you."

Julianne swallowed her annoyance. Perhaps she could assign him some mindless task. Or demand he put on some clothes. But it occurred to her he would not be easily put off, and that moreover, with his easygoing smile and knowledge of Summersby, perhaps there *was* something useful he could do. "Can you ensure the needs of the guests are met?" She pulled a smile out of her arsenal. Knew it was working when he perked to attention. "Patrick wished them to be permitted to stay as long as they wished, and I confess I lack the capacity to play the doting hostess at the moment."

"Of course, Julianne." He breathed her name, almost reverently, and his straight white teeth flashed like a mirror in sunlight. "It is the very least I can do. I am completely at your disposal."

A ruffle of unease shifted through her, like a change on the wind. She needed to focus on Patrick's defense, not worry about how to deflect Willoughby's panting adoration. But there was little she could do at the moment besides smile benignly and hope his "disposal" kept him well out of her path.

"HAD ENOUGH YET, Haversham?"

Jonathon Blythe's voice reached through the red-rimmed haze and yanked Patrick back to vivid consciousness.

His eyes slowly focused on the gaol's damp stone walls. The smell of urine clung about the place, a testament to the gaol's more common use as a place for Shippington's less cautious souls to sleep off a bender. Hell, Patrick had spent his own sixteenth birthday in this very cell, urged to ill celebratory judgment by Eric and a barkeep who was far too deferential to refuse the earl's sons anything. But today, the stone walls he remembered had been turned over to a more formidable use.

Patrick spit out a mouthful of blood onto the gaol's dusty, disused floor, his ears still ringing from the last blow Blythe had delivered. He ought to feel helpless, tied to a wooden chair while his cousin used him as a punching bag. In a fair fight, Patrick could have acquitted himself well. He'd done more than just study at Cambridge.

This, however, was not Cambridge, and this was nothing close to a fair fight.

Still, Patrick did not regret turning himself over to this arrest. His relatively peaceful surrender had pulled his pistol-waving cousin away from Summersby. Patrick could do nothing more now except wait for MacKenzie and pray that Blythe did not become more unhinged.

And for every blow that fell, he'd be glad his cousin was here, swinging at him instead of Julianne.

Blythe circled to the left, and Patrick braced himself

for the coming blow which—if he was to reach for any sort of a silver lining—came and went quickly, and ensured the unpleasant ringing in his right ear now had a matched partner in the left.

"*Enough*, Mr. Blythe." The magistrate's disapproval rang sharply throughout the cell. Farmington leaned closer, his face white around the edges. "The inquest has already determined the charge of murder. There is no need to continue in this vein."

Blythe cracked his knuckles. "There is still the matter of the earl's death to sort out."

A denial set up in Patrick's ears, even as he gingerly tested the movement of his jaw. "I did not kill my father or my brother, Blythe. A beating will not change that truth."

"The truth?" Blythe barked. "What do you know of the *truth*? It's as plain as Hades you've married the only witness to keep her from testifying, and orchestrated the whole thing to subvert justice. Thank goodness the coroner saw fit to see justice served."

Patrick set his thankfully unbroken jaw against his cousin's accusation. He might have started out with such an indelicate mission in mind, but so much had changed between Julianne and himself that he could scarcely identify his original reasons for marrying her.

Not that she seemed inclined to listen to him on that front.

"You always thought you were smarter than the lot of us," his cousin went on, "but this time your bloody arrogance has caught up with you. Because the inquest didn't need her testimony after all, did it? You murdered your brother, and then poisoned your father, all to acquire the title." He drew in a ragged breath. "The title you never deserved."

Anger welled up, hotter than blood. "By the balls, I didn't kill my brother, *or* my father."

"You certainly benefited from their deaths, though." Jonathon Blythe's voice shook, and for the first time Patrick caught a glimpse of the man's motivation in moving these charges forward. Grief was etched there, in the lines around his eyes and the tremor of his hands.

"I had no hand in my father's death, Blythe. I've been in Scotland the past eleven months, and have witnesses who can place me there." Damn, but he needed Mac-Kenzie right now. What in the devil was keeping the man so long?

Farmington leaned in, and Patrick could smell the man's sour distaste for the proceedings roll off him. "Haversham, I do not like seeing you so ill-used, but Blythe raises a serious accusation. It will go better for you if you simply tell us the truth. Did you have a hand in your father's death?"

Patrick leaned back, knowing the truth was not what they sought. He'd hoped to be able to reason with the magistrate, but with Blythe's right hook flying so indiscriminately, it seemed that polite discourse was the furthest thing from either man's agenda—unless the discourse involved confessing to a crime he hadn't committed.

"This line of questioning is finished," he told them, even as he braced himself for another blow. "I will speak no further without my counsel present."

Chapter 24

SHIPPINGTON WAS A town of two lazy streets and a few hundred people. Despite arriving in the middle of an apparent market day—complete with a parade of sheep through the middle of town—it took Julianne approximately three seconds to find the magistrate's office. She headed toward the stone building with its blue-painted shutters. Her feet might be on a collision course with mayhem but her constitution was proving more reluctant. She'd felt nauseated most of the morning, but was it any wonder?

Patrick had spent last night in the town's gaol, while she had laid her head on a pillow that seemed to gradually—maddeningly—lose his scent.

She leaned her hand against the door frame to Farmington's office and breathed in deeply, trying to settle her faithless stomach. The door opened without warning. Scrambling back, she put a hand to her mouth—as much to cover her explanation of surprise as ensure nothing unforgivable came out of it.

Dr. Merial stepped out, pulling his hat down over his brow. He stopped when he saw her. "Good morning, Lady Haversham. Is anything amiss?"

Julianne shook her head. "I've come to ask Mr. Farmington for permission to visit the gaol." She swallowed the bile still lingering in her throat. "I'm not sure if you've heard, Dr. Merial, but my husband was arrested yesterday." It made her feel ill just to utter the words. She'd scarcely ever given Britain's prison system a moment's thought beyond the fact it kept madmen and criminals from bothering innocent citizens, but everything she'd ever read in the *Times* came flooding back now.

The doctor's face betrayed his prior knowledge. "I've heard," he answered grimly. "Mr. Blythe was in the King's Widge last night, sharing all the sordid details." He eyed her speculatively. "Truly, you look terrible. Have you been sleeping?"

"It is just a little nausea. But why are *you* here?" Worry speared her, worry that she might have come all this way only to find Mr. Farmington discomposed. "Is the magistrate ill?"

"No, I was summoned for a different matter entirely." He cocked his head, as if sorting out a puzzle. "Have you any fever?"

Julianne shook her head. "Truly, Dr. Merial. I'm already feeling much better." She tried on a too-tight smile, the sort Patrick—but no one else—would have seen right through.

He smiled encouragingly. "Ah. Well then, nausea without fever is not a cause for alarm in a young married woman of otherwise good health. But, if I may offer a word of advice . . . I do not recommend using Shippington's midwife on these matters. The woman is one hundred years old, if she's a day."

Julianne's cheeks warmed. "I've been married but a few weeks, Dr. Merial. I assure you, it is premature for any discussion of that nature."

"Of course." His dark eyes flashed with humor. "But just in case, you might try eating something bland, such as dry toast, upon first rising. It . . . er . . . helps."

Oh good heavens. It seemed Mr. Blythe had discussed more than just Patrick's arrest at the King's Widge last night. "That is *not* why I married my husband," she insisted. Truly, it was for a far less palatable reason. She might have preferred the rumor as truth.

The doctor smiled, which had the grave misfortune of making him appear even more handsome. Julianne stared at his straight white teeth, mesmerized by the flash of them. Good gracious. No wonder the entire house had been atwitter during the dinner party.

She fished for a diversion, anything to draw his attention away from her and what might or might not have been the cause of her hasty marriage. "It is said you were of great comfort to the earl in the hours before he died. The family is grateful for your kindness."

"I only wish I could have done more. His rapid decline surprised me greatly. He was, by all accounts, a man in excellent health, even a week before his death."

Julianne's stomach rolled precipitously. "Are you saying there is some truth to the rumors that the earl's death might have been caused by something untoward?"

Merial's hands tightened around the handle of his bag. "I am new from university, and have little enough experience in determining such things. But in truth, I am hard-pressed to deny his decline might have been assisted by something more mortal. I am afraid that is why I was summoned to the magistrate's offices today. Mr. Farmington wanted to question me on the matter. I was asked here this morning to provide a statement under oath."

Fear threaded its way through her. "Do you believe my husband was involved?"

"No." He offered her a small shake of his head. "But I cannot prove it, one way or the other. And regardless of my opinion, all that matters is that others clearly do."

"I see," she said.

And unfortunately, she did. Was it not enough to hang an innocent man once, they needed to charge him with a second murder, just to be sure?

She fought off a fresh wave of nausea as Dr. Merial tipped his hat and took his leave. This was not the time to be ill . . . this was the time to *act*. Because as she knocked on the magistrate's door, her thoughts tripped over the chilling realization that not only had there been one murder at Summersby, there had likely been two. But whoever had killed Patrick's father would have needed to be at Summersby *before* the funeral.

And that meant the list of potential suspects was smaller than they had imagined.

MORE THAN THE silence, Patrick hated the rats.

Not because they skittered over him as he lay on his bunk, jarring him awake with a whisper of toes. Not even because they gnawed at his food and fouled his drinking water when he tried to stretch those precious commodities. No, he hated the rats because they were free to come and go. They appeared out of nowhere, flattening their rib cages to squeeze through holes no bigger than a fingernail. He could respect such creatures of stealth and wisdom, even as they mocked his own desperate straits.

But he didn't have to like them.

He had no idea how much time had passed. Two hours, two days, it all blurred together with the removal of sunlight. But now the sound of the door to his cell opening sent him scrambling to his feet and the rats scuttling for holes. A light was lifted aloft, and his eyes blinked warily against the breached darkness.

But the sight that greeted him as his eyes adjusted to the light's intrusion was neither Blythe, returning for another piece of him, nor another awful meal to replace the congealed porridge he'd been given earlier. It was Julianne, accompanied by Mr. Farmington, and the sight of her in his filthy cell proved as sharp and breath-robbing as the light from her lantern.

For a moment Patrick could only blink, his eyes running over her swoop of a chin, lifted in challenge. When Farmington stepped out and the door swung shut behind her, she set the lantern down with the slightest hesitation. And then she flung herself into his arms with a sudden rush of movement. He could do naught but catch her up, having neither the strength nor the good sense to push her away.

He held her a long, trembling moment, though he was sure he would sully her merely with the air he exhaled from his lungs. He absorbed the feel of her, shored up his reserves in preparation for the time when that door would swing shut on her and he would be wrapped in darkness again. Her hands scraped against his injured ribs, and the slight groan of pain gave him away.

She drew back and peered up at him. "What have they done to you?" she whispered, her hands cupping each side of his face. "What have *I* done to you?"

He winced against the stark questions he saw there, and the way her fingertip traced some unseen injury below one of his eyes. "It is nothing, Julianne." He set her away from him with jaw-gritting determination. "Why in the devil did you come here? I specifically asked you not to. These are not kind men who hold me."

"You didn't ask me, Patrick, you ordered me about as

if I hadn't a choice in the manner. Which, of course, I do. Mr. Farmington was not pleased with my request to visit you this morning, but I eventually talked him around." She untied the string to her bonnet and removed it carefully from her head. "We've a quarter hour. I would not spend it arguing with you over whether I should or should not have come."

Her mention of the magistrate made his teeth grit in anger. Of *course* the man had permitted her this visit, particularly after Patrick had refused to confess during his interrogation. Farmington probably had an ear to the door just now, listening for clues that might be used in the eventual trial. And what did she expect to *do* in this hard-won quarter of an hour, with naught but his bloodied person and a squalid cell to entertain her?

He breathed her in as if she were the very air, but she was a gift he could not have, and a distraction he did not want. Even now, her body held in stiff defiance, he could see the cogs in that pretty head turning with ruthless intent. He didn't want her putting those hidden freckles to the ground and sussing out more danger, not when he wasn't there to protect her.

"I asked you to stay away for your own safety, not because I didn't want to see you." He'd told her not to come, not to meddle. Yet here she was, in his cell, and damned if she didn't smell like a bloody cake, fresh from the oven, which only sent his temper—and other unnamed emotions—spiking higher. "Jonathon Blythe is not opposed to using violence to achieve his goals, and Farmington proved little better yesterday."

They faced off, two determined souls, neither willing to give an inch. "I am perfectly safe, Patrick," came her firm retort.

"The very fact that you are here suggests otherwise.

You could fall ill, or be charged with conspiracy." He stared down at her in growing irritation. Christ, she looked . . . exquisite. Like a flame-haired ghost, haunting his private hell. Impertinent gown she had on too, some confection of air and lace that made her skin glow to perfection, even here in the squalor of this cell. "I do not want you anywhere close to their crosshairs, Julianne."

A long, wordless moment passed before she spoke again. "I spoke briefly with Dr. Merial this morning. He told Farmington he believes your father might have been murdered. Were you aware such accusations were being lodged against you?"

Her words burrowed into his brain. It was not a new idea, and so he did not react as he might once have, but it *was* new to hear it fall from Julianne's lips. "Are you asking if I killed my father?" he asked hoarsely.

"No." She shook her head, and raised her voice. "It never crossed my mind. I think the more logical presumption is that whoever killed your brother also killed your father."

"Please, Julianne." He glanced toward the door. "I would ask you to keep your voice down."

"But whoever killed your father would have needed to be at Summersby *before* your father died," she whispered, still far too loudly. "Which narrows our list of suspects down quite a bit, don't you think?"

Patrick tried to find his voice. He'd hoped Avery's warning would come to naught, that it was nothing more than a rumor, a twisting of facts against him. He hadn't truly *believed* his father might have died from unreasonable circumstances. But Dr. Merial was an excellent physician, as well as a friend. If the doctor believed the earl had been murdered, Patrick was inclined to trust the man.

Julianne had cobbled together a logical, chilling explanation he had not previously considered. He'd initially presumed the person who had wanted Eric dead was someone from whom his brother had borrowed money. But she was right. The pieces of this puzzle could easily fit into a far more sinister shape. He could come up with *two* men who made sense. Always underfoot. Always wanting more than they had.

A person who murdered an earl was mad, desperate, or stupid. Truly, either of his bloody cousins could fit the bill.

"It could be Blythe," he admitted. "Or Willoughby."

Julianne shook her head. "I cannot believe it of George. He would never do such a thing."

The air between them stilled. "George, is it?" Patrick's voice deepened with distrust. "I do not like how close you have become with Willoughby."

"He believes you are innocent. And I think we both know that George Willoughby is far too simple to be involved in such a complex plot."

"There are layers to both men you don't understand," he warned her. Hell, he was beginning to suspect there were layers to both men *he* didn't understand, and he'd practically grown up with them. George Willoughby might be too simple to conceive of a murder plot, but he was proving devilishly clever sidling up to Julianne.

But he shook off the pull of petty jealousy, and concentrated instead on the facts as he knew them. He could not deny that, given their history, Blythe made more sense as the killer.

"I need to find Prudence." Julianne's voice echoed rudely across the low stone ceiling.

Patrick glanced toward the door. He could see a light hovering, in the crack just above the floor. "I am not yet ready to discuss such things with Farmington," he warned.

"She saw the killer pull the trigger, Patrick," she argued, though she at least lowered her voice. "If I can put her in front of Blythe, she can identify him."

"No. If Blythe is our man this is infinitely more dangerous. It is not safe for you to be involved." Hadn't his cousin already proven himself capable of violence, especially when expended in the name of a cause he believed in? But what was the cause here? Patrick could think of little by way of human emotion that could justify such an urge as murder. Love and family certainly knocked around at the top of that list. In this moment, he could well imagine killing someone who threatened those he loved.

He refused to be moved by the flash of hurt surprise on his wife's face. After so much recent loss in his life, the thought of losing her was untenable. Quite simply, saving her neck was worth risking her ire.

"I am more capable than you credit me." Her voice remained calm, though her words were thickened with distrust. "I would not say anything that would alter your defense."

"Christ above, Julianne." The devil take it, she made him feel bloody powerless. "I am not worried about the danger in what you might say. I am worried about what the killer might do. To *you*. Whoever this is, he is a dangerous man. I will not have you in harm's way."

The door swung open. Farmington's shadow fell across them, dividing them more effectively than any fence. "Your time is up, Lady Haversham," he told her, his face unreadable.

Patrick shook off the thought of the coming darkness and the rodents that would emerge with it. Any thought of his own discomfort paled in comparison to the worry that sliced through him now. "For God's sake, please do not investigate this any further on your own," he told her, not even caring that Farmington could hear every word of their exchange now. "It is too dangerous."

And I do not want to lose you too.

"I will be careful," was her only response. And then she stepped out of the cell and the darkness closed in once more.

Patrick stared at the place where she had just stood, imagining he could still see her, still smell her unique fragrance. It was a hell of a thing to be locked in gaol while your wife ran amok. Impotent rage streaked through him as he reimagined their conversation and still arrived at the same maddening conclusion.

She was going after Prudence. He could see it in the tilt of her jaw. Fear was a paralyzing thing, and he was undeniably afraid for her.

Because if she insisted on investigating these events on her own, he was terrified she could very well find herself the killer's next victim.

Chapter 25

Two things soon became clear. Prudence was proving devilishly difficult to find.

And George Willoughby was trying to drive Julianne mad.

Whereas the gentleman had once been content to merely offer his smiles and besotted glances, he now turned himself over to the business of making himself indispensable. He fetched her slippers. Insisted on reading to her, as if it was too taxing for her brain to hold a book *and* be female. He used words like "rest" and "gentle" and "please." In his efforts, she could see echoes of those men of the *ton* who had pursued her these past three Seasons, men who saw her only as an object to be admired, petted, cosseted.

Far from making her feel better, it made her miss her husband. Not because she required male attention, but because she was beginning to realize why she had been attracted to Patrick in the first place. In contrast to Willoughby's fawning attentions, Patrick treated her like an equal. Oh, he argued with her. Ordered her about rudely at times, and railed against her at others. Pushed her against walls and kissed her senseless. But never did he treat her as though she was some fragile flower, bound to be crushed beneath his boot with a single misstep, not even when he was truly—and reasonably—worried for her safety.

Worse, she'd been unable to locate Prudence, despite two more trips into town. The former maid had completely abandoned her post at the seamstress's shop, and it seemed likely that she—and Julianne's five sovereigns—were now in Leeds, blending into the working-class woodwork there. With MacKenzie not yet returned from London and Farmington refusing her requests to see Patrick again, she felt shackled by ineptitude, and desperate to do something. *Anything.*

Anything except tolerate Willoughby.

"You should accompany me to church today," George said as he followed her to the breakfast table on Sunday morning.

Julianne glowered at him as she settled into her chair. When had he stopped asking questions and begun presuming he knew her mind? "Actually, I had thought to take a trip into Leeds."

"Is that wise?" He moved to pour her a cup of tea at the sideboard. "You seem out of sorts. And Leeds is some distance away."

She couldn't deny she *felt* out of sorts. A faint sense of nausea had trailed her all week, but it seemed to have grown claws this morning. "Nonetheless, I have business there. You should ask someone else to accompany you to church. The dowager countess, perhaps. And I feel sure Aunt Margaret would be willing to accompany you, if you ask her."

"Sitting in church with Aunt Margaret would make it difficult to pray for her departure." George set a cup of tea down in front of her and smiled, one conspirator to another. "She's the only one who refuses to leave, you know."

Julianne glanced down at her cup, staring at the innocuous curl of steam hovering about the porcelain rim. "Not the *only* one, surely."

After all, *he* was still here, handily underfoot.

The tea was a perfect example. George had taken to bringing her cup after cup of the vile beverage, this one sweetened with honey, that one flavored with rosehips. The thing was, she didn't *like* tea, however unpatriotic a sentiment that might be. She would have much preferred chocolate. But she clamped her lips around the thought as George sat down beside her, because to give voice to it would surely result in an avalanche of the sweet drink.

"Aunt Margaret is the only one who has decided to stay on, despite my encouragement otherwise." George reached for a piece of toast and spread it with jam and clotted cream before laying it on Julianne's plate. "The last of the guests left this morning."

Julianne looked up in surprise over the rim of her cup. For the first time, it occurred to her that the table stretched empty on either side. It didn't matter that she couldn't normally see her guests with any clarity beyond the fifth or sixth seat—there were clearly no faces to be seen this morning. She eyed the man who had orchestrated it all. George *looked* his usual benign self. Brown eyes, mild smile. His clothing had been selected to accentuate—if not outright exaggerate—the breadth of his shoulders, and his brown hair had been carefully combed into compliance. But he sounded like someone else entirely.

"You've evicted them?" she demanded. She'd scarcely thought of Aunt Margaret these past few days beyond someone to generally avoid, but the woman was not being particularly troublesome at the moment. In fact, given the choice of Willoughby or Aunt Margaret's company this morning, she'd be hard-pressed not to pick the latter. "Without consulting me first?"

"You were the one who put the idea in my head, asking me to see to the needs of the guests."

She drew a deep breath. "My husband clearly indicated he wished to extend our hospitality, as his father had always done. You had no right, George."

"Your husband is not here. And you need to rest." George reached over and tucked a napkin across her lap. "But do not worry," he said, ending on a smile. "I think I can hurry Aunt Margaret along in another few days."

"I did not ask you to hurry her along. I do not require your protection, George."

His hand moved suggestively from the napkin to squeeze her thigh. "Julianne, I want to protect you. And should the worst happen—although I am sure we can all agree we hope it doesn't come to that—I want you to know that I would fight to keep the title within our family, and offer you the protection of my name."

Julianne stared at him, incredulous. "What *name*, George? If Patrick is found guilty and hanged, the title will revert to the Crown."

The hand in her lap shifted from a squeeze to a patronizing weight. "I was as devastated as anyone when it seemed the title was in jeopardy. But Jonathon Blythe has spoken with several influential people in London during these past difficult months. He assures me the Crown would likely consider a close relative's petition to be awarded the title."

Julianne eyed George Willoughby with a dawning horror. Blythe was making inquiries into whether he might qualify to be considered for the title? As far as motives went, it was every bit as logical as the one people wished to pin on Patrick.

"But until it comes to that, I'll not have you dance attendance on a woman who should have left a week ago," George blundered on. "Not when you are expecting."

For heaven's sake. Shouldn't *George* have left a week ago? She opened her mouth, about to snap that she was most assuredly not expecting anything but his own swift departure, when Mr. Peters stepped into the dining room and cleared his throat.

"Mr. James MacKenzie has arrived, my lady. I've brought him straight in, as you requested."

"Oh, thank heavens." Julianne twisted around in her seat, grateful for a reprieve from the unpleasant surprise George Willoughby was turning out to be. Her stomach cartwheeled at the sight of James MacKenzie, looming tall behind the butler's shoulder. His clothes bore the imprint of travel, and his face was marred by a new slash of beard. But she had never been so glad to see a dusty, dirty soul in her life.

"Mr. MacKenzie." She gained her feet. A rush of dizziness made the floor slip beneath her feet, and she placed a steadying hand on the back of her chair. "I am so relieved to see you. I trust my father explained the current situation?"

"Aye. I came as soon as I could. Your father will be a day yet, some business in London." MacKenzie's gaze swung across the table, his eyes narrowing on George. "How is Haversham?"

"He's still being held at the Shippington gaol."

MacKenzie frowned. "I had hoped he might have been transferred to North Riding, at least. Is he well?"

"I do not know," Julianne admitted. "I visited him

the day after his arrest, but the magistrate has refused my requests to see him again."

The solicitor uttered a brogue-rich curse, then spun on his heel. Julianne scrambled to follow him down the hallway into the foyer. "Let me have the coach called up, and we can take it into town together."

"No, lass, that's a poor idea all around. I've a horse I rented from Leeds that will carry me there well enough. You'll only slow me down. Patrick's been rotting in gaol for almost a week, not knowing where I am. I'll not have him thinking I've abandoned him too."

Julianne's leap to understanding was swiftly cruel. "I have not abandoned him!"

"No?" MacKenzie jerked his chin toward the dining room, and Julianne imagined she could see disappointment in his green eyes. "Your cozy breakfast suggests otherwise."

Julianne gasped, though her outrage was tinged with guilt as well. "George Willoughby is Patrick's cousin. There is naught between us that is improper."

"The gentleman had his hands in your lap. Your mind does not seem on your husband, Lady Haversham."

Julianne gathered herself for a proper denial, but just as her mouth was opening, she was struck by an unexpected maelstrom in her gut. She pitched for the umbrella stand, the contents of her stomach ejecting in great, heaving rolls. Embarrassment and nausea colluded against her, and a long moment passed before she had the courage to look back up at her guest.

"How long have you been feeling poorly?" he asked, a curious expression on his face.

A gray cloud crept in on the edge of her vision. "A touch of upset, nothing to be concerned about. Probably the clotted cream, at breakfast. Although . . . I don't know how I am going to explain the umbrellas to Mr. Peters."

He lifted a dark brow. "Georgette keeps a chamber pot at hand when she feels poorly. Of course, I try to keep a wide berth on those days." He pulled on his hat and reached for the front door. "If you are feeling ill, all the more reason to stay here instead of taking the coach to Shippington. Patrick needs your strength, Lady Haversham, not your theatrics."

Chapter 26

Patrick had come to dread the scrape of keys at his cell door.

Beyond what the opening of that door meant to him, he lived in continual worry of what the scrape of those keys might mean for Julianne. He'd dreamed, on more than one occasion, the door might swing open to reveal someone bearing news of her injury or worse. And so, as the unmistakable sound reached his ears, he gained his feet, readying himself for the worst.

But the worry Patrick carried on his shoulders lightened as James MacKenzie ducked his familiar dark head into the cell, a lantern in one hand.

"Bloody hell, MacKenzie." Patrick grinned around the sight of him. "At last you decide to grace me with your presence. I figured you'd decided I was guilty after all."

James chuckled. "The only thing you are guilty of is questionable hygiene." He enveloped Patrick in a back-slapping hug as the door swung shut behind him. "Still refusing to bathe, I see."

Patrick twisted out of his friend's bruising grip, his ribs healing, but still not quite up to the task of such an enthusiastic greeting. "I'm glad to see you."

James snorted. "I'm pleased *someone* is, because your gaoler seems to be of the opposite opinion. Mr. Blythe nearly tore off a limb when I informed him your solicitor was here to see you, and moreover, to demand your removal to North Riding." James eyed the closed door with an upraised brow. "Is Shippington so small they must conscript your cousin to serve as guard?"

"I assure you, the man is more intent on keeping me locked away than any hired thug," Patrick said dryly. "Where in the blazes have you been?"

James hesitated, and glanced toward the closed door again. "Things in London took longer than I expected, but I was able to settle the matter of your petition. Can we speak freely, or is there someplace else I should request you be moved?"

Patrick shrugged. "I am not sure we'll be given an opportunity for anything more private. Let us talk, but try to keep your voice low."

James sat down on the narrow cot, and set the lantern down beside him. "Your petition has been filed, and they are preparing to convene a special session in the House of Lords, although I'll not be permitted to defend you there. I've found you a serjeant-at-law, though given what the man charges, it is likely to be a painful experience." James's eyes narrowed. "Although I suppose pain is relative. You look as though you're in need of more than just a bit of soap to set you to rights. I see they've been trying to beat a confession out of you."

"I've given them naught."

"Good lad." James hesitated a telling moment. "And how are you getting on with the delectable Julianne?" He grinned. "Still inhabiting separate rooms, I see."

"I'll admit, things could be improved at the moment."

Patrick winced. "Being here is certainly not helping my circumstances."

"No, I'd imagine it isn't." James's grin fell away, and he studied him with eyes sharp as talons. "Haversham . . . about your wife. Do you trust her?"

Patrick knew not even a second's hesitation. "Aye. She's proven herself loyal, I'd say. Refused to testify against me. Tried to take on the whole of my relatives, merely for voicing a few negative opinions. I think the bigger question is whether she should trust *me*."

"Oh?"

"She knows why I married her." He dragged a hand through his hair. "I would not be surprised if she hates me now. I've been a terrible husband, all told. But why would you ask such a thing?"

"Because I've come from Summersby this morning, and she is acting deucedly strange."

Patrick's thoughts jerked hard to center. "What in the hell are you talking about?"

"She took ill this morning. Cast up her accounts, right in front of me. I've seen it happen to people who are struggling under a tremendous amount of guilt."

Patrick's hands balled to fists. "Damn it, man, why didn't you say something from the start?" He had never struck his friend in anger, though they had certainly engaged in their share of good-natured sparring. He stood on the verge of rectifying that oversight now. "If she is ill, you should have told me immediately."

The Scotsman shrugged. "Your wife's condition is not my primary concern. *Yours* is, and seeing you released. Although . . . I am not sure that illness or guilt are the only possible explanations for the theatrical bit of nausea I saw this morning. Georgette had much the same look about her during the early part of her pregnancy. Couldn't stand to look at food, and even ordinary smells would send her running." James offered him an indelicate sniff. "Perhaps it's a good thing she isn't here to see you. You're enough to turn *my* stomach, right enough."

Patrick stilled against his friend's suggestion. "Are you implying Julianne may be pregnant?" The idea rolled around in his head. Gathered speed. "It is far too early," he protested, even as hope began to strangle logic. "We've been married only a few weeks."

"She's a dramatic sort. You've admitted as much yourself. Perhaps such things might affect her earlier than other women." MacKenzie's matter-of-fact observation made Patrick want to plant a fist in his friend's mouth, never mind that his statement was deadly accurate. "Of course, you might want to make sure it's yours. Because she's become very cozy with your cousin George Willoughby."

Bloody hell. Patrick had meant it when he'd said he trusted Julianne. He did not think her infatuated with his cousin. But he'd not ruled Willoughby out as a suspect—certainly not with enough assurance he felt comfortable knowing Julianne was so close to him.

But of course, MacKenzie didn't know any of this.

And so Patrick told his friend everything. About Prudence, and the fact that his brother's gun had never been fired, and the suspicions about his father's death. And as he related the course of events, he became increasingly consumed by desperation.

"So your cousin, Jonathon Blythe—who even now is sitting outside this cell, while you rot inside it—is your primary suspect for Eric's death?" James asked, close to incredulous.

Patrick nodded grimly. "And my father's, as well."

"And Blythe is also the party responsible for bruising your ribs?"

Another nod. "Julianne's illness . . ." Patrick's voice rang hoarse, but oh God, it hurt to think of what this all could mean. "It could be something more sinister. My father was *poisoned*. And I am not there to protect her."

A frown spread across his friend's face. "Well then." James rose to his feet, his hands balled to fists. "It sounds like we need to fetch the magistrate."

JULIANNE AWOKE IN a state of confusion, blinking against the gray light threading its way through the bedroom window. She lay a moment, the air in the room too still, too heavy for comfort.

And then she remembered. She'd taken ill in front of Mr. MacKenzie, casting up her accounts in the umbrella stand, of all things.

Someone—Aunt Margaret, perhaps?—had brought her a ginger water to rinse her mouth, which had helped, but then had come the awful vertigo that had sent the walls spinning like a child's toy and forced her to lie down on the bed and close her eyes. And that was the last she remembered until waking in a room as quiet as a tomb.

Gingerly, she tested her limbs, which were thankfully in working order. Her stomach seemed to have quieted dramatically, thank the stars. The stillness was odd. Summersby was never still. There was always someone about, servants chattering in the hallway, or the girls' feet pounding in the upstairs nursery. Shouldn't there be someone about? A dog, or a maid, perhaps?

The ever-lingering George Willoughby?

The first splatters of rain began to pelt her window, and she pulled herself from bed to peer out at a building storm. It seemed the weather today was determined to match her health. Or perhaps her condition had soured on account of the gathering clouds. Of course, she didn't need a gray sky to justify her black mood. Though her poor, pitching stomach was much improved over its performance earlier this morning, she had a perfectly reasonable reason to feel emotionally out of sorts.

James MacKenzie had accused her of unfaithfulness, and then gone on to see Patrick in the gaol without her.

She made her way downstairs, her feet unsteady enough that she had to grip the banister for support. How she felt made not a whit of difference. Whatever she might have hoped to salvage of her marriage would surely be lost the moment the Scotsman mentioned his suspicions. She needed to go to Patrick immediately, to explain that Mr. MacKenzie had dreadfully misinterpreted whatever he thought he'd seen.

But Mr. Peters shook his head, clearly nonplussed at her request to have the coach called up. "I am terribly sorry, my lady, but I was not aware you were planning to travel today. The coach has taken the household into Shippington to attend Sunday services." He hesitated. "We were led to believe you were resting above stairs and were told not to disturb you. But if you are feeling better, you've a visitor, just arrived. She was most insistent on waiting for you. I've installed her in the green salon."

"Mr. Peters, I do not think I am up for receiving anyone today."

"Shall I turn Miss Smith away?"

Julianne's senses marched toward alert. "Miss *Prudence* Smith?"

He inclined his big head, kindly concern in his eyes. "Yes, my lady. But if you are not feeling up for it—"

But Julianne was already hurrying toward the green

salon, as fast as her unsteady feet could carry her. Her eyes fixed on a familiar dark head, pacing nervously near the windows. "Prudence," she said, closing the doors behind her. "I am so glad to see you have not gone back to Leeds after all."

The former maid bowed her head. "No, miss. I . . . I've been hiding in my rooms, trying to decide. I thought more about what you said. And what I did. Or, more what I *didn't* do." Prudence frowned. "You are right. So much of this is my fault, for being too frightened to say anything. But I'm far more frightened now than I ever was in November. I can't eat, I can't sleep. I'm too afraid the killer might strike again. I've been afraid to go back to Leeds, even. Surely he could find me there, if he wanted to. That's why I'm here." She fairly shook beneath the weight of her teary confession. "The only way to be safe is to see him arrested, isn't it? That's what you've been trying to tell me all along."

"Yes." Julianne nodded. "You know we would protect you here at Summersby."

"That's just it, miss." Prudence darted a glance toward the door, and her voice hushed to a whisper. "I don't think you can protect me at Summersby. Or yourself either. I went to church today to pray on it. And . . . and I saw him again."

"You saw the killer at church?" Awareness charged in like a runaway horse. "Do you know his name?" Julianne asked frantically.

"No, miss. But . . ." Prudence's breathing hitched, coming faster now in a series of quick pants. "He was sitting in the Haversham pew, next to Lady Haversham."

Julianne was seized with an awful, knee-buckling certainty. "You did not speak to him?" she asked sharply, suddenly afraid for the girl.

"No. I panicked. Slipped out of church and ran back to my rooms, right in the middle of the opening prayer. But after I thought about it a moment, I realized I needed to tell you, and that I had this one chance to do it before church let out. So I rented a carriage, and came straight here." She hesitated. "Oh, please, *please* tell me you know who it is. I couldn't bear it if after all this, we still had no idea."

The room seemed to tilt beneath Julianne's three inch heels. "Yes," she admitted, though her gut wanted to deny it. "I'm afraid I do know who it is."

Prudence worried her lower lip between her teeth. "Then you can tell the magistrate?"

"*You* need to tell the magistrate," Julianne corrected, already bundling the frozen girl toward the door.

"I . . . I couldn't miss."

"They won't take my word for it, Prudence. The gentleman who would have been sitting with Lady Haversham in church this morning is George Willoughby, my husband's cousin. We *must* return to Shippington immediately and tell the magistrate everything you have told me."

Prudence tensed. "I know I've caused a good deal of trouble, but I am not sure I can . . ."

For a moment Julianne was afraid she might be facing a repeat performance of the girl's prior disappearing act. She forced her voice to soften. "We both caused the trouble, Prudence. I should never have claimed to have seen something I hadn't." She hesitated. "In truth, I should not have pretended I could see so well on any number of occasions."

Julianne knew, however, that if she got a second chance at this, she would proceed far differently. There was no shame in admitting a deficiency. The only shame to be found was in hurting people she loved, because of little more than vanity.

"I know this will be difficult," she told the former maid, "and you have every right to be afraid. But I want you to know, when this is through, you shall have a position here at Summersby. I am still searching for a proper ladies' maid, after all."

The girl's eyes widened, though her face was still a sickly white. "Truly?"

Julianne nodded, and squeezed her hand. "Quickly, then."

Chapter 27

JAMES MACKENZIE PROVED remarkably talented in the art of persuasion. Within a quarter hour, he'd seen the magistrate fetched from church and had Farmington and Blythe sitting on two chairs they'd brought into the cell, ostensibly waiting for a promised confession.

Of course, Blythe had no idea who the intended confessor was.

"I understand Mr. Blythe assisted with my client's arrest," James said easily. *Too* easily, considering his friend looked all too ready to break a law or a leg or both.

Farmington had the good grace to at least look chagrined. "We do not have a constable here in Shippington. Mr. Blythe has been most helpful in that regard."

"What does this have to do with Haversham's confession?" Blythe demanded.

"I did not say the confession was my client's." James smiled patiently. "We have invited you here, actually, because I wanted to ask *you* some questions, Mr. Blythe. And we wanted Mr. Farmington to be present in case you say something . . . *interesting*."

Blythe turned pale at the thinly veiled threat. "I have nothing to hide."

Patrick stepped closer to the seated man and put a hand on the back of Blythe's chair. Time to tell the truth, at long last. "There's a witness who can prove I didn't murder my brother."

The little cell fell quiet, except for the hypnotic drip of water somewhere in a hidden corner. Finally, Farmington's voice severed the disarming silence. "Do you speak of your wife?" he asked slowly. "She has said she will not testify."

"There is a second witness," Patrick admitted. He kept his eyes trained on Blythe, trying to read his cousin's frozen face. "Who can name someone else as the killer."

"Have you been withholding this piece of it, Haversham?" Farmington's strangled voice finally pulled Patrick's attention away from Blythe.

For the first time since this whole business had started, the magistrate sounded truly, legitimately angry. Not that Patrick could blame the man. Even though he was magistrate of little more than a sleepy Yorkshire town, it was still Farmington's job to sort out the truth, not field the bits and pieces of it someone saw fit to gift him. Patrick suspected the beleaguered magistrate was already viewed somewhat precariously because of the long-delayed inquest. He was poised to look more than merely foolish if a second witness could be produced.

Patrick could almost—*almost*—feel sorry for him.

"Who is this witness?" Farmington demanded. "I'll have his name."

But Patrick hesitated to reveal any more. His whole point in mentioning the second witness had been to use the element of surprise as leverage against Blythe, and the bloody man had barely blinked. "All in due time, Mr. Farmington. But on the matter of witnesses, you should also know Mr. MacKenzie can place me in Scotland during my father's illness. Which brings us back around to our original reason to call you both here." Patrick leaned down, closer to Blythe's ear. "Perhaps we should direct the question of my father's death to *you* then, cousin. Because it occurs to me that you have as much to gain by his passing as anyone."

Now, finally, Blythe's stony gaze cracked. His eyes swung wildly between the men in the room. "What? *No!* Why would you have cause to think such a thing?"

"The chance at a title, and the accoutrements that come with it."

Blythe stood, bristling ominously. "Then I bloody well would have killed you too, wouldn't I have? Far better to see you dead than hanged. At least then the title wouldn't be in question. The fact I haven't killed you yet ought to prove I'm not capable of it."

"Do not try to tell me I should presume you are innocent," Patrick snarled as James grasped his cousin's shoulder and shoved him back down forcefully in the chair. "You proved long ago what you were capable of."

Blythe's eyes flashed. "Is this still about those damned puppies? For God's sake, Haversham. You're a grown man. To accuse me of Eric's murder is outrage enough. But the earl?" His voice cracked. "Nay. Never. The man treated me as well as a son."

Patrick narrowly controlled the urge to wrap his hands around the young man's neck. He could allow that strangling his cousin might make him feel a sight better, but it was unlikely to free him of a murder charge. "Where were you when my father fell ill?"

"I was in London."

"Can you prove it?"

Blythe drew in an unsteady breath. "There are any

number of witnesses who can place me in London in the weeks before he fell ill."

"You'd best enumerate them," Patrick warned.

"My mistress, for one. The patrons of the club I frequent." Blythe hesitated. "You really think I could have done something so terrible?"

"History is a damnable thing," Patrick countered. "And none of the witnesses *you* mention are here for us to question. Rather inconvenient, wouldn't you say?"

"My mother was staying at Summersby all through September, and she can stand as witness I was not here in Yorkshire. She sent me a letter when the earl fell ill and I rushed to Summersby, worried for his health." Blythe's chin lifted, a hint of his usual arrogance suffusing his earlier panic. "It was the least I could do for the man, given that you were still playing the prodigal son. I didn't kill the earl. You *know* he was like a father to me."

"That sort of familial thinking seems to have slipped your mind when you accused me of the deed," Patrick all but growled. His relationship with his father and brother might have been strained eleven months ago, but even at its worst it had still been based on love and respect. He could see that now, and regret the profound loss of it.

But *someone* had killed them, and he was not going to rest until he proved it.

"Your mother is not here at the moment either," he reminded Blythe.

"Damn it, Haversham, *noone* is here." Blythe swallowed roughly. "But Mr. Farmington can attest to the fact I was not at Summersby in the weeks before the earl's death. He spends a good deal of time there with my mother."

Patrick glanced away toward the magistrate, surprised.

"I . . ." Farmington looked muddled, his gray brows pulled down unhappily. "That is . . . I take dinner there, regularly, when Margaret and Jonathon are visiting Summersby. Your aunt and I have . . . an . . . understanding, of sorts. And I am afraid Jonathon is correct. He did not arrive at Summersby until after your father fell ill."

Patrick's thoughts wrapped tight around that. *Margaret.* The use of his aunt's given name was rather telling, all-told, never mind that they were both consenting, unencumbered adults. But if Blythe was telling the truth, things were far more tangled than he had imagined.

Could it really be Willoughby after all?

Patrick glared down at his cousin. Damn Blythe's ready answers, Patrick was tempted to believe him. The young man's angst at being accused was too authentic, his anger too real. No matter his hot temper and his past mistakes, Blythe's affection and respect for the earl was something Patrick had seen firsthand. It was almost as though his cousin had wished—or coveted—Patrick's father as his own. He could well envision the rage that would have enveloped his cousin at the thought of someone murdering the man.

It would not be far off from the anger he felt himself.

But if he was wrong about Blythe, he was wrong about other things as well.

"Was George Willoughby at Summersby during September?" he asked Farmington, panic bumping up his heart rate.

The magistrate mopped his brow with a white kerchief. "Yes, but it is the shadiest leap of logic—"

"He was also there in November, and out with our

hunting party that morning, though he hung back from the others. He has every bit the motive Blythe would have."

Farmington shifted uncomfortably in his chair. "I don't see how this line of questioning is helpful. You've no evidence against Mr. Blythe *or* Mr. Willoughby, and you are facing a charge of murder, handed down by the coroner's jury. This is conjecture, at best."

"I need to go to Summersby," Patrick insisted. "Willoughby is there. He needs to be questioned." When the magistrate did no more than shuffle his feet in discomfort, Patrick felt near to exploding. "Damn it, Farmington, if Willoughby is our man, Julianne is in grave danger!"

"You're under *arrest*, Haversham." Farmington seemed to shrink against the back of his chair. "I cannot just release you on such little evidence—"

"You certainly have the right to move a prisoner," James pointed out. "*Move* Haversham to Summersby. You'll be with him, so no one can claim he's been freed."

Farmington's last remaining bit of color fled at that. "This is all highly irregular. I could not bring myself to circumvent the requirements of my position—"

Blythe rose from his seat. "I find myself in agreement. Willoughby should be questioned, if nothing else."

Though Patrick was quite sure he would never like the man, given their fractious history, he discovered that he appreciated his cousin's verve a good deal more when it was directed toward a common goal instead of against his jaw.

"There are still guests at Summersby who could be in danger," Blythe went on. "My *mother* is still there. Or does she suddenly mean so little to you?"

Farmington's mouth moved a wordless moment. When he spoke, it was with a voice that seemed fraught with uncertainty. "The rules, you know. I am still expected to adhere to them."

James stepped closer to Patrick, his big arms folded menacingly across his chest. After a tension-fraught moment, Blythe stepped in beside them. Together, they all faced Farmington down. "Hang the rules," James said vehemently.

And for once, Patrick didn't mind the word.

THEY WERE ALREADY too late.

As Julianne and Prudence careened out onto the flagstone front steps, the man in question stepped down from the mud-splattered coach, shielded by an army of umbrella-wielding footman. Julianne muttered a foul oath, something so incongruous with a young lady's vocabulary she ought to have her Almack's voucher revoked. But she had neither the time nor the inclination to apologize. They were caught, like moths in a spider's web.

And the spider had already seen them.

A prickling awareness ran the length of her spine as George Willoughby grinned up at her. Lady Haversham exited next, Mary and Eleanor tumbling out behind her, turning their innocent faces up to the sky and trying to catch raindrops on their tongues. Aunt Margaret rounded out the group, lifting her skirts high against the muddied drive.

The pulse in Julianne's ears pounded in time with the rain accelerating on the overhead roof tiles. Willoughby didn't *look* malicious. In point of fact, he looked disastrously ordinary, if a bit presumptuous. Stepping down from the mud-splattered coach emblazoned with the

Haversham crest, his necktie starched to perfection despite the wilting weather, Patrick's cousin seemed far too assured with his position and his future.

He herded the church-going brood toward the house under the canopy of umbrellas. Julianne struggled against her rising ire at the evidence of the young man's now complete intercalation into the family. He'd escorted Patrick's sisters to church, for heaven's sake. *Bastard*. Not that George Willoughby was a bastard, per se.

Life would have been so much simpler if he was.

The dogs came streaking up from wherever they had been down near the lake, covered in mud and heaven knew what else. They slid to a raucous halt on the front steps and shook, each in turn, earning shrieks from the girls and a glower from Aunt Margaret. George, however, remained unruffled as he strode toward the door under his umbrella.

"You missed a delightful sermon today, Julianne." He spoke loudly to reach over the rain, and smiled wide enough to swallow the sun, no matter the near-opening of the heavens. But that smile faltered somewhat as his gaze moved on to the young woman standing quietly beside her. "Have we a visitor?"

Though Julianne was relieved to hear that George did not precisely recognize Prudence, fear refused to loosen its hold. A man depraved enough to kill his relatives and then eat breakfast placidly at their table was a man who would think nothing of killing a simple servant if he felt he had been recognized. If he found Prudence remotely familiar, the situation could rapidly turn from unpredictable to desperate.

To Julianne's surprise, Prudence delivered an unswerving performance that belied the fear the girl ought to have felt. "I was just leaving." She looked up at Julianne. "Were you coming with me, Lady Haversham?"

Julianne hesitated, unnerved by the girl's stalwart recital. She was not sure she could manage the same now that she was facing the man who had killed Eric. She settled a hand against her stomach, praying for divine inspiration.

It came in the form of George Willoughby.

"Is something wrong, Julianne?" he asked, raising his voice to be heard over the raindrops drumming overhead. He stepped closer. "You looked a bit peaked, truth be told. Do you feel faint again? You gave us quite a scare this morning."

His nearness kicked her protective instincts higher. "Er . . . yes." She widened her eyes purposefully in Prudence's direction. "I do not think I should travel in my condition. But *you* should go ahead and discuss the matter with the relevant parties, without delay."

Prudence paled somewhat. "Are you sure?"

"Yes." Julianne nodded firmly, praying she would not argue. "Just as we discussed. Quickly, now."

The girl picked up her skirts and—eschewing the footman's offer of an oilskin umbrella—dashed off through the downpour toward her rented cart. Willoughby watched her go, a perplexed look on his handsome face. "She looks deucedly familiar, doesn't she?"

Merciful heavens. If he recognized the former maid now, before she'd even left the front drive, all would be lost. "Would you please help me inside, George?" Julianne said hurriedly.

He offered his arm, though his face screwed up in thought. "Miss Smith, you said? She dresses like a servant. Was she once employed at Summersby?"

"Oh," Julianne moaned. "I am feeling so faint."

As George helped her back inside the house, she peeked out from lowered lashes to judge the impact of her subterfuge. Aunt Margaret was watching her with a frown, and the worried faces of Patrick's mother and sisters swam into view. Julianne was reminded, in that moment, of what she stood to lose if she failed at this most basic task of distracting the gentleman. If Willoughby felt he was threatened, there was no telling what he might do, or whom he might hurt. Patrick would want his family protected, above all else.

"Why was Miss Smith here?" George pressed, handing his dripping umbrella to Mr. Peters.

"She has just started working with Dr. Merial," Julianne said, desperately stretching for an answer that avoided suspicion but circled Willoughby's attention squarely back around to her. She needed to give Prudence every chance at a firm head start, before George's suspicions caught up with him. "She was here about my . . . *condition*." She splayed a hand across her abdomen. "Perhaps . . . perhaps I should lie down."

Gemmy immediately—and uncharacteristically—dropped to the floor, his muzzle quivering between his two front paws. Constance, however, knew her mistress better. She cocked her head as if to acknowledge the fine bit of acting unfolding before her eyes.

Surprisingly, it was Aunt Margaret who clucked into action. "George, be a dear, and help the poor girl back up to her room, before she pitches over. She should not have left her bed today, feeling as poorly as she has. Lady Haversham, perhaps you ought to take those girls right upstairs and get them out of their wet shoes. Possibly even call for a bath."

"A bath?" exclaimed Mary.

"We've just *had* a bath. Last night," echoed Eleanor indignantly.

"Your new sister is ill," Aunt Margaret chided. "Do you want to contract something terrible?" She shooed them on, and then added, "I'll summon the housekeeper to make a hot tisane. I know that always makes me feel better when I am out of sorts."

Julianne watched it all unfold like a runaway carriage, unable to even insert her own opinion into the mix because she was *supposed* to be wretchedly ill. The dowager countess herded the whispering children up the stairs, presumably to put as much distance between them and a source of possible contagion as possible.

Aunt Margaret's plan was brilliant in at least one respect. If George was busy helping *her*, perhaps he would be too occupied to think about Prudence. But halfway up the stairs, George leaned in low to murmur in her ear, "Are you sure Miss Smith was not the ladies' maid who helped you during the November house party? I recall someone who looked just like her—"

Julianne promptly wilted, praying he was naïve enough to catch her, if not believe her.

George scooped her up. The feel of his hands on her body was close to agonizing. This was, after all, the man who had killed Eric and possibly the old earl. The man who had stood by and let Patrick be blamed for a murder he hadn't committed, all to save his own sorry hide.

Instinct told her to bite. Kick. Scream.

Instead, she summoned every bit of theatrical skill she had obtained at the hands of the *ton*, forcing herself to stay limp as George Willoughby carried her to her room. She could hear Constance's nails, following steadily on the floor beneath her, and swallowed the urge to send the little dog to safety with a sharp word.

If she spoke now, it would give her away.

As George settled her atop the coverlet on her bed, she felt him smooth a hand down one arm, coming dangerously close to one breast in the process.

Clearly, this was not a man a woman ought to faint around.

"Where am I?" she asked, injecting her voice with just the right amount of grogginess. Time to rouse herself before Willoughby took it upon himself to loosen her corset.

"I've taken you to your room. Are you . . ." George leaned in, and the motion seemed somehow all the more ominous for the fact he looked concerned. "Is there a chance you could be losing the baby?"

She tried to affect a distraught look. "Please . . ." she croaked in what she hoped was a pitiful voice. "I should like some water."

"I think tea is better called for in a situation like this." Aunt Margaret bustled into the doorway, blurry but unmistakable in her turban. She came closer, slipping into Julianne's grateful line of vision bearing a tray and tea set. "George, I imagine Lady Haversham would prefer the company of another woman at the moment."

"But—"

"*Now*, George."

Still, he hesitated.

Julianne added her agreement through artfully lowered lashes. "I confess, I would prefer if Aunt Margaret stayed with me, if you do not mind. But please, stay close, if you would." She offered him a tremulous smile, praying her request would hold him to Summersby long enough for Prudence to be safely away. "In case I need you."

George's eyes searched hers. "Of course, Julianne. You know I would do anything for you."

Aunt Margaret locked the door behind him with a deft turn of her hand, and slipped the key into a pocket in her skirts. "There," she muttered to the door. "Now that beef-witted boy will not bother us."

Julianne exhaled in relief as Constance jumped up on the bed and nudged at Julianne's hand. She could not imagine how Aunt Margaret understood to do it, but she was relieved at the woman's astuteness. George could not reach her through a locked door. The girls were safe with their mother, she hoped, being scrubbed down from whatever miasmas to which they were feared to have been exposed.

And Aunt Margaret's reassuring presence was blotting Willoughby from the room, at least for the moment.

She dutifully tried to sip the tea Aunt Margaret brought her, but after the first bare taste, she found herself unable to stomach it and surreptitiously tossed it into a nearby vase of flowers. She continued to pretend to sip it, wanting to ensure she did not hurt her aunt's feelings, and needing her to remain as a buffer against Willoughby's return.

Now began a waiting game: waiting for Prudence to reach the magistrate, and for the magistrate to reach Summersby. She prayed Mr. Farmington believed the girl.

Because she had no plan for managing Willoughby beyond a few hours' delay.

Chapter 28

PATRICK HAD BELIEVED he was used to rain. He'd presumed the sorts of showers he'd become accustomed to in Scotland, storms that bore in from the coast and anchored themselves in the hills above Moraig, would have immured him to the drudgery of a dour English drizzle.

But as they began the last push toward Summersby in Farmington's unfortunately open-topped carriage, Patrick was forced to acknowledge that the storm battering them was no typical English rainstorm. It poured down from a dark slash of sky, obscuring their vision and roaring in their ears. It slowed them down, but with Blythe at the reins, the carriage continued to lurch across the mud-soaked ruts with a vigor just short of reckless.

Patrick could feel the knot of worry tightening in his chest as they turned onto Summersby's long, muddy drive and Blythe pushed the horses harder, faster. Far ahead, rising up through the trees, the manor house could be seen, a Gothic nightmare come to life. Slate-tipped turrets watched their progress like great, mythical eyes, and even from this distance, the gray stone walls gleamed slick with rain and moss.

With such a spurious welcome, it seemed easy to question the wisdom of their rushed approach. No one with an ounce of sense in his head would be out in weather such as this. But Julianne was somewhere inside those damp walls, and he would not be able to rest until he reassured himself she was well.

As fate would have it, they weren't the only ones lacking good sense. Less than a quarter of the way up Summersby's rambling drive, they came across a single-horse carriage mired in mud. The driver—a lone figure in a soaked-through dress—waved at them from atop the dangerously tilted curricle, and Blythe pulled their team to a stop a safe distance from the muddied dip of the road, where a nearby creek had overflowed its bank.

Patrick warred with two competing, animalistic instincts. To pass the stranded woman by and leave her to the elements was a thought so cruel as to be villainous. But to add even a moment's delay to their push toward Summersby was untenable.

"She's stuck, all right." Blythe raised his voice to be heard above the rain. "If she'd a proper team she might have been all right."

"She's in a hired livery," Farmington said. "I recognize the horse from Shippington."

"Right then," James said, leaping down with a formidable splash. "We need to get her out if we've a hope of getting our carriage past in this weather. Patrick, let's see if we can get our shoulders behind helping this poor woman out."

Patrick climbed down, cursing fate, the rain, the day. Julianne was in danger, and Willoughby was an unpredictable fool. He didn't just want to get to Summersby. He *needed* to be there, to protect his family and the woman he cared for enough to charge through an autumn downpour.

"Oh, I am so glad to see you," the stranded woman gasped, blinking through the pelting rain. "I'm in ever so much of a hurry."

"You shouldn't be out in a storm like this," Patrick told her gruffly.

The driver was a slip of a girl, dark hair plastered against her head. She looked vaguely familiar, but then again, most of Shippington's residents were people he had seen in one form or another over the course of his life. The woman shrank against his curt observation, pulling her arms close around her, as if she could ward off his glower with the rain.

Neither was even a remote possibility.

James climbed up onto the cart seat and took over the reins, while Patrick put his shoulder to the rear of the carriage—little more than a curricle, really, and infinitely inappropriate for the weather. He dug his boots into the muck, pushing with all his might, rocking and cajoling until the wheel came free.

As the mud finally gave way with a loud groan and James urged the horse to take over, Patrick went down to his knees in the filthy water. "The devil take it," he cursed, clambering heavily to his feet, his boots squelching through the mud.

James hauled back on the reins and grinned down at him. "A fine sight we'll be, descending on Summersby like this. This Willoughby fellow's likely to laugh himself to death and save us the trouble of a trial."

The woman stared at James, her eyes flashing through the rain. "Did . . . did you say George Willoughby?"

Patrick tensed, suddenly more alert to hear his cousin's name on this young woman's lips. "Aye. Do you know him?"

The girl paled beneath the curtain of rain that enveloped them all. "I . . . I have a message about George Willoughby. I must deliver it to the magistrate. 'Tis an emergency, and the only reason I am out in this terrible weather."

Patrick swiped a hand across his face, although the water ran back into his eyes almost immediately. "What is your name, miss?"

"Prudence Smith."

Patrick stood frozen as he realized he was speaking with the second witness, the girl who—thank God— had not disappeared into the teeming cesspool of Leeds. She was the key to everything. And she was here, in front of him, the magistrate only steps away.

"What is the message?" he asked, forcing himself to remain calm.

"I've strict instructions from Lady Haversham to deliver it only to the magistrate, sir."

"I am the lady's husband," he told her, impatience sinking its teeth into him. "I assure you, it will be fine to share it with me."

The girl's lip trembled in indecision. "I . . . I am sorry, my lord. But I would prefer to speak directly with the magistrate."

Patrick bit back a snarl of frustration. Beside him, James climbed down from the cart and beckoned to the cowering Miss Smith. "Well, despite the inauspicious start to your drive, you are in luck, Miss Smith. We've the magistrate with us, in our carriage just over there. If you've a message for him regarding Willoughby, you need go no further."

"Oh." She blinked and then jerked to awareness. *"Oh."*

But as they slogged their way through the mud toward Farmington's carriage and the two men waiting inside came into clearer view, the young woman suddenly planted her feet and looked wildly between Patrick and James. "What sort of trap is this?"

Patrick bit the inside of his cheek at what appeared to be yet *another* delay. The girl was clearly frightened, though of what he could not tell. "You wanted to speak with the magistrate," he growled, anxious to be done with this. "He's just there. Mr. Farmington. The older gentleman, to the right."

"But . . . that is George Willoughby," Prudence gasped. "Isn't it?"

Patrick and James glanced at each other over the young woman's head. "Er . . . no. Do you recognize him?"

Prudence closed her eyes and nodded. "I saw him this morning, at church."

Patrick offered James a telling look, then slowly chose his words, feeling his way toward the truth the way a blind man would find his bed. "I believe you might be confused, Miss Smith. The older gentleman you have pointed out is not Mr. Willoughby. That is Mr. Farmington, Shippington's magistrate."

She turned deathly white, then whirled in a shower of rain-soaked skirts and splashed back to her carriage, scrambling back up into the seat like a cat with a singed tail.

They plunged after her. "What in the devil has you so spooked?" Patrick demanded. "You cannot leave, Miss Smith. We need your testimony."

"I cannot deliver it to *him*," she moaned.

"Why ever not?" Patrick grabbed hold of the girl's reins, trying desperately to slow her panicked flight.

Damn it, she couldn't leave. Miss Prudence Smith—hysterical or not—was the key to this whole damnable puzzle.

The carriage whip sliced down on Patrick, and the unexpected pain on his arm loosened his hold. The carriage lurched forward and then it was pulling away.

But the girl's voice wavered, faint and ominous against the steady clap of rain. "Because *he's* the one who killed Lord Haversham's heir."

JULIANNE LEANED BACK into her pillows, rubbing the silky fur of Constance's ears absently between two fingers. Aunt Margaret seemed in no hurry to leave, floating around the room, straightening, shifting, touching.

Julianne would have preferred to be alone with her thoughts, but she also knew that as long as Patrick's aunt remained, George Willoughby would be held at bay. Aunt Margaret hummed an indiscernible tune as she rearranged the service. Straightened the teaspoons. Repositioned the sugar dish.

"Have you finished your tea?" the older woman called absently over her shoulder.

"Er . . . yes. Your kindness is appreciated." Julianne held out her empty cup. She realized, then, with the degree of difficulty that accompanied the simple motion, that her head felt strange, as though it were stuffed with wet cotton.

"Did you enjoy it, dear?"

Julianne squinted at her aunt. Usually, at this close proximity, she could see people quite clearly, but Aunt Margaret's round face was out of focus. Or perhaps it was that Julianne's eyes would not be still. Whatever the cause, she felt quite odd. "I think I would have preferred chocolate," she murmured distractedly.

Aunt Margaret placed the cup on the tray. "Tsk, tsk, child. I can't think such a rich drink would be good for you, given your condition."

"My condition?" Julianne tried to raise a brow, but the motion felt disastrously slow.

Aunt Margaret peered closely at her. Whatever she saw in Julianne's face seemed to cheer her immensely. "Yes, your condition. Rather inconvenient, Haversham reappearing to face his murder charge with a pregnant wife in tow. I scarcely think any of us is looking forward to another heir to stumble over."

Julianne blinked her way back into focus. "Aunt Margaret . . . I think . . . I think George must have put something in my tea."

The older woman smiled patiently. "George would never be so pragmatic. Why, the very idea you might be expecting has sent the poor young man into a veritable paroxysm of panic. How could he manage something requiring actual planning?"

Julianne struggled to wrap her head around her flying, disjointed thoughts. Why did Aunt Margaret have cause to dislike Willoughby?

It scarcely signified that Julianne no longer liked him either.

"Willoughby is—for want of a better term—a short-sighted simpleton," Aunt Margaret continued. "Ask yourself, why would he want to ensure your comfort, when the very child causing your illness is a threat to his own future? It would be a shame if the earldom was given to a man like that, when my son is so much more deserving of the title. And when the time comes, I am confident Willoughby's lack of ambition and mental acuity will ensure the Crown views my own son's petition more favorably."

Julianne recoiled against the woman's words. Her leap to understanding was slower than usual, but it carried the horror of perfect clarity. Her nausea this morning had not been the result of the clotted cream. She could feel the remnants of that same illness now, churning back to vicious life. "Oh dear God," she swore, not even caring that she had uttered the unladylike curse out loud. "*You've* put something in my tea."

Aunt Margaret's atrocious turban bobbed agreeably. "I've put something in your tea much of the last week. A touch of arsenic. Yet another advantage of poor George Willoughby's oblivious nature. I was originally hoping for a slow erosion of your health. The poor, new wife, wasting away while her husband was tried for murder. I learned with the earl that too sudden a decline could raise undue suspicion. But your pregnancy has now given me the perfect excuse for action. You shall lose the child, and die yourself from complications."

"*You* killed the earl?" Julianne gasped. "Did you kill Eric too?"

Only that couldn't be right. Her brain was befuddled, but she was *quite* sure Prudence had said the killer she had seen was a man.

Aunt Margaret leaned in, so close Julianne could see the fine lines radiating out from the woman's narrowed eyes. "We've made too many mistakes, but I *will* salvage it now. Your husband is next—whether by noose or deceit, I care not a whit. He should have been killed back in November, had the deed been properly finished. But if you think I will sit placidly by while you poke your nose about Summersby, stirring up trouble, you are mistaken in the extreme. The cup of tea you just finished had enough belladonna in it to fell an ox. I probably ought to apologize for that." She shrugged. "I could not take any chances."

Julianne swallowed the bile that pricked the back of her throat. How much of the poison had she consumed? Not the entirety of the cup—not that Aunt Margaret knew any better.

Certainly enough to affect her.

But enough to kill her?

"Why are you telling me this now?" she rasped, wondering if Prudence had any hope at all of reaching help before the poison took its full effect.

"Why should I not? The older woman smiled, and the sight of it sent a chill through Julianne. "It is not as though you will be able to tell a soul. Of course, I shall be sure to claim I did everything I could to help you, short of fetching your chocolate. How about some more tea, instead?"

Julianne thrashed her head mutely.

"No? Well, you're in no position to negotiate, dear. In fact, I quite insist on it."

Chapter 29

*B*LOODY HELL.

Farmington had been his father's friend. The man had taught him how to tie fishing lures for God's sake, and had spent many a memorable night in Summersby's parlor, moving chess pieces across a board with Patrick's father.

For a brief moment, the utter sense of betrayal Patrick felt threatened to drown him far more effectively than the howling wind and rain. But then anger lifted his feet and carried him back toward the carriage. James followed close on his heels, as if reading his thoughts.

"Who was the girl?" Farmington asked as they swung up onto the wet seat. Weary lines of cold and exhaustion peered out from the dripping brim of the magistrate's top hat. "Not from Shippington, I should think. I don't recognize her. Whoever has the charge of her ought to be shot, letting her traipse about in a storm like this."

The man's casual reference to violence snapped whatever finesse Patrick had thought to manage here. He grabbed Farmington's arm and twisted it, wrenching a shout of surprise and pain from the older man's mouth. Blythe lurched around, the reins bunched in one fist. His face darkened when he saw what was happening.

He reached into his jacket, pulling out his revolver, but James had already anticipated it and wrenched it from his hand before Blythe's thumb could reach the hammer.

"Bloody hell," Blythe swore as he realized his vulnerability. "I *knew* we shouldn't have trusted you, Haversham."

"I'm not the one who has breached an essential trust here." Patrick directed his bitter glower toward the magistrate. "She was the missing witness, Farmington. And she's just named you as the man who pulled the trigger on Eric."

For a moment, Patrick thought Farmington would struggle, or at least offer a word of denial. But instead, he sagged against Patrick's punishing grip, offering no resistance at all.

"For God's sake Farmington, tell them it isn't true!" Blythe blustered.

Patrick ignored his cousin. "Have you any rope, MacKenzie?"

"No." The sound of a pistol cocking rang out, distinct over the merciless sound of the rain. James pointed the barrel toward Farmington's chest, cupping his hand over the top of the piece to protect it from the weather. "I've something better."

"You can't point a bloody weapon at a magistrate!" Blythe objected. "He's not been charged with any crime, for God's sake. There's a process to follow."

James illustrated his opinion of the "process"—and stopped the man's tirade—by pointing Blythe's own weapon toward him. "Are you going to make me secure you too, Mr. Blythe?" the solicitor drawled, his voice deceptively low. "Because I confess, I've a mind to give you a taste of your own methods. A few cracked ribs should shut you up. I won't even tie you up." He smiled wickedly. "Not that I need such an advantage. Unlike you, I know how to aim my fists without hog-tying my target."

"Put it away, Mr. MacKenzie. There's been enough violence." Farmington's voice rang out, thick with sadness and pain. "I'll not have more deaths on my hands. Eric's was hard enough."

"It's true then?" Blythe blinked, almost stupidly. "It's been you? All along?"

The magistrate nodded. Only once, before his lips settled into a firm line that refused to budge. Clearly, Farmington was through talking.

But he'd said enough to take the starch from Blythe's sails. When next his cousin's eyes met Patrick's, he appeared shocked, but newly resolute. "Do we travel on to Summersby then?"

"We have Farmington in custody, and Lady Haversham's safety is no longer a question." James shook his head. "We should take the prisoner back to Shippington."

A sound plan. Logical. The sort of thinking Patrick was usually wont to do.

Except he couldn't shake the feeling they were missing something vital in their understanding of the magistrate's involvement. By all accounts, Farmington was a man without motive. He was a close friend of Patrick's father, had known both Patrick and his brother their entire lives. What had possessed him to take the lives of people he ought to hold dear?

The answer, Patrick felt, would be found at Summersby. If they were going to question the man, he wanted to do it where it had all started.

His father's study.

Only this time, Patrick was going to be on the business end of the interrogation.

"I must make sure my family has not been harmed," he ground out, motioning for Blythe to drive on. "We can arrest him properly later."

They pulled up to the manor house just as the rain started to slacken and clattered through Summersby's front door in sodden boots, their coats dripping puddles onto gleaming floor. Gemmy greeted Patrick as if he'd been gone on a three-month sea journey, leaping in wild circles around Patrick, but he sidestepped the dog's exuberance.

"Julianne!" he shouted, his voice echoing across the marble floor and high ceiling.

Instead of his wife, Mr. Peters appeared from a side hallway, hurrying forward. "My lord," he said, breathing hard, "you've returned without notice?" He caught sight of Mr. Farmington, held fast in Blythe's grip, and his eyes widened. "And in a far different manner than when you left, I see."

"Where is Julianne?" Patrick demanded.

Mr. Peters hesitated. "She was not feeling well, my lord. In fact, I am rather concerned about her. She's gone above stairs—"

"Thank you, Mr. Peters." A feminine voice rang out. "That will be quite enough."

Patrick's attention lifted toward the stairs. Aunt Margaret was descending, one purposeful step at a time. "I saw your arrival from an upstairs window, Haversham. Am I to presume this means you have been released?"

"In a manner of speaking," he said slowly, trying to

sort out why his aunt was issuing the staff orders instead of his wife.

Aunt Margaret's gaze fell questioningly on Farmington as she reached the final step. Patrick's mind scuttled backward to a conclusion that made sense. He had long struggled to conceive of any motive that would justify his brother's murder, and drawn a blank for all save one. *Love.* A desire to protect, to nurture at all costs. Some shade of the same breath-robbing emotion that drove him here, desperate to see Julianne, and willing to kill anyone who might think to stop him. The pieces fell into place with alarming alacrity.

Patrick shoved Farmington into the center of the foyer. As the man fell to his knees, Aunt Margaret's gasp of dismay rattled his ears. "I should have never been arrested," Patrick ground out. "As I am sure you know, Aunt Margaret."

"What are you talking about, Haversham?" Blythe demanded, whirling on Patrick with knotted fists. "*Farmington* has admitted killing Eric."

"Aye." Patrick kept his attention directed toward his aunt. "But he didn't admit why. Given how reticent he's been to talk about it, I'll wager he's protecting someone. And while he has admitted a role in Eric's death, he has not confessed to killing my father. It would take someone close to the family to accomplish that. Someone who stayed at Summersby, whom the staff trusted. Someone a bit more bloodthirsty, and with a stronger degree of motivation." He took a step toward his aunt. "Someone like *you*, Aunt Margaret."

Farmington struggled to his feet. "Is Haversham correct, Margaret?" His voice rang thick with emotion. "Did *you* kill the earl?"

Aunt Margaret's hand closed over the mourning

brooch at her throat. "Do not say another word," she warned.

Farmington's throat worked convulsively. "You swore to me—*swore*—that after Eric, you were content to wait for the order of things to progress. But if you have killed your brother—"

"You are the one who cocked it up to begin with, not killing Patrick when you had the chance. I was only thinking of my son—"

"For God's sake, Margaret. I do not want to hear about your blessed son!" Farmington straightened, his face blooming red. "I *killed* a man for you. The least you can do is be honest with me if you have done the same."

Her reply was only silence.

That is, until the sound of a scuffle broke out behind them. Patrick turned to see MacKenzie and his cousin battling for control of the gun. Though his friend was stronger, Blythe had the advantage of surprise this time, and in less than a second, Blythe had the pistol in his hands. And then he pointed the weapon straight at his own mother, the engaging of the hammer unmistakable. "Answer Mr. Farmington's question, Mother."

Aunt Margaret gasped. "You cannot be serious, Jonathon."

"I assure you, I am deadly so. You see, I can well believe you might have coerced Mr. Farmington into pulling the trigger. I should know—I've found myself at the receiving end of your schemes more than once in my life." The barrel of his pistol did not waver. "I grow impatient for your response."

"Yes," she finally hissed. "I knew you would never conceive of doing such a thing for yourself, or agree to the plan. But I did it for *you.*"

Blythe swayed unsteadily, clearly horrified by his mother's confession, despite his steel-edged demand for it. "My God."

Patrick eased closer to his cousin. "She's admitted it, Blythe," he said, in what he hoped was a soothing voice. He, of all people, knew the toxic consequences of absorbing guilt that was not yours to take. "This is not your fault."

Blythe shook his head, his eyes blinking rapidly. "No. It is, you see. She's my *mother*. I knew her heart was dark. My entire life, I've sought to distance myself from that darkness. Do you recall, that summer, with the dogs?"

"Aye," Patrick said, trying to sort out whether he could slip the wavering pistol from his cousin's hands without risking it going off. "'Twas the start of the animosity between us."

"She caused it. You thought I had drowned those puppies to punish you, but it wasn't my idea, Haversham. We were all of, what, nine years old? She *made* me drown them. To teach me of duty, she said." Blythe renewed his grip on the pistol, holding it with both hands now. "I knew then . . . knew there was evil in you, Mother." His voice cracked. "But to take a human life . . . your own brother's life. How could you *do* such a thing?"

Patrick held up a cautious hand. It was far too easy to be riveted by the unfolding drama . . . for once, thankfully, not his own. He could see James sidling closer to Aunt Margaret, and the thought that his friend was stepping closer to the path of a potential bullet made his chest tighten.

"I did not trust my brother would leave this world in time for you to see the title." Aunt Margaret shook her head. "And he was beginning to ask questions. Beginning to suspect. I could not risk it, not after waiting for so long."

"Damn it, Mother. I ought to kill you." Blythe's voice cracked.

"But you won't," she whispered, lifting her chin. "I am your mother."

"You killed your brother. Who is to say I don't carry the same lack of morality in my blood? Who is to say I am not like you?"

The moment stretched to silence, long and hard, seconds ticking away.

"Jonathon." Patrick laid a careful hand on his cousin's arm. He could feel the tension in the younger man, coiled and ready to strike. "You are in charge of your own decisions, your own life. Family history cannot force you to be someone you are not."

"That's a sodding lie, and you know it." Blythe shook his head, almost desperately. "You are your own worst example, Haversham. Here you are, titled and miserable, forced back to Summersby where you never wanted to be."

Patrick recognized echoes of his own confused choices in his cousin's anguished voice, but he knew one clear truth. "No. No one forced this of me. I could have remained in Scotland, hiding from it all. But I chose to take on this responsibility, Jonathon, to return and face a murder charge I did not deserve. This is not your fault, cousin, any more than Eric's death was mine. And you can *choose* to not be like her."

He could see his cousin hesitate, see his words slip through the young man's confusion. Patrick stepped closer still, and then he was lowering Blythe's weapon-wielding arm and pulling the pistol from his cousin's hand. From the corner of his eye, Patrick could see James seize Aunt Margaret by the arm.

And just like that, it was over. The danger was defused. His future was returned.

Patrick stood unsteadily in the middle of Summersby's foyer, watching as James secured Aunt Margaret with a length of hastily produced rope. He *ought* to be glad. His life was waiting for him to gather up the pieces and craft them back into something whole. He couldn't bring his brother and father back, but he could make damned sure he well honored their memories. But happiness—and relief—were hard to find when his wife was still very much missing.

"Where is Julianne?" he demanded.

"I believe she is in her room, my lord." Mr. Peters bowed his head. "She has been ill, and Mrs. Blythe insisted on attending her, this hour past."

Willoughby chose that moment to bumble out of a side hallway, a cold leg of chicken in one hand. "I've asked the cook to send up a tray to Julianne's room, to go with Aunt Margaret's tea." His face settled into open surprise as he encountered the group in the foyer. He wiped his mouth with a guilty sleeve. "Oh, I say. What have I missed? And why is Haversham here, instead of gaol? Has Julianne lost the baby after all?"

But Patrick was already off like a shot. He took the stairs two at a time and reached his bedroom door in record time. His hand rattled the latch, confirming its locked state. Beyond the looming barrier, he could hear Constance's anxious whine, the scratch of the little dog's nails against the door, but no answering flow of human voice.

Fear speared his gut. Aunt Margaret was unstable—that much was clear. She claimed she would do anything for her son.

But how much harm had she done?

He set his shoulder against the door, splintering the wood around the latch in two hard slams. Constance greeted him on the inside with a ferocious growl, charging at him with her hackles raised. But he sidestepped the danger of the protective little dog and rushed toward the bed, where his wife lay still as death itself.

A thousand thoughts swam through his panic at the sight of Julianne's pale face, but one thought pushed insistently to the surface of that vortex. Aunt Margaret had poisoned his father. *Surely* she would not have left Julianne untouched.

He collapsed beside the bed, seizing his wife's thankfully still-warm hand. Constance leaped up on the bed beside him and nudged her mistress's arm. Julianne's lack of response to either touch sent Patrick's gnarled lungs into ever tighter contortions. He leaned over her, searching for some trace of poison, some odor, that might provide a clue.

"Julianne." His fingers instinctively searched the base of one slender wrist, seeking evidence she yet lived. "We know about Aunt Margaret. She and Mr. Farmington are in custody. You are safe now." His voice cracked around the impossible words. "But I need you to wake up and tell me what she has given you, or I am afraid I shall lose you too."

She remained deathly pale, eyes closed, no discernible response. He could feel her pulse thumping merrily along beneath his fingers, but its steady bump could not reassure him when she remained so still. He sagged against the mattress. He felt jerked backward in time, to a mist-covered glen, his brother's blood spreading out on the ground. The same feeling of helplessness he'd felt then enveloped him now.

Four years at Turin. Countless medical texts studied. He'd not been able to save Eric.

And now he faced losing Julianne, and quite possibly his unborn child. He had no means of knowing what Aunt Margaret might have slipped in her tea. No way to quickly sort through the hundreds of potential possibilities.

Still, he had to try. There was so much he regretted already.

He did not want losing her to be the worst of it.

Chapter 30

JULIANNE STUDIED HER husband's profile through barely closed lashes.

The feeling of his fingers on her wrist was a fine thing, but the sight of him proved even better. Her eyes lingered over the curve of his nose, the strong line of his jaw hidden behind a week's growth of beard. His hair hung in wet clumps, and his mud-splattered clothing was soaking through her own, raising the gooseflesh on her arms. Once upon a time, such a sight as this big, mud-encrusted man looming over her would have sent her scrambling away, calling for a bath, demanding an entire year's worth of soap.

But the raw emotion on his face kept her still as a statue, lying on the bed.

Hadn't she dreamed of disrupting this serious, studious man's composure? Hadn't she wanted to shatter his calm and yank against the chains of his careful restraint and prove, once and for all, that he was capable of terrible feelings?

Well, apparently feigning death was one way to accomplish it.

Oh, but he was going to be angry with her. But her

performance had fooled Aunt Margaret, and likely saved her life. She could not bring herself to regret the subterfuge now.

He lowered his ear to her chest, closing his eyes, listening. She held her breath, enjoying the feel of him pressed there against her breast. Had it really been only a week since he had touched her there last? It felt like an eternity.

But then his eyes cracked open and she was swept up in the suspicious brown warmth of his gaze. "Julianne . . . are you . . . *pretending*?"

Her eyes fluttered full-on open. "I am merely timing my entrance for maximum effect."

"Bloody *hell*, woman." He pushed away from her. The air between them hummed with his anger, and Constance—her faithful companion through the last hellish half hour—jumped down from the bed to seek calmer quarters.

"Do you know how scared I was?" he demanded. "I've lost my brother and father, for God's sake. I thought . . ."

Julianne struggled to a sitting position, still a bit dizzy from her close brush with Aunt Margaret's special recipe, though the effects had been muted by lying so still. Her heart did a pathetic little jump in her chest as she watched him glare at her.

"You thought . . . ?" she asked, leadingly.

He offered her a fresh, muttered oath and slicked a hand through his rain-soaked hair, sending clumps of mud and dirt splattering to the floor. "This isn't a game, Julianne. If you are trying to punish me, you've picked a drastic means of achieving that end."

The sharpness of his words dug under her skin, rooting for a foothold. "I did not do this to punish you, Patrick, or to coerce you into confessing some ill-timed romantic notion of your regard for me." *Although that would have been nice to hear.* "When I heard someone crashing through the door, I presumed my performance was still required for survival. Aunt Margaret had already tried to poison me once. I didn't want her thinking I was ready for another dose."

He paled beneath the ragged growth of beard. *"Another* dose?" And then his big, mud-splattered hands were on her face, lifting her eyes wide, turning her head from side to side.

"Patrick—" she protested, trying to squirm free.

"Your pupils are dilated. What did she give you?"

Julianne sighed, well-recognizing the clinical fervor that now had hold of him. "Belladonna."

He released her face, only to hold three fingers in front of her eyes, tracking them slowly back and forth. "How many fingers am I holding up?"

"I did not consume the entire dose she intended for me."

"Answer me, Julianne."

She glared at him in response. He ought to be kissing her. Instead he'd devolved into the veterinarian, and she was his latest beast of burden. "Oh, for heaven's sake. Three. And if you bring them any closer, you'll find yourself missing one." She tucked a curl behind one ear. "I had no more than a taste of it. Surely too little to effect any lasting damage if I am awake now. I poured the cup out, when she wasn't looking. Truly, the arsenic she'd been slipping in my tea over the past week affected me far more."

Patrick paled beneath his scruff of a gaolhouse beard, and Julianne almost found a smile at his distress.

"Her mistake was poisoning my tea. If she'd brought me chocolate instead . . ." She shuddered to think that she might very well have been fooled into consuming the entire dose. "I think it is safe to say I shall not be accepting another cup of tea anytime soon, no matter how desperate my thirst nor how prettily packaged the offer."

Patrick leaned back, and though he did no more than place a few inches between them, she felt the loss of contact acutely. "She and Farmington are in custody now," he told her. "You do not have to worry about them anymore."

"Mr. Farmington?" Julianne drew in a surprised breath, trying to process it all. "But . . . I thought . . . once it became clear it wasn't George, perhaps it was Jonathon Blythe."

He frowned. "Blythe is innocent, as it turns out. Farmington has admitted he killed Eric, although he appears to have done it for Aunt Margaret." He lifted a hand, his right palm hovering over her abdomen. "Julianne," he asked, his voice lower now. "I have to ask. Something George Willoughby said, below stairs. Are you pregnant? Because both arsenic and belladonna can have harmful effects on the womb . . ."

Julianne sighed. "No. I am not pregnant. I had my courses the day you were admitted to gaol. Honestly, why does everyone think that?"

"George Willoughby implied you were. And Mac-Kenzie suggested it as a possible explanation for your illness this morning." His eyes narrowed ominously. "Or have you been pretending to be pregnant too?"

"That," she snapped, shoving him aside and swinging her legs over the bed, "is less my fault than everyone else's. My uncertain stomach can be laid at the hands of your aunt and her pharmaceutical skills. Everyone seemed determined to presume the fact of my pregnancy, as though it could be the only possible explanation for our quick marriage. But I am not with child." She stood up, swaying as her muscles readjusted to their new permission to move. "And that was not the reason we married. There is nothing in that vein that would irrevocably tie you to this marriage. Nothing at all."

Julianne gathered her courage into a tight ball, and shaped it into the weapon she needed to guard her heart. After the initial rush of euphoria she had felt upon discovering it was Patrick bursting into her room, instead of the frankly terrifying Aunt Margaret, reality and disappointment were once again intruding into her world. This was her husband, and despite all odds, he'd just been handed back his future.

If she did not do this, she risked having him hate her every day for the rest of their lives.

She was a woman used to pursuing and acquiring what she wanted, whether it be the latest fashion from Paris or a husband whose kiss made her heart fling itself against the walls of her chest. She had married Patrick because she had wanted to. She had wanted *him*. Her body was even now leaning toward him, wanting the reassurance of his touch.

But now that she knew she loved him, she faced a far more difficult choice.

She drew herself up, though she leaned against the bedpost for support. "You only married me to ensure I could not be compelled to testify against you."

"Julianne, you cannot know—"

"Don't." She threw up her hand, shielding herself from the sting of his certain protest. "Do not try to spare my feelings on this matter. I will not have another falsehood between us, now that we are finally being truthful with each other. You have been freed of the murder charge. You are home, with your family, your title returned to you. You no longer *need* me. It would not be fair to hold you to the vows you made."

He flinched backward. "What are you saying?"

A half hour of feigning death with Aunt Margaret watching over her had given her a long time to consider the future. She had reacted harshly to his confession, that day by the lake. She was shallow and selfish and spoiled, things she had never regretted in her life, and had always understood. She feared she was selfish enough to keep him.

But those were not things a man like Patrick would want in a wife. He deserved a wife he wanted, one he chose without the press of a noose about his neck.

He deserved a chance to find his happiness.

And so she faced her dripping, disheveled, muddied husband and lifted her chin with a courage she did not feel. "Given that you are safe now, I suppose we ought to discuss the possibility of an annulment."

SURELY SHE WAS pretending this bit of it too.

Any moment now, her mouth would curve upward into a real, heartfelt smile, and Patrick would be able to sort out what she was actually thinking.

Except, damn her flashing eyes, he had a sinking feeling she was all too serious.

He tried to school his lungs to breathe normally, tried to force his hands to unclench.

All his efforts failed.

"You would end it?" He was startled to hear the hoarse tenor of his voice, wrapping itself around those terrible words. "After all we have been through, you would simply walk away?"

Her lips stretched the merest fraction of an inch. "I

don't blame you for marrying me, Patrick, truly, I don't. You were desperate, and I was willing, if a bit naïve. There was no coercion, no outright lie on that front. But the circumstances that drew us together no longer matter. We've spent scarcely a few weeks in each other's company. There is no child to be affected by the decision, no reason to delay the inevitable. Everything has changed. And because of it, I would not force you to honor our original arrangement."

By the devil's balls. It sounded as though *she* didn't want to honor their original arrangement.

Patrick drew a deep breath, feeling his way through this unexpected quagmire of emotion. "I don't think an annulment is possible," he told her. "At least, Mac-Kenzie warned me it wasn't."

She inhaled sharply. "So you've discussed the option with your solicitor?"

He stood stock-still. Damn it, this was her idea. Why did she sound so irritated?

"You've been poisoned, Julianne. Perhaps the belladonna has confused your thoughts. Give it some time—"

"I do not need time to know what is right, Patrick," she interrupted. "If we are truly tied to each other, I suppose we could deal with an unwanted marriage the same way everyone else in the *ton* does. 'Tis no small matter for me to live in London. I know your heart would keep you at Summersby. And your mother and sisters, certainly, need you here."

Her words slid into him like a freshly sharpened knife. *An unwanted marriage*, she called it. He had thought it so himself, once upon a time. Had envisioned just this means of escape, handed to him on a silver platter. But for Patrick this had ceased to be an unwanted marriage almost from the start. All through his time in the gaol, through the endless press of day into night, he'd thought of her. Of the stunning gift of her love, and the promise that awaited him when finally he fought his way free of the charges.

Of how he had hurt her with his silence, and how he could make it right.

He'd come through hell, dreaming of this opportunity to prove himself to her, only to find that what waited him on the other side was infinitely worse.

"You may think that an admirable solution, but what of my need for an heir?" Patrick took a step toward her, reaching for her, sure that if he could only take her in his arms, he could prove why this was a poor idea.

But she flinched as his hand brushed her cheek. He could feel her muscles tense, ready for flight. Imagined he could see the revulsion floating beneath her skin.

"You've cousins who could fill that role," she told him, her voice shattering the last of his hope. "And apparently, though it strains the imagination to consider it, they are both of the innocent variety."

Patrick's hand fell away. She didn't want him. Her eyes had been opened, and her heart had been closed.

And it was no less than he deserved.

Chapter 31

PATRICK SLAMMED INTO his father's study, still stunned by Julianne's ruthless request and his own reaction to it. She had stood in front of him, still swaying unsteadily from the effects of her near-poisoning, and told him she wanted a goddamned annulment. There was naught for it but whisky and the solitude of his father's chair.

Or, more correctly, *his* chair.

But neither solitude nor whisky were to be found in that chair, because James MacKenzie was sitting in it, his muddy boots propped up on the desk, the ever-present decanter of brandy uncorked in one hand.

"The whisky bottle was empty, so I sought my sins elsewhere." His friend eyed him a long, studious moment, then held the decanter out. "You look as though you could use a drink. I presume this means your wife has awakened to torment you anew?"

Patrick snatched the decanter from his friend's hand. "I thought you were heading back to Shippington, with Blythe and the prisoners."

"Your butler dispatched an entire army of footmen to see them on their way. And your cousin Blythe seemed more than willing to see his mother to gaol. Blood-thirsty fellow, that."

"Righteous, I would say. He was always so. Only now it seems he had reason to be." Patrick shook his head. "I have misjudged him somewhat, I'm afraid."

"Well, it seems with your poor, wee, misjudged cousin so eager to guard his mother I was . . ." James paused and waved his hand about. "Superfluous."

"I understand the feeling." Patrick shoved his friend's boots to the side and perched on the edge of the desk. "Only it turns out the person who considers me *most* unessential is my wife." He obviated the search for a glass in favor of more immediate salvation, and tipped the decanter up to his lips. The long, sweet draught of brandy ought to have calmed him.

Instead, it sharpened his pain like a damned whetstone.

"She wants an annulment," he said, as much to the wall as anything.

"Pregnant women can be a touch unpredictable." James shrugged. "Georgette told me she wanted me to grow my beard back, just last month. And then turned around the day after and said I needed to shave." His lips twitched. "There is naught for it but to let it blow over."

"She is not pregnant," Patrick said, realizing that the admission hurt. "She was ill because Aunt Margaret was trying to poison her, although she seems well on her way to recovery now. And I do not believe this is going to blow over."

James leaned back, his dark brows bunching. "Well, she can't bloody well have an annulment. Tight as a drum, that contract is. I ought to know. I orchestrated the thing."

Patrick glared at his friend. "You've made that perfectly clear. And I was willing to accept that ours might not be a happy union, at the start. Only . . . and here's the rub . . . I didn't expect to feel this way about her."

"Driving you crazy, is she?"

"Crazy seems a euphemism, at best. My brain goes to rot around her. It's like I cease to be the person I thought I was the moment I see her. Think on it. Have you ever seen me this way? More or less breaking out of gaol, wrestling pistols out of people's hands? It is as though I cannot remember who I'm meant to be because of her."

"Perhaps she has turned you *into* who you are supposed to be," James unexpectedly countered. "She is a challenge, to be sure, but in my experience, one needs a little challenge to grow in life. Do *you* want an annulment?"

"For shite's sake, no." Patrick waved the decanter about, trying to express how she made him feel. "She's maddening and unpredictable and a little bit vain, but the damnable thing is, every one of those . . . flaws, if you will . . . contribute to something more than just their sum. I enjoy her, MacKenzie. She makes me want to stick around to discover what unexpected, brilliant thing she might do next."

"Ah." A knowing grin claimed his friend's face, even as his head shook in the universal gesture of sympathetic friendship. "Shouldn't you be telling her these things, instead of me?"

Patrick glared down at him. "You aren't helping matters. I am not someone who finds it easy to express my feelings."

"If you want my advice—"

"Which I don't."

James's brow winged up. "But if I were to give it anyway—"

"Which, of course, you will."

"Then I would say you need to find a way to tell her everything you just told me." James's mouth pulled down into a frown. "Unless you *want* to give her an annulment."

"I've already said I don't want an annulment," Patrick snarled into his decanter, before slugging down another throat full of regret. He wiped his mouth on his shirtsleeve, the incongruity of the motion with the expectations of his new title be damned. "But I don't want her to be unhappy either."

"You would grant it to her? Even if it made you miserable?"

Patrick floated a moment on the terrible thought. When he thought he had lost her, his world had razored into focus. His future had ceased to exist for that frightening slice of time.

And he knew. Knew in his gut. Knew in his heart. He loved her.

He would do anything to make her happy, and the sacrifice of his own happiness in pursuit of hers barely scratched the surface of it. If Julianne told him the key to her happiness was in his recusal, he would give it to her. Because he didn't just enjoy her. That implied pleasure over pain. This thing he felt for her . . . by God, it *hurt*.

But it was the kind of hurt that made him happy to suffer it.

"I would," Patrick told his friend, cold with the truth of it. "If it was within my power, and I could not convince her otherwise."

James lifted a dubious brow. "You would accept her

right to leave you and seek another husband? You can be sure your cousin George Willoughby would be first in line, slavering for a chance at her."

The very thought clawed at Patrick's conscience. "If she wanted him, I could not deny it of her," he said, more slowly this time. Truthfully, this was a bit of a stretch. He could accept that Julianne could not be happy with him. But he was not at all sure he could accept her being happy with George Willoughby.

James sat back in the chair, rubbing a hand across his chin. "Bugger it all, you're well and truly smitten." His friend eyed him with something approaching respect. "All right then. You should give her one."

Damn it all to hell. What was MacKenzie about here?

"I don't see how," Patrick protested. "From the start, you told me the only way to do this was to be sure she could not press for an annulment. I followed your instructions to the letter, down to the requisite, awkward wedding night. The deed is sealed in blood."

"She cannot press for an annulment. But *you* can. On the grounds of fraud."

Patrick grappled with a growing unease. Damn MacKenzie's black soul, he looked deadly serious, no matter that his words completely contradicted his earlier position on the matter. "How can I accuse her of fraud, when *I* am the one who lied to her about my motives in marrying her?"

"I was your witness, and managed the settlement papers, if you recall. I was not sure, when all was said and done, you would want to stay married to her. She'd ruined your life once, already." He smiled in a self-deprecating manner. "But she was also far too trusting, signing whatever I slid in front of her. She misrepresented her age."

"Her . . . *age*?"

James cleared his throat. "The papers she signed may have indicated she was born in the year 1802."

Patrick's imagination kicked at the absurdity of it. "No one will believe she is forty years old. She's just come off her third Season. The whole of London knows she's just shy of her majority."

"No one needs to believe she is forty, Patrick. They just need to believe *you* believed it. The chit signed the papers without looking at them. She's as culpable as anyone. It is a petty thing, I know, but enough to take before the Commissary Courts to request an annulment."

"I thought you prided yourself on your honesty," Patrick protested, still trying to wrap his head around it.

"Do not mistake me—I do not recommend this course. It rubbed me wrong to do it then, and it rubs me wrong to tell you of it now. But if you are serious—and by God, you'd better be if you decide to pursue it—you can claim you did not realize she was under age. If Julianne is the one who so desperately wants this annulment, she could claim she willingly lied. Or, if you would rather offer some version closer to the truth, you could claim that I was the fraudulent party."

Patrick fixated on the last of his friend's offer. As a solicitor in Moraig, James MacKenzie was well known for his fair dealings, and his sense of social justice. But now he was offering to destroy that reputation, all to help a friend. "That's a big risk to take, MacKenzie. What about your reputation you are always harping about?"

James shrugged, damnably unrepentant for his sleight of hand. "My reputation seems a small sacrifice if it saves your miserable arse. It was my decision to orchestrate it, and is my consequence to face, if it comes to it. I only envisioned this means of escape employed as a matter of last resort, and had hoped to never need to tell you. Truly, I see much potential between you and Julianne."

Patrick swiveled a disbelieving eye on his friend. "I thought you said you engineered this entire bit of lunacy on the basis that we might not suit."

"I didn't know her when I penned that settlement. But traveling with you both down from Moraig, I saw a different side of her. She is funny and smart, and yes, maddening if you don't take the time to sort out that beneath that fashionable exterior lies a sharp, loyal mind."

"You told me this morning I ought not to trust her."

"I was testing you. Anyone with a pair of eyes can see you each care for the other. She is fierce in her desire to help you, and puts your needs above her own comfort. That is an admirable prelude to love."

"So you *don't* think I should grant her an annulment?"

"I think you need to *think*, Haversham."

Patrick studied his friend a long, tense moment. "I suppose you think I should thank you for this. You'll forgive me if I am not feeling all that gracious."

James slipped the decanter bottle from Patrick's hand. "It remains to be seen whether you will thank me or hate me later. But regardless of how you feel toward me, you have the means to grant your wife the annulment she wants." He shook his head and refilled his glass. "But I'll be damned if I can see why you'd want to."

•

Chapter 32

Patrick pushed his way up the long, winding staircase and pointed his boots toward his bedroom door. Far from steadying his nerves, the brandy had obliterated his resolve to approach this conundrum in a civilized, cerebral fashion.

The denial that had sent him searching for a bottle had been displaced by a howling sort of anger since his conversation with MacKenzie. He was livid with his friend, for machinating such a damnably brilliant fix. He was angry with his wife, for wanting it.

But most of all, he was furious with himself, for lying to Julianne in the first place.

The weather, it seemed, had spent itself out, and through the windows at the far end of the hallway he could see the beginning of what promised to be a significant sunset. But the lingering storm still seemed to hang in a bit of indecision, with gray-tinged clouds boiling low on the horizon. Long fingers of amber light splashed across the hall's carpet runner and played about his feet, and he knew, like those shadows, he needed to make a decision which way things would go. He wanted Julianne to be happy. He had not lied to MacKenzie about that.

But he was beginning to think that he had lied to himself. Because while it might be selfish, he wanted Julianne to be happy with *him*.

He opened the door to his room, and the belligerent bump of his pulse shifted toward confusion. Because instead of packing her things in a mad dash for London, as he had half feared she would be doing, Julianne was standing over a steaming bath.

She looked up as he stepped inside, and the light from the fireplace danced across her face. She had changed into a nearly translucent wrapper, and it swung like a gossamer pendulum about her body. The room was bathed in heat, thanks to the fire that had been laid. She'd let her hair down, and it streamed down her back like the flames in the grate, halos of red and amber and always, always, those endless curls he wanted to wrap up in his fist.

"You have returned." Her voice was steady, giving no hint as to her state of mind.

He closed the door as best he could, given that he had so recently smashed through the latch in his quest to reach her side. "I am sorry. I should have knocked." He could think of no excuse for his poor manners, beyond the fact that his thoughts had been fixed on the dilemma of his wife's future happiness, rather than his wife's breasts.

Though they were certainly on his wife's breasts *now*.

He'd come to talk, to dissect their options. To determine if even a spark of the passion she had shown him that night in the folly might still be glowing beneath her skin, waiting to be kindled back to life. But as she straightened over the bath, the hopeful evening light danced about the thin fabric and tripped across the outline of the lithe body against which it floated. And that frantic, gasping glimpse told him—beyond any shadow of a doubt—she was wearing nothing beneath that wrapper.

Bloody hell. This was no way to end a marriage.

The physical demands of his body were already colluding against the analytical arguments he needed to make. "I have interrupted your bath," he said, rather stupidly. "I can return when you are . . . er . . . presentable."

"'Tis your bedroom, Patrick," she said, and her lips lifted in a manner that skirted into dangerous territory. "You have no need to knock, or to leave. And this is not *my* bath. I ordered it for you."

Her smile became as translucent as her wrapper as she stepped toward him. The diaphanous white hem billowed out around her ankles, and his eyes felt burned by the glimpses of curves beneath it. She stepped closer still, until she was upon him and his nostrils were filled with her feminine, cinnamon scent. "We must decide what our future holds. You are covered in mud, and look as though you haven't bathed since your arrest. I would have the conversation with a cleaner version of my husband."

He swallowed. "Even if the conversation is about whether I will no longer *be* your husband?"

She held out her hand. He watched it come, transfixed by the sight of Julianne reaching for him. Patrick struggled to comprehend the incongruity of what she seemed to be offering. Not an hour ago, she had flinched from the merest brush of his fingers, but this seemed a seduction of the highest order. Was this yet another demonstration of her superb dramatic skills?

Or something else entirely?

Her fingers uncurled slowly and his breath lodged deep in his throat. In her palm lay nothing more seductive than a bloody cake of soap.

"Do you really think a bath is a higher priority than this discussion?" he asked.

"*Your* bath is," she told him, her lips turned down.

He reached out his hand and took it. The soap warmed in his hands, releasing its scent. It smelled . . . well, "heavenly" was the word that came to mind. He could see now why she always smelled like cinnamon. She was a cosseted, perfumed, damnably inconvenient intrusion into his easy, ordered, unhygienic life.

And he was convinced of the need to keep her there.

He sat on the edge of the tub and began to pull off his boots. At the moment, he was anxious to plunge into the arguments of keeping their marriage intact, not plunge into a bath. But if dislodging the worst of his dirt would help her sit quietly through this coming conversation, he supposed he ought to delay the inevitable another five minutes, even though every instinct in his body told him that this reckoning needed to be taken by the throat.

As he began to work on the buttons of his shirt, the scrape of heavy furniture across the floor caught his attention. He turned to see Julianne shoving his reading chair in front of the door. "What are you doing?" he asked, perplexed.

"Ensuring we will not be interrupted. You've destroyed the latch, after all."

Patrick shouldered out of his shirt. There was that damned "we" again. Maddening, perplexing woman, when she had just demanded her freedom.

How was he going to do this? If she was going to strip him down to his most vulnerable and settle in to watch, she was going to see that he was fast becoming interested in doing things more intimate than talking.

She glided toward him, her hand held out for his shirt. "I'll take that now, thank you."

Instead of dropping it on the floor, as he would usually do, he placed it hesitantly in her open palm. Incredibly—*inconceivably*—she accepted the filthy thing, folded it carefully, and laid it on top of the bureau. "Now the trousers," she said, then treated them to the same exacting process.

"Why take the time to fold clothes that I probably ought to burn?" he protested.

"Because it is the natural order of things. And it hurts my eyes to see them tossed about on the floor." She beckoned with her fingers. It was to be smallclothes next, then.

Oh bloody, bloody hell.

"If we are discussing natural order, you should know that a gentleman usually shaves before his bath," he told her, turning over his smallclothes and the last shreds of his dignity. Any hope of wrangling his unruly body into something approaching respectable was lost. He'd been at attention from the moment he'd stepped into the room, and that interest had no hope of flagging now that at least one of them was naked.

"I thought it was well established sometime ago that you were not a gentleman." She raised a brow. "Should I shave you then?"

He shook his head. Julianne and sharp objects and his neck were a combination of events best avoided in the heat of an argument. "If you think I am handing you a razor, given the conversation we are about to have, you are mistaken, *wife*."

If she was startled to hear his proprietary claim, she hid the emotion well. Her lips pursed, and he felt the scrape of her eyes against his jaw as acutely as any straight razor. "That is just as well, because I find I rather like this rakish, unshaved look."

And then her gaze arced downward, sliding along his body to pool somewhere far too low for comfort. "And the rest of it as well."

"JULIANNE." THE SOUND of his voice echoed like the snap of a whip, jerking her gaze in a more northerly direction.

Her cheeks flamed warm against his stern, knowing gaze. Did he know what the sight of his body did to her? Did he understand that despite her offer to end this marriage, to give him his happiness, the loss of him—if it came down to that—would cripple her?

"Yes?" she answered hoarsely.

"What game do you play here?"

Julianne swallowed. "I wish to test a theory."

He swore, something filthy and flush-inducing. "You've said you wish to end our marriage, and yet you are sending rather mixed messages in that regard. For God's sake, have a bit of mercy here, wife."

Julianne moistened her lips, which felt as dry as glass paper. He had called her "wife" again. And he had not yet said *he* wished to end the marriage. "If you would think back to our discussion before you stormed out, I did not say I wished to procure an annulment. I said we ought to discuss the possibility." She paused, her heart in her throat. "Have you? Given it any thought, I mean?"

He jerked away from her with a snarl of frustration. She had a meager, heart-stuttering glimpse of the bare arse she had once ogled from Summersby's foyer, and then he was lowering his tall frame into the bath. Water sloshed heavily at the sides as he worked the soap into a frenzied lather. "MacKenzie says there may be a way." He scrubbed up one arm, and then down another. "Your age is misrepresented on the wedding documents."

She stared at him. "I beg your pardon?"

"Apparently you are forty. Or else, pretending to be."

"But . . . that is ridiculous. I do not even reach my majority until next month."

"You signed a document stating otherwise. MacKenzie has suggested it could be used to argue a claim of fraud." He lifted his soapy hands to his head and scrubbed his hair for a long moment. "Apparently, I must pretend I've a taste for older women. You are to be a disappointment to me." His lips firmed. "Or something of that ilk."

Julianne felt as though she were being pushed under the very tub in which he sat. As he submerged his head to rinse the soap from his hair, her eyes fixed on the sloshing, brown water. She had hoped—prayed, actually—that Mr. MacKenzie would tell Patrick the contract was unbreakable. That they were well and truly sewn into this marriage, despite her offer to free him. She had hoped there would be nothing for it but to regroup, accept their situation, and fall back into each other's arms.

But apparently, this marriage could be dissolved as easily as the blasted soap.

He came up sputtering, groping a hand for a towel. She snatched it up and stepped forward, dangling it in front of him. "And are you really willing to lie about this?" she demanded. "You knew exactly how old I was when we married. There was no fraud involved in the negotiation of that contract. And you seemed remarkably *pleased* with me that night in the folly."

He reached for the towel, but she jerked it higher, angry now. How *dare* he contemplate an annulment that required her to lie to procure it for him?

How dare he contemplate a blasted annulment at all?

"It is the only way." His brown-eyed gaze shifted

from the towel to her face. "And yes," he told her. "I am willing to lie for you."

"What do you mean, lie *for* me? I am not the one about to destroy this marriage!"

A very clean hand snaked out of that very filthy water. And then she was seized in his grasp and tipping into the tub, towel and all.

"Aren't you?" he all but growled as he hauled her against his damp chest. The shock of the water was nothing compared to the shock of his skin, humming through the meager layer of wet muslin. "I am not the one who broached this subject."

"You spoke of an annulment with MacKenzie before I ever mentioned it," she protested, her hands pushing ineffectively against the wall of his chest.

His hands came up to cup her face, holding her still to his gaze. The horror of the used bathwater fell away to the thrill of his touch. "That conversation happened before we married, before I even knew you. I married you with the understanding it could not be undone."

"You married me for revenge—"

His fingers gripped tighter. "What kind of lunacy is that? I've *never* wished to hurt you, not even in the worst of it. Do not pretend to me an annulment is logical, or necessary to right a great wrong. You married me knowing I didn't love you—I never pretended otherwise. But how can you leave me, knowing I love you now?"

His words swam upstream in her brain, seeking a coherence that continued to outwit her. "You . . . *love* me?" she asked.

"Yes." His eyes darkened. "Christ. You really can't see a thing in front of your face."

And then his lips slanted over hers, warm and brandy-touched and violently *right*.

She sank into him. Shimmered there, floating, until the press of his mouth was no longer enough. He loved her. Merciful heavens, how had it come to this? She'd imagined only convincing him to keep her. This was a gift beyond hope.

She lifted her hands into his damp hair and yanked him closer into her. They clashed there, wet heat and open mouths and pounding hearts. "I love you as well," she gasped against his mouth. She sucked in a breath, unable and unwilling to take it back. "But I thought . . . I thought you would no longer want me, now that you had been freed of the murder charge."

"Bloody hell, Julianne, I want you in my sleep. You are the only thing that kept me sane over the last week, during those long, dark days in gaol. When I thought you were in danger, I was tossed back to hell, staring down the barrel of a rifle with no future in sight." He tipped his wet head against hers, breathing hard. "And then, just as I was clawing my way out, just when I could see the end of this nightmare, you told me you wanted to live apart. But I can't face it. You belong here, with me."

Julianne choked on a sob. "Say it again."

His lips curved up, mere inches from her own. "The part where you belong with me?"

"The part where you love me."

He laughed. "I love you, wife."

She pressed her finger against his lips, determined to commit the act to permanent memory. "Again."

"I. Love. You." The rumble of words against her finger sending a skitter of warmth through the whole of her. "I will say it every day, if that is what it takes to keep you here. I can't do this without you."

"You don't have to," she told him.

And then she pulled him in for a kiss.

Chapter 33

Though he'd spent a good deal of time tonight trying to see through it, Patrick's *affair de coeur* with Julianne's wrapper was at an end.

The damned thing had to go.

He stood up from the tub, his wife in his arms, water streaming off them both. The towel was now soaked, but he found he did not care. The air in the room was languorous and warm, thanks to the fire blazing in the grate. Neither of them risked being felled by pneumonia as a consequence of what he was about to do.

Because while the next sensible step might have been to cover up her wet body as quickly as possible, he wasn't feeling entirely sensible at the moment.

He carried her, soaking wet, to the bed and set about peeling the wet, transparent wrapper from her skin. The fabric stymied him at every turn, clinging to her shoulders, sticking to her arms. Slowly, slowly he tugged, until it bunched about her waist and the pale perfection of her breasts tipped into his greedy view.

A word took a claw-hold in his mind. *Mine.* A simple enough sentiment, one that even a fool like himself could understand. And yet, it was so much more complicated than that.

She was finely molded, peaks and valleys tempting a man to chart his own course, a fever dream one wished to never wake from. He leaned in and feathered a kiss down the slope of one breast before running his tongue up the other.

She squirmed beneath him. "I've decided I like it when you meander," she gasped.

"Meandering has its place, certainly." He lingered over the damp scent of her as his mouth explored her body, moving up to brush his lips against the soft skin on the underside of her jaw. "But I confess, this particular waiting has come close to killing me." He slipped the robe completely off her and rocked her gently back onto the bed.

He stared down at his wife's flushed face, then tripped down to her toes and back again. Lord, but she was beautiful. She was pale, smooth perfection, and vivid red curls. The mere curve of her collarbone was eroticism redefined. He ran his hands down the still-damp length of her, pausing over the gentle flare of hip, stroking up the lust-provoking curve of her calf until he found the sweet, secret indentation at the hollow of her knee. He wanted to explore every inch of her, from the high arch of her foot to that lovely mouth that could slice a man in two or take him to heaven, depending on her mood and fate's whimsy.

He hoped fate was feeling whimsical tonight.

He eased his own body onto the mattress beside her and trailed a finger down her abdomen. His hand brushed the tempting curls waiting there at the juncture of her legs. He found her more than ready to receive him, and his body jerked painfully at the discovery.

"Do you know how often I have dreamed of seeing you like this, naked beneath me?"

She shuddered beneath his touch, and her legs fell open in a silent but unmistakable invitation. "It cannot be that often. We've only been married three weeks."

A chuckle built in his throat. "Oh no, love." Slowly, slowly, he found the hidden place that made her tremble with pleasure and arch upward into his touch. "You've occupied a place in my mind for far longer than the length of our marriage. Almost a year now."

"So long?" she gasped.

He pressed more firmly, enjoying the way her breathing had accelerated to quick, hard pants with just a touch. "Aye. Ever since that damned waltz. Devilish thing, that. I almost refused you. I knew you were trouble, sure enough, and looking for more. And I was right. When it was through, I couldn't get you out of my head."

"I thought you hated me," she protested, thrashing her head with the pleasure he was determined to coax out of her.

"I *wanted* to hate you." He slipped a finger inside her, and almost groaned from the contrast of silk and heat. "But I also wanted to tup you. Whenever I thought of you at night, in my lonely bed in Moraig, I imagined you flushed and panting beneath me, eager for whatever I had in mind. And that was after a single dance and a murder accusation. Imagine what I want to do with you now that I've had a taste of you."

JULIANNE WANTED TO collide with her husband in damp, twisted sheets. She wanted to dive into madness and never come up.

And she wanted to do it now.

Desire snaked through her in a delicious, erotic pulse. His confession loosened some critical tether in her soul, and she pulled him down hard toward her mouth. She licked the space behind his ear almost experimentally. The taste of him—salt and subtle spice and the distinctive tattoo of her own soap—was a heady, forbidden thrill. Next she scraped her teeth across the skin at the base of Patrick's neck, smiling as the gesture ripped glad laughter from his throat.

She had a feeling she was going to like tupping. Very much, indeed.

"Are you trying to mortally wound me, wife?" He chuckled, and the sound of his amusement was the most intimate thing imaginable.

"I am trying to get you to hurry," she admitted.

Not that her body objected to the pace of her husband's ministrations, per se. He was brilliant in his leisure. But the blood hummed in her veins. The argument that had led them here had left behind a thrumming heat demanding something more than the gentle press of her husband's hand. They'd meandered enough on their way to this startling bit of happiness.

It was time to finish the journey.

"I don't want to wait," she told him, ready to beg if it came down to it.

"I've no objection to hurrying," he told her, threading his fingers through her hair and anchoring her tight. "As long as we are hurrying together."

He captured her lips in a deep kiss as he entered her. She yielded to the sweet torture that began where he joined his body with hers and ended somewhere in the vicinity of her heart.

She clung to him, reaching for the release she knew hovered, just out of reach. It was a far different journey now that she understood the fire beneath her skin was merely the prelude to something more portentous. He drove her there, with the feel of his hand at her breast, and the impossibly sweet sound of her name on his lips.

She was in awe of the emotion he'd unleashed in her, in the strength of her love. She let herself go, trusting him, trusting herself. Her body was tutored now, aching for that peak, willing to expend whatever was needed to find it.

"Please," she begged him.

He obligingly bent his damp head and captured her nipple in his mouth, and that was all it took to hurl her right over the edge. She broke apart in his arms, her eyes blurring with the pleasure-pain of it. The cry that was wrenched from her throat would have sounded feral, but for the sound of his own lashing release.

Her return to sanity was blissfully slow. The room came back into focus in slow measures. First the fire, burning low in the grate. Then the floor, where Patrick's boots lay tossed about like so much rubbish, and the water soaking the carpet beneath the tub. And finally, her husband, with his unkempt sandy hair and lovely, lean body and smug, smug grin.

Although, surely if anyone ought to be a bit smug, it was she.

She smiled through the remaining fog of pleasure. "Why are you grinning in such a lascivious manner?"

He gathered her back against his chest. One big hand trailed down her arm, raising gooseflesh anew. "You are sweating. I am not sure I realized before tonight that ladies might sweat."

"I imagine most ladies don't," she admitted, knowing she ought to take offense. But how could she object to her state of dishevelment, when she wanted only to indulge in the act again? "Although they probably don't tup either."

His chuckle floated, just behind her ear. "More fool they."

She wanted only to stay here, safe in his sweat-slick arms, the world held at bay by nothing more than a busted latch and a heavy chair. But reality tried to nudge that delicious logic aside. "I suppose I ought to call for another bath."

"Whatever for?"

"Why, because I am sweating, of course. As you have been so kind to point out."

He lifted the damp curls off her neck and pressed a kiss against her heated skin. "You might want to wait until I've finished with you." He pressed into her, and she could feel him already stirring to life again against the small of her back.

She closed her eyes and turned herself over to the delicious sweep of longing that once again began to displace good sense. "I suppose I could delay it a bit longer," she gasped as his mouth once more began its sweet, busy assault on her senses. "Until you've finished."

He laughed against her shoulder, and his chuckle reverberated through her. "I will never be finished with you, Julianne. So best be careful, love. You may never bathe again."

Epilogue

October 1843

ᕼE WASN'T IN the mood for a proper English miss.

Not that those words precisely described the red-haired infant Julianne delivered into Patrick's arms that full-moon October night.

Their new daughter's entrance into the world was timed, of course, for maximum effect. The baby was a good two weeks earlier than predicted—the better, Patrick supposed, to surprise them all. And more to the point, she arrived a mere five hours after announcing her intentions, with the onset of labor during the second course of dinner.

Once the first blush of panic had worn off and Patrick realized his wife was not inclined to take a leisurely, rational approach to childbirth, he had elbowed the housekeeper aside, rolled up his sleeves, and proceeded with the decidedly un-earl-like behavior of delivering his firstborn.

Patrick held the slippery bundle in his hands and

stared down into his new daughter's scrunched-up face, thinking her quite possibly the most beautiful thing he had ever seen. He wiped her tiny nostrils clean with the soft cloth the housekeeper handed him, willing his daughter to breathe. She did so with a short, soft gasp, inhaling her first taste of life.

And then the new Lady Sarah Jane Channing let loose a high, warbling wail that reminded Patrick very much of the child's mother.

He reluctantly turned her over to the housekeeper. While his medical skills had rendered him perfectly capable of delivering his daughter, the scrubbing and swaddling part of the experience was admittedly beyond his scope of experience. When baby Sarah was finally presentable in a manner befitting the offspring of a peer of the realm, Patrick carried her back to Julianne. He stood beside them, humbled to silence by the experience of seeing his daughter's cries subside as she nestled tight into the crook of his wife's arm.

He wondered, for a breathless moment, how his normally squeamish wife would react to the sight of a newly born human, which admittedly lacked the innate softness he knew the baby would later acquire. But Julianne looked down on her daughter with as much awe as Patrick felt himself, and he felt something slip in the vicinity of his heart.

"You amaze me, wife."

She looked up. "I do?"

"Aye." He had memorized every feature, and every nuanced emotion of his wife's beautiful face, and damned if there wasn't something missing. "I don't know a single other woman who could come through childbirth with her freckles still carefully hidden from view."

"A lady does not like to be reminded of her flaws," Julianne said, her voice ringing with amusement and weary happiness. "I confess, this little one took me by surprise. 'Tis unnerving to find yourself at the whim of another person, even one so sweet and little."

Patrick chuckled. "At last you know how I feel, almost every day."

His wife's eyes flashed like green ocean glass, tumbling in water. "Then you are now saddled with two unpredictable females. Whatever deity did you insult to be so blessed?"

"Never let it be said I do not count myself fortunate in that regard. You've a way of making me look forward to the unknown. And while baby Sarah took us all by surprise, it is better for you, certainly. The faster and earlier the delivery, the less difficulty you were likely to encounter." He cleared his throat. "Er . . . at least . . . that is the way of it with horses."

That made her laugh again, which made the baby stir in annoyance. "Well," Julianne said, smiling over their daughter's head, "I am glad to see your medical skills and good humor have not rusted during the months of disuse, at any rate."

"Oh, I've found plenty by way of diversion about Summersby to keep those old skills sharp," he assured her. Indeed, he'd found a heady mix of responsibility awaited him as the new Earl of Haversham, a unique concoction of affairs that involved as much or as little veterinary knowledge as he wished to apply to the business of managing—and improving—his estate.

And with every night spent in Julianne's arms, his good humor was by now firmly established.

"Can you fetch my spectacles?" she asked, nodding to the bedside table. "I want to inspect her thoroughly."

Patrick picked up the delicate wire rims. He settled them doubtfully on her nose. "You only need these to see at a distance. Why do you want them now?"

"I don't want to take any chances on missing anything about her," she said, squinting down through the lens at her daughter. After a short moment, she sighed and pulled them off. "You are correct, as you almost always are. I can see her far better without them."

Patrick grinned. "Until she gains her legs. Then I suspect you shall find yourself relying on them more than you want." He leaned down to kiss the tip of his wife's nose, and the love he felt for her almost dragged him under with the force of it. "Does our little Sarah fit your mother's name, as you had hoped she would?" he asked.

Julianne smoothed a gentle head over her daughter's still-damp hair. "That she does. My mother would have been so pleased. But . . . are you disappointed I have not delivered you an heir? I know you had hoped for a son we could name after Eric."

Patrick shook his head, as sure of this as anything in his life. "No, love. I am not disappointed in the slightest. She is absolutely perfect. I can already see her chasing Gemmy and Constance, and twisting her grandmother 'round her little finger. She's bound to lay waste to hearts from here to Scotland in about twenty years."

Indeed, Patrick had a feeling the little waif was bound for trouble. After all, she had a head full of red hair and her mother's demonstrably healthy lungs. And she might be tiny, but she'd already disappointed many a fortune-seeking bounder. Half of London had been waiting breathlessly for her appearance, the gaming books heavy with wagers on when she would arrive, most erring on the side of expediency over caution.

"We certainly showed the cynics, didn't we?" Julianne lifted a brow, dragging his heart along with it.

And well they had. It was a good twelve months after the date scrawled on the blacksmith's register in Moraig, and ten from when they had repeated those vows at the parish church, ensuring no one could ever challenge the validity of their union. No one could claim any longer that their marriage had been made in the worst sort of haste, or orchestrated to cover an imprudent night of passion.

"Yes, love. We've shown them all. You no longer have to chafe against the whispers."

"Idiotic gossip. The fools making such wagers deserve to be parted with their money. You shall never, ever put stock in such things, will you?" Julianne crooned down at her daughter. "You shall be brave, and bold, and true to yourself. And above all, you shall marry for love."

Patrick smiled. Because in truth, he knew that as time went by, they would quiet the gossip with more than just baby Sarah's timing. Anyone who saw him with Julianne could not fail to see the rare affection between them. They had more than just the appearance of a love match. They had one in actuality.

And that was a rumor he was all too willing to prove.

Next month, don't miss these exciting new love stories only from *Avon Books*

How to Lose a Duke in Ten Days by Laura Lee Guhrke

When the Duke of Margrave agreed to her outrageous proposal of a marriage of convenience, Edie was transformed from ruined American heiress to English duchess. She's delighted with their arrangement, with her husband on another continent. But when a brush with death impels Stuart home, he decides it's time for a real marriage with his luscious bride, and he proposes a bold bargain: ten days to win her willing kiss.

It Takes a Scandal by Caroline Linden

Abigail Weston's parents hope she'll wed an earl but she longs for a man who wants her desperately and passionately. Sebastian Vane is not a fit suitor for anyone, let alone an heiress. But Abigail lights up his world like a comet and it might end happily ever after . . . until Benedict Lennox—wealthy, charming, heir to an earl— begins courting her.

Redemption of the Duke by Gayle Callen

Adam Chamberlin was known for gambling binges and drunken nights. But when tragedy strikes and Adam becomes the Duke of Rothford, he is determined to right his ways. Faith Cooper is surprised when Adam offers her a position as a lady's companion to his aunt. Although Faith refuses to be beholden to Adam, with passion simmering between them, will she surrender to forbidden desire?

*G*ive in to your Impulses!

These unforgettable stories only take a second to buy and give you hours of reading pleasure!

Go to *www.AvonImpulse.com* and see what we have to offer.

Available wherever e-books are sold.

2018/6

AVONIMPULSE

IMP 0811